Jumper and the Bones

By Kenn Amdahl

Jumper and the Bones

Copyright 2011 By Kenn Amdahl

First electronic version released 2011.

First printed version released 2014

ISBN-10   0615997724

ISBN-13   978-0-6159977-2-8

Clearwater Publishing

P.O. Box 778

Broomfield, CO 80038-0778

CONTENTS

3

CHAPTER ONE

In which I start my art career and tell you about me and get a pretty good job which ain't gonna last that long if you read the next chapter

Some people say I ain't smart enough to have did what I done. But some of the guys who say that ain't exactly Einstein Bagels themselves and probably ain't as smart as stuff they done either. Sometimes smart and lucky is the same thing, which a guy should not get credit for even if they want to.

OK, so getting in a fight with the meanest gang guy in Denver wasn't smart or lucky, I'll give you that one. I shouldn't of done that and I ain't got excuses. And any time you see a murder, you got to figure you done some dumb stuff to put you in the wrong spot at the right time. So it would be fair to take off some of my brain points for being a murder witness, on top of the points for the unfortunate gang incident. But then you got to add some luck points for not getting killed myself, and some on account of the turtle. Since smart and lucky is a lot alike, as I already explained, I think my luck points raises my brain points back to a level playing field.

I'll get to the gang guys and the murder in a minute. But if I just told you the interesting parts of my life and none of the boring stuff, this would be like a show-off letter from a guy you didn't know from atoms, which you wouldn't read, plus it would be real short. So I'll fill in some blanks about me and then in your book you can talk about you. I won't hold it against you if you ain't had as interesting a life as me. I bet you got some natural gifts I ain't got, if you thought about it. Like, maybe you can play ping-pong.

I'm an artist and now, obviously, a writer too, which is both interesting jobs except for if you want to get paid. The part of my life I'm going to write for you started with a guy on TV who said some famous genius artists used mirrors to paint stuff. We all seen a windshield reflect a spot of light on a wall. The TV guy said that a curved mirror can reflect a picture of something that's out in the sunshine onto a wall inside your apartment. Guys like Leonardo da Vinci, who drew Mona Lisa and who everyone called a genius – this guy on TV said maybe Mr. Vinci used a shaving mirror to reflect onto his paper and then just traced her. It don't take a genius to trace, but you can bet Mr. Vinci probably made a fortune and drove fancy cars, and had pretty girls all round him, like those guys on MTV.

7

The guy on TV pissed a bunch of people off. People get used to their geniuses and don't like it if you call them ordinary guys with shaving mirrors. So I seen right away that even if he was ordinary in every other way, Mr. Vinci was a genius one way: he didn't tell nobody about the shaving mirror. I thought that was pretty cool of him. I don't tell people stuff much either, so we was like twin brothers, Mr. Vinci and me.

I wondered how Mr. Vinci thought to use his shaving mirror in the first place. Did Mona need a shave and so he loaned her his mirror and then seen what the mirror was doing? I don't mean to sound ignorant and politically uncorrect, but she's got black hair and them big black eyebrows like the social worker lady who talked to me when Mom died. You might be too polite to ever say it, but you know what I mean. That social worker lady could of used a quick shave. Genius or not, maybe Mr. Vinci should of painted a pretty girl instead of a social worker.

Or maybe he got the idea when he was drawing one of them sunflowers, except I don't know why he'd take his shaving mirror out in the field. Either way, I bet it was an accident, the whole bit with the mirror. It wasn't some genius thing. Keeping it secret, that was the smart part.

So the next day I watched the news to learn more details, but it was like they forgot the whole story. Not a word, which surprised the heck out of me. O.J.'s trial was on TV every day and he was just an everyday actor, if you ever seen one of his films. This was Leonardo da fluffing Vinci, who is in art museums. But not a word.

After I wasted a couple more days of watching a lot of news about people in other countries, I got this idea: Why not get a shaving mirror and try it myself? I got plenty of time and my favorite thrift store might have one of them curved mirrors.

I put ten ones in my shirt pocket and went down three flights of stairs from my apartment and started walking. It was a sunny day, but even sunny days in April can feel cold here in Denver, so I walked fast. Some of the trees was getting leaves, but there was also little piles of snow in shady spots. It took about eight minutes to get there.

"Hey Jumper," the man behind the counter at the thrift store said when I walked in.

"How ya doing, Jim?" I said back.

"Can't complain," Jim said, though he's only got one leg and I'd probably complain about that.

8

So now I should explain my name. People always called me Jumper since I was a kid because I loved to jump off things and after a while it got to be my name. I jumped off chairs when I was three or four years old, and my mom said I giggled like a idiot every time. When I got bigger I jumped off tables and cars and anything I could climb up on. By the time I was in eighth grade I was jumping off the roof of the garage. People said I ought to go out for track, maybe be a long jumper. But I never got around to that. Them hours of a coach yelling at you never much appealed to me. Plus I knew I ain't a distance jumper, I'm a height jumper. Other kids busted their ankles when they jumped off a garage roof. But they hadn't been practicing like me. I jumped every day, sun or snow, rain or shine and I still do, only I seen that people thought it was weird so now I mostly jump at night and don't talk about it much. Now I'm full grown, with lots of interesting stuff in my life, and a good apartment and hobbies and sometimes I go out with girls. Everybody still calls me Jumper, but most people don't know how come.

Jim, the thrift store guy, didn't know and he never asked. Jim's cool. Sometimes he'll find a pair of jeans or a shirt he thinks I'd like and he hides them in the wrong size until I show up. Rich people go to fancy department stores and don't get that kind of service.

"So Jim," I says. "I need me a shaving mirror. You know, one of them curved ones."

Jim looks at me, thinking hard. He don't ask why I need it or make a joke on it. He just closes his eyes while his brain checks things off its list. Then he nods.

"Got two of 'em," he says. "Aisle 13, back between kitchen and bathroom stuff." He thinks another minute. "Three bucks each but one of 'em has a loose stand. Make you a deal, five bucks for the pair."

Jim is about as skinny a man as I ever seen outside a TV special on Africa. He ain't skinny in a vegetarian way, but skinny like a man who don't eat enough. He likes cars and looks at car magazines a lot. Sometime I'm gonna ask how he lost his leg but it ain't never come up yet. It might of been in a war, because sometimes he says the word shrapnel, which means pieces of metal that stick in you when something blows up. But then lots of things blow up so you can't tell by that. Jim uses crutches to walk, but his brain is extra good.

"Man, I don't know how you do it, Jim," I said, and he looks down kind of embarrassed. He must hear compliments all day long about his

9

memory, but he always acts surprised and shy about it. Mom always said it's just as easy to make somebody feel good as feel bad, so I try to remember that, even if it don't always work.

Sure enough, down aisle 13 there was two shaving mirrors. And sure enough, if you set one of them up it slides down real slow. Most people wouldn't look at it long enough to notice.

I sure didn't need two mirrors, and I'm not so rich I just throw away two bucks for nothing, but Jim didn't need to tell me about that loose mirror either, or offer me a deal. So I carried both of them up to the register. In case Jim makes a commission, that extra two bucks might as well show up during his shift. I put the mirrors down on the counter, plus five ones.

While he's putting the mirrors into a little plastic sack, I took off my backpack, which I pretty much wear all the time, and pulled out a shiny apple.

"Man, I done it again," I said with a little laugh, putting the apple down on the counter. "Got one of them New Zealand apples by mistake. I don't know why the store puts 'em side by side with the deliciouses."

Jim's eyes lit right up. He loves them New Zealand apples.

"It's yours if you want it," I told him. "I'll just throw it away. They don't even taste like apples to me."

"You know if you'd just read the little sticker you'd save yourself some money," he says. I can see he's already tasting that apple.

"That's a good idea," I said. I put the sack with the mirrors in my backpack and started walking home on Colfax Avenue.

Colfax is a great street which runs all the way through Denver. If you keep going west, you get to the mountains. Go all the way east and pretty soon you're on the prairie. If I ever get me a car again I'm gonna drive the whole thing a few times. Lots of the buildings are old, so you got your liquor stores and beat-up motels and dry cleaning shops and adult businesses. Old buildings make the nice suburban folks nervous, so they don't get out of their cars when they drive through my neighborhood. Women drivers don't even look left or right. They stare straight ahead like they're driving through a tunnel, which maybe in their brains they are.

Sure, you got some hookers and some homeless folks, and sometimes a guy selling weed, or a little group of young guys who watch too much MTV and try to act tough. About once a week you hear a gunshot when you're trying to sleep, but then some weeks you don't even hear one. Mostly it's just regular folks like me and you who mind their own business. Sometimes I run into gang guys who pull out their guns or knives and want my money. So I keep ten ones in a old wallet, plus business cards of people, which you can get easy, to make it look full. When gang guys want my money, I just give them the wallet, like an insurance payment. I can get me another old wallet at the thrift store for fifty cents and ten bucks plus a wallet seems pretty cheap. It makes them feel like big shots that they got my money, but pretty soon they figure out I'm a hard lemon to get much lemonade out of and leave me alone. Lots of people spend more than ten bucks on insurance and don't get no more for it than me, so what the heck.

An old guy was sitting on the sidewalk staring straight ahead. His hair hung down to his shoulders, real stringy and dirty, brown and gray. He wore a red flannel shirt with a big rip in the sleeve. I never seen him before. He didn't even ask me for spare change which bothered me.

"Hey, man, you OK?" I asked. He turned his head slow to look at me, like a guy who was sleeping and I woke him. He took a long look at me, focused for a minute, then turned back to stare at the street. His face was all sun-wrinkled and thin. I couldn't tell if he was OK or not so I sat down next to him on the sidewalk.

"Nice day, huh?" I said. "My name's Jumper."

He didn't move or say nothing.

"Nights still feel like winter, but it sure feels good when the sun's out, don't it?"

He still didn't say nothing. If he was one of them guys who just don't talk much, he'd picked a good spot for not talking. The sun was warm on us. Across the street a tree had little white buds on it. I think it was a peach tree. In a couple weeks them buds would be little white flowers, and before you know it, little peaches. Or maybe apples.

The tree could of been in a painting at the Denver Art Museum a half-mile away. Some of the cars driving past was probably on their way there, but the drivers didn't notice that their minivan was going through a Van Go painting, since they thought they was driving through a tunnel and all. If this old guy chose this spot for the view, he was pretty smart. If he just happened to sit there, he was pretty lucky. Like I say, sometimes smart and lucky is the same thing.

Either way, I liked the old guy. You gotta like guys who don't talk too much. So I sat there with him for maybe a half-hour, looking at that peach tree and not talking.

11

But I was anxious to try out the shaving mirror idea, so finally I got up.

"It's a good spot," I said. "You're a lucky guy." He just stared straight ahead. He probably already knew he was lucky. But that give me an idea. I felt like I owed the guy something for being so friendly. "Tell you what. I ain't that lucky myself," I said. OK, so that was a little white lie. I'm really a pretty lucky guy. I took five ones out of my shirt pocket. "I was gonna blow this on Lotto tickets, but I won't win nothing. I bet you could get yourself some breakfast and a Lotto ticket besides. If you win, you can buy me breakfast some time." I stuffed the bills into his shirt pocket. As I turned to go, he kind of grunted so I looked back. He was pointing at his hat. It was a red baseball cap with the words "John Deere" on it. I smiled at that. "Pleased to meet you Mr. Deere," I said. "Like I say, I'm Jumper. Cool hat. See you around."

John Deere was just a homeless guy I sat with on a sidewalk looking at a tree. It ain't everybody you meet turns into your best friend, or an enemy, or your girlfriend, or the guy in the movie who killed the butler. Mostly you sit on the sidewalk next to some guy you ain't never gonna see again. So since I'm writing a true book instead of a TV show I'll just tell you right now I never seen Mr. Deere again. I could of made up that he won the Lotto and then tracked me down and give me a bunch of money but that would be a lie. I ain't a good enough writer to try that big a lie. Maybe he got himself turned around and cleaned up and got to be President of the United States, only I don't know for certain it happened so I ain't gonna write it, even if I got suspicions.

Back at my apartment I got out my new mirrors. The guy on TV had demonstrated Mr. Vinci's art method, so I knew what to do. The thing I wanted to draw had to be out in the sunshine, the paper had to be inside, and the room had to be dark. No problem making the apartment dark. It's only one room to start with, and only has two windows, so pulling down the shade on one made it pretty dark.

The other window's in the little kitchen area and if you open it you can climb out onto a little balcony that's big enough for one chair, or in my case a wood apple box that's just as good as a chair. There's a ledge around the balcony with a daisy plant on it growing in a coffee can. That daisy blooms all summer and since I took it inside this winter it already had a nice flower. My idea was that if Mr. Vinci could get rich and famous drawing sunflowers, which is a weed here in Denver, a daisy ought to work even better. But if not, it would be a good science experiment anyway.

I moved the mirror around and sure enough, it made a circle on my ceiling with something in it that could of been the daisy. Right away I figured out that's how Mr. Vinci got the idea to paint the cistern chapel ceiling, which you probably heard of. The guy on TV had called the mirror thing a name that sounded like "camera of squirrels" or "camera of Skura", which is probably named after one of Mr. Vinci's girlfriends besides Mona. Unless he really liked squirrels. Either way, I had just made me one.

I moved the mirror some more until that circle was shining on my refrigerator. If it was just the right distance away, you could actually see the coffee can and flower pretty good, only they was upside down. I put the mirror on my table and moved it to the best spot. Then I stuck a piece of paper up on the refrigerator with a real estate company magnet, found a good sharp pencil, and started my art career.

Now, when you look at something regular, you just see the whole thing, like a rock or a coffee can. But when you look at it with a camera of squirrels, what you see is all these little lines. Some light and some dark, straight ones and curved ones, thick ones and thin ones which ain't all that ordinary. Plus, if you try to get real close, your head blocks the light and you see a shadow of your own head. So you have to stand a little bit to one side and hold your pencil so it don't block the light too.

I started at the top, which was the bottom of the coffee can, since it looked upside down. It took me three hours to do the whole thing. By about the middle I noticed that on the parts I'd already drew my lines didn't match up with the reflection from the camera any more. The sun was moving across the sky which was probably screwing with me, but there wasn't much to do about it. Anyway, this was just a experiment and if I practiced I bet I could get faster. Art is like jumping off things, the more you do it the better you get. If I'd figured out jumping off garages, I could figure out art.

It was fun. My feet got tired of standing in one place so long and my hand hurt a little, cause I was squeezing the pencil so hard, but it was nice anyway. I had to sharpen my pencil about four times. I bet a guy like Mr. Vinci could do it in two sharpenings.

When you draw something upside down for three hours, you get so it don't look upside down at all. That was something I never would of knew, but when I opened the shade on the other window and stood back from my picture, the drawing looked right to me. I flipped it around and even if my brain told me it was right side up, now it looked upside down to me.

13

I laughed out loud. This was about the coolest thing ever. In a few minutes it fixed itself, and that was cool too. I had to admit, it looked about perfect.

By now the sun was setting and I was hungry. I opened a can of spaghetti, washed a fork and opened the window onto my balcony. I took the can out there and sat on my apple crate to eat dinner. The sky had big fluffy summer clouds even if it was only April. The setting sun did its own painting on them, turning them orange and yellow, while the blue parts of the sky got darker. I bet everyone in Denver was watching that. Even a genius like Mr. Vinci never got to throw colors onto clouds, but at the same time, even poor people like Mr. Deere could afford to look at it.

Before it got dark, I looked over the edge of the balcony. I'm on the third floor, but there's an old garage right below my balcony. Somebody stores an old car in there, but nobody really uses it. It's got a flat roof and right after I moved in I hauled an old mattress up there from the alley. It's just a little more than one story from my balcony to the garage roof, which ain't a big deal for jumping, but since I mostly practiced at night I liked to land on something soft. It's easier on my ankles, plus it made my landings quiet. A pipe from the roof gutter runs down the wall right past my balcony. It has good strong brackets holding it, which made it a no brainer for climbing back up.

The mattress was right where it was supposed to be and nobody had threw a beer bottle or anything up on to it.

I went inside, made myself a nice glass of ice water, and went back out to sit on the apple crate and wait. Pretty soon stars would be coming out, which is always cool. I like to wait until everyone has their lights on before I start training, since then they can't see outside.

I'm especially careful about Holly. Holly lives right below me and is a pretty nurse who sometimes talks to me in the hall. The last thing in the world I wanted is to freak out Holly by flying past her window, or climbing up the downspout just when she's looking out. By now I can climb pretty quiet, of course, so I don't really think it would bother her, but maybe. Just to be sure, I always close my eyes when I'm climbing past her balcony. I mean, I can see right into her apartment and if she happened to look out and seen me looking in, she'd think I was snooping on her. Then she'd think I was weird for sure and might stop talking to me.

But five nights a week she works the evening shift at the hospital, five to two, so I usually train on them nights. She'd be working tonight. So I

14

watched the stars come out and lights come on in the building across the alley. I wasn't in any hurry. There ain't many things better than watching the stars come out while the air gets chilly.

After a while, the night felt like it had put itself together. I climbed up onto the railing and stood up. I couldn't see the roof below me, or the mattress, but you don't have to see things to know they're there. It might make some folks nervous to stand on a railing and jump into the dark but that's OK. It's just because they never done it before. You can't hold it against them.

I stood on the rail for maybe a minute. I figure it's good for my balance and you can't be a jumper if you ain't got good balance. Then I practiced standing on my left foot by itself, and then my other foot. That was tricky the first time I done it at night, but by now it was pretty ordinary.

After I done my balancing work, I raised my arms about as high as my ears, closed my eyes and jumped.

Now, you might think that since I've wrote this book that I'm pretty slick with describing things. But even I can't describe jumping in words. Somebody might say it was like flying, and that's pretty good. Or you might say it was like swimming, on account of everything going slower while you're in the air. The main thing is that it feels like just the right thing for me to be doing that particular minute. That's all I can say. You should try it sometime, if you ain't yet. Maybe it's just the right thing for you too.

I done eight jumps that night, which is about average, then went to bed. It had been a good day. Met Mr. Deere, my new friend who don't talk much, made the camera, did my first drawing, learned that thing about seeing upside down, had a good dinner, saw some stars and got in a good workout. That's a lot of stuff for one day but it didn't bother me.

About 2:18 I woke up when I heard Holly come home downstairs. Right on time. I smiled and the sentence come into my head that art is looking at life through a camera of squirrels. Then I went back to sleep.

The next morning I ate my oatmeal with a banana mashed up in it, took a shower and put on a clean T-shirt and jeans. I would of liked to try another drawing, but I had an appointment.

Now, I'm not a guy who never had a job. I had lots of them. I swept floors, and picked up trash by the highway and washed dishes and cut lawns. You name it, I done it. I always show up on time and I always done my best,

15

that ain't my problem. My problem is I tend to get interested in things, even if it ain't exactly what my boss would prefer me to get interested in. I just can't help it. Like once I was picking up trash by the side of a road with a crew of other guys and I seen this dragonfly land on a blade of grass. I never seen a dragonfly up close, so I laid down on the grass and crept up on him real slow until I was maybe a foot away. Anybody would get interested in a dragonfly. They got all these little bitty parts put together like a toy helicopter, all shining different colors, and these wings that look like plastic, and a big flat circle on their chest which looks like a satellite dish and so is probably a big ear. But I knew they wasn't paying me to stare at bugs. I would of got up after I had a good look but, just when I was about to, a tiny little green bug crawls up another blade of grass and that dragonfly zaps over to him as quick as you could see and grabs him. Then he landed again and ate that bug right in front of my eyes.

Now if you went to college, you probably seen stuff like that a lot, but I never got around to college so this was brand new to me. He chewed on that bug like it was a Big Mac and when he was done he just sat there waiting for his fries.

About then I realized my boss was standing right over me watching me the way I was watching the dragonfly. He was nice. He didn't yell or nothing, but just said he wouldn't be needing me the next day, so that was good. Some bosses will yell at you when they fire you and make you feel bad, but he was professional. He paid me for the day and thanked me when I give back the orange vest they made us wear. So it was a good firing, but not as good as keeping the job. I couldn't argue with him either, because he was right. They wasn't paying me to watch bugs. Still, that dragonfly was pretty cool.

After a bunch of jobs turned out to be more temporary than I thought they was, I figured out I'm more of a renaissance guy than a career guy. A renaissance guy is like Mr. Vinci; he spent time inventing submarines and helicopters and drawing social workers and designing buildings and lots of other stuff. So he had trouble keeping jobs too.

A guy can keep himself in groceries just by going up and down the alleys picking up cans to recycle, but it's seasonal work. When there's a foot of snow on the ground the kids don't hang outside much and families don't picnic, so the can business goes to heck. You might find a can or two, and I always keep my eyes open, but you can't count on it.

Sometimes you can pick up twenty bucks cleaning out an apartment when somebody moves out, but some months nobody moves out. I been cleaning apartments for Mr. Levy ever since I first started living on my own, and now I have three other guys I do it for sometimes. The good part of that is that Mr. Levy is cool if tenants leave stuff behind that you could use and so he don't mind if I take it. I asked him at first, but now I got a good sense of his rules and don't need to. I got my apple crate that way, for one example, and sometimes I get a week's food money just from the pop cans laying around. Plus they usually leave some food behind, and if there ain't bugs in it, or it's cans, I can't see throwing it in the trash. It's usually stuff like cans of pumpkin they was gonna make a pie of, or beets which I ain't that crazy about, but then I ain't paying for it either. Mostly it's just trash. Mr. Levy is strict that you turn in any money you find to him, or liquor, but he don't mind if you keep cans of pumpkin or beets, or three by five cards, or pencils.

When people know they're leaving, they stop cleaning. It can take me two days to get all the burned food off the stove and the refrigerator all clean and bleached, and the bathroom looking like no one ever used it before. If the faucet's dripping I put in new washers, which Mr. Levy gives me for free, and which takes about five minutes. I like to do my best job and I feel good when I'm done and the apartment looks better. Anyway, the pay is good, when you count all the free stuff I get, and I'd hate for Mr. Levy to give the next job to somebody else. Mom always said she thought I'd be great some day, and being great means doing your best job. If she was still alive I'd want her to think I done great, so I always do my best job. Everybody wants to be great.

When the cleaning business is slow, and the can business is slow, sometimes I sell blood, just like everybody else does, but it always makes me feel a little guilty. I mean, there's guys out there in a lot worse shape than me, guys who got in accidents and can't think so good any more, or alcoholics, or maybe regular guys who just ain't got ambition. Some of them don't even have an apartment, and selling blood is their only steady money. I always worry I'm taking their gig away from them. But then I never claimed to be a saint, so if I really need the twenty-five bucks, I go down to the clinic and sell some blood, drink the glass of orange juice they give you, and remember that somebody in a car accident or something is going to be real happy I did.

But today I had an appointment down at Colorado General Hospital for an even better gig. Eight hundred fluffing dollars for being in some test.

17

See, the big drug companies, when they come up with a new medicine, they have to do all these tests to make sure it's safe. First they test it on animals and if none of the animals die they have to test it on humans. Someone told me that if they think it still might be dangerous they test in on people in real poor countries, where they can get lots of volunteers for not much money. Plus, if any of them die, they don't have good newspapers to report it, and even if they did they ain't in English so nobody will ever know about it. But if any of the people die, they just stop the test and it never gets over here until they fix it.

But if they want to sell it to Americans, they gotta test it on Americans. Since nobody's gonna just pop a bunch of brand new pills for free, they pay you to do it.

They don't let just anybody into the study. You can't be an alcoholic, or crazy, or be sick. You got to stay in the hospital during the study, so if you got a regular job you probably can't get time off. They prefer guys like me who are healthy, in good shape, pretty smart, and self-employed. From that description, you'd think a bunch of lawyers would do it to make some extra cash during weeks they didn't have a trial or something, but I never seen one. I think it's because most of them work for the drug companies that write the checks and they probably have a rule about that.

At first I was nervous about it myself. But then I decided that by the time they got around to testing a drug on Americans they already tested it on animals and French guys and nobody died so it was mostly safe. I said what the heck and signed up. I did two studies last year, at four hundred a pop and never felt a thing.

Now if I'm honest about it, I'd have to say there was a bunch of reasons I was excited about the gig. First the money was better than a whole month at most jobs and it was only going to take a week. That one is obvious. Then there was the walk to the hospital which takes about an hour and which I don't do every day. You always see somebody you know, or some pretty girls, or a neat car. Sometimes you'll find something cool just laying on the sidewalk, like a hat or a quarter. Then at the hospital, it's just like a fancy hotel, with TVs and big meals and real clean beds. But if I was under oath and had to tell the truth, the whole truth and nothing but the truth, I'd have to say the other reason I like the hospital was that Holly worked there. I mean she's not my girlfriend or anything. I'm not crazy, I'm not gonna pretend that to you. I mean pretend she's my girlfriend, not pretend I'm not crazy. Which I'm obviously not, but then you don't know me so you might not know. She just lives downstairs from me and is real nice, and also smart, maybe even smarter than me, being a nurse and all. You can like someone pretty much without them being your girlfriend.

I never seen Holly at the hospital anyway, so it wasn't like I was planning on seeing her this time either. She worked on a whole different floor than where they done the studies. But I liked it that I'd be in the same building as her, with a chance we'd run into each other, I had to admit that. So I guess that is crazy, just a little.

The week before, I'd went in and they'd tested my blood and a bunch of other crap and said I could be in the study, so now I was gonna go do it. I put some extra T-shirts in my Nike bag, which somebody thrown out just because the zipper don't work. I watered the daisy and after I thought about it a while I moved it inside onto the window ledge. Now that it had a flower, I didn't want it to freeze and it was still early in the year. I put my toothbrush in the bag and that was it. Don't take me long to pack, plus with the zipper broke, something could fall out if I stuffed the bag too full.

Then I seen the drawing I done on my refrigerator and thought what the heck. So I rolled it up and put a rubber band around it and put it in my Nike bag. No rule against decorating the wall by your bed at the hospital. Then I locked the door and started walking.

The walk was pretty ordinary. I didn't get interested in anything so much I had to stop and watch it, so I got there about seven.

The nurse reminded me of my mother but more serious, with some gray hair. She looked like a real sturdy woman. She was the one who had took my blood last week, but she still looked surprised to see me. "Are you here for the study?" she said from behind a little counter. She kept pushing her glasses up on her nose.

"Yes ma'am," I said.

"Well, you certainly are punctual. We didn't expect you until eight."

"The walk was kind of ordinary," I explained.

"Yes, of course," she said, looking through some file folders. Then she took one out. "Here we are. John Cable, right?"

"Yes, ma'am." I said. "But everyone calls me Jumper."

"Good. Follow me."

I carried my bag and walked behind her. She was a fast walker for an older woman.

"You use that lemon cleaner, don't you?" I said.

19

"I'm not sure what they use," she said, sort of formal.

"Smells like lemons, I use it myself sometimes," I said but she didn't answer. I decided she was just thinking about doing her job, which is good. "Really cleans good," I said, mostly just to be polite. "Like if there's a dead mouse or something. Makes it smell a lot better. After you get rid of the mouse, of course." One thing cleaning apartments had did for me was I knew my cleaners. But after I said it I felt bad in case she thought I was saying their nice clean hospital might have dead mice. So to make her feel better I said "Or dried vomit. It's really good on that too."

"I'll make a note of that," she said and so I felt better. I was gonna tell her that TSP works even better and is cheaper, but I didn't. Nobody likes you to tell them how to do their job. Better to say the compliment about the cleaner they used, which would make them feel good.

She led me back to a little room where she took more blood and weighed me and looked in my ears and eyes. They always did that stuff, so now that you know about it I won't keep telling you every time. Like, OK, now it's Tuesday and they took more blood and weighed me again and then they looked in my eyes and ears. And then, OK now it's Wednesday and they took more blood and all that other stuff. Since it's pretty much the same every time it might be less boring for you if I don't just keep saying the same stuff over and over even if genius writers tend to do that. Like the guy who said miles to go before I sleep and then said the same dang thing again, like we wasn't listening the first time. And since it don't matter to what I was going to tell you about anyway, in case you forget about them weighing me or whatever, it really don't matter.

She give me a sheet of paper to read about the drug and another paper to sign that said I read the first one and if I died I wouldn't sue them. Then she left.

Now I'm a pretty good reader, but I admit I couldn't understand that first paper much. The drug was called ML629, which don't tell you much. It was what they called a perception drug, which either meant you couldn't get it unless a doctor said you could or else it had to do with the way railroad tracks look closer together the farther away they are. Either one was fine with me. I never could draw railroad tracks, so maybe it would help me with my art. Of course, with my camera deal I could probably draw railroad tracks OK, so I didn't really need it. But if I died I didn't plan to sue anybody, so I signed it.

After a while the nurse come back, took the paper and led me down the hall. The room where us study guys stayed was big with about ten beds in it. I was the first one there so I took the bed closest to the window and put my Nike bag on it. The windows don't open, probably for safety. It was the fifth floor and not even me would jump five stories, but a beginner might think he'd try it. From my bed the view was great. You could see parking lots and houses and warehouses and the smoke from a refinery. The view alone was worth the whole thing.

Plus they had a couple of TVs in there, hooked to cable so there was more shows than a guy could watch in a week. Down the hall they had a room with two pool tables and some video games and a couch, so in some ways it was even better than home. Which is good because it was kind of boring staying there for a week.

Then I remembered my drawing. I took it out and unrolled it. I wished I had brung some tape to put it up with, but I hadn't. I looked through my jeans pockets for a stick of gum, which would work as good as tape, but no luck.

The nurse brung in the next guy who looked like a college guy. He was tall and had on a REM T-shirt, who I guess are cool again, and he had a big bag of clothes and a laptop computer and about six books. He was ready to stay there a lot longer than a week. The nurse brought him over.

"Michael, this is John. John, Michael. Just pick a bed and when everyone's here we'll get started.

"Nice to meet you Michael," I said, shaking his hand. "Everyone calls me Jumper." He raised one eyebrow, like Spock would, or like he never heard the name before. I get that a lot. I turned to the nurse.

"Excuse me, ma'am. Do you have any band aids?"

"Did you cut yourself?"

"No, no," I laughed. "I just wanted to hang up my drawing."

"We have special tape for that. I'll bring you some."

"Thanks," I said.

By this time Michael had picked the bed farthest away from mine and was unpacking stuff. Boy, you would of thought he was moving in forever, as much stuff as he had. I got the feeling he wasn't in the mood to talk much yet, so I let him alone. Maybe this was his first study and he was nervous. I decided to keep an eye on him in case he got worried. Sometimes

21

all a guy needs is someone to be friendly to him, especially a guy like me who's a little older and done more stuff. Don't cost me a thing and I got the time, so I see it as my job, except there ain't any pay. So it's more like a hobby. Besides, he probably knows stuff I don't know, like computer stuff, so you can't look down on him if he gets nervous. Everybody gets nervous sometimes, just for different things.

The nurse brung more guys in there and everybody said their names and we all shook hands, but you probably don't need to know all their names. She also give me this tape that was sticky on both sides and helped hang my drawing. Then we stepped back and looked at it.

"What is it?" she asked. I knew she was joking on me but I played along. Right away I liked her better, having a sense of humor and all.

"It's a daisy," I said.

"Hmm," she said. "Very modern."

"Thanks," I said, and then she walked off to get more study guys.

When all the guys had showed up the nurse come back in with a doctor. You could tell he was a doctor because he had on a white coat, plus he had white hair that was extra neat, and a nice suntan even though we hadn't had enough sunny days to get that from playing golf yet. Doctors go get their suntans different places from where they work, so that's a clue right there.

"Thank you all for participating in our study," he said, and we all sat on the edges of our bed and listened. Nobody fooled around or anything.

"The drug we'll be testing this week is designed to help people with certain rare mental disorders. None of you show any symptoms of this disorder, so you should experience nothing at all related to its efficacy. We're simply going to monitor you for unexpected side effects. The drug has been tested extensively on laboratory animals with no apparent deleterious effects. It's also been tested on humans in other countries and has so far proven completely innocuous." I smiled. If it didn't bother French guys it probably wouldn't bother Americans either. At least I think that's what he was saying.

"It may reassure you to know that the drug itself is completely organic, a combination of chemicals normally found in everyone. The drug merely provides a higher concentration than normal, which the manufacturer believes will offset the deficiency noted in people afflicted with the disorder."

One guy raised his hand and the doctor nodded at him.

22

"So, what exactly is this disorder?"

I ain't even gonna try to repeat the name of the disease. It sounded like some long foreign word, probably French, which I don't speak that much of except for "we" and "French fries."

"The symptoms are similar to clinical depression and it's often misdiagnosed accordingly. Luckily for us, very rarely it also affects members of the porcine family." He stopped and looked around at us. "Pigs. Approximately one in 100,000 pigs exhibit the same deficiency, accompanied by analogous symptoms. The drug has shown remarkable success in alleviating the symptoms."

One guy started to laugh, even if the doctor was being serious. "Sorry," the guy said. "But if it can cheer up depressed pigs I want double doses." Everyone else laughed too. The guy was kind of fat, so he was making a joke on himself, which you have to like. Even the doctor smiled a little.

The college guy Michael raised his hand.

"How can they tell when a pig is depressed?"

Everyone laughed at that one too. This seemed like a good bunch of guys.

"Porcine physiology is similar to human," the doctor said, as if he was gonna answer the guy's question. The fat guy's name was Gary, which would be handy for you to know if I'm gonna talk about him. So the doctor was answering Michael's question, but Gary was the one who got them started talking about the pig part of the study. The doctor seemed serious. "Pigs that seem listless or easily frightened are candidates for further diagnosis. One symptom unique to pigs is that they seem to lose their fear of heights. They often jump off things."

Suddenly I got a lot more interested. I'd never thought of a pig jumping off something, which is funny because I thought a lot about jumping. But then I never knew that many pigs.

But he didn't say anything more about that and somebody asked him another question and everyone forgot all about pigs. Except me. I kept thinking how if a pig jumped off something they thought it was crazy. Or maybe the doctor was just getting in the joke mood with everyone else and he made it up to be funny. Sometimes if you go to school for a long time, like college and medical school, you said jokes nobody thought was funny. I seen it a bunch of times.

Or maybe he was serious. Maybe some pigs like jumping, kind of the way I do, and they're regular pigs who just like to jump. If this drug cured them of something they loved to do, I got a little nervous maybe it would cure me too. Eight hundred bucks ain't near enough to give up jumping for.

Like I said, everybody gets nervous about different stuff, and now you see I ain't any better than anyone else like that. But mostly you worry and then it turns out the thing that got to you ain't near as bad as how you thought it would be. I seen it lots of times, so I decided to just wait and see what happened.

Still, when they lined us up to take the pill I was breathing a little fast, like the first time I done a night jump and couldn't see where I was going. But I didn't say nothing, I just swallowed the pill and went back to my bed to look out the window.

I felt pretty ordinary, so I decided maybe I was OK. I watched the smoke from that refinery way out in Commerce City, but I was also kind of watching myself. I said I was just doing my job. We was supposed to notice if we felt anything and tell the nurse and that's what I was doing. But the whole truth and nothing but the truth was that I was nervous too.

For my own little experiment, I thought about jumping off my balcony and it still sounded cool. If I would of had a good place to do it I would of gone and done a few jumps right then to relax. That seemed like a good sign. Anyway, the doc hadn't actually said the drug cured the pigs of jumping and he probably would of if it did. Maybe it just made them happier when they trained.

All day we watched TV, or shot pool or played video games. Some guys played chess, which never seemed that fun to me. Michael typed on his laptop and read his books and stuck to himself. I watched him but he seemed OK so I didn't go over and talk to him. They brought our meals on trays like we was sick people staying in the hospital. One thing you had to like was how they usually had Jell-O in most of the meals. I've made Jell-O and you don't just put that stuff together in five minutes. You gotta heat water and mix it up and pour it in a bowl, but then you ain't done. You gotta let it cool in the refrigerator for a long time or else it's just a gooey drink. So all that Jell-O took some planning to make it ahead of time. But it ain't real hard to make either, and they tell you how on the box.

Different nurses come in a lot and asked how we was doing and took our temperatures and wrote it down. Nobody got sick although the fat guy,

24

Gary, always oinked like a pig, which the nurses who hadn't been there in the morning didn't get. But Gary thought it was funny, and some of the guys did too. It just reminded me of the jumping pigs, but I didn't spoil his fun. When he oinked at a nurse I always laughed to be polite.

One time I thought I might read something, since Michael the college guy was doing that a lot. I ain't got nothing against reading, if you like it, but you gotta admit most stuff you read is better if they also put pictures in with the words. They had some magazines and I picked up a Harpers, which don't have that many pictures. It had a thing in it about some new book, to tell you if you should read it or not. This guy John Leonard wrote it, and I started about in the middle because it takes writers a while to get themselves going full speed and it seems a waste to read what they wrote before they was up to full speed. So he says, 'Those critics who insist on looking under Morrison's skirts for Faulkner's boll weevils will be confounded to learn that Love is more like a Scott Fitzgerald. Not that her black Gatsby would go tender into any night.'

Well, obviously I put the magazine down and give up on reading for that day. This guy was writing in code, and it was like the code we all used in high school to make the teacher think we read some book when we really was out looking for skirt weevils like Mr. Leonard. Some guys can write about girls without their face getting red, and I ain't criticizing them, but I ain't got the gift.

But if you was going to write a book, you'd probably read one first to see how real writers do stuff. Then when you wrote your own you'd do the things you liked but you wouldn't do the bad stuff. Plus you might get ideas that you wouldn't of got on your own.

I done that myself when I realized I was writing this book. You write down a list of the stuff that goes on and pretty soon if you got enough pages, it's a book. I been writing a book without really knowing it, so I figured I better read one. I didn't want to read a bunch of bad books so I went to the library and picked a couple that had won prizes and read them. Might as well learn from prize winners, I thought.

After about a month of reading the first one I decided that idea was more hassle than it was worth. You could read three or four pages in a row without anything happening, so what was the point of that? I thought they must of cheated to win the prize and so it would be dumb to copy them too much. But then I tried to read the second book, which was by a whole different guy, and it was the same deal.

That was a discouragement. I couldn't write that boring if there was free pizza in it for me. If that's what it took to win book prizes, I was out of luck.

Then I decided that maybe there was two different kinds of books, the ones you read and the ones that win prizes. I wrote down the stuff I noticed and stopped reading. I decided to throw in a couple of their writing tricks just in case I ever wanted to enter a contest, but mostly I'd write how I liked, which was the opposite of them.

One thing them books did is tell you a bunch of stuff you didn't need to know about people. Like if a guy was walking down the street and found a million dollars, they'd spend about ten pages telling about walking down the street, and what it looked like, and what the guy was thinking about and what he would of thought when he was a kid if he walked down the street, and what his father would of thought if he'd come over from Ireland because of bad potatoes and had found the street and started walking down it, and how it reminded him of bad potatoes or whatever and so he'd stop walking and start crying.

By the time he found his million dollars you were sorry all that money was wasted on a boring guy like him.

So I ain't going to go hog wild on adding a bunch of extra stuff but I guess I'll try to add some. Them books like to tell you a bunch of crap about the people and maybe they got a reason for it I don't get. But if anybody's got bad potatoes in their story I'm going to leave them out, because I already had enough of them. If you put too much stuff in a book that ain't about what happened, pretty soon you forget where you was when you started adding stuff. So in case you forgot, I was in a hospital doing a drug study.

CHAPTER TWO

in which I tell about the hospital study, and meet some gang guys, and have to make a insurance payment I'd rather not of had to make.

That night I couldn't sleep even after everyone else was. Some of the guys snored and mumbled things you couldn't understand. Gary oinked a couple of times in his sleep, which I about laughed out loud at, but it might wake people up so I tried not to. Sometimes I can't sleep after an exciting day, which you'd have to say this was. Plus I really felt like training. I hate to skip days but sometimes you got to.

Now I knew they didn't like us to go wandering around the hospital. They had made that pretty clear. But I got to thinking about Holly working somewhere downstairs and how surprised she'd be to see me if we run into each other. But I knew that would be weird so I put my foot down on that idea.

I decided what I really needed was a glass of milk. There was a cafeteria somewhere in the hospital. I'd been in it once before, but I was with Jim the thrift store guy and he knew where it was so I didn't pay that much attention while we walked there. I had my old wallet with ten bucks in it and nobody was going to mug me in the hospital. And they wouldn't hide a cafeteria so I figured I could probably find it. I could always go to a different floor where they didn't know I was in the study and just ask someone. They'd probably think I was a new doctor or something and figure they had to tell me.

The more I thought about a glass of milk the thirstier I got. If I didn't wake up any patients it wasn't going to hurt anybody.

OK, I know I was making up reasons to do something I wanted to do anyway. They told us not to wander around and I was working for them, so they was like my boss. You can make up reasons for anything you want to do, even if there's better reasons on the other side. But sometimes the good reasons have quiet little voices and the reasons you want to win have these big opera-star voices.

So I got up, put on my clothes and went out in the hall. Nobody was there. The elevators was down the hall to my left, but you had to walk past the nurse station, so I turned right and walked real quiet to the stairs. I opened the door and closed it slow so it wouldn't be noisy and started down.

I only went down about three steps when I had a idea and stopped. The stairs went down to a landing and then you'd turn around and more stairs went down to the left. It was a funny angle, not like jumping straight down, but each set of stairs was only half a story so that was nothing. There wasn't room at the bottom to roll like you do on a long jump or if you jump off something that's moving, like a train or a pickup truck, and I'd be going forward when I landed so I'd have to use my arms against the wall. So this wasn't an ordinary jump like I always did, which made it extra interesting. I practiced it once in my head, how I'd land and all, and in my head it worked great.

And then I jumped.

It worked just like I seen it in my brain, except I jumped a little too hard and got too close to the wall, so even catching myself with my arms my nose banged into the wall. It hurt like heck, but didn't start bleeding, so that wasn't too bad. I rubbed my nose until it didn't hurt so much and then I jumped down the next batch of stairs.

I tried to land soft so I didn't make much noise and except for that first one, I did pretty good. I don't think I woke anybody up. When I got to the bottom, I ran back up the stairs and started over. I was feeling a lot more regular, plus I was getting better and better at it from practice.

I had run up partway to start over a third time when I remembered the glass of milk. Right away I felt guilty, because the glass of milk was the reason I was out there at all. So I stopped and tucked in my T-shirt to look more like a doctor, and opened the next door I come to. I'd spent some time already and if a nurse come into our room and seen me gone I could kiss that 800 bucks hasta la vista. So I decided to go straight to the nurse station and just ask where the cafeteria was. It wouldn't be smart to waste any time.

Most floors have a big sign that says what they are, like "maternity" which means babies, but this floor didn't have no sign at all. Plus, nobody was at the nurse station. She was probably in a room with a patient, so I walked down the hall to find her. The doors were all open so you could see the patients, who was mostly pretty old and had real white skin. Most of them was hooked up to tubes and had plastic over their mouths. A few mumbled in their sleep, but nobody oinked. Still no nurse.

Then I heard someone calling out in a real soft voice. I had been looking right but now I looked left. This old lady patient was staring right at me from her bed. "Doctor..." she said. Her arm was laying flat on the bed but she was motioning me to come with her hand.

Well, shoot, I thought. I woke up somebody after all. She said it again and kept motioning and even if her voice was pretty whispery I got nervous she might wake somebody else. So I went in.

Now I never pretended to her I was a doctor. I just figured maybe she needed a drink of water or something. No way was I going to take out her kidney even if she asked me. I stood over her and she just stared at me. This lady was scared of something, I could see that by the way she looked at me. Only there wasn't nothing scary in the room. Didn't take much to figure it out.

"It was just a bad dream," I said and took hold of her hand so she'd know she wasn't still dreaming. Now she was real old and skinny and she couldn't even hold up her arm, but if I looked at her just right I seen how pretty she was when she was young. Not as pretty as Holly, but pretty enough you'd look twice if she was walking down the street. You know how sometimes you look at people and see different versions of them. So I smiled at her young version and squeezed her hand, like we was on a date and I was flirting with her. Her eyes kind of relaxed, like she was forgetting the bad dream and even though her mouth didn't really move, I knew she was smiling back at me. "How about some water?" I asked and she nodded. There was a little plastic thing with ice water on the table and some paper cups so I poured about half a cup and held it up to her lips. She drank about three drinks.

"Thank you, doctor," she said.

"Well, I ain't really..." I started, but I didn't finish. You don't need to be a doctor to give someone a drink of water, so I was pretty sure I didn't have liability issues. And I don't think she cared that much who I was. She turned to the table on the other side of her.

"My garden," she said.

Now that fooled me for a little bit, because there wasn't nothing on the table. But she seemed pretty regular so I didn't know what she was talking about. I went around to look at the floor in case something fell off it, but didn't see anything. So I layed down on the floor, which surprised me how cold it was, and sure enough there was a picture of a garden in a little frame under the bed. I hauled it out, dusted it off with my shirt and set it back on the table.

"Thank you," she said, and this time even her mouth smiled a little. Before I could say anything more, she closed her eyes and was asleep again.

I admit I was tempted to help myself to some of her water. After running up all them steps I was thirstier than when I started. But that wouldn't be right and I knew it. That was this old lady's water. So I just left and went back to my room and crawled into bed.

The next day was just like the first one except the doctor didn't come in, and I didn't try to read nothing. Mr. Leonard had cured me of that for a while. Guys watched TV and played pool. I was sitting on my bed watching cars out the window, five stories below and thinking how the people in them each probably had five stories too, like stories of stuff they'd did, but I didn't know what they was. That's one of them interesting ideas that could keep a guy busy all afternoon, except someone come up to my bed without me hearing them.

"What is it?"

I turned around and seen who was talking. Gary was standing by my bed staring at the picture.

"It's a picture," I said.

"I mean what's it a picture of?"

"Oh. It's a daisy." I started to tell him about my camera and how I done it, but then I remembered Mr. Vinci not telling anybody. But I was already started to talk so it was hard to stop all the way. I decided I could tell him just a little.

"I drew it upside down."

Gary nodded. "Right," he said. "So what does it look like if you hang it right side up?"

I stared at it. I'd got so used to looking at it upside down that now I wasn't all the way sure it was hanging right.

"It looks kind of the same," I said. "A drawing is just lines. It's how you look at it."

"Let's see it the other way," he said. So I got up and pulled it off the wall and switched it. That tape was good, it didn't rip or anything and it stuck up there again. Now it looked upside down to me.

"Just watch it for a minute," I said. Sure enough, pretty soon it looked OK to me again. But Gary shook his head. "I don't get it," he said and then he walked away. Well, you can't make somebody see something they ain't gonna see. Some people look at a river and see where the trout's gonna be, and some people think they can but they're just guessing and they don't catch no fish. So I guess art is like that.

I went down the hall to watch guys playing pool. When I come back, Gary and Michael was standing by my bed. Gary was pointing at the picture and they was both laughing. I got the feeling they was laughing at the picture, even if it wasn't funny. When they seen me they quick walked away. I went to my bed and when I passed them, Michael said, "Nice picture," but was still smiling so I didn't know if he meant it or not.

I laid down on my bed. If I tilted my head back I could seen the picture on the wall, only upside down, I was pretty sure. It made me feel good looking at it. But it bothered me there was something funny about it that I couldn't notice. Was it funny because it was in a coffee can, which you don't see that often? No, some guys draw soup cans, which ain't any better than coffee cans if you think about it. I didn't like that somebody might think it was a goofy drawing when it still looked pretty good to me. It felt like there was something wrong with those guys that made it so they couldn't see art, but they was making fun of me because of something wrong with them.

Then I thought, maybe it's the drug we was testing. Maybe it was having a side effect on them. Right away I felt better. You couldn't hold it against somebody if they had a side effect. Still, I started thinking about taking it down. You don't want to hang up your art where people just think it's funny even if it's a side effect. You might as well hang it down at the humane society, where the dogs would think it looked like a newspaper on the wall. But then you also hate to take it down and have it go to waste.

That old lady downstairs would probably like it, I thought. She liked the picture of her garden pretty much, and a daisy is kind of like a garden. Just about as fast as I thought that idea I knew what I was going to do.

That night I made myself stay awake again until everyone else fell asleep, then went back to the stairs. Only this time I had my daisy picture rolled up in one hand. I didn't even jump down the stairs, in case I got interested in that and forgot what I was doing, but just walked down real quiet. When I got to the right floor, I opened the door just a little. I seen a nurse at the station, with her back to me, so I waited until she went to do something. Then I went through the door and walked fast to the old lady's room. I admit I was breathing fast even if I hadn't done any training, like I was going to steal something, only I was really going to give something away.

31

She was wide-awake, just like the night before so I walked right in.

"Howdy, ma'am," I said and grinned at her.

"Hi," she said softly. She didn't look all that good but you could tell she remembered me.

"I brung you something." I unrolled the picture and held it so she could see. She stared at it for a minute and I kind of held my breath with my face getting hot.

"I love daisies," she said.

Well, that made me smile, that she could tell what it was right away and didn't want me to turn it upside down.

"Well, it's yours then." I looked around to see where I could hang it that she could see it. You could see she wasn't doing a lot of rolling over onto her side, and there was machines over by the wall anyway, so I tried to imagine myself being her, laying on her back and decided the best place was on the ceiling right over her bed.

"How 'bout if I hang it up there?" I asked. Her eyes brightened up and she nodded.

Well, there wasn't any way to get up there except standing on the bed with one foot on each side of her. Obviously I wanted to be careful about that. First, if a nurse come in she might think that didn't look exactly ordinary. They might even have a rule about that which would be a bigger deal than the one about not wandering around the hospital. Second, if I slipped and fell on the lady it would probably kill her outright and that was about the last thing I wanted. But like I said, I got pretty good balance, so there wasn't an incident. I just stood up there and was glad that tape was so good, because it stuck right away. Then I jumped to the floor. That part was probably a little bit of showing off, but as you guessed by now, jumping off a bed ain't a real big deal to me so it wasn't a real big showoff.

"I gotta get back to the study," I said.

"It's lovely," she said. "Just beautiful."

"You can take it home with you when you're better," I said. "That tape comes off real slick."

"I will," she said. "Thank you."

I started to go out of the room, but a nurse was standing in the door with her hands on her hips blocking my way. Uh-oh, I thought. Before I

32

could think of a good way to explain what I was doing there, the nurse said, "Jumper?"

That was an extra surprise that she knew my name, right on top of her being there in the first place, so I couldn't think of anything good to say except "yes, ma'am." But there was even one more surprise, which was that her voice was familiar, but the hall lights were bright behind her and the room was about half dark so I couldn't see her that well. Plus, I was looking down at the floor trying to think of something better to say.

"What are you doing here?" she said, sounding mad.

Now that was the question I was working on a good answer for, but I hadn't thought of one yet. But just then I remembered her voice.

"Holly?"

"Come on out of there, Jumper."

She turned around and walked out to the nurse station and I followed her. My face felt pretty hot and I was really breathing fast. This wasn't much like the way I pictured running into her at the hospital. She was going to think I was weird for sure. I wondered if she seen me standing on the bed? Now I'd put her in a bad spot, having to turn me in. When we got to the nurse station she turned around and I remembered how pretty she was.

"Now, Jumper," she said. "What were you doing in Mrs. Murphy's room?"

"Just visiting," I said, which was as close to nothing but the truth as I could think of without going into the whole truth.

"Do you know her?"

"I met her once," I said. "She likes her garden.,"

"So you came down here in the middle of the night just to visit her?"

Like I said, Holly was smart, and she was asking me questions that was hard to answer without turning yourself in, just like lawyers on TV did. So I decide to throw myself at the mercy of the court.

"I'm in a study."

"You're in a drug study?"

"Yes ma'am."

She looked at me like to see if I was joking on her, or like she was waiting for me to say something else, but I'd pretty much told the story. I tried not to think about standing on Mrs. Murphy's bed, which is the part

33

of the story I hadn't said, because it would make my face get even hotter than it was and she was smart enough to notice that. Plus, if you think of something, you're pretty likely to say it even if you wish you didn't. Holly's hair was about to her shoulders and she wore it in a ponytail, which I like because you don't see it that often. Finally she kind of flicked her head and the ponytail went to the other side and landed on that shoulder. I knew right then if she asked me more questions I'd just have to tell her the whole truth. But I could tell right then too that she was done asking me hard questions "They don't like you to wander around the hospital. Didn't they tell you that?" Her voice wasn't so lawyery any more.

"Yes, ma'am. I just wanted a glass of milk. And then I seen Mrs. Murphy and her garden picture had fell down." OK, so that happened the night before, but it was still the truth, and you don't get in trouble for telling the truth.

"She had a picture of a garden?"

"Yes ma'am. Only it had fell under her bed where she couldn't see it. So I got it out for her."

Holly nodded. "No one could figure out what she was talking about," she said, looking at the wall. "She just kept saying 'my garden.'"

"It ain't a garden, it's just a picture. You can see it for yourself."

"Well, thanks for finding it for her. I know you didn't mean any harm. But you have to get back to your room before they miss you."

"Are you going to turn me in?"

Then she smiled and I felt my face getting hot all over again. I wanted to look down at my feet at the same time I wanted to keep looking at her face.

"No, Jumper, I'm not going to turn you in. But you need to stay in the study area so they can monitor you. Will you promise me you'll do that?"

I nodded about eight times, which probably looked pretty dorky. "I promise."

"Well, go on then."

I walked out of there fast and run up the stairs to the study area. I had extra energy so I jumped up most of the steps three at a time. Even at that I wasn't breathing fast. Just as I was going into our room, another nurse was coming out with a clipboard. I nearly run into her.

"Mr. Cable!" she said, all surprised. "So there you are."

34

"I was thirsty. I was looking for a glass of milk." It sure wasn't the whole truth, but it's what I said anyway.

"You're not supposed to leave the study area."

"Yes ma'am," I said and didn't say any more. Lots of times you get in more trouble if you keep on talking. I could write a whole other book on that one.

"Well, fine." She said and erased something on her clipboard. "I'll have them send up a glass of milk. But if you want anything else you just let the duty nurse know. OK?"

I nodded. It wasn't that long until I had my milk, which was real good, and then I went back to bed. Only I couldn't get to sleep for a while, even with the milk. I should of been thinking how lucky I was not to have got busted, and how in handy that eight hundred bucks was gonna come. But the whole truth and nothing but the truth is I kept seeing Holly flip her ponytail from one side to the other. And after that I seen her smile right at me and say she wasn't going to turn me in.

I've had some good days before, but none that ended as good as that.

The rest of the week just went by. Nobody asked how come my picture was gone. I mostly watched TV, like those old black and white westerns. I didn't try to make friends and I admit I kind of stopped watching out for Michael, the college guy. That was probably wrong of me, but I just couldn't do it. Anyway, Gary and some of the others took to him pretty good, so I figured he'd be OK. Nobody tried too hard to make friends with me either. I didn't go downstairs to visit Mrs. Murphy and I sure didn't do any jumping. I'd promised Holly I'd stay in the study area, and a promise is harder to break than a rule any day. I didn't have no side effects. Gary pretty much stopped oinking. I thought about telling the nurse he'd had a side effect that made it so he couldn't see art, but I didn't do it. Maybe he couldn't see art even without the pill so it wouldn't be a side effect. At the end of the week they paid me my $800. I went straight to the bank and cashed it and put it in my shirt pocket.

When I walked home from the bank I thought about art and how it's a lot like a different version of regular life except your brain can't explain it as easy. I must have been thinking pretty hard since I didn't notice these gang guys who was on the other side of the street watching me crossed over to my side so they'd be in front of me. I knew this would be a good time to think up a plan so I didn't get beat up, and my eight hundred bucks stole

35

from me, and I started to, but in the middle of that I started thinking about words, which happens to us writer guys pretty often.

If you get serious about words, like where you're careful to use the right one all the time, or if you was writing a book like I am (which you are reading) and somebody who read it was extra serious about that kind of stuff (like you might be) then a guy would explain how he uses some words that might not be the same to you.

So take "gang guys" for one example. I used it a minute ago. You pretty much know what I mean by that except you might think I was talking about guys who was in a gang. And they might be, or they might just be guys who act the way guys in gangs do, which is trying to be all cool and tough all the time. I know guys who work in the stockroom of Wal-Mart all day, for one example, and they talk as educated as me or you and say please and take breaks when they're supposed to, but then at night they put on leather jackets and sunglasses and whatever else they think is cool and they go hang out with their buddies who work at Dairy Queen or the post office. You call them gang guys and that cheers them right up.

Then there's other guys who don't have a gang, but they're drug dealers or criminals. So they might dress all cool just so they don't stand out from the Wal-Mart guys while they sell weed on a street corner. Then there's other guys who actually joined a gang, so they gotta wear the same clothes just like the Dairy Queen guys do when they're at work. The gang makes 'em do it, just like the DQ manager does. You can't hold it against them.

So you got a bunch of guys hanging out looking tough and talking crude and some of them are as nice as anybody, and some are pretty mean. To me they're all gang guys. It's smart to act respectful, but you mostly don't need to get too nervous. Only a few of them will hurt you just for the fun of it. To them guys, it don't matter how nice you act to them. They're gonna do what they want anyway.

So that's what I mean when I say "gang guys."

There's about three other words that you hear every day that my mom told me wasn't that polite. I try not to use them myself, unless I hit my thumb with a hammer in which case the rule book is out the window. But you can see the pickle it puts me in. I'm writing a true book, so if someone says one of them words that ain't polite, I gotta write the word they said or else it ain't a true book. But it don't seem fair they should make me write in an impolite way if I don't want to just because that's how they talk. So sometimes I might write a word in code, by using a word that sounds like

36

the word they said but ain't so impolite. Like if "hat" was a bad word, I might say "cat" instead and you'd know what they really said. If a guy says, hey, it's cold outside, I'm gonna wear my cat on my head, then you know he really said "hat." That way it's a true book, but with the code it ain't so impolite. It just seems fair to let you know right up front so you don't think I don't hear good when people talk. I always code them three bad words and sometimes others if I think it's a part that a kid might read. Like if there was a puppy in one part, kids would like that part, so I'd be extra careful about coding bad words. I hope it don't piss you off.

Just so you remember where we was, some gang guys had crossed the street so now they was ahead of me and I was walking toward them. By the time I done all that thinking, I had got pretty close to them without really coming up for a plan of how not to get beat up.

OK, once they make a point to cross over to be in front of you, you're pretty much gonna have a conversation when you get to them. So I just kept walking down the sidewalk toward these gang guys and them walking toward me, but I didn't know if they was selling drugs, or if they worked at Dairy Queen and this was just their hobby. They was about a block away, which ought to be enough time to think of something good to say, so I started thinking about that. But every time you should think about one thing, that's when you start thinking about something else.

I started thinking about how to tell one gang from the next one. Sometimes you can tell by their clothes. It used to be every gang would choose a color they liked and they all wore something with that color. I heard that colors used to be a word for flag, and so when you showed your colors, you showed your pirate flag, or your France flag or whatever. Gangs is like that. They don't like other guys to wear their colors. It helps keep track of their turf. That idea worked pretty good in the olden days, before gangs was such a popular hobby. If you think about it, there ain't that many colors, and even if you get two of them per gang, you gotta figure red and blue are gonna get took on the first day and by the time you get to pink and tan it gets hard to look mean in your outfit. You might as well just wear the Dairy Queen uniform. So now they do other stuff, like wear tattoos, or one kind of haircut.

What's bad is a lot of that stuff is secret, which is why gangs is fun. But it makes it so sometimes you just can't tell.

That's what I thought about when I was going to be thinking up something good to say so these guys wouldn't beat me up. By now they was right in front of me. There was four of 'em and they stopped and blocked the sidewalk. They happened to be white guys, maybe twenty years old. They wasn't wearing the same color, or a tattoo, and their hair was all a little long but I couldn't see exactly what the uniform was. But they all had the mean look on their faces down pat.

"Where do you think you're going?" the main guy said.

"Down to the thrift store," I said. The guy wasn't very friendly; he was looking me over trying to decide if I was tough or stupid or a plainclothes cop or what. I wished I had spent the time walking up to them using my whole brain on a plan not to get beat up. But a lot of times plans don't work all that well anyway, so sometimes you're as good off not making one. By now the guy decided I didn't look too tough, or like a cop.

"Give me your money," he said. He sounded just like a lawyer, all sure of himself.

"I ain't got that much money," I said

He punched me about as hard as he could in the stomach and I bent over.

"I said give me your money."

OK, so I wasn't hurt as bad as I let on. I seen his punch coming so I tightened my stomach and pulled back a little when it hit. I could of punched him back, which would of surprised the heck out of him, but then he'd think he had to protect his honor by having his three friends beat me up. I didn't think his honor was worth that much to me, so I held my stomach with both hands and coughed and tried to look really scared. He smiled and took a step toward me. I shook my head, like I couldn't talk and reached into my back pocket for my wallet. He took it from me.

"Ten bucks! You gotta be joking."

"I ain't that much of a joker," I said, remembering to stay bent over. "You ain't modeling proper behavior for your buddies," I said. "You hit a guy, then they think it's OK to hit a guy, and pretty soon everybody's hitting people and pretty soon you have a war. You don't want to have to explain starting a war, do you?"

"I ought to mop up the sidewalk with your head for wasting my time," he said and his buddies smiled like that sounded fun to them too. They moved around so they surrounded me. There ain't nothing you can say back to a comment like that without making things worse. I didn't have no chance against four guys. Mostly the smart thing is to just let gang guys

38

feel like they won and they leave you alone. The second best thing is to run away and hope they ain't faster. The last thing you want is to let them mop up the sidewalk with your head. Sometimes that ain't as fun for them if you manage to land a few good kicks or punches. But against four guys who was a little younger and in pretty good shape you had to figure I'd wind up in the emergency room again, with another doctor bill that wasn't likely to get paid very soon and not feeling good for a while.

But then, that's just part of life and you can't do much about it. It happens to everybody. They was too close around me to run. So I made a decision. I'd already given him my insurance wallet and that was all they deserved. If any more fighting happened, I'd have to do some of it myself. The guy took a step toward me. I stood up straighter so I'd have a good shot at him if he started to throw another punch. I stared back at him this time, and he was deciding how fun it might be to beat me up while I'm deciding if I could kick out his kneecap before his buddies could grab me from behind. I figured I probably could, and if I ducked low afterward I could probably tackle one of them other guys and hit my head right into his stomach while I did. In football that's called "leading with your helmet" and it ain't legal, but in a fight it's just a smart move. Trust me, it hurts like heck and you don't want to do much fighting for a minute after you get tackled like that. That would only leave two of them, which seemed a lot more fair. They'd still probably beat me up, but there was no way I wouldn't land a good punch or two against only two of them, so that cheered me up quite a bit.

The guy staring at me must of figured out that I was making a plan and he took a step backward. "Not worth our time," he says. "Let's get out of here."

And just like that they walked away. I watched them for a minute, then walked back to my apartment.

39

CHAPTER THREE

In which I tell you what I look like, and do some jumping, and Holly makes me nervous with questions. Which sounds pretty boring, but it ain't a real long chapter.

Back at home I watered my daisy, opened up a can of minestrone soup and took it out on my balcony and sat on my apple crate to wait for it to get dark. Maybe tomorrow I'd do another drawing, I thought. But for right now, I liked the way the can felt in my hand, and the way the sky looked as it got dark. I'd seen enough TV to last me a long time and I had the big part of $800. Best of all, in a little while I'd do some training. I was pretty sure that drug hadn't cured them pigs of wanting to jump. It sure hadn't cured me. But since I was just thinking about all that, it might be boring for you to watch me doing nothing. You might as well watch TV. So this would be a good time to fill in more blanks about me and the other people I'm writing about while it gets dark.

You already know everything about me, so I don't see much blanks to fill in. My hair is brown and I keep it a little longer than some people think is in fashion, but not long like a girl. My eyes is brown to match my hair and I don't wear glasses or contacts. I mostly wear jeans and running shoes, which my dad always called sneakers, so I do too. I know how to swim, and I can ride a bike, only someone swiped mine and I ain't got around to buying me a new one. I can drive a car pretty good, and I had one for a while. It was a Pinto, which was a good deal because people thought their gas tanks exploded, but mine never did. Sometime I'll get me another car, but I ain't decided which kind fits my style yet. Lots of guys in towns don't use cars because of parking issues, and buying gas, and fixing them. It don't slow you down much not to have one. You got to sell a lot more cans if you want to pay for owning a car and that don't make sense. It'd be like working two jobs so you could hire a butler. I'd rather just give my butler that second job and open the door myself when somebody knocked. A car would be handy if you wanted to go somewhere and maybe a butler is handy like that too in some way I don't get. I ain't saying there's something bad with having a butler, I just ain't felt the need myself. But then my door don't have no tricks to it.

There's a lot of stuff you might know more about than me. Like politics for one example, which makes sense to some people. Guys apply for the job of running the country who ain't ever run a country before. I think America should buy a little country somewhere, like one of them little ones by Mexico, and if you want to run America you got to practice by running that one first. You wouldn't hire a doctor who never operated on a brain before just because he swore up and down how good he thought he could do it. No way. You make him practice on rat brains first, and if most of the rats come out OK, you might hire him. So I think we should make politicians practice on little countries too.

In a way it was good I give away the daisy picture, because I was anxious to do another one, but I hadn't thought of what the next one should be of. Since the daisy one turned out so good, but I didn't have it any more, it made sense to do another one. Plus, now it had two flowers on it, which was even better.

While I was getting the mirror set up, and putting the paper on the fridge, I was thinking how lucky I was to be a renaissance guy instead of a career guy. If I was a doctor, for one example, I couldn't just take a day off to do art or other stuff I wanted to do that didn't make money. My appointments wouldn't let me. That's not saying there's something wrong with being a career guy. Doctors probably really enjoyed sticking their hands up a guy's butt or whatever. You can't hold it against them, doing something they love, even if to you it ain't that appealing. I went through all the careers I could think of and they all seemed pretty ordinary. I gotta admit being a doctor seemed about the worst.

I tried to draw a little faster this time. Three hours seems a long time to take, even if you was doing masterpieces. I bet Mr. Vinci couldn't get Mona to sit still for three hours. If he was real slow, she'd have to come back the next day and wear the same clothes. One thing I know is that girls don't like to wear the same clothes two days in a row.

Maybe if I got real fast I'd ask Holly to be Mona for me. That's a picture I wouldn't ever give away, unless she wanted it herself.

"Don't be stupid," I said out loud. I'd probably never be good like Mr. Vinci and, if I wasn't, I had no business even thinking about doing a picture of Holly. But you can think things that probably won't never happen and that's OK. If you don't think up things you might do you won't ever do nothing. But I'd have to be a lot faster. I couldn't even think up asking Holly to wear the same clothes two days running, except for her uniform.

41

So this time the drawing only took about two hours and ten minutes, plus a break to eat a peanut butter sandwich and it was just as good as the first one. Maybe even better. Same deal this time. I got so used to seeing it upside down it looked wrong when I switched it. It also looked tall and skinny at first, but pretty soon it looked regular to me.

I had let my groceries get pretty low, so after I looked at my new drawing for a while, I put twenty bucks in my shirt pocket, plus a ten in my back pocket where my wallet used to be and walked over to the store. I got all my usual stuff, peanut butter and bread and milk and some cans. I started to get in line to pay when I thought of something I forgot. I went over to the fruit at the back of the store. I was feeling pretty rich, but I didn't want to be show-offy. I asked the guy working there what other apples tasted like them New Zealand ones and he showed me some. I bought five of them, paid my money and went home. After I put my groceries away, I went outside and walked to the thrift store.

"Hey, Jumper, what's new?" Jim said.

"Had another insurance claim," I said back.

"Geez, Jumper, are you OK?"

"Yeah, I'm fine. Just doing my part to trickle down my money. Keeping guys off welfare. But I need a new wallet."

"You're pretty smart, Jumper, with that wallet trick. But if they ever catch on they'll be pissed."

"Them guys ain't too bright. Your wallets in the regular place?"

"Aisle six, halfway down on the left. Couple real nice ones."

"Old and beat up is better for me."

"Got a couple of them too. Fifty cents, three for a dollar."

"Thanks."

Sure enough, they had a bunch of old wallets. I grabbed up three, took them to the counter and got out a five. While Jim was counting out my changed, I put the bag of apples on the counter.

"You ain't gonna believe this one," I said.

"Oh no, Jumper, not again."

"I was real careful this time and got all the same ones. These is American apples, I asked and everything. But I never heard of this flavor, and it was a mistake. Taste like stick to me."

That's a case where I used one of the three impolite words which I should not of, but I ain't gonna make it worse by writing it. So stick is a code word. Code words is real popular in books these days. Mr. Vinci even had a code, but his book of it was so big I ain't got around to reading it yet. But since I'm a fan because of his mirror trick, if I ever hear he needs the money, I'll buy one of his books.

Aside from the code part, what I said to Jim was a little lie. I didn't taste any of them apples, so I ought not to have pretended I did. But then I ain't that crazy about any apples, so I probably wouldn't of liked these either. So it was kind of the truth too.

"Geez, Jumper, you got five of them."

"I come into a little cash, so I was feeling pretty flush. Can't return em, they got a policy, so I gotta throw them away. Yours if you want 'em."

"At least let me pay you for them."

"No way, man. I'll never learn my lesson that way. You try to pay me and they're going right in the dumpster. I'm gonna leave 'em right there, what you do with 'em ain't my business."

I put my ten-dollar bill into my new wallet and put the spare wallets in my backpack.

"How's the leg doing, by the way?" I asked. It was about the weirdest thing in the world, but sometimes his leg that wasn't there hurt.

"Not bad. Glad the weather's warming up. It's better in the summer."

"Well, you take care," I said and walked out the door.

"Thanks for the apples," he hollered after me and I waved my hand above my head.

By now you kind of know how my days go, so I won't write 'em all down one after another. Some days I went out looking for cans, some days I drew, some days I cleaned up apartments or other jobs like that. Even if you make some extra money you gotta be productive or else you'll forget how to. You can't be great if you don't show up. Even if you ain't got a regular job like a career guy, you gotta show up, even if you just made eight hundred big ones.

Most nights I trained, at least the nights Holly was working. Sometimes when she was home I'd go out and train other places, like at the park. They got some pretty good trees at City Park, which you could climb partway and then jump down on the grass. But you gotta watch out for people

43

taking walks. Once, about 11:13 at night, I jumped from a tree and this man and woman was about ten feet from where I landed. I hadn't even seen them. Lucky for me they was kissing each other right at that second and never seen me either. I stood real still and then they walked past. I could of reached out and touched them, but of course I didn't. They was pretty lucky too, if you think about it. If someone was gonna jump out of a tree and land where they was walking, it could just as easy been a weird guy instead of me. After that I was careful to watch out for people walking.

I never seen anybody else jumping, but that don't mean they don't. If I figured out to be careful and not to tell people, I bet they done that too. For all I know, everybody in the world is a jumper. Maybe somebody famous, like Jay Leno, will start talking about it and then everyone else will too. But it's a private kind of deal so maybe no one will ever talk about it. It ruins things when everybody starts talking about them. Like if someone seen a movie and talks about it, it ain't as good if you see it after that since you know stuff that happens in it already. But I don't think Mr. Leno would spoil jumping for people, because he seen lots of movies and heard people talk about them, so he knows how that works. I ain't so sure about Mr. Letterman, though. He drops watermelons off buildings which could give a terrorist an idea to do that too, which is one of the ways they win. By having other people think up their ideas for them. There ain't any terrorists as smart as Mr. Letterman so he shouldn't give them ideas. But except for that, he seems like a pretty regular guy too.

I was drawing different stuff now, like my apple crate, and a trash sack. One time a bird landed on my balcony and I tried to draw him. I drew the fastest I ever did, because I figured he'd fly off pretty soon, which he did. So I just got the big lines drew. I gotta admit, even I have to stare at that one for a while before I see the bird. I had pretty much decided to draw an apple and give it to Jim, but I wasn't all the way sure. If he just thought it was funny I'd feel pretty dumb. I drew on a lot of days when I didn't have other appointments, and by now I had 27 pictures and could do one in about 58 minutes.

Before I knew it, it was summer and the can business had picked up. I was walking home with a full trash sack of cans when I seen Holly walking toward me. She was in her nurse clothes, so I knew she was going to work. I didn't want to make her late, so I just said hi and kept walking. But she stopped right in front of me.

44

"Jumper," she said. It wasn't like a "hello jumper" kind of voice, but a voice like teachers use trying to get your attention, which I admit was a voice I heard once or twice in school myself.

So I stopped.

"Hi, Holly," I said again and looked down to make sure I hadn't did something dumb like put on my T-shirt inside out.

"Do you remember Mrs. Murphy?" she asked.

"Yes," I said and didn't add no more words. The less words you say when you broke a rule the better off your case goes. I had figured they wouldn't find out about me standing on her bed after all this time, but now I got worried again. So I didn't want to keep talking and get in worse trouble.

"She went home," Holly said, watching my face extra careful, like maybe I had peanut butter on it. She didn't say nothing else, but just waited. It would of been smart for me to say something real short back, like, "Oh?" and then shut up. But it was hard for me to be my smartest around Holly. If she was using lawyer talk on me again, it was way too slick for me to see what she was up to. But by now, after I thought all that, I knew I'd waited too long so I didn't have the choice of saying just "oh" because then what took me so long to think up that answer? So I had to just answer as natural as I could and then next time she asked something I'd answer real short, now that I thought that strategy up.

"That's good. She was a nice lady. I hope her garden is good. She likes her garden."

"She wasn't supposed to go home."

"Where was she supposed to go?" That seemed pretty short, plus it wasn't about standing on her bed.

Holly stared at me some more and didn't talk again for a minute. Her being quiet felt like a whole new kind of cross-examining. You always got the right to remain silent, but they always know you're guilty if you do. Just don't say something about standing on the bed, I told myself. She kept watching me careful, then she answered.

"People on that floor don't go home. They don't go anywhere."

"She didn't seem like someone who would break rules. I bet she just didn't know."

"She didn't break any rule. She went into complete remission."

45

"I didn't even know she was Catholic." That was short, plus it probably made me look smart.

Holly stared at me some more. Her ponytail looked extra nice, and her nurses outfit was all ironed and neat. I would of been just as happy if we could of just stood there while she talked and I looked at her, only that wasn't her idea right now. She wanted me to do my part of the talking too.

"She said she started feeling better after your visit."

"Well, I felt better too." I thought it might be good to aim the conversation a different direction. That's what the President of the United States does when someone asks him a question he don't want to answer. He aims them in a different direction, which is a gift he's got. It might be the gift that put him ahead of the other guys who wanted to be President. Plus, he's a Einstein Bagel if I ever seen one. So I ain't saying I got the gift like him, but it was worth a shot.

"She was real pretty when she was younger, wasn't she?" I said.

"Did you see a picture of her?"

Right then I knew I'd already talked too much.

I never seen a picture of Mrs. Murphy younger, but I didn't need to. Sometimes you see stuff someone else ain't looking for, like other versions of a person, and if they don't see it themselves, they look at you like you're joking on them. I could look at Mrs. Murphy and choose whether to see her younger version or her current version, just like you can. It was pretty easy to see what the older version of Holly would look like too, which was still good. But if you ain't thought about it, you can't see it, so you'd think I was making it up.

"I was just guessing," I said, which ain't exactly the truth, but I figured if I thought about it long enough I could come up with a reason it was at least part the truth.

"Yes, I'm sure she was pretty," she said. "So what exactly did you do to Mrs. Murphy?"

That word "exactly" had a real lawyer sound to it. With Holly I knew I couldn't fudge on "the truth" or "nothing but the truth" so I had to bet all my marbles on skipping "the whole truth." Just don't mention standing on the bed, I thought. Or jumping off it. I'd almost forgot that part.

"Well, let's see," I said. "It's been a couple months now so I might of forgot some details."

"You don't forget a thing, Jumper."

"Everybody forgets stuff…" I started to say when she interrupted me.

"Who missed the interception in the Broncos playoff game in 2002?"

"Mobley." That was an easy question. "But it just surprised him, it was coming so fast…" then I stopped. Geez, she could of been Perry Mason.

"About Mrs. Murphy?" She crossed her arms over her chest. But even if she was Perry Mason, I wasn't about to say the part about standing on the bed or jumping off.

"Well, let's see," I frowned like I was thinking real hard. "She called me, that's the first thing. I didn't go in there on my own."

"She called you?"

"Well, she sort of called me. She was staring right at me and she was saying "doctor" and waving for me to come with her hand, like this." I pretended I was motioning me. "And she kept calling and I thought she'd wake somebody. So I went in. She looked scared, so I held her hand and told her it was just a bad dream. Although that was a guess on my part, but there wasn't anything else in her room, so it seemed pretty likely. Then I give her some water. Then I found her picture for her."

Right then I about had a heart attack when I remembered that all that was the first night, but I actually visited her twice. If they found out I'd been wandering the halls two nights they'd probably want their 800 bucks back. I'm careful with money and the can business was pretty good, but I sure didn't still have all that $800. So the "whole truth" part I was trying to skip just got a new section to not talk about.

"Anything else?" she asked, like she was reading my mind.

"I give her a drawing." That seemed a smart way to answer. No lie in there, I just hadn't mentioned that I give it to her the second time I visited. I started to think maybe I could be a lawyer myself. But only if they didn't make me wear a tie. I ain't real big on formal dressing up, so if that was a condition of the job, like wearing a hat at the hamburger place, I'd just as soon pick up cans.

Holly nodded, like she just figured something out.

"You drew the daisy picture?"

"Yes ma'am."

47

"She loved that picture." Then she looked down at the sidewalk and her ponytail fell forward by her neck. The next thing she said was real quiet, so I ain't sure I heard right, but what I think she said is, "I did too."

Well, even if I didn't quite hear her right, which I maybe didn't, I felt about a million percent better just from the fact that maybe that's what she said. Then she looked up again.

"Well, I don't think there's anything there we need to report to the medical journals. You've been collecting cans?"

I didn't know what she was talking about so I just looked at her, waiting to understand. She pointed at the garbage sack I was carrying. I'd forgot all about it.

"Yeah," I said. "Summer's good for that."

"Well, it's good you do that. Keeps the streets a little cleaner."

"Thanks," I said. "You going to work?" As soon as I said it I knew it was the dumbest thing I ever said. Where else would she be going in her uniform? A costume party? But she didn't make a joke on it.

"Yeah, I better go or I'll be late." She looked at her watch. "You do any other drawings?" she asked.

"Twenty-seven," I said.

"Really? Twenty-seven?"

"If you count the bird. He flew away before I finished."

"Could I see them sometime?"

I couldn't keep looking at her face once she said that, so I looked at the house across the street and tried to sound casual.

"Yes ma'am. Whenever you want."

"Thanks," she said. "See you later." And then she walked past me.

I tell you what. That night I done twenty-two jumps and wasn't any tireder when I finished as when I started.

48

CHAPTER FOUR

In which I practice my art, and tell you about playing Dr. Hudson with my dad, and learn a new trick with a sack of trash. I know what you're thinking. But I bet your life would sound pretty boring to me, too, if you just said it like that.

Someone asking to see your pictures don't make her your girlfriend or anything like that, but it does put a little pressure on your art. If Holly was gonna look at my drawings I wanted some extra good ones in the stack. So I bought me a new pencil and practiced like heck. Plus I wanted to have some pictures of things a girl might like. If you think about it, most girls might not like a picture of a garbage sack, for one example.

Being summer and all, there was lots of flowers blooming. But you can't really just pick flowers out of somebody's garden, so I tended to go for wildflowers, which some people might call weeds, that I picked in the cracks of parking lots or in the grass someone was going to mow down anyway, or in the alleys where nobody really owns 'em. Plants is like people. They're pretty much everywhere, but if you ain't noticing them, they're weeds. Paying attention is what makes them flowers. Or, if you have to buy them you think they're special. If you had to buy dandelions everyone would like them. You think I'm making a joke, but I seen it with blackberries. Here in Colorado you buy a blackberry plant, which ain't cheap, and people think they're cool. But in Oregon, where we went once when I was a kid, they grow everywhere and they pay people to get rid of 'em. To them, they're weeds, even if they're easy to grow and taste great. If roses grew up like dandelions in your grass, people would say they was weeds too, even if you could still put them in a vase and look at them. Seeing weeds is like seeing art: it ain't so much the flower itself as what state you're in.

That idea give me another idea. I could practice just as easy on weed flowers as anything, but if I was gonna do a real special picture like, say, one a girl would like, maybe I should do a bunch of roses. Girls really like roses.

So every day I done practice pictures of weed flowers. They mostly died real quick, so even drawing my fastest, my pictures all had some good flowers and some pretty sick looking flowers. Some of the weeds drooped so fast I had a flower in it twice, once while I was doing the top part, with the flower all fresh, and again at the bottom of the picture all stooped over. It

49

didn't bother me though. It was like different versions of the same flower.

When I had did thirty flower pictures I decided I was ready to do some roses. A dozen roses is pretty standard, and I knew the grocery store sold 'em. So first thing one morning I put ten bucks in my pocket and walked over to the store.

They had three kinds, the real dark red ones, the pink ones, and the yellow ones. A girl maybe 18 years old was messing with the flowers. I went up to her.

"How much for a dozen roses?" I asked.

"Thirty dollars," she said without even looking up. At first I thought she was joking. I could eat for two weeks on thirty bucks. But then I looked at the sign and sure enough it said three dollars each, $30 per dozen. No wonder people liked roses so much. I didn't have an extra thirty bucks in my budget, plus I'd got spoiled by drawing all the free flowers. So I stared at them for a while, thinking about some gardens I know where they had so many roses they'd never miss a few. But then, if you got flowers worth three bucks each, you probably count them every day.

Then I had a idea. I could draw one, and then move it a little and draw it again. Even if I only had one, I could draw it twelve times.

"Have you decided yet?" the girl asked.

"Which ones is the best?" I asked.

"Depends on your taste," she said. "Can't go wrong with red. Red roses say I love you."

"Which ones says I like you pretty much?" I asked.

"Any of them. Maybe a nice combination?"

"Yeah, that's a good idea. I'll take one of them yellow ones. And one of them pink ones. No, I tell you what. If it's in a combination it don't matter so much, and I like the red ones for my purposes. A yellow one and a red one."

"The pink might go with the red a little better," she said.

"Well, it's gonna be in a pencil drawing, so the actual colors ain't that big a deal. Except if their personalities come through."

"Right," she said. She wrapped up my two roses in plastic and handed them to me. I paid my six bucks plus tax and went home. I walked extra fast, because I didn't want them to die on me and I didn't know how long

50

they'd last out of water. Plus it felt like people might look at me like I was weird from carrying flowers down the street.

At home I got out a big water glass, put my roses in it, set it on the balcony, and started drawing. You can bet I drew my fastest, because if you think about it, I had to draw six pictures on the same sheet of paper. The good thing is that roses last better than any weed I ever drew. My feet really got sore, but I kept up my concentration. This was the first drawing I ever did that was kind of for somebody else, and also the first time I paid money for a model, so I wanted it to be extra good. I didn't even stop to eat lunch. Just sometimes I'd have to stop and sharpen my pencil and shake out my hands.

It took me all day to do the drawing and by the time I was done, the sun was about to go down. I was hungry as heck and my feet was really tired and I didn't want to look at another rose for a long time. They'd almost become a weed to me, but I'd get over that.

The picture was a little odd, even I have to admit that. Some of the roses had sun on the front of them and some had it on the back. Plus, where the stems crossed each other you could see through them to the leaves and stems I'd already drew. But that seemed OK. It was like different versions of the stems and leaves, one visible and one invisible, only there at the same time. It just depended on which one you was looking at. Some of the flower parts was like that too.

I thought about bringing my new picture down to Holly but I didn't do it. Maybe she was just being polite when she said she wanted to see my drawings. Plus, even if I had her in mind when I drew the rose picture, you can't ever tell if that's the one she'd like best. I decided to wait and see if she brung it up again. The roses still looked pretty good and I thought about just giving the actual flowers to her, but that would of been a little weird. If you act like you like somebody and it turns out they don't like you all that much, it just makes them nervous. So if you like somebody and you don't want to make them nervous, the smart thing is to act like you don't like them that much. James Bond done that all the time.

I opened up a can of Dinty Moore stew, which is about my favorite, and took it out on the balcony. It was warm out there, but not as warm as my apartment and there was a good breeze. I didn't look at the roses much, but just having them out there was nice. Classed up the whole balcony.

I said to myself that I should skip training because I knew Holly wasn't working that night. But the other reason was that my feet hurt like heck

51

from standing up all day and jumping off my balcony didn't sound all that good to me, which is unusual. So I took off my sneakers, which felt good, and ate dinner. When it got darker I got some ice water and took that outside too. The breeze slowed down and I had to shoo mosquitoes away from my feet, but the sky looked cool. No clouds at all, but it felt a little damp out, which is also unusual for Denver. Maybe tomorrow we'd have Apache Fog, which the weather girl mentions sometimes. I don't know how to recognize that from regular fog, unless there's Indians in it, but it sounds cool. I was tired but it had been a good day. You spend a whole day drawing and you feel like a real artist. For some reason I started thinking about when I was a kid.

There's this thing called karma you might of heard of which my dad told me about. I don't remember too much about him, my dad I mean. So the things I do, I remember pretty hard. For example, once he decided I wasn't going to hurt myself jumping off monkey bars or swings, he always just laughed and thought it was cool. Another thing I remember is he told me that in far away places, like the kind in fairy tales and National Geographic Specials, they believed in karma. What it is, is that the universe treats you the way you treat other people, and animals of course.

Well, that made me laugh, but he said, no, really, lots of people believe that. I said it didn't make no sense, just like you're probably saying, and I wanted him to prove it.

"Can't be proved," he said.

"So why believe it?" I asked.

"Because you'll have a better life if you do," he said.

Well, that don't make sense either, but it was easy to remember so it stuck with me. It ain't any harder to act like there's karma and I'm pretty lucky, so maybe there is. But then maybe there ain't and I won't hold it against you if you think it's a funny idea.

My dad died when I was seven and a half years old of a disease that gets you pretty fast once it decides to. So I ain't got a lot of childhood memories about him. If you read many books, that probably gives you a sigh of relief on account of I ain't gonna spend a lot of time telling old stories. But if you're a girl, you're probably hoping I tell you a couple anyway because girls really like that crap. So I'll tell you what I remember.

He never made much money except I didn't figure that out until he died and I was older. So I guess it didn't matter much either way. And he didn't teach me much either except we watched football on TV together and we played catch with a football. He was sure my biggest jumping fan, that I remember real good. If I jumped off the coffee table or something in my pajamas with feet in them and did a good roll out of it, he'd laugh and clap like I just scored a touchdown. That always made me feel 100 percent good, like everything in the world was perfect. And if I done a drawing of a frog or something, he'd say it was great because I done my best on it and stick it on the refrigerator with real estate guy magnets. That made me feel like drawing and it also made me remember to do my best job all the time.

Dad had this karma game he liked to play and sometimes he let me play too, which is called Doctor Hudson.

We lived in a pretty nice apartment back then, and ate pretty good meals at home. Sometimes on a Saturday morning instead of eating at home, if he didn't have to work, Dad would take me out to McDonald's for breakfast, which made me feel like a movie star. We'd sit there talking about football, which I didn't know too much about because I was so little, or school, or something on TV. He talked to me like I was another grown up and didn't tell me to sit still or stop dunking potato cakes in my orange juice or stop dripping ketchup on my shirt. That was pretty cool.

The McDonald's was in a part of town where there was people less fortunate than ourselves, including guys who didn't shave much and old women with grocery carts full of their stuff. To play Doctor Hudson, you picked out someone who needed something and you figured out how to give it to them without them knowing you did. So being someplace with a lot of people less fortunate than ourselves made the game easier.

I don't even remember the first time he let me play the game with him, but I'm pretty sure it didn't sound like a very fun game at first. Here's how it would go.

We'd finish our breakfast and talk about football for a while and then it would be time to go. Then he'd say, "OK, Doctor Hudson, what's the game plan today?"

And I would have been planning the whole time and I'd say, "I think that guy out by the dumpster. He looks hungry."

And he'd smile and say, "You noticed him too? You got sharp eyes, Doctor Hudson. But he looks like a cagey one."

Then I'd say, "Yeah, he does, but he ain't suspecting a little kid."

And he'd say, "Interesting. Go on."

And I'd say, "If we got us a meal to go and they put it in a sack, I could go out there with it and sit down like I was waiting for someone. But I'd sit where he could see me. Then you could come and find me and yell for me to come, like, hey Jumper, come on now, time to go. And when I got up I could accidentally forget the sack."

"That's a pretty good plan, Doctor Hudson. Are you sure you're only six years old?"

Then I'd giggle a little because he knew how old I was as good as I did, and we'd sit thinking about it to make sure there wasn't hidden flaws. And he might think of one like, "OK, so what if he yells at you that your forgot your sack?"

"I'd say, that's OK, you can have it."

"Maybe. But then he might figure out that was the plan all along." My dad was really smart. We'd think a while longer and maybe I'd say, "OK, if he yells that, I'll just pretend I don't hear him."

"That's a good idea. But wouldn't that be like lying?"

I had to think about that one.

"I don't think it's a bad lie if it's part of a good game."

"So it's OK to lie if you got a good enough reason?"

"Yeah, I think it probably is."

"Jumper, is that what Mom tells you?"

"Well, not mostly. Mostly she says I ain't supposed to lie. And if I tell a lie I get consequences, like maybe I have to go to my room or miss dinner."

"So you can't lie to that homeless guy."

"Sure I can. I just got to take my consequences. If he gets a sack full of food, that seems like a good deal. Specially if I just got to go to my room. But even if I had to miss dinner it seems OK."

Then he laughed out loud, not in a mean way, but in a happy way, like he thought of a joke and was about to tell me. But instead of a joke, he told me about white lies, which is when you say something which ain't the truth, the whole truth and nothing but the truth, but it don't hurt nobody either. Like if you told the lady down the hall that the fruitcake she give you was good and that you ate it all instead of throwing it in the trash. She'd feel a lot better with a white lie.

54

White lies seemed like a pretty good loophole to me even when I was little, but you gotta be careful about them. It's easy to pretend to yourself that it ain't hurting no one, even when sometimes they do. White was the only color lies I ever learned about, but if you listen to guys in suits on TV you can tell there's other colors too, with more rules. If I ever meet a lawyer who ain't trying to tell a judge I was speeding or loitering I'm gonna ask him about the other colors of lies. A lawyer can make you sound like a criminal even if you was just standing in front of the liquor store smelling some kind of liquor that a guy had spilled on the sidewalk because you never smelled it before. A good lawyer can use words like "drain on society" and make it sound like you come from Mars to eat kids, which must be some kind of lie, only I don't know what color. And if you get elected to something they give you the whole playbook of colored lies. But I ain't never gonna meet someone who was elected.

My plan to give a McDonald's sack to the homeless guy worked pretty slick. He didn't yell at me so I didn't even have to waste one of my white lies on him by pretending not to hear. We tried it a bunch more times after that because it was fun.

Doctor Hudson is a fun game. It's easy to figure out things to do, especially for people less fortunate than ourselves. The hard part is not letting them know you done it. And the other hard part is that you can't tell nobody else either. At first I'd come home and tell Mom, but then later Dad explained that rule to me again until I remembered it. Even if I can't tell you any stuff we done without breaking the rules, it must be OK to tell you about playing the game or else Dad couldn't of told me.

At first I just wanted to buy homeless guys meals, or sneak a dollar into their pocket. Dad said that was OK when we was playing as a team, but I didn't need money to play. I didn't get no allowance, so that was lucky. If some kid was wearing cool shoes, and I said, "hey, those are cool shoes," it would make him feel good and wouldn't cost me any money. OK, in that example I wouldn't get full Doctor Hudson points because he'd know it was me saying it, but you get the idea. Mostly there's ways to help somebody that don't cost money and they won't know you done it.

I ain't saying you should play Doctor Hudson. If everybody started doing it then everybody'd also know about it. Pretty soon you couldn't find someone to do something for and nobody could play. So it's OK for you to know about it, just don't tell no one else.

55

After I thought all that, the night was getting chilly, and I didn't have a jacket on, so I shivered out on my balcony for a while and then decided it was time to go to bed.

When I went back inside, I seen my trash can was full and starting to smell a little. I knew I ought to take it downstairs and back to the dumpster in the alley. But like I said, my feet hurt, I already took my shoes off, and I was tired, so I admit this quiet little voice was saying to me to take it down, but this big opera voice was saying go to bed.

Then I thought, I wonder if I could just throw the sack from the balcony, across the back yard and into the dumpster? It wouldn't of been a long throw for John Elway, the best quarterback the Broncos ever had, but then trash sacks probably don't throw as good as footballs, and it would have been a pretty good throw for every other Bronco quarterback, which don't mean it was all that far, but we had some delicate throwers at quarterback.

Most people don't throw their trash like that, so I knew it was a little weird, but then it was dark so nobody'd see me. It's only weird to do stuff if people seen you doing it. And I'm a pretty good thrower so I thought what the heck. I made a bargain with the soft little voice first. If the lid was closed on the dumpster, I'd just carry the sack down. If I missed and the bag exploded on the grass, I'd go down and pick up all the trash and throw it away ordinary. If you make a good enough deal with yourself, it's OK to do about anything. And this seemed like a foolproof deal.

There was still enough light I could see the lid was open and it wasn't overflowing with trash. I got up on my balcony rail, where I'd have a good swing, and threw it pretty high and far.

The trash sack landed right in the dumpster. It scared the heck out of a cat who was on the other side, which yowled and ran down the alley like somebody lit its tail on fire. I laughed out loud. All this time I'd been carrying my trash down three flights of stairs when this was easy and fun and took less time. If you want to be great you gotta think up new ways to do stuff sometimes. I didn't mean to scare that cat, even if it was funny, but he wasn't supposed to be playing around that dumpster either, which somebody probably told him a million times and he knew better. Him and me both learned a lesson we should of already knew.

Sometimes you gotta listen to that big opera star voice.

56

CHAPTER FIVE

Which would sound pretty interesting if you said it like this: there's a black widow spider, and me when I was a kid playing with matches, and some gang guys want to beat me up but I ain't saying whether they do or not until you read the chapter.

After Dad died, Mom and me moved into a little apartment. Our building had a spot out back, behind the dumpster, that had some dirt and then some wooden steps that went up to where a door had been but they'd bricked it up. So the stairs didn't go nowhere and you had to be skinny and little to squeeze past the dumpster to get back there. Nobody knew about that spot, so nobody went back there except me.

There was a kind of room at the bottom of the steps. Well, it wasn't really a room, it was just the place under the steps, but it was closed in with boards so it was like a room with a dirt floor and steps for a ceiling. The last board by the brick wall was loose and you could pull it back and get inside. Sometimes if I wasn't in the mood to go to school I'd go there instead. It was dark, but some light come in between the boards so after a minute you could see. In the summer it was cool from being shady, and I liked the smell of the dirt and the old wood. Spiders and other bugs liked it too, especially black widow spiders.

You probably heard that black widows is poisonous so I don't need to tell you that. But they ain't all that mean. Some people see a black widow and they start yelling like that spider the size of a quarter was going to eat them up. And I gotta admit mom had told me about them being poisonous enough times that the first time I seen one under the steps I got pretty excited myself. Her body was big and shiny as a wet black marble.

I was sitting on the dirt under the steps thinking about stuff while my eyes got used to the dark. Once they did, I started looking around and seen some old boards and a couple beer bottle lids and some busted glass. Then I turned my head to look to my left, and there she was, about six inches from my face in the middle of a perfect web. This big old black widow. I'd been sitting right next to her the whole time and didn't even know it.

For a minute I wanted to yell and get out of there. But I already knew from dogs that if you start yelling and waving your arms, that's like saying,

57

OK, now you can bite me. So I just stayed real still to see what the spider wanted to do.

After a while you could tell she decided I wasn't a fly or a beetle that would make a good lunch and if I didn't mess with her nice web she worked so hard on, she didn't care about me one way or the other. And I didn't have no issues with her either as long as she wasn't gonna bite me. So we just sat there looking at each other.

The first thing I noticed is that she wasn't a fast nervous spider like you see if you pick up a board off the dirt and a spider's under there and runs light-speed away. This black widow was calm. She moved real slow, like a dancer or one of them mimes who pretend they can't talk. She didn't move much, but when she did, it was like a dancer on TV in slow motion. At first I just kept watching her, in case she was trying to fool me and if I looked away she'd run over and give me a poison bite. Then I decided she was probably as nervous as me. I could step on her easy, or squirt her with bug killer a lot easier than she could bite me. After about a half hour of watching real careful, I started looking away and pretty soon I about forgot she was there. Just because something can hurt you don't mean it wants to. You can't explain that to a spider any way except not to step on him.

The next time I went under the stairs I brought a candle and some matches. Even though Mom wasn't crazy about me using matches, I didn't have much choice. I wanted to make sure there wasn't more black widows under there I hadn't seen before so I didn't sit on one. I also brought a fly I caught to give to the spider.

It's easy to catch flies once you get the trick of it. You curl your hand so it's half closed and move slow to a fly that's landed. When you're pretty close, you quick grab the air an inch or so above the fly. When the fly sees you make your move, he jumps up right where you're grabbing. So he's quicker than you, but you got a better plan. I used to have to catch flies all the time for my pet turtle. He wasn't much bigger than a ping-pong ball and he come in a glass bowl with water. He mostly liked to eat stuff that was moving in the water, so I didn't have much alternatives but to catch flies and throw them in there while they was still wiggling.

I got pretty good at catching flies without killing them. Sometimes I'd squeeze too hard and there was some mess, so mom started a rule than anyone who caught flies had to wash their hands afterward. It was an easy rule and it didn't bother me much for as good as it made her feel.

58

I crawled under the steps and lit the candle. I didn't see no spiders except the one I was used to so I sat down. I'd kept the fly in my hand the whole time and once I felt pretty comfortable and my eyes was used to the dark I flicked the fly into the spider web.

You might think it was gross to hear about a black widow eating a fly, so I won't tell you about that, except for a couple of cool things. First, a black widow can move pretty quick when something lands in her web. I was glad I hadn't poked the web with my finger. And second, they don't eat the wings and legs and hard parts of a fly. They kind of suck on him like he was an orange and they only wanted the juice. So that was interesting.

With the candle burning you could see the area under the steps lots better. The only spider was the one I've been talking about and I felt pretty good about her. I'd brought her a gift of lunch, and she ate it, so there wasn't much reason for her to give me a poison bite. I liked the way the wood looked on my ceiling, which was the bottom sides of the steps, and I liked the brick wall on one side and the board walls on the other sides. It felt about as comfortable as my bedroom. And when you count that I had matches, and a candle and a dangerous spider in there, it felt a lot more grown up than my bedroom, so I started calling it my office. If mom was home when I went outside I told her I was going to my office. She'd smile and say, well, be home in time for dinner. And I'd say OK and leave.

After my dad died, she wasn't home so much any more, so it wasn't as big a deal what time I come back inside. She had to work extra jobs to pay the bills, so when she was home she was mostly sleeping or tired. I did my part by remembering rules, like to wash my hands if I caught flies, and don't talk to strangers and make a lunch sandwich before you go to school. Most of the time she didn't get home in time to make dinner or put me to bed, but it didn't stunt me none. You don't have to be an Einstein bagel to open a can of food or crawl under your covers when you get sleepy. If she was going to work that hard it was fair for me to do my part.

School was the only thing I had trouble doing my best at. I didn't like to read all that much, and it seemed that's the main thing they wanted you to do. In September there was lots of hot days when you could see out the window that it was more a summer vacation day than a school day. Sometimes I'd start thinking about that and pretty soon my head was on my desk and I was taking a little history class nap. The teachers didn't like it when you took a nap, but they got used to it. There was so many kids in each class, with a lot of them rude and noisy all the time they decided that if I was resting my eyes for a minute that was one less kid they had to fool with. I got me a pretty good education anyway, mostly from watching TV.

Mom got sick just before I went into ninth grade, so I was already used to being the man of the house. She took the bus to the hospital for treatments every week but they wasn't doing much good. I went with her so she wouldn't be alone or scared which meant I missed some school days and got a little behind even in the classes I was pretty good at. Then one day the treatment was taking extra long and I was sitting in the hallway when a doctor come out and told me my mom died in the middle of the treatment.

At first I didn't believe him, but then a lady from social services come and said it too. Then I was mad but they said they was sorry and they done the best they could, which is all you can ask. They asked who I was staying with, but when they asked they was too interested in my answer. Most times, people don't care too much when they ask a question about you, so when they do, it makes you nervous, like it's a trick question. Especially right then. I mean, my mom had just died so what did anything else matter? So I told a little white lie and said I was staying with my aunt and she was coming to get me. They asked me some more questions like that, and wrote down what I said, but the social worker seemed like a teacher when she's busy and the class is noisy. A kid who was living at his aunt's house in a different town was like a guy sleeping in history class. You crossed him off your list and were glad you had one less kid to fool with.

They told me there was a chapel in the hospital I could wait for my aunt in, and I said thanks, so they told me where it was and I went there.

The chapel was a little room with benches for sitting on and a colored glass window at the front. It wasn't a window to the outside, but just glass on a wall with a light on behind it so it looked like a window with different colors. I went in and sat down mostly so the social work lady would leave me alone. I didn't have an aunt so I wasn't worried abut missing her. I figured I'd just sit there a while and then go home.

Even if Mom was dead, about the only thing I could think of was to talk to her and so I did. Nobody really knows how dying works, so maybe she could hear me.

"So, OK, Mom, I wished you hadn't died, that's the first thing. But I don't blame you or nothing because you told me that when it was your turn you'd just have to take your turn and maybe you wouldn't even be able to say goodbye. See how good I remembered you saying that? But it's still about the worst thing that ever happened to me. Or probably to you either.

And I already miss you and I just seen you a couple of hours ago. I remember how you want me to do my best job all the time, so it's a no brainer I'll do that. And if there's anything you need, if you can figure out how to tell me, I'll sure get it for you. But I sure wish it wasn't your turn."

Then I cried for a while, which there ain't nothing wrong with if you're sad. Then I said "Amen," like people do in church, and got up and went home. I opened a can of chicken chili and ate it. Then I went to bed and started crying again. I cried for quite a while but finally I went to sleep. It was about the worst day of my whole life.

Now I'm back telling you about myself as a grown up. The last thing I told you was about throwing the trash sack from my balcony and practicing that.

The next morning I ate some oatmeal and decided to go to the grocery store to buy another pencil. I thought maybe there'd be some cans down by the Platte River, which ain't much of a river but runs right through Denver anyway. It's like six inches deep, so people that come here from wet states think we're joking calling it a river and building bridges over it, but it's what we got. Anyway, there's a jogging path by it, where sometimes you see pretty girls jogging along listening to their headphones, and grass where people eat lunch, so it's a pretty good place to find cans. I put a garbage sack in my backpack. I hadn't really did any work yesterday, since I drew all day, and I'm not so rich I can take too many vacation days.

OK, so that's what I said to myself, but the rest of the whole truth is that it looked like it was gonna be a nice, hot day, like the kind in school where you just want to put your head down on your desk and take a nap. So a walk sounded pretty good. I put a banana in my backpack for lunch and started walking. If I felt like taking a nap, I'd just take one. That's one big advantage to being grown up. You can take a nap whenever you want.

So I went and bought the pencil, and walked to the river. There was several interesting things along the way, so by the time I got there I was ready for that banana. I sat down on the grass by an overpass and ate it. Probably because I'd been thinking about taking a nap I got sleepy so I said what the heck and laid down.

After a while I realized I'd been sleeping when I heard some voices and woke up. These three young guys was about fifty feet away, talking that crude MTV way, with a lot of fluff this and fluff thats thrown in. The biggest one was black, with nice clothes. The other two was white, but with good tans, like they might be some other ethical group you ain't supposed to discriminate against because they talk with an accent. They was looking over at me, which didn't seem like a good sign for my new wallet. Some of those guys will discriminate against you pretty fast, even if you ain't supposed to do it back. I've got pretty good at noticing when they're thinking about discriminating against me and this seemed like a hundred percent chance of being an incident about to happen.

I didn't look at them, cause that just pisses 'em off, but I got up, put on my backpack and started walking up toward the overpass. These was not guys I ever seen before, which was probably good if I give them a wallet with ten bucks in it. They might think that was a weird coincidence. I walked as casual as I could up toward that overpass.

Their voices didn't get any softer as I walked away which meant they was following me, but I was also getting close to the road and guys like that are a little shy about beating you up where a cop car might come by. They was saying things about me, and you could tell they thought I was a homeless guy who slept under the bridge. Their voices was getting louder now and they were calling me names. They always say stuff like that, working themselves up to be mean. They don't mean it personal, it's more like cheer leading themselves.

Now, I been beat up before, and though it ain't my favorite thing, it don't worry me too much either. But if you make things too easy for these guys it just encourages 'em and the next time they might beat up somebody who ain't as used to it. Better to try to get away if you can. If the job of being a gang guy starts being more of a pain than a real job, they might consider a career change. I could probably outrun them, because I'm pretty fast, and sometimes I do that but, if you try and then a bus gets in your way or something and they catch you, they take your wallet and then beat you up anyway. This time I thought if I could just get up to the road they'd lose interest. They had in their heads I was a homeless guy, and the most you get out of a homeless guy is some cigarettes and three bucks, so they didn't have the incentive to invest too much effort in chasing me down. Or you could probably fight back, which would discourage them the next time too, only mom always made it pretty clear that fighting wasn't the way to solve problems, so I mostly did the rope a dope like Martin Luther King did and let them hit me 'til their arms got tired and they went away.

The gang guys was closing fast. As soon as I got to the road I started across the bridge on the sidewalk and they followed me. There was a bunch of cars coming about a block away, which I thought might work to my advantage if I used my brain. When the gang guys nearly caught up to me, about half way across the bridge, I ran real fast across the street just before the cars got there.

So now these guys couldn't cross until there was a break in the traffic, and that pissed them off as bad as if I'd run away. My plan was to start running across the bridge toward home and the traffic would give me a head start. I knew they wasn't fast enough to catch me if I got a head start, 'cause nobody is, so it was a great plan. The hidden flaw with my plan was there wasn't a sidewalk on my side like there was on theirs. There was only about a foot between the line on the road and the railing on my side so I had to edge along it sideways to keep from getting hit by a car. Every single car honked as it went past me and I could see one of the guys chasing me had already got to the other side of the bridge and was waiting for me. The big black guy was just strolling along across the street from me on the bridge's sidewalk, and the third guy had gone back in case I tried to escape off that side of the bridge. So although they wasn't in a circle, they had me surrounded, with just the cars between us.

Then I seen that after the next three cars, there wasn't any more. So, in about ten seconds, those guys would just walk across the street, beat me up, and swipe my wallet. They was pretty mad by now and then I seen the black guy pull a knife out of his pocket and snap it open.

I try to be polite pretty much all the time, but I admit that knife kind of pissed me off. It should of scared me, that would of been the smart reaction. But like I said, I ain't no saint myself and every now and then something just hits me wrong. Maybe it was the uneducated way they was talking, or the way the guy with the knife was smiling and the cars honking and all, but I just decided these clowns wasn't getting a insurance payment today.

But there was no way I could fight three guys and have any percentage in the deal. Like I say, I'm pretty fast and jump training makes you pretty strong, but I ain't a practiced fighter, cause it ain't the way to solve problems. So I had to even things up a little.

OK, so I say that now like I thought it all up like James Bond, but the whole truth is I don't remember doing much thinking. When that last car was going by and there wasn't another car in sight, I climbed up on the railing. If you're gonna be outnumbered, you want to be higher, that's a easy rule. The guy laying on the ground ain't got much chance against the guys standing over him, for one example, and the guy up on the railing can

63

see what's going on better. Plus, being a jumper and all, I ain't nervous up on stuff like some people, and I got good balance, so if they decided to get up on the railing too I could outrun them easy. If there's something you're better at, that's the thing you want to do. But it was more a instinct told me get up there than a big plan. I gotta admit that.

The black guy started casually crossing the street, cussing and waving that knife around. One tan colored guy come walking from the left side of the bridge and the other from the right. I got that feeling of being surrounded a lot more without the cars between us. The guy with the knife walked straight toward me cheer leading himself pretty loud so his buddies could hear.

"Looks like the mofo backed hisself into a fluffing corner," he said. The other two laughed. You could tell it surprised them, me climbing onto the railing, but it had a flat top about six inches wide, so I was pretty comfortable. It was a lot steadier than my balcony railing which was more for decoration than this one, which was for keeping cars from going over the edge and down onto the grass or jogging path or river below. So being up there, I didn't feel really scared, but still kind of pissed. The black guy was just about to me, and if you got to fight three guys you want to do them one at a time so I ought to start before his buddies got there. But you don't want to start a fight without giving the other guy a good chance to get out of it. That's just being polite.

"Why don't you go home before you hurt yourself?" I said as nice as I could. He didn't look so big or tough from up above him like that, even if he really was a lot bigger than me and probably tougher too. Plus, of course, he had the knife. But even if he beat me up, if I decided to fight back he'd probably get hurt too, so it was at least partly the whole truth. And I'd mostly made up my mind to fight back at least some, even if it never solved problems. A guy with a knife could wind up killing you by accident.

"You're full of sticks! You the one fluffing in my house," he said, even if we weren't really in anybody's house. We were on a bridge. I was mad but I didn't correct him, cause that would of made it harder for him to not fight. Nobody likes it if you tell him they used words wrong. He kept talking loud and fast. "Now you dis me. No one dis me in my house. You gonna be a fluffing example, what I'm talk about. Then I'm gone find your stupid ass mama and make an fluffing example of her too. Just like I done last night."

64

The smart part of my brain said that they did not know mom, and being dead and all there was no way they could do a thing to her. They just say stuff like that to get you mad so you'll do something stupid and they can beat you up easier. So a really smart guy, like the President or something, would just ignore that they said that.

But I was already pissed at these guys. And then I was trying extra hard to let them skip the fighting part, which a gentleman should always do but they wasn't making much effort to do their part toward that issue. And then they started making fun of mom who never fought anybody except for yelling at my teachers when they laughed at stuff I said that wasn't a joke. Thinking about that made my face get hot and the smart part of my brain was getting pushed back where it wouldn't get in the way of the mad part. You never do your best thinking when that happens, but I kept trying to think anyway. Only when I tried to come up with a strategy for solving the problem of the guy with the knife I kept remembering mom getting mad, and the teachers not being polite to her like she was to them, and this guy started to look like one of them teachers to me. I could feel my face getting hot, and especially my ears, and I heard a little buzzing sound that I sometimes hear when I get pissed. The smart part of my brain ain't got much chance to vote when I hear that buzzing sound.

"You shouldn't of said that," I said as polite as I could, but it might not of come off as sounding very polite. "I ain't got nothing against your buddies. Why don't you tell them to go on and you and me can finish this however you want." That seemed fair to me, but the guy just laughed again.

"You ain't got thing one to say about it, stick-head," he said. "They gone watch me slice you up like a dang fish, then they gone watch me fluff your mama. Heck, we gonna take turns. Then we slice her up too."

He poked at my ankles real fast with his knife, but I moved them out of his way by hopping from one foot to the other. He was trying to cut me and make me fall off the ledge. He poked again, but I was still too fast. He kept jabbing, but I was in jump mode and my ears was buzzing, and it was like he was moving in slow motion. He couldn't believe he kept missing, and it made him mad, but it wasn't his fault. He just wasn't in jump mode. His hand moved like it was in a jar of honey and I seen each jab come from a mile away. I could of done that all day, but the smart part of his brain must of stopped working about then and he decided he'd just slash both my ankles with one big move so I couldn't hop out of the way.

Well, he drew back the knife too far, that was his big mistake. He wanted to make sure his friends saw him swing at my ankles, so he made his motion real big. Anybody might show off for their friends, we all done it ourselves. But for him it was a mistake. On a guy who wasn't a jumper it might of worked, but it looked like slow motion to me, so it was a no brainer to jump straight up. His hand would of swung clear, but the knife hit the rail and stopped dead and I landed right on his hand. The knife went over the edge and landed on the grass twenty feet below. I felt some bones crunching under my feet. They was like chicken bones breaking, if you ever crunched up a leftover chicken body with your foot to take up less room in the trash. This made that same familiar sound, so I was pretty sure something got broke.

For about one heart beat he just looked surprised, then his eyes got big and he started swearing every swear word he knew, which wasn't that many. "Fluff! Sticks! Dang! You fluffing stick-head! You broke my fluffing hand!"

I moved off his hand and he stepped back, grabbing his broke hand with the other one and then screaming even louder.

But I was still pissed. My face was still hot and my ears was still buzzing, and even if I got his knife away from him that didn't fix that he'd wanted to slice me like a fish, and mom too. So the next thing I done wasn't necessary, and was probably wrong. I jumped straight off the railing and landed one foot on top of each of his. I heard some more cracking sounds. Now I was standing right in front of him, with our belts touching, but me standing on his feet.

"Still want to fight?" I said right into his face, but real quiet because I was pretty sure he didn't. He just kept screaming and when I got off his feet he fell to the concrete. It wasn't until that minute, when he fell, that I thought maybe I broke his feet too, which I hadn't planned. But then, like I already said, I didn't start out with a big James Bond plan, even if it would make a better story if I did. Anyway, I had other issues to worry about right now.

His buddies hadn't got to us yet when the black guy had started using his knife. When they seen him swing it they froze to watch. But when he fell they started running toward us. I still didn't have much issues with the two tan guys, and I felt bad maybe I broke the black guy's feet, which would understandably piss them off. Now that my ears wasn't buzzing so bad anymore, the smart part of my brain started chiming in with its opinion, which was to leave the scene in a orderly fashion.

66

The railing was only maybe three feet high so I just did a standing jump to get back up there. The grass down below looked nice and soft, so I picked a good spot, just in case. I tried to explain to the other two that I was only acting in self-defense as they run toward me, but they didn't pay attention. When one of the tan guys got to me and started to swing his blade at my legs, I spread my arms out and jumped.

The jump itself was pretty ordinary, even if it was a little higher than I usually practice. And the grass made for a good landing. I saw the knife laying there, so I picked it up. Even from down there I could hear the guy screaming and then I heard cars honking. The two other guys stared at me from up on the bridge. One had his mouth open. I wiped the knife off, since it got some grass and mud on it, and put it in my pocket. I wasn't even a little pissed anymore, but I wasn't giving back the knife.

Between the cars and their hurt buddy, they had their hands too full to come after me, so that was the end of that. I'd probably never see those guys again, which was fine for all of us. We hadn't got off to a good start. I waved at them and then started jogging down the bike path.

That bridge had been a pretty good place to jump. I might have to use it again.

CHAPTER SIX

In which I do some laundry, but it ain't that boring because Holly comes in, and then she asks about my drawings.

Sooner or later, everybody's got to wash their clothes. My building has a room in the basement with two washing machines and two dryers. It takes four quarters for a wash and four more for a dry, so you want to wait until you got a full load. About every month I load up a trash sack with dirty clothes and take 'em down there. The room don't have anything else in it, and the light is just one bulb hanging down from the ceiling, so most people don't spend much time in there. They bring in their clothes, put in their quarters, and go back to their apartment until it's time to dry. People in my neighborhood are pretty honest, so you don't worry much about somebody swiping your clothes.

Sometimes I sit on a dryer and wait. The dryer is nice and warm and the sound it makes is like a drum. When the washers and dryers are all going at once, it's like a whole tribe in Africa drumming for rain or something. I sit there listening until one of them stops, then I leave. I never seen anybody else sit on a dryer, and when a machine stops you know somebody's gonna come in for their clothes. Might be nobody else thinks the sound is cool so they'd just look at me funny. No reason to make them feel bad just cause they never paid attention to that sound before. Everybody's different. Some people like jazz that's so weird you can't even tell what the song is, but maybe if I knew how to listen to it I'd think it was just as good as the laundry room. It's hard to imagine, but maybe.

One night I was sitting on the dryer with my eyes closed, pretending I was in Africa, when Holly walked in.

"Jumper," she said and my eyes snapped open and I jerked more upright. She laughed. "Sorry I startled you."

"Hi, Holly," I said. "I'm doing laundry."

"I can see that. You look like you were meditating, too."

"Nah, just thinking."

"What are you thinking about?"

Well there was no point in lying about it. Sitting on a dryer ain't that weird.

68

"I like the sound."

"What sound? The sound of the machines?"

"Yes, ma'am. Sounds like drums."

She kind of nodded at that, listening but not saying anything. Then she put her clothes in the washing machine, added soap, stuck quarters in the slots and started it.

"Drums, eh?" she said.

"It does to me. If you listen right."

Believe it or not, she climbed up on the other dryer. She was wearing a regular shirt and sweat pants instead of a uniform. Even though I didn't look right at her I could see her pretty good out of the corner of my eye. She closed her eyes and listened. Then she smiled.

"It does sound a little like drums," she said. So we just sat there for a while, listening. It was even better listening with somebody else there. After a while she said, "I've been thinking about Mrs. Murphy." She said it kind of quiet.

"Thinking is good for your brain," I said. Her saying that made me nervous all over again. I had thought that whole part of the story was done and I wouldn't have to write any more on it, but when she said that I seen I could still be in hot water over it. Like if they figured out I stood on her bed and jumped off it right when I wasn't supposed to be even wandering around the hospital. And if you think about it, a real good detective like maybe Columbo might ask how I taped the picture to her ceiling any other way than by standing on the bed? It would be smart to steer the conversation away from that, but I'd have to do it gradual so she didn't notice.

"There was a chair in her room," I said.

"Right. She seems to have made a complete recovery."

"That's good," I said, trying to keep my mouth shut for my own good. You got the right to remain silent, everybody knows that. But if you ever say something, they'll use it against you. Although I don't think Holly would.

"I was wondering," she said, looking off like she was talking to the wall across from us. "When you gave her a drink of water, you didn't happen to put anything in it did you? Like maybe extra medicine from a study or something?"

Your first idea is to quick say "no" because you know that's the correct answer, plus with the advantage of being the truth. But I didn't remember even telling her about the drink of water. So I might of forgot that, or this might be a trick question. If Holly was asking me trick questions then maybe the only reason she was sitting on the dryer was to play good cop bad cop on me and I done something way worse than jumping off a bed without even knowing it. But if you use your right to remain silent too long that's just the same as saying you're guilty. It's extra hard to remain silent if you don't know what crime you're supposed to remain silent on. But her comment gave me a pretty good idea, so I answered real careful.

"Only doctors and nurses can give you medicine," I said. "Everybody knows that. Oh, by the way, I think I just remembered something I was supposed to do up in my apartment. I better go do it." Even if it was nice sitting on the dryer with her, I didn't know how long I could remain silent on something I didn't know, not being a lawyer myself. Lawyers can talk or remain silent on stuff they don't know and it don't make no difference to them. Either way it sounds the same, and their face don't get hot. But not me. I could already feel my face getting hot and all I done was give a lady a picture.

I slid down off the dryer, but Holly reached out and put her hand on my sleeve. That stopped me like she'd shocked me with a taser gun. Which, if you ever been loitering and disorderly without meaning to just when the cops show up, you know what that feels like. Even through my shirt her hand was real warm and a lot better than getting tasered.

"When are you going to let me see your drawings?" she said, and kind of smiled.

"Probably some time you're not working."

"I'm not working now."

"Unless you call washing your clothes working. Which a lot of people would."

"The washing machine does most of the work. I'm just sitting here with my friend listening to African drums."

"It's pretty cool, ain't it?"

"Very cool. But you promised to show me your drawings."

"They ain't that good. They're mostly practice drawings…"

"And I bet your never break a promise, do you?"

70

"They're a lot harder than rules."

"So why don't you do whatever you have to do in your apartment and then bring them down here? I'll watch the laundry."

"You mean now?"

"Why not? I bet you could be back down in seven minutes."

"About four and a half," I said. "Only..." I seen I'd backed myself into a corner on that one. There wasn't a good reason to not bring the drawings down. I wanted to show them to her, and I'd even said I would. It's just not the way I pictured it. But that's not a good reason to skip doing something. Plus I was glad she was off the Mrs. Murphy subject.

"OK," I said.

I ran up the stairs, picked up the stack of drawings and neatened them up. At first I put the bird picture on the bottom, so if she didn't look at all of them she'd miss that one, since I never finished it. I put the rose one on top, in case she only looked at one and then she'd see the best one. Then I thought again and switched them back. That way, by the time she got to the good one she'd of forgot the bird one. I carried them out into the hallway and down the stairs. Just before I went into the laundry room I changed my mind and put the bird one in the middle. No need to scare her off with that one right away.

I handed her the stack and got back up on the dryer. She looked at the top one for a long time. "It's another daisy, isn't it?"

"Yes ma'am."

After she said what it was, she smiled and looked at it some more before putting it down on the dryer. Then she looked at the next one. I looked at the drawing too but I was mostly paying attention to her face out of the corner of my eye.

"You drew a garbage sack?" she said about the next one.

"Only one," I said. "They're kind of ordinary." She nodded. I had already figured girls wouldn't like that one too much. I probably should of put more of the flower ones closer to the top. When she got to the bird one she frowned and looked at it for a long time. Why didn't I just leave that one upstairs, I thought? Then she smiled again.

"It's a meadowlark, isn't it?"

"He flew away before I could finish. Sometimes you can make them stay if you whistle back the song they sing at you. But his got too compli-

71

cated and he figured out I wasn't a bird and so he flew away. It's the worst one."

"It's nice," she said. "Just a little different from the others."

"I didn't plan it. He just landed on my balcony."

"All these were on your balcony, weren't they?"

That comment made me a little nervous, since I'd already decided not to tell people about my shaving mirror camera and if she kept asking questions like that I'd be in a pickle.

"It's convenient," I said. Luckily she just put the picture down and went on to the next one. She was saying what each one was a lot quicker now. Some she'd just look at for a second and say, "dandelion" or "bindweed" or whatever. Even if she was just pretending to like them it was nice of her to pretend.

When she turned over the last one, her eyes got big and she inhaled quick so it made a sound. "My god, Jumper," she whispered. She stared at it for a minute then whispered the same thing all over. "My god, Jumper." She turned and looked at my face like she'd never seen me before, which creeped me out a little. "How did you do this?"

Even though I'd been trying to think of a good answer in case anyone ever asked me that, I hadn't thought up anything I really liked. But now I had to think up something in like ten seconds. The only line that come into my head was what a guitar player had said on TV. I don't like to steal somebody else's lines, and if some other words would of come to me I'd of used them, but none did.

"I don't like to talk about my process," I said.

She laughed out loud at that, but it wasn't a mean laugh. She tilted her head back so her ponytail waved around and did a nice happy laugh. "I don't blame you, Jumper," she said.

I felt good that the line had worked, but bad that I'd stole it.

"This clears up a little mystery," she said. "A couple of weeks ago I was looking out my kitchen window. I didn't want to go to work and I was in a bad mood. Then out of the clear blue sky, a red rose petal came drifting in the breeze and landed right on my hand. Nothing like that ever happened before and it cheered me right up."

"That's cool," I said, but it didn't seem that odd to me. Stuff blows in my window all the time.

"It probably came from one of your roses," she explained.

"Oh yeah, well, it's cool if it cheered you up. Maybe it means you're supposed to have the picture. It's yours if you want it."

"I couldn't take your picture, Jumper. You could sell this."

That panicked me for a second. I had been trying to be real casual and now she didn't even want it.

"I don't sell 'em. These are just practice pictures. I want you to have it." I tried to picture myself James Bond cool and all, but it was hard selling my brain on the idea.

She stared at it. "Are you sure?"

I shrugged my best James Bond shrug. "The paper didn't cost a nickel, even, and I already had the pencil. Cheaper than a get-well card which I'd buy you if you was sick. You take it now and it saves me two bucks if you get the flu or something. That's a pretty good deal for me."

She smiled at that. "Thank you," she said.

We sat there for a while and then she asked, "Do you ever draw pictures of your family?"

"I ain't got any family that's still alive."

"I'm sorry. Do you ever draw them from photographs?"

"I ain't got any photographs. We had some when Mom died, but then when I couldn't make the rent and had to move into a littler apartment, the guy who owned the building threw all that stuff out. If I'd been older I would of stood up for my rights. But you can't blame a kid for not knowing his rights, even if the kid was you."

"You don't even have one photo of your parents?"

"Not any more. We took a family picture one time down at Broadway Photo when I was little. I can still remember it in my brain pretty good."

We was real quiet for a long time. That bothers some people but it don't bother me. I can be quiet as long as about anyone. I was glad she wasn't talking about the incident in the hospital, and glad she liked her picture. The dryers seemed to be playing an extra cool drum song. You can be quiet for a long time when you're having fun. After a while she started talking again.

"Speaking of get-well cards," she said. "There's a little girl at the hospital who likes to draw. I bet it would cheer her up if you visited her. Two

73

artists who don't like to talk about their process and all. What do you say? If you time it right, I'll buy you a cup of coffee on my break. I know right where the cafeteria is. We can't get her to go to sleep before about 10:30 anyway. What do you say? Tomorrow night about 9:30?"

"Nine-thirty at night?" It ain't ever a stupid question to be sure you got the facts right.

"Yes, nine-thirty at night."

"Sure," I said. Just then my dryer stopped. "OK, I better go then." I scooped my laundry back into the garbage sack, picked up the rest of my drawings, and ran back up to my room.

That was one of them nights it's hard to go to sleep. It just goes to show that sometimes things you don't plan out all the way work out even better than the plan you had in mind. I was glad I hadn't got stubborn about deciding ahead of time how it was going to work.

CHAPTER SEVEN

It ain't really like a date, and then there's a pregnant woman, and then I start doing art therapy, which is more fun than it sounds, like almost everything is.

The next night I started walking to the hospital about 7:32. Sure, that was too early, but like mom always said, a person's got to know how they are. I'm a guy who notices stuff, which is maybe why it was easy for me to become a writer-guy. Writer-guys notice stuff so they can write it down, but it takes time. When I walk someplace, even if I try my hardest, something might be interesting along the way, and I'd start noticing it, and then I'd be late. So I give myself extra time just to be sure. That's different from how a kid might do it, or even some grown ups, but I always do my best job. That means knowing how you are and taking that into account when I make my plans.

Several things was interesting. Like there was a broke stoplight flashing red in both directions. You'd think it wouldn't be a big deal to the drivers, they'd just take turns crossing. But sometimes a guy would try to sneak across before his turn and that pissed everybody off and they'd honk at him. Other times some lady was either scared or polite, or didn't understand taking turns and she'd wait to go even if it was her turn. People honked at them too, and then some other guy would try to sneak across so there was more honking. People trying to turn left confused everyone and then no would remember whose turn it was.

I could of stood and watched that all night, but I didn't. Holly had said she'd buy me a cup of coffee, plus there was something else about a little girl, and I remembered the 9:30 at night part extra hard. It was just a cup of coffee, but this was as close to a date as I'd had in a while. About the last thing I wanted was to be late. Before I left my apartment I'd looked in the mirror about six times, made sure I hadn't forgot anything, like if my T-shirt was right side out and my zipper was closed. I took two showers and brushed my teeth for five minutes. So I was pretty sure I was OK.

I only watched the broke stop sign for a little bit. If I was lucky it would still be broke when I come home and I could watch all night long if I wanted. But walking away from all them cars honking and the drivers yelling was a big deal to me. It was like leaving the circus early, like if your mom had to get up early to go to work the next morning and the last bus

75

was about to leave so you had to miss the part where there's somebody doing different stuff in each of the three rings. It wouldn't be professional to make a fuss about it, but that don't make it easy.

I admit, I kept thinking about having coffee with Holly. I tried to think up interesting stuff to say and said them to myself, and then in my brain I'd see her tilting her head back and laughing. I even practiced some jokes I'd heard so I could remember them right, but mostly the ones I'd heard seemed a little off-color to say to a girl. But then James Bond never said too may jokes, and girls liked him all the time, so I decided not to risk any jokes. There was lots of things I didn't know about Holly, like what it was like to be a nurse, and if she had hobbies, and where she grew up. So I hoped I didn't have to talk too much and could just ask her questions a lot of the time. Anyway, a break don't last that long, so I didn't have to memorize a Shakespeare play or anything. Which is lucky, because I never done that.

Plus the whole truth is, if you stepped back and looked at it, it wasn't really a date. It was real casual, just having a quick cup of coffee with someone. I could pretend it was sort of a date, there wasn't nothing wrong with that, but the big opera star voice inside me knew better.

I got to the hospital about nine and sat down on the grass in front to wait. It's extra hard not to pay attention to things when that's what you're trying not to do. It was mostly dark out, except for car lights, and building lights and some streetlights. One streetlight was flickering, like it was going bad and that was pretty interesting, but I just looked away. Somebody else was going to have to be the one who seen that light go out. A guy was walking back and forth on the sidewalk saying stuff to himself, but the sole of one of his shoes was loose, so it made a clapping sound every time he stepped on it. I pretended he wasn't even there. There was some moonflowers by the grass, which are really big and white and smell like perfume, but they only open up at night. They wasn't open yet, so it was tempting to go sit by them and see if I could watch one of them open. I was real proud when I decided to put them on my list to do a different night and just stayed where I was. It was safer to watch the cars go by, because even if one of them did something interesting they'd drive on by and be gone.

I kept looking at my watch, which I bought at the thrift store for six bucks, so I could see how close it was getting to 9:30. It was about 9:23 when I seen someone walking down the sidewalk. They caught my eye because they was walking funny, with their legs spread far apart. So I looked harder and seen it was a lady about as pregnant as she could be. She was a block away, so I couldn't tell much, but I seen her holding her stomach. She'd stop for a second, then take a couple more steps, then stop again.

It didn't take a professional intern to know what the deal was. She was having a baby right then and trying to get to the hospital. I got up and ran into the hospital to get somebody, but there wasn't anybody there. Just a lady behind a counter across the lobby. I knew that lady wasn't going to leave her post. She'd just call somebody and we'd all wait for them to get there, and by that time there'd be a new baby on the sidewalk. But there was a wheelchair just sitting in the lobby, so I pushed it out the door and down the sidewalk until I got to the pregnant lady.

Only she wasn't there anymore. OK, Jumper, I said, you're in trouble now. They'd think I swiped their wheelchair. Grand theft wheelchair is probably about as bad as grand theft auto and I knew guys who went to jail for that. So I turned the wheelchair around and started to go back when I heard a girl's voice off in the shadows kind of moaning. She had crawled off onto somebody's grass and was in the bushes. That streetlight had finally gone south, so I couldn't see her. I followed her voice until I found her.

"You OK?" I said.

"My water broke," she said, and then she made a sound like somebody punched her in the stomach. "About an hour ago. No car."

"Me either," I said. "But I got a wheelchair. Maybe we should get you into it before they arrest me about it."

"OK," she said. "I don't know if I can..."

"No problem," I said. "I'm pretty strong."

She wasn't all that heavy, even being pregnant and all. She was probably only fifteen years old, but you can't ever tell with girls. I set her in the wheelchair and pushed her to the hospital.

The lady behind the counter took one look and right away she knew what was going on.

"Maternity is fifth floor. Elevators right down that hall. I'll call ahead." She had already picked up the phone and was talking, so I pushed the girl to the elevator and took her to the fifth floor. When the elevator door opened, a bunch of nurses came at us like linebackers on fourth down. I stepped back, out of surprise, and they ignored me and went right to work on the girl.

77

Now, them nurses knew what they was doing. They grabbed the wheelchair and started talking to her real soft while they pushed her away down the hall. "You're going to be just fine," they said. They was taking her pulse, and pushing her hair back out of her face, and doing other stuff I don't remember.

One nurse took my elbow and pulled me out of the elevator.

"Looks like we don't have much time," she said. She grabbed a clipboard off the nurses' station desk and started right in asking me questions. "Name?"

"Jumper," I said.

"And your wife's first name, Mr. Jumper?"

"I ain't married."

"I mean the mother's first name."

"Ann," I said. I'd always liked my mother's name, and it was nice of this nurse to ask about her. Ain't so many people ask what your mother's name was before they get to know about you. Maybe this nurse was going to be a writer-guy like me some day. She was noticing stuff like crazy, and asking questions, and writing lots of it down. That's pretty professional.

"Any history of illness?"

"I don't get sick that much."

"I mean Ann. Does Ann have any history of illness? Any allergies?

"I don't think so." My mother had always been pretty healthy too. And being dead cured her of any other illnesses she might of got, including allergies. But they were asking about history, which is stuff that already happened. "No, I can't think of any."

"Responsible party?"

"You mean for the kid? You'd have to ask her. I wasn't there."

She raised her eyebrows and looked over the top of her glasses at me. Then she went on, but she sounded kind of testy, like I give her a wrong answer. But she was asking questions about as fast as I could answer, so if I screwed up a answer, part of that might be on her as much as me. You can only answer questions as fast as your brain will let you.

"How about insurance?"

"You mean my insurance wallet?"

"Yes. I'll need the insurance card in your wallet."

78

"You heard about that? I got several cards in there. I try to keep my insurance for emergencies only. The hospital's got pretty honest people, I don't think I'll need it here..."

"I want your insurance right now!"

Well that surprised me, cause she'd been polite before that. But like I said, she'd seemed to be getting testy for a while now, so maybe she'd just had to deal with some difficult people, which will make anyone testy. You can't hold it against them. Then I thought that maybe if you weren't in a study, the hospital had a cover charge just for coming in. Hospitals was fun enough, that made sense. I pulled out my wallet with the ten in it and handed it to her.

Right then I remembered about Holly and looked at my watch. It was 9:43.

"Geez, I gotta go," I said and turned back to the elevator.

"You've what?" the nurse said. She left her mouth open after she said it.

"I got an appointment." The elevator door opened and I stepped in. The nurse stared at me while she held my wallet in one hand and the clipboard in the other. She hadn't thought to close her mouth yet when the door started to close, but she didn't say nothing. So I waved at her, kind of up and down so she could see my hand, just before the door finished closing. Then I pushed the button and the elevator jerked a little and started going.

From all my activity, I probably wasn't as fresh as I'd wanted to be when I got to the right floor, but Holly was standing at the nurse station. I hoped she hadn't already took her break.

"I'm sorry I'm late," I said.

"Jumper," she looked up from her papers a little surprised and looked at her watch. "No problem. Linda's looking forward to seeing you. She's ten years old. Come on."

I followed her down the hall. I'd almost forgot I was supposed to meet some little girl. To Holly that might have been as big a part of the date as the coffee part.

"You didn't already take your break did you?"

She laughed. "No, I usually go about 10:15. I'll come and get you." She led me to Linda's room.

"Linda, this is Jumper. He's an artist too."

79

The little girl was skinny with big brown eyes like a golden retriever dog. She wore a baseball cap that was a little too big for her head, which just made her look even cuter. I could see she didn't have no hair underneath the cap. Some medicines make you lose your hair and she probably felt funny about that. So I didn't say nothing about it.

"Nice to meet you, Linda," I said and shook her hand. "I see you're a Broncos fan." Her hat had the Bronco horse on it.

"Their defense stinks," she said. "We keep wasting draft picks on lazybones defensive ends. If they don't wise up pretty soon I'm switching to Jacksonville. At least they have cool uniforms."

"But not the Raiders?"

She stared at me real disgusted that I'd think of a thing like that. When I was a kid, girls in my class used to look at me like that pretty often from stuff I said. It's just how girls are, you can't hold it against them. Weird stuff disgusts them before you even decided if it was interesting or not. "They're not even a football team," she said. "They're just a bunch of thugs."

Holly laughed. "I have to go back to work, but I don't want you two arguing about football and bothering the other patients. It's past visiting hours you know. Maybe you could show Jumper some of your drawings."

"That'd be cool," I said. Linda shrugged like she was bored but, when Holly left the room, she got into a drawer in the bedside table and pulled out a stack of pictures.

"They're not very good," she said. "But there's nothing else to do in here unless you want to watch dumb TV shows." She handed them to me and I sat on the bed. Linda pretended not to care if I looked at them or not, but you don't do that many pictures unless they're important to you. There was a lot of pictures of families and monsters and kitties. She didn't put in lots of details, like she might just have a dot for an eye, or one line for an arm, but I could tell right away what they was. I took some time looking at each one and I didn't say nothing in case I hadn't exactly understood the drawings and guessed wrong. Pretty soon I figured out that they wasn't just drawings, they was stories, but without the words. When I got done looking at all of them I started over, to get the stories. Some was hard to get, but some was easy.

"OK, let's see if I get this one," I said. "The dog lost his toy, which the cat has hid up on the roof, and the little girl is trying to get him interested

80

in this new toy. It's something a dog wouldn't like too much, like a potato, and she's pissed cause she don't get what the dog's thinking. So it's like a joke."

She smiled just a little. "It's an orange," she said. "But it could have been a potato. I just like oranges better. You're the first one who's got it."

I smiled. "It's pretty funny," I said. "Only I didn't want to laugh in case I was wrong. She's never gonna get that dog interested in a orange. They ain't got much appetite for fruits."

She nodded. "I know. That's why it's funny."

I turned to the next one. It took me a minute.

"OK," I said. "There's a little girl on a beach and her mommy and daddy and a boy, who's maybe a brother or a friend, are on a boat going someplace cool, only they don't know where. It's pretty far away, and kind of blurry, and their faces is confused. And the little girl is waving goodbye to them. She looks like she feels two opposite feelings at the same time, which girls can do even if boys don't believe it. She's happy they're going on a vacation, but she's sad because she's not going with them. And then in the water is the dog, who's also confused cause he don't know if he should swim out to the boat or back to the girl. Plus she's got some peanut butter sandwiches. Either she really likes them sandwiches or she's gonna be there a while cause she's got a bunch of them."

Linda's eyes looked at me real big and she nodded her head.

"If it was me," I said, "I'd draw me a rope out to the dog. Cause maybe she thinks she can't swim to the boat, but I bet if that dog was pulling her too, she could. I bet it would be easy. Only I don't know what to do with them peanut butter sandwiches."

"I do," she said; and she took the drawing. In about ten seconds she'd drew a zip-lock baggie around them sandwiches and a rope to the dog too.

"I never seen anybody draw that fast," I said. Plus she didn't have a shaving mirror or anything.

"It's just a rope," she said, like I was her little brother who said something dumb.

"Yeah, but it's a good rope. You got knots in it and everything. I like the picture better now."

"Thanks," she said. "Me too."

When I get interested in one thing I forget other stuff, like appointments, or doing the job I was hired to do, and her drawings was all cool little puzzles. So I didn't pay attention to the time and I admit I forgot about my date with Holly. I kept figuring out each drawing, and mostly I was right. When I was wrong, sometimes Linda smiled at me for being silly, and sometimes she rolled her eyes and give me that disgusted look girls do so much. Once I heard a bunch of people running down the hall, pushing one of them metal carts on wheels. A different night I would of got up to see where they was going as fast as anyone, but the picture I was looking at made me feel weird, so that was interesting. I kept working on figuring it out. It had more stuff in it than the other drawings, so that was a clue right there. Only I didn't know what it was a clue to.

"So the kid in this one is a Broncos fan, that much is obvious." I said.

"Because of the hat."

"Yeah, that was a giveaway. And these other people, they don't have hats on, but they seem like decoys kind of. They ain't really in the story, but they're there to fool you into thinking they are. Decoys is also called red herrings by writer-guys. Of which I am one, by the way. A writer-guy that is, not a red herring."

She didn't say anything.

"That's OK," I said, holding up my hand like to stop her from saying something. Columbo done that sometimes. "It wouldn't be fair giving me clues."

She closed her mouth real tight, so her lips were thin together.

"But this big old monster coming down the hill. He's got me fooled. It's like nobody can see him except the kid. Or else they'd be all scared. But they ain't even looking at him."

She nodded but kept her lips closed tight. I kept looking at the picture. It was a hard one.

"I don't think I like that monster much," I said. "He looks pretty serious and all. I mean, it's your drawing so it's up to you. But if it was me, I think I'd give him some big old floppy rabbit ears."

"I can't do that."

"They ain't hard. You got more paper?"

She handed me a sheet of paper. I drew a circle for his face and then made these really big ears on it, all drooping down. "See? OK, so they look more like cocker spaniel ears, but then I done 'em pretty quick. Maybe if

82

they went up more before they went down." I did another circle and tried again. "OK, so that ain't right either."

"I'll show you," Linda said. She drew some great big old floppy ears on the monster. "See? Like that."

We both looked at that monster for a minute. Them ears was pretty funny. I tried not to laugh, her being a kid and sick and all, but I couldn't help it. I tried to keep the laugh in, but it started coming out anyway. I bit my teeth together real hard and it started coming out my nose. So I pinched my nose together with my fingers but it didn't do no good. I didn't want to hurt her feelings by laughing at her drawing, plus Holly had said to be quiet. But it wasn't that I thought it was dumb, it was just funny. So finally I had to let that laugh out so I didn't explode from it. At first I only let a little giggle out, but the giggle made a goofy sound, with my nose pinched shut and all, and that was funny too. So finally I let go of my nose and just started laughing.

You know how it is when sometimes you start laughing and you just can't stop? Well, this was like that. I bent over. I should of been real quiet in case other patients was sleeping, but I just couldn't stop. I have a pretty loud laugh when I get going and I really was going this time. I was loud as a cow and my stomach hurt from laughing so hard and I couldn't stop enough to talk.

Linda looked at me pretty surprised and then she looked back at the picture. And then she started cracking up too. Pretty soon she was laughing as hard as me and for such a skinny little girl she had a loud laugh too. When I could breathe a little I put one finger over my mouth to say 'quiet' and managed to say, "They'll kick us both out of here," and that seemed funny at the time and got us going all over again.

"How about a big nose?" she said and drew a big clown nose on the monster and that set us off again.

"Or one of them ballet dancer skirts?" I said.

She nodded and quick drew one on him and we about fell off the bed from laughing. Then I heard something behind me.

"OK, Jumper, what did you give that little girl?" Holly had come into the room. Her voice was more confused than lawyery, but Linda and I cracked up all over again at it.

"I didn't give her nothing," I finally said. "She don't need goofy pills to make her goofy."

83

"I think you did," Holly said, real soft, and still kind of confused, cause obviously there ain't a thing called goofy pills but she wasn't sure I was joking on her. "But I don't think it's anything we sell here. It's Linda's bed time."

"I'm always in bed," she said. We both was trying to be serious now. She put her hand on my arm.

"Will you visit me again?"

I didn't even think about it, but put my hand on top of hers. "I have to," I said. "We ain't done looking at your pictures. But I gotta rest up my laughing muscles first."

"Maybe Mr. Jumper can come back next week," Holly said.

"Cool," Linda said. "Can I see some of your pictures when you come back?"

"Only if you don't laugh at 'em," I said and winked at her. She giggled.

"I promise," she said. And so Holly and I went into the hall.

"I didn't know she could still laugh," she said.

"She laughs about as loud as a horse," I said. "She drew a funny picture."

"Listen Jumper, I was looking forward to having a cup of coffee with you. But we're short-handed and we've got a situation with one of the patients. Will you take a rain check?"

I was still thinking about the little girl, so I guess I was slow answering. Holly thought I didn't know what a rain check was, so she said it again a different way and slower. People do that if they think you're dumb, or if you don't hear good, or if English ain't your best language. The President does it sometimes in case someone who's listening is dumber than him, which we must all be since he's the President and we ain't. Holly probably thought I had hearing issues.

"I can't take my break tonight, so I can't buy you that cup of coffee I promised you," she said real slow. "Can we do it next week when you come back to see Linda?"

"Sure," I said. "No problem. I gotta admit I'm kind of tired anyway from all that laughing. You just let me know when's a good day for you."

"Thank you, Jumper. Linda's parents come to see her most nights except Tuesdays, so that's the best night. I'm really sorry."

84

"Tuesdays are usually pretty good for me too," I said. "I ain't usually got appointments."

"Thanks. I've got to go." She turned and walked real fast down the hall to where some doctors was.

OK, so I didn't get my date with Holly, but that little girl Linda had been pretty fun anyway. Plus, walking home the stoplight was still broke, so I got to take my time watching it. There wasn't so many cars now, but there was guys working on fixing it, so that was interesting too. It didn't even feel like the same corner as before. Funny how, when something's broke, one time you get a whole circus of flashing lights and honking horns and people yelling like it was the end of the world, and then another time you get a few guys who just work quietly to fix it. Then pretty soon they get their job done and it ain't no different than if it never broke in the first place. So it seems like a lot of wasted honking for something that's only going to last a little while anyway. Unless you love to honk, in which case them folks earlier had themselves a big-time party of it and probably got home feeling great. Some folks ain't happy if they can't honk and yell, so a broke stoplight is good news for them.

It was about 3:31 when they finally got it fixed. Then I walked the rest of the way home and went to bed.

CHAPTER EIGHT

Officer Mike tells me about the Bones

The next morning I kept thinking about that little girl Linda. She wanted to see my drawings, so I decided I ought to do a picture a little girl might like. I thought of lots of different things, but I admit they was mostly things a little boy would like. For one example, I thought of a fire truck cause every kid likes them, but then I thought maybe that was more of a boy thing. I thought about drawing a Denver Bronco, but I didn't happen to know any of them personally and they make so much money I probably couldn't afford to rent one of 'em, even if I drew my fastest.

So I decided on a teddy bear. Linda didn't seem exactly like a teddy bear kind of girl, but maybe if I made it silly, with a Bronco hat, it would be OK.

I put a ten in my shirt pocket and walked down to the thrift store. On the way down there, I run into a policeman I know.

"Hey, Officer Mike," I said.

"Hello young man. You staying out of trouble?"

"I got to or you'll throw me in the pokey."

"I might do that anyway, just as a preventative measure."

Officer Mike has been walking up and down Colfax for as long as I remember. He's about fifty, with a pretty good gut for a guy who walks so much.

"Ain't you getting about ready to retire?" I asked.

"Forty three and a half days. But who's counting?"

"Well, I am for one. Some new guy might not watch me so close."

He laughed at that, a big old friendly laugh. Officer Mike had been on the job a long time, but it didn't make him a hard case. If there was trouble, he could usually just talk people into behaving, and if there was a robbery or something he was pretty quick to call for backup. Anyway, except for the hookers and gang guys, there wasn't much crime in my neighborhood. Everybody knew Mike kept his eyes out for stuff, so just having him walk around made people careful. Nobody wanted to cause him a hassle.

Once upon a time, Officer Mike was in the Army and has one of those green hats like French guys wear that the Army give him and he showed me once. But he says that was a whole different lifetime and he don't talk about it much. Anyway, he says him and me got to keep our relationship professional, since he's a cop and I'm sometimes suspected of alleged loitering. But that's more like him making a joke than meaning it. He makes a joke on it so I don't ask him about being an Army guy if he don't want to talk about it. I'm cool with that. Him making a joke on it makes it more like we're buddies instead of professionals. The way I see it, we're secret buddies who don't ever hang out with each other. It's his way of saying he don't like talking about the Army even if it sounds like he's saying he don't want to be my buddy.

There's one thing I might say about Officer Mike if we was talking in a bar that I probably shouldn't say in a book on account of it ain't like all the rest of the stuff about him so it might confuse you. Before he went into the police business, he was in the Army, which I told you. But before he was in the Army he wanted to be a dancer.

Now I don't know how you make money as a dancer unless you're a girl, or maybe you're on a MTV video, but Mike was too old for videos and too fat to pretend to be a girl, so you can see some reasons he went a different way with his life. But I know he thought about it cause he give me two clues.

The first clue was that he told me that when he was young he wanted to be a dancer. He even took some lessons at a college and when I didn't believe it he told me the names of about ten dances. A guy could look up the names of dances to tell you, and he could make up names to fool you, like "the pumpkin squash dance" and if you didn't know you'd just go along. But he said names like tango and waltz and marimba that all sounded like dance names. Anyway, he ain't a guy to joke on you much and didn't wait between names like he was thinking them up.

So I got that clue at about 11:53 one night. Officer Mike had got off his shift at nine. He wasn't in his uniform so I about didn't recognize him coming out of O'Hurley's Bar in regular clothes. He wasn't drunk, but he had a beer or two to celebrate Mr. O'Hurley's 80th birthday and when I seen him come out of the bar I yelled, "Hey Officer Mike!" He seemed in a friendly mood, so I walked with him toward the bus stop and we had a nice talk. When Officer Mike was a kid, Mr. O'Hurley was already grown up with gray hair. Mr. O'Hurley had a daughter named Katie that went to school with Officer Mike before I was even born, but you could tell that when Officer Mike said her name he was thinking about her pretty face. Then we got to the bus stop so our talk was over and I never decided if Officer Mike married Katie and she was still his wife, or if they never even dated. But I could tell he still thought she was pretty.

The other clue about him wanting to dance also involved Mr. O'Hurley, who I don't have to tell you much about because he's dead. The Friday night after he died, they had a party at O'Hurley's Bar which he owned, and Officer Mike went to it. I wasn't on the guest list, but I was walking past at about 12:33 at night when Officer Mike come out. It was raining pretty hard, which I already said ain't that ordinary in Denver. I was across the street when he come out. I didn't holler out or go over because I ain't sure about the rules for parties you throw when a guy dies. I just watched for a minute trying to decide what was the correct thing to do. Mike had a umbrella out, which was good planning ahead, and he walked for a ways real slow, like a guy even older than him. More like a guy as old as O'Hurley. Then he stopped and leaned up against a building and started crying. I could see his shoulders shaking and that made his umbrella shake too. He cried for a while and I didn't want to let him know I seen him, in case he was sensitive about that, so I pushed myself back into a doorway. There wasn't anybody else on the street and it made me feel sad watching him all by himself leaning against the wall. I remember it like it was in a movie: there was a street lamp on the corner making shadows on the wet street and big puddles. His umbrella was black and shiny wet. The air smelled fresh, like it does when you ain't had rain in a long time and then it cuts loose. Some cars honked a couple blocks away, but it sounded like hearing them through a pillow.

After Officer Mike cried for a while he done something that surprised me. It was something I won't ever forget if I live to be fifty years old. Even if it was still raining full blast, he folded up his umbrella and held it like a cane. And then he started singing.

I think it was an old song since the tune went up and down a lot, and which I think I heard on TV before. You could tell it was probably called "I'm Singing In the Rain" on account of how much times it said that line. He started off singing soft and his voice sounded like a guy who'd been crying, all weak and cracking. As his hair and clothes got soaked he got himself cranked up until he was singing as loud as the opera star singer doing Oklahoma. Then he started moving his feet in time and swinging his umbrella and jumping up steps and down into the street. He splashed right through big puddles and swung around the street light. The whole time he kept singing as easy as if he was sitting down. Then he got to the corner and sang his way around it and I couldn't see him anymore.

Now maybe you wouldn't call it dancing because there wasn't like a few steps you done over and over again, but it looked cool to me. I was about the most surprised I ever been in my life. I couldn't say nothing to him since then he'd know I seen him crying. But it was a good clue that even if he didn't know exact steps like waltz steps they taught us in school, he probably had more interest in dancing than a lot of guys. Plus, he could move around a lot better than most older guys. I decided maybe knowing the rules and following the correct steps ain't as important as feeling a dance inside you that you gotta let out. Although my sixth grade teacher would not have bought that story off me when the only thing she wanted to let out of me was a waltz. Which she finally figured out I didn't have one inside me. After the Singing in the Rain incident, I decided that you can't tell how good somebody's dancing just by watching them.

So now, if you remember from when I started talking about Officer Mike, I just run into him when I was going to buy a teddy bear so I could draw a picture of it for that little girl Linda in the hospital. I said hey, and he asked if I was keeping out of trouble, which I already explained to you. Then he put his hands behind his back and looked up in the sky.

"I heard something interesting a week or so ago," he said, like he was talking to the clouds. "Gang banger got his wrist broke and a foot too."

I didn't say nothing. The whole truth only counts if somebody asks a question. You always got the right to remain silent. Mike shook his head.

"Strangest thing I ever heard," he said. "He says three guys cornered him on a bridge, threatened him with knives and then jumped on his hands and feet. But the weird thing is he said that just when his friends came to help him, his attackers ran away. Except the ringleader. He just jumped off the bridge and walked away. What do you think about that?"

"Was he under oath when he said all that?"

"No, but he was going under anesthesia at the hospital. His two friends signed corroborating statements."

Well, obviously I was working pretty hard to keep my face from getting red, but I could tell I needed to start working harder on that. Officer Mike had caught me one night jumping off somebody's garage into an alley. They had been painting or something, so they had a ladder leaning up to the roof, and it was about midnight so it was too hard to resist. I done

89

ten jumps off it, and I don't know how many Officer Mike seen, but when I landed that tenth one, he walked over from the shadows and started talking to me. He might not even of seen one jump, because he didn't mention that at all. Just talked about what a nice night it was and how pretty the stars was. Then he started talking about private property, not in a mean way, but just how people feel invaded when other people use their stuff without permission. While he talked he started walking down the alley, a real casual strolling kind of walk, and to listen to him I had to walk along with him. Pretty soon we was on Colfax, with all the lights and stores and traffic. Then he said how part of his job was protecting people's private property, shook my hand, and told me to have a good night. I figured that was a close call, so I went on home.

I was careful after that not to do any invading of people's private property and whenever Officer Mike seen me on the street he'd stop and talk for a minute. But I had to guess he maybe seen me jumping, so he knew I liked to jump off stuff, and now the police was looking for a jumper. It was circumstantial, so you couldn't worry about it too much but I was going to be careful what I said anyway.

"You hear anything about that incident?" he asked, still looking at the sky.

"No sir," I said, which was the truth. Nobody had said a word to me about it.

He nodded. "How's that guy's story sound to you?"

"Well," I said. "If I was to imagine something like that I don't think I'd imagine it the way he said."

"It doesn't sound quite right to me either. Say you were going to imagine how it might have happened, how would it go?"

"Well, first off, since you say they was gang guys, they probably had knives or something. And I bet they kind of turned the story around to make themselves sound good in it."

"I was thinking the same thing. I was thinking maybe they tried to pick on the wrong guy."

"I could imagine that easy," I said. "Them being gang guys and all, that sounds more right."

"You think they tried to mug some guy?"

"That's the way I'd imagine it," I said. "I'd say the three of 'em was try-

90

ing to get one guy's money, cause gang guys do that all the time. And that guy tried to get away, and that pissed them off. So he got himself backed up on the bridge and when the first guy got to him and swung his knife, the guy on the railing jumped up and landed on his hand. Then he jumped off and landed on the gang guy's feet, but kind of in self-defense. So when the other two got there with their knives he jumped off the bridge and landed on the grass. Once he was down there, he found the guy's knife. It was muddy, so I cleaned it off and walked away."

Officer Mike nodded. "That's about the way I imagined it myself," he said. "But if I find the guy, whoever he is, I'd tell him to be careful. These guys are bad news. They're in a gang called "The Bones" in Chicago, where they take their gang stuff serious. I hear they're looking for this guy to pay him back. They don't know Denver too well yet, though. They probably assume the guy hangs around the Platte River. So I'd tell him to stay away from there for a while. If I was to find him."

"That's probably some good advice."

"Well, you have a good day, young man," he said. Then he walked away.

I felt pretty good that I kept Officer Mike from knowing I was the guy without having to tell any fibs. Plus without even knowing, he had give me some good information. I decided to stay away from the Platte River no matter how many cans there was, and no matter how many pretty joggers.

CHAPTER NINE

In which I do some art, and learn a whole new trash sack trick the hard way, and then of course there's the turtle part. Which is all good. But then The Bones shows up again, so that ain't so good. But I come up with a plan.

I never spent much time in the toy section of the thrift store, so I was kind of surprised they didn't have no teddy bears.

"Health Department," Jim said. "They could have germs. Maybe you could find one at a garage sale." He didn't even ask how come I wanted one.

"Well, maybe I'll just look around for a minute then," I said. I went back to the back and when I was sure he couldn't see me, I took a little pack of peanuts out of my wallet and put it on the floor. Then I put a scrap of old newspaper over it to hide it. I knew he'd be sweeping before he closed up, and then he'd find them peanuts. You had to worry about a guy as skinny as Jim. But you can't just give a guy something he needs because then it makes him feel bad he needs it. But if he just stumbles onto it, he feels lucky about it. So us guys who are more fortunate, like we got two legs and make pretty good money, we gotta think about it a little before we help 'em. Like I already said, I ain't no saint. This was more like a hobby to me. It makes you feel good to make a guy feel lucky.

I hit two or three garage sales before I found one with a big old silly teddy bear. He was the biggest teddy bear I ever seen. He had a couple of rips in him but I figured I didn't need to draw them. Anyway, he was only a buck so I bought him and paid three bucks for an old Broncos cap, before they got the fancy new design.

On my way home I hit one more garage sale cause I'd got myself used to stopping at them by then. They had the weirdest thing I ever seen, which was a little bitty suit coat, like a baby would wear if you dressed him up to go to church. I figured it would be a little big on the teddy bear, but it was only two bucks so I decided to gamble on it. So now I was getting excited about my drawing because I never seen a teddy bear in a suit before wearing a baseball cap of a football team, so that should be pretty cheerful. It would be like he was going to a costume party, and parties are fun. I was walking extra fast, thinking about it and I come to the grocery store where I shop and had one more good idea. If he was at a party he ought to be holding a balloon. I went in the store and spent two more bucks plus some change on a little bag of balloons.

The rest of the way home I kept thinking about my new picture and how cool it would be. I bet all the famous artists planned out their pictures like that, unless they were of a girl like Mona or something, in which case you was pretty much stuck with whatever mood they showed up in.

Well, sometimes guys like me who think a lot think up one thing too many. If they're artists, like Mr. Picasso, you can just get a bunch of stuff going on that don't necessarily make sense when you get 'em all together. After I got the teddy bear all dressed up and had a couple of balloons blew up and tied with string to his paw, I thought I'd did one thing too many this time. I mean, he looked cooler than heck, and he cracked me up just looking at him, but what I hadn't counted on was the wind. Them balloons wouldn't sit still for one minute on my balcony.

So this was going to be one of them artistic challenges you hear about. I sharpened my pencil extra sharp and started drawing.

The teddy bear part wasn't no big deal. After all them weeds and roses I was pretty good at drawing stuff that stood still. But them balloons was a whole 'nother can of fish. I'd get one about half drew and then it would fly off somewhere else. Finally I decide to draw as much of them as I could before they moved and maybe it would turn out cool, like different versions of the same balloon. You look at some drawings Mr. Picasso drew, for one example, and you gotta figure he done that too. Found something he couldn't really draw that well so he kept adding stuff and hoped it might be cool. Which, if you're pretty drunk, it might be. Anyway, if it didn't work, I'd just draw the teddy bear again without the balloons and nobody'd have to see that first one, unless I got so famous I could sell even my dumb pictures and pretend they was what I was going for all along.

The drawing was like Mr. Picasso's more than Mr. Vinci's in the fact that it wasn't all the way ordinary but I couldn't decide if I liked it. I could tell what the balloons was, but then I already knew, so maybe somebody else would just see a bunch of lines. The art ain't in the lines it's in looking at the lines, but it don't count if you already know what it's supposed to be of.

So I sat on the floor and stared at it for a long time imagining I never seen it before. Sometimes I imagined not seeing it before pretty good, but I might of been fooling myself. After a while it got hard to see, because of it getting dark and I didn't have no light turned on.

93

So I ate my dinner and started to do my training. After about three jumps I remembered it was time to throw my trash in the dumpster. Before I tied up the sack I looked at the picture again, wondering if I should just throw it in the sack and start over tomorrow, but when I looked at it that time I kind of liked it, so it stayed on the refrigerator.

By now I'd got pretty good at tossing a garbage sack from my balcony into the dumpster, so I decided to make it more interesting. I carried it out on the balcony and got up on the railing. But this time I waited until I jumped and was already halfway down to the garage before I threw it.

Well, hitting a dumpster with a trash sack while you're falling through the air in the middle of the night ain't as easy as it sounds, if you never tried it. I didn't need no streetlight to tell I'd missed pretty bad and the bag had broke open in the back yard. I could hear cans go rattling around every-where. So now I had to go clean up the mess. I jumped off the roof of the garage and went to where the sound had been. I found some of the cans by stepping on them even before I found the sack.

The next problem was that the sack had a big old rip in it like you can imagine. Mostly the trash was soup cans, but the week before I had bought me a cantaloupe and the skin that was left wasn't all that fresh anymore. I always thought if I forgot what it was called I'd remember by thinking it's like antelope in a can, but I never forgot its name so I never got to use it. Like Holly said, I remember stuff pretty good. I put them cantaloupe skins in the trash sack by feel, even if it wasn't all that pleasant.

I held the ripped part together with both hands and walked around to see if I stepped on any more cans or whatever. When I didn't find more trash, I figured I got it all. But that sack was slippery and the rip was a good one, so sometimes some cantaloupe or a can would fall out and I'd have to find it all over again

The obvious thing would of been to carry the sack over to the dump-ster and throw it in while I was handy. But it kind of pissed me off, missing my throw, so I took it back upstairs to try again. I couldn't climb up the downspout, what with holding the bag with both hands, so I went around to the front door and went up the stairs. This old lady, Mrs. Johnson, was coming down the stairs when I went up, which seemed unusual, because it was late, but it wasn't none of my business. She was dressed nice, like she was going out on a date, but I reminded myself it wasn't my business and just said, "Hi, Mrs. Johnson." She looked at my ripped trash sack with stuff trying to fall out and walked right on past me. That kind of distracted me so I didn't notice a cantaloupe skin getting loose on me. It fell on the stair and I stepped on it and slipped, so I fell and let go of the sack, which spilled stuff all over the stairs. A few of them cans tried to make an escape and went bouncing down the steps, making a lot of noise. That was pretty funny, so I started laughing at that. After I was done laughing, I picked up all the trash and stuffed it back through the rip and went the rest of the way to my apartment.

A different guy would of put the whole sack in a new sack and finished his training and brung the trash out tomorrow morning in the light. But nobody's the same and you gotta do stuff your own way. It seemed a big waste to use two sacks on one load of trash when it was ready to get thrown away anyway. So I used some duck tape to fix the rip and went back on the balcony. This shouldn't be so hard. I mean, I'm a good thrower and a good jumper. No reason I couldn't do both at the same time. Just in case, I brung the roll of duck tape with me on the next jump. One thing besides being good at remembering stuff is that I learn pretty quick. If I had to patch that sack again it was smarter to do it before I carried it up the stairs again. Mrs. Johnson would think it a little unusual if she seen me carry a broke sack up the stairs two times in one night. She'd think I was stealing trash or something, which even I think ain't ordinary.

It was a good thing I did, too, because I missed on that second throw too and the sack got a whole new rip in it. But I patched it up and brung it back upstairs. By now I was pissed at missing so much and made a deal with myself that I said I'd just keep trying till I got it right.

On my eighth jump I heard it land right in the dumpster, where even if it did break them cans couldn't make much of a getaway.

That felt good and so I had me a can of Fresca before I went to bed. I don't drink much pop because it's so expensive, but landing that throw seemed a pretty good reason to celebrate. So I sat on my apple crate next to the teddy bear in his suit and watched the clouds move past the stars and drank me a cold Fresca.

The next day I went out collecting cans and made about $6.20. The next day I cleaned an apartment and made twenty bucks plus a can of beets which I put in my cupboard next to three other cans of beets which I will eat if there's a snowstorm and nobody can get to the grocery store. But if I ain't eaten them by Christmas I'll put them in a box at church to give to people less fortunate than ourselves. It would just be mean of me to hang onto extra beet cans when they ain't even my favorite if some body else

95

don't even have one can of beets. Especially at Christmas, when God is watching and all.

On Tuesday, when it was time for me to go visit Linda again I put all my drawings in a brown paper grocery sack and left a little earlier even than last time. You probably don't run into a pregnant girl every day at the hospital but it just goes to show you can't ever tell. There's always something interesting and you never know when it'll show up so you gotta give yourself time. It was probably only a half hour walk, if you had horse blinders on, but you don't see many people walking around with them. Not even too many horses, which they was designed for, but you'd probably get places faster if you didn't notice stuff. Even with a funny little girl to visit, and maybe a cup of coffee with a nurse waiting for me, two hours hadn't been enough time last time, so I wasn't taking chances.

So this time I left about 7:02. During the whole walk I practiced real hard at not noticing stuff. It ain't so hard as you might think, if you never done it. You just got to concentrate on stuff in your own life, and on where you're going, and just pretend the rest of the world ain't out there. I bet anybody could do it if they tried. It ain't much fun, but it could be a useful skill to develop, like throwing a trash sack in the middle of a jump.

I had me one close call at noticing stuff, even with concentrating. You ain't gonna believe it, but I seen a turtle walking out of an alley and aiming toward Colfax. He wasn't some little bitty water turtle like they used to sell in pet shops, but a big old land turtle, the color of an avocado and about as big as most of my foot. He come marching out of that alley like he went to sleep on the prairie a hundred years ago and woke up with all these buildings grown up around him, and now he was gonna go find him a fat grasshopper for dinner.

Well, you can't blame me for noticing that. He didn't look scared or anything. He knew where he was going and wasn't about to let a city stop him. Only it was clear that where he was going was right into the street. So he was brave enough, but about as smart as a dinosaur and you know what happened to them.

I didn't see no choice but to rescue him. You would of done the same thing. He'd like it a lot better down at City Park, which was an easy walk but in the wrong direction, He hissed when I picked him up, because he thought I was keeping him from dinner, so you can't hold that against him. Living was a better choice than dinner even if he didn't know any better, and one of us had to be the human here.

96

You probably already seen the pickle it give me. Should I take him to the park, and then go to the hospital, or should I bring him with to visit Linda and then drop him off afterward? If I carried him to City Park first, you'd think there's still be plenty of time to get to the hospital. Which there would be if nothing else was interesting. And if I waited, he'd miss his dinner and that didn't seem right. So I should take him to the park first. But there's a lot of interesting stuff in the park, and that would cut out my spare time for being punctual. So I should take him to the hospital with me then turn him loose in the park after my visit. But they might have rules about bringing turtles in during visiting hours. So then I went back to the idea I should take him to the park and then go to the hospital, but if another stoplight was out I was a cooked goose. So there was advantages and disadvantages to both plans.

I stood on the sidewalk for a while thinking it all out. I could tell some of the people walking past noticed me doing that. They probably never seen a turtle up close. I held him in one hand, because my sack of pictures was in the other hand. You would of thought somebody would of said something, like "Hey, nice turtle," but nobody did.

Finally I come up with a good plan. There was a little health food store on the way to the hospital and stores always have some boxes out back by the dumpster. I'd put him in one of them, so the hospital people wouldn't notice him so much, and then after my visit I'd take him to the park. Maybe that store would even have some food a turtle might like, so he wouldn't be irritated at missing dinner. Plus, I could show him to Linda and then take him to coffee with Holly so we'd have one extra thing to talk about.

Sure enough, there was several good boxes with lids and everything. I put him inside the best one and left him in the alley while I went inside to get him some food. I figured no one would swipe him with the lid on and all.

I never made dinner for a turtle before, so that took a little thinking right there. I ruled out all the tofu stuff right away because I ate some once. Maybe it tastes like grasshopper to some people, but it tasted about like cardboard to me. Then there was different sprouts, which I considered for a while on account of them being easy to eat, but they didn't look too good to me. There was nuts and stuff like a turtle might see in nature, but I couldn't imagine my turtle eating them, so I give up on them too. Then I come to the fruit part and that seemed a better idea. A guy I talked to down at the bus station once had talked about turtles in Oklahoma loving mulberries and how their faces got red from the juice. But this was a pretty

97

small store and they didn't have mulberries. Only thing they had that was red was raspberries, organic ones they'd got in Oregon. They looked real good, which they should of from the price, which was six bucks for a little basket. I would of kept looking for something cheaper, since they was for a turtle I didn't know all that well, but it was already about 8:02 and some of the stuff in the seafood area looked pretty interesting, so if I kept looking I might get distracted and get myself late again. I took a real quick look over in that direction and seen stuff with tentacles and claws and decided not to risk looking closer. I bought the raspberries, the girl put them in a little sack, and I walked back out to the alley.

So now I had my picture sack and my raspberry sack in one hand and this big box in my other hand with the turtle inside. The box was about as big as I could get my arm around, and I couldn't use my other arm to help much since it had the sacks. I sure didn't want to drop any of it either, so I had to walk extra careful. Which just made it harder to concentrate on not noticing stuff. But a guy's gotta learn to do several things at once, so I figured it would be good practice. I walked slow and just looked where I was going.

That made the walk seem a lot longer, of course. By the time I got to the hospital it seemed like I'd been walking an hour, but when I looked at my watch it was only about 9:07 so I was still plenty early.

I set my stuff on the grass and sat down cross legged. The turtle was fine, but you could tell he was pissed. "Chill, bud," I told him. "We'll feed you when you're inside. The little girl I'm going to introduce you to might like to watch you eat." Then I closed up the lid, because I knew what would happen if I started watching him.

I could tell I was getting tired from working at not noticing stuff. For a minute I closed my eyes, but that was worse on a couple counts. First, when you close your eyes, you pretty much can't help noticing sounds and we had cars and birds and crickets and people talking when they walked past. And you start to notice that new mowed grass smell, with some clover and weed smell mixed in, plus a little gasoline smell from the mower. And you notice the breeze on your face shifting around and you start to wonder how come whatever made the breeze in the first place don't make it just keep blowing the same all the time. I mean whatever it is, and it's probably a scientific thing, it probably don't have a brain to keep changing ideas, so that's pretty interesting right there.

98

Second, when you close your eyes you start to think about things and one thing leads to another and pretty soon you're asleep.

So I opened up my eyes and kept on concentrating. I did a good job of it, and at 9:21 I picked up my stuff and went inside.

Holly wasn't at the nurse station, so I walked down the hall to Linda's room.

"Hey, Michelangelo," I said to her. She looked a little better. Sometimes people like it if you call them somebody famous, and Michelangelo was a famous artist. Plus he was a man, not a girl, so it was kind of a joke. Linda rolled her eyes like girls do when you say something, but she smiled a little bit too.

"Hey, Mr. Jumper," she said. "Did you bring some drawings?"

"Yes ma'am," I said. "Plus I brung another visitor." I set my sacks on the floor and put the box on the bed and opened the lid. "It's a turtle."

"Ooh, cool!" she said, which made me feel good cause I'd been a little nervous a girl wouldn't enjoy a turtle too much. "What's his name?"

"I don't know," I said, "We just met and he ain't told me. He seems pretty feisty though. He was about to jaywalk Colfax when I found him."

"Can I pet him?"

"He might have germs."

"He don't have anything as bad as I got already," she said and reached in.

"Watch out for his head," I said. "He ain't been housebroke for little girls."

"I'm not scared of no turtle," she said, and petted his shell real soft. At first he opened his mouth big like to scare her, but even being dumb he knew he couldn't reach his neck around to get her. After a minute he closed his mouth and looked like he kind of enjoyed the attention.

"He's nice," she said. "But you're right, I bet he gets into trouble a lot. Only he must get out of it too. Since he's still alive, you know. Kind of like Bart Simpson."

I never heard of that guy, but figured he must be a politician or something. She said he was a TV guy, but on cable, which I don't get.

"How you doing, Bart?" she said. Of course the turtle didn't say nothing.

99

"Only problem with calling him Bart is that if that reminds the doctors of a troublemaker, they might object to his visiting you. If one walks in."

She frowned. "You're right. How bout this? You and I will know his name is Bart, but if anyone else walks in we'll say he's Bartholomew, which is the big name for Bart."

"That's a good idea," I said. "Bartholomew is a big enough name even for a doctor. I got some stuff for him to eat. You want to feed him?"

"Can I?" she said.

"Sure. I got some raspberries, only I don't know for sure if he's gonna like them. Plus, he's probably nervous being in a strange box and all, so if he don't eat you can't take it personal."

"Everybody likes raspberries," she said. She took one out of the little basket and dropped it in front of him. We was both real quiet and watched him. He didn't exactly move, but you could tell he was thinking about that thing in front of him. After a minute, when the raspberry didn't do nothing suspicious, he cocked his head to one side to get a look at it from his other eye. Then he started walking real slow toward it, like he was stalking it. When he got close, he pushed his nose into it and thought about the smell for a minute. When he was sure it was OK he turned his head half sideways, opened his mouth and grabbed it. He shook his head from side to side while he chewed on it, like he was trying to confuse it by shaking and in a minute it was gone. Sure enough, his mouth was all red.

"Cool," Linda whispered. She dropped in another. Bart had done all his thinking about raspberries already, because this time he went for it right away. He ate ten raspberries. When she dropped in the eleventh, he ignored it.

"I think he's full," she said.

"I think you're right. You got the touch with turtles though, I gotta say that.,"

"Thanks. We better look at your drawings now before they kick you out."

I put the lid back over Bart's box and set it on the floor.

"They have rules against you eating turtle food?" I asked.

"Probably," she said. "If not, it's just cause they didn't think of it yet. They've got rules about everything."

"Well, I sure don't want to carry them raspberries back home with me, so I think we need to eat them."

"But what will you feed Bart?"

"I was thinking about taking him over to City Park. I bet he'd find lots of good stuff over there."

"You're going to turn him loose?"

"Well, he seems more of a park turtle than a box turtle. Nobody ought to live in a box."

"I live in a box," she said in a pouty voice.

"Then you get what I mean. It ain't the best deal for nobody. Anyway, you'll be out of here pretty soon. So he should be too."

"I wish I could watch you turn him loose."

I had to think about that one for a minute. She wasn't strong enough for the hospital to let her have vacation days yet. But my building don't allow pets, and even if I said he was just visiting until we could turn him loose together, they'd probably call him a pet anyway. Plus, even if I'd got lucky on them raspberries, I gotta admit I ain't really a biologist or anything, who knows about turtles. But all that was being said by the quiet little voice in me which I don't always remember to pay that much attention to.

"OK," I said. "I'll just keep him until you're out of here and then we'll go turn him loose together. But it would be mean to keep him too long, so you gotta work extra hard at getting better. Deal?"

"Deal!" she said. "So you want to take the raspberries home for Bart?"

"Nah," I said. "He'd probably like something different tomorrow. Let's look at some pictures and eat turtle food."

So we did.

It was fun looking at my pictures with Linda cause she got 'em all right away.

"I like dandelions," she said as soon as she seen that one. "It's like they have two flowers, the yellow one and then the one you blow."

"Me too," I said. "They ain't rated as high as they ought be."

"It's cause nobody pays attention to them," she said. "I don't know why everybody wants their lawn to be just green. Boring."

101

Well, I liked her even better for saying that, since I'd already said it to myself before. You always like people who say the same stuff you do. But I was holding my breath about the teddy bear picture. I'd stuck it right in the middle so it wouldn't seem special just because of where I put it, and she was about to get to it. I was acting James Bond cool, but I watched her careful when she come to it. When she turned it over she started grinning right away.

"It's Benson," she said. "When he was all new. Mommy's keeping him until I come home, because the neighbor cat ripped him a little and she didn't think he should come to the hospital. She bought me this doll instead." She pointed to a plastic doll on the table who looked pretty grown up if you ask me. "Barbie's nice and all, but she isn't Benson. How did you get to meet him?"

"Well, they probably made a bunch that all looked about the same," I said.

"It's Benson," she said. "How did you do the balloons? They look like they're moving."

"I don't like to talk about my process."

She looked at me like a schoolteacher might look when you said some excuse that wasn't exactly nothing but the truth. Something that sounded official but had a hidden flaw in it that blew the story the minute you said it. Like, "I had to go to the Tuesday night church service," but you didn't know they didn't even have one that night. So her look made me wish I'd remembered to come up with a better answer when people asked about how I drew something.

"That's puppy pooh-pooh," she said. "You just heard somebody say that."

I wondered if every little girl was Perry Mason waiting to grow up.

"It's kind of complicated and boring," I said.

"Are you saying I'm too dumb to understand it?"

I felt like I was about to get a firm talk from the judge about purging myself before he held contempt on me.

"I'd never say you was dumb. Especially not after how you got Bart to eat and all."

"OK then," she said and just waited.

102

So there I was in this corner and I didn't see much alternatives. "I seen it on TV," I said, and come clean about the shaving mirror. She watched me real careful while I talked, looking for the whole truth, etc. "And that's how I done it."

"Cool," she said, looking back at the picture.

"Only I told myself I wouldn't tell anybody, just like Mr. Vinci didn't, but now I did." I felt bad I'd broke a deal I made with myself. You start breaking your own deals and pretty soon you won't know whether to believe yourself or not on the next deal.

"I won't tell," she said. "I promise. I didn't mean to make you feel bad."

"It's OK," I said. "I can tell you take promises serious. You can have that one if you want. Seeing as how you know Benson and all."

"I can?" Her eyes got big so I knew she wasn't just being polite.

"Sure. It wasn't that hard. Benson was a real easy model to work with."

"Thanks," she said. She set it aside. "I got one for you, too." She got into the drawer on her bedside table and handed me a drawing. It was a guy who looked a lot like me, with a backpack and sneakers, who was drawing pictures. He had a big grin on his face which made the picture pretty cheerful.

"I don't have that much muscles," I said.

"Sure you do," she said. "Or else I wouldn't have drawn it that way."

"I love it," I said. "Nobody ever done a drawing of me before."

"I was going to make it funny, like the monster picture, but this is just how it came out."

"It's plenty funny just the way it is. It's about my favorite picture I ever seen. Thanks."

"You're welcome," she said. "Let's look at the rest of these." She went back to looking at my stack of pictures. She thought the one of the trash sack was funny, which by now I did too, so that was OK.

"How come you didn't finish this one?"

I didn't even need to look to know what she was talking about.

"He flew away."

"But he was still in your mind."

"That ain't the way I draw. With my process and all."

103

"Well, I can still see him. Even the parts that aren't there."

"OK, then, Michelangelo, I'll just leave him here and you can finish him. Then we'll sell it for a hundred bucks and split the money."

"OK, I will." She set that one on top of the Benson one.

"I thought I heard voices down here." Holly had walked into the room.

"Look at the picture Mr. Jumper gave me," Linda said. She held it up. Holly looked at it a minute but you could tell she didn't exactly get it yet. "It's Benson," Linda said. "With balloons."

"The butler from the old TV show?"

That set me and Linda to giggling.

"My teddy bear," Linda said.

"It was the suit coat that fooled you," I said to Holly. "Anybody could make that mistake."

Holly looked at the picture for a minute more, smiling like she seen the teddy bear, but you could tell she didn't. "It's nice," she said. "But it's time for Linda to go to sleep. And I promised Mr. Jumper I'd buy him a cup of coffee."

"Next week?" Linda asked.

"You bet, Michelangelo. And I could sure use that fifty bucks, so you gotta work on that."

"I will," she said. I put my pictures back in their sack, picked up Bart's box and followed Holly to the cafeteria. We sat at one of the little tables. She looked even prettier than usual, like she put on her makeup extra careful or something. I figured she must have a meeting or something.

"What's this fifty bucks you were talking about? You're not gambling with my patients are you?"

"It's kind of a joke. She's gonna finish that bird picture for me, and if we sell it for a hundred bucks we're gonna split it."

"I see. Listen, Jumper, I want to give you some advice and I want you to listen carefully."

"Yes, ma'am."

"Well, first, thanks for visiting Linda. I haven't seen her this happy since she got to my floor. So you're doing her a lot of good. She breaks my heart."

104

"She don't mean to. She can't help it if she's sick. She's a pretty funny girl."

"I know. But Jumper, you've got to protect yourself. I learned that a long time ago. You have to keep a little distance. If you get too attached to people and then..."she looked at me careful, "and then if they go away, you'll feel too sad. Do you understand what I'm saying?"

"You can't keep that much distance if you're looking at pictures together. I don't think I got germs or anything. They tested me for the study. But if you got rules, I could sit a little farther back."

"I'm not worried about her. I'm worried about you."

"Shoot, I'm pretty healthy. If there ain't rules I'm breaking you don't need to worry about me."

"You're not breaking any rules." She drank her coffee like she was trying to think of something else to say. Finally she shook her head. "What's in the box?"

"Now that could be a rule I'm breaking," I said. I opened the lid. "It's a turtle. His name is Bartholomew."

"He's bleeding," she said, but I think she was mostly surprised to see any turtle at all.

"Nah, we was feeding him raspberries. That's just juice around his mouth. Linda has a good knack for turtles, even though she never had one. She's a natural."

"I didn't know you had a turtle."

"I just found him on the way here tonight. I was going to turn him loose in the park, but then I thought Linda might like to see him, and then she said she wanted to turn him loose with me. So I guess he'll be staying at my place for a little while, till she feels better. Only he's not a pet, he's just visiting."

Holly turned her face away and put her hand up to her mouth. I seen her eyes get wet so I knew she was trying not to cry. I done it again, I said to myself. Now she's gonna have to turn me into the building supervisor for having a pet, which she naturally wouldn't like to do. I put her in a bad spot by telling her.

"It's OK," I said. "If you gotta turn me in for having a pet, I'll find him some temporary place. I got lots of friends, and some of 'em don't have rules about pets where they live. So you don't have to feel bad about that."

105

She didn't say nothing for a minute, then she smiled even if she was still kind of crying.

"I'm not going to turn you in, Jumper," she said. I guess she'd worked it out in her brain how a turtle visiting wasn't the same as a pet. "How's your coffee?" she asked.

"It ain't bad," I said. "It ain't as good as what they do down at the shelter on Thanksgiving, but you can't hold that against them. It's cold then, and coffee always tastes better when it's cold out."

"Do you spend Thanksgiving at the shelter?"

"Yes ma'am. They can always use a little extra help then, what with all the poor people. I usually give out the mashed potatoes. Unless the Broncos are playing, of course."

"Of course."

Way across the cafeteria two guys walked in and went to the counter, got some coffee and sat down. They looked like someone I knew only I couldn't think of their names, which is unusual because I'm good with names. They was tan with black hair, like a guy from Mexico or Arabia and I was sure I knew them. Maybe from the thrift store. I was gonna go over and say hi when I figured out how come I knew them. They was the two guys who was with the black guy I had the incident on the bridge with. Maybe the guy whose feet got broke had some complications or side effects and he had to come back to the hospital so they come with him.

A good detective pays attention to stuff that some people miss, and he figures out ways to notice that ain't that obvious. Like in a crowded cafeteria, people only listen to the person they're sitting by and the rest of the noise is like bees humming to them. But if you watch somebody's lips a couple tables away, pretty soon you hear that person's voice just as good as if they was sitting by you and then you can listen to them instead. It ain't really polite to do that, but sometime it might come in handy if you was detecting a hard case. If someone's saying private stuff I pick somebody else to practice on but, if they're just talking about TV shows, I figure they don't care that much. This seemed like a good time to risk invading somebody's constitutional rights by listening to them if I could.

Up to the time I recognized them, I had been pretending Holly and I was on a date, even knowing it wasn't exactly one. But when I seen them two guys that whole idea went out the window. I didn't want to be rude to Holly, but part of me thought the smart thing was to sneak out before they

106

seen me. I tried to think up some good reason I had to leave, but I knew if she got into her Perry Mason way she'd figure something was goofy and start asking hard questions about it.

But before I even thought up a bad story I seen one of them look right at me and say something to the other one who turned and looked too. I knew I was busted, cause I focused in on his voice and he said, hey, it's the guy from the bridge. Only they didn't get up and come over, so I didn't either. This was one of them times you had to use your whole brain on one idea, but I also had to talk to Holly, so maybe I didn't do the best job on neither. Them guys wasn't going to let me leave peaceful, but they wouldn't want to do nothing where there was witnesses and security guards, which I could tell from the parts of their conversation I could listen to. They'd wait till we left and then follow us. I thought about them dark areas outside and wondered if that streetlight was still broke. Even thinking hard about that, I answered a question Holly asked me and my answer made her laugh and she tilted her head back, which made her neck look cool, and her hair moved, so that broke my concentration for a minute.

"I guess I'd better go back to work," she said.

"I'll ride you back up the elevator," I said.

"You don't need to do that."

"Well, just part way then."

She laughed at that, but by now I was thinking pretty hard about them gang guys. They'd watch the elevator lights to see what floor we got off on and then take the next elevator after us. Holly worked on the sixth floor, so after she punched that button, I punched the third button and got off there. OK, so if these guys seen many movies they'd know that was a pretty ordinary trick, and I hated to steal it, but it was the best idea that come to me.

"See you next Tuesday," Holly said as the doors was closing.

"You bet," I said. "Thanks for the coffee."

There was two elevators there and by watching the lights above them I seen the other one was already going down. Now on most days my plan would of been easy. Once that elevator started going up, I'd just go down the stairs. Nobody could run down 'em as fast as I could jump down 'em, so I'd be out the front door and running light-speed away before they ever got up to the third floor. But holding Bart's box in one hand and my drawing sack in the other was a complication. I hadn't thought up that part of the plan yet. The other complication was they seen me talking to Holly. If

107

they didn't find me, they'd go looking for her to get answers about me. If she wasn't going to turn me in for having a pet she wouldn't turn me in to them guys, unless they said they was my buddies or something. But if that didn't work they might try getting mean with her, which was about the last thing I wanted. The best solution was to make them forget about her by letting them chase me. People forget to be smart if you give them what they want in the first place. I went into the first room I seen, which had two guys sleeping in it. I put my stuff in their closet and went back out to the hall. It was room 306, which I needed to remember so I could come back and get Bart and my drawings. The elevator dinged and I started walking real casual toward the stairs.

"There he is," I heard one of them say behind me, but I pretended not to hear and just kept walking.

"Hey man, we wanna talk to you," they said. By now I could hear them running, but I got to the door to the stairs and went through it. I jumped down that first bunch of steps and was just going down the second one when I heard them open the door. They wasn't all that stealthy, which is a cool word you don't hear that much. I wasn't too nervous by then, because I was jumping pretty good and unless they was jumpers too I didn't figure they could catch me. So I just took my time, jumping each bunch of steps and practicing my form and listened to them coming down as fast as they could. Even taking my time, I got pretty far ahead of them and had to wait by the front door till they come out of the stairs. When I was sure they seen me, I went out the door.

They wasn't in that good of shape, from how hard they was breathing already, but I knew they had knives so I didn't want to take no chances. I figured it wouldn't be all that smart to run in the direction of my apartment cause that would just give 'em a clue. So I run the other way, south down Colorado Blvd. At first I ran fast, but when I turned around I seen them falling behind, so I stopped and walked. When they caught up a little I started running again, but pretty slow. I felt bad for them, being that slow and all, but not bad enough I was gonna let 'em catch me. I could of run all night long that slow but even at that I had to stop and walk a few times so they could keep up.

We only went about a mile when I could see they was losing enthusiasm. We was in an area with some tall apartment buildings now and I seen an older woman with a grocery sack heading for the front door of one.

I jogged up to her. She was trying to get her key out of her purse and having some trouble because of the sack. I kept jogging in place like you see runners do at stoplights.

"Want me to hold your food for you, ma'am?" I said. She looked at me suspicious, but I smiled and then she seen them gang guys about a block away coming toward us. One had his knife out.

"Thanks," she said. She opened the door and I followed her in and give her back her groceries. The door snapped locked behind us. I heard them guys out there so I waited near the door to hear what they might think up, but it didn't sound like they was doing much thinking. They cussed a lot, but it wasn't a proud, mad kind of cussing so much as just tired. The building was easy to figure out, with a big lobby and then a hall. At the end of the hall was a back door. Every building's got a back door if you look for it. I went out it and started jogging back to the hospital to get my stuff. I went a little faster now, more cause it felt good to be running more than I thought they might beat me back there. I got the feeling they'd probably stop at a bar on the way back for a beer and tell the guy with the busted feet they chased me longer than they did. You could tell by the story they told the cops about the incident on the bridge that honesty wasn't their favorite idea. It would be easier to make up a new story than to chase me some more so I figured they got that out of their system for a while.

I got my stuff without another incident and walked home. I decided not to notice stuff while I was walking and used my whole brain to think about the situation, in case I forgot stuff. The guy with the busted feet would still be pissed at me, that one is obvious. The other two could go either way. When I'm mad, a nice run always made me feel better, so maybe they'd be like that. But then, I always enjoyed running. At school I remember some kids not enjoying it so much and when the gym teacher made us all run laps some guys got so pissed they egged his car. So if they was like that, which they seemed, they wouldn't be liking me any better than before we started. They'd probably spend some time staking out the apartment building I went in, in case I lived there. OK, that's one thing that might happen, but it'd be smart to keep thinking of what Plan B or Plan C I would do if I was them.

I didn't like the thought that come into my brain next. If I was looking for clues, I'd follow Holly home. Knowing her name on the mailbox and where she lived would be extra clues, and if they seen a name like Jumper on a mailbox, they might put two and two together. And if it was me, I wouldn't wait about it. I'd just hang out outside the hospital tonight and start my plan.

CHAPTER TEN

Duck tape and a gunshot wound. That's all I'm gonna say.

I put the turtle box down on the floor and put my sack of drawings back on top of the refrigerator. It was almost 12 and Holly got off at two so I didn't have time to do much more thinking. If there's a chance you might have to fight two guys, you ought to think about bringing a bat or something, especially when they had knives, but I didn't own a bat, being more of a football fan. But there's usually stuff laying around anywhere, so I didn't worry about that too much. The only thing laying around my apartment was my roll of duck tape, which wouldn't be that good for fighting, but always comes in handy, so I put it in my backpack and went downstairs.

When I got near the hospital I cut down a alley so if they spotted me I'd be coming from the wrong direction again. So obviously, I'd thought this out pretty good. My plan was to find them without them finding me and then wait till about five till two and distract them again so they didn't see Holly go to the bus stop. My plan didn't go so far as how I was going to distract them. They was tired of running after me so that idea wouldn't be all that tempting. But I get ideas pretty often so I figured one would turn up.

From all my night training, I'm good at walking real quiet. Lots of times I gotta admit I done training places where some folks might think it was unusual, so it was handy to walk real quiet and not upset them. You put your feet down soft, with the toe part first. I call it Indian walking, since they was good at it. I'd also got used to staying in the dark shadow places mostly, even if sometimes you step on a cat or something. So I was pretty comfortable wandering around looking for them guys and not making much noise and staying hid.

They was sitting on this metal bench by the sidewalk, one on each end, and they still seemed a little tired. But they was talking tough again, so that wasn't a good sign. Plus they had a bottle in a paper bag, which they passed back and forth to each other. You had to figure they'd been drinking for a while now, so they wasn't at their best, but they might also be more dangerous. Whiskey gives your brain about four opera star singers telling the quiet little smart part what to do.

110

The door to the hospital was off to their right and behind them and they kept looking over there which confirmed my suspicions. The best distraction would be on their left, to make them look away from the hospital door. My first idea was to roll the duck tape over there. Anybody's gonna go pick up an $8 roll of duck tape if it just happens by.

That idea give me an even better idea. When a noisy truck went by I pulled about three feet of duck tape off the roll and held it in my teeth. Duck tape comes off the roll noisy, and this was a time to be stealthy. When another truck went by I walked up behind them in the shadows and lay down on my stomach. Then I crawled under the back of the bench. One guy's foot was right next to the other guy's foot. As stealthy as I could, I wrapped a strip of tape around each of their pants and taped them together, not tight so they would feel it, but more like looped around them. It didn't matter that the tape wouldn't stick very good to their pants, but it stuck to itself as good as if it was a rope knot. If you ever seen a three-legged race you know having your leg stuck to someone else's is distracting even if you expect it. These guys didn't know their legs was taped to each other. So I'd distract them to get them to stand up, then that tape surprise would interest them while Holly left the hospital. They might even think it was funny and laugh. I only needed it to work for about eleven seconds. After Holly was gone, they'd still have to deal with cutting it off while I made my getaway. It seemed a foolproof plan.

Then I crawled back out again and snuck around to some shadows to their left and watched the hospital door. They was still talking when Holly come out the door, so they didn't see her that instant. But they could of turned around any second and seen her.

"Nice evening," I said, stepping out of the shadow and onto the sidewalk.

"You!" they both said. Then one said, "You got to be the stupidest mother fluffer in the world!"

The next thing surprised me. They both pulled out guns and pointed them right at me. It was just instinct made me step back. Another instinct said this would be a ideal time to start running, but I'd already decided that wouldn't be a good distraction. I took a couple more steps back.

"That ain't all that friendly," I said.

The next thing surprised them. They both stood up real quick and tried to come at me, which I didn't think they'd want to do any more, only that duck tape tripped them and they both fell flat on their faces. While

111

they was falling I seen some fire come out of the front of their guns and heard two shots. Holly heard the shots so she turned and run back into the hospital. I felt something like a real hard punch in my side and the guns rattled across the sidewalk.

Well, the only thing I ever did to these guys was lead them in some laps around the neighborhood, which might of been worth a car egging, but it sure wasn't worth a shooting. So that pissed me off. But guys who got guns is likely to use them, so the smart thing was to take them guns with me. I picked them up and put them in my backpack. The two guys was rolling around holding their noses, which was both bleeding. They was cussing and yelling worse than any guy on MTV, so you knew they was still mad. But they was also confused, so before they figured out exactly what the deal was I pulled their hands behind their backs and taped them together. They wrestled me a little trying to resist, but they wasn't too strong in that position, so it wasn't much of a problem. A jumper has to keep in shape by doing two hundred sit-ups every night after training, and some other stuff, so I ain't the weakest guy in the world. But it was mostly the advantage of their legs was taped together, and their noses were broke and they was laying on their stomachs. It ain't like I beat them in a fair fight. Plus them gunshots got my whole brain working and I felt about as pumped up as I ever felt. I could see they had knives in their pockets, which they might of figured out how to get and cut the tape, so I pulled them out of their pockets and put them in my backpack for good measure.

They wasn't all that pleased when they finally understood the situation. One said something you don't even hear on MTV.

"Hey, kids might walk past here," I said. "You don't improve your language you'll get your mouth duck taped too," I said.

But they hadn't learned their lesson yet and they called me a name I ain't never heard before but which you could tell wasn't polite. I ain't even gonna code it for you. So I put a piece of duck tape over their mouths too and started walking away from my apartment again.

In about a block I noticed that my shirt was wet. I pulled it up and seen a big old cut bleeding to beat the band. About then I noticed that it hurt like heck.

"Dang it," I said. That punch in my side had been a bullet but I figured it must of hit my belt or something cause it wasn't how I thought a bullet would feel. It had been hurting, but once I seen that the bullet sliced me as it went past, it hurt like heck. It looked like a long knife cut. Part

112

of me said I should go back to the hospital and get some stitches. But if I done that, Holly would figure out I had a incident with gang guys and think maybe I was a gang guy too. Plus I ain't got medical coverage right now, and hospitals is expensive. So I used one of their knives to cut off the bottom part of my shirt, which I had just washed, and pushed it on to my gunshot wound. With my teeth and other hand I ripped off some more duck tape and used that to hold the cloth on the wound real tight. Some sirens was coming closer so I crossed the street and went home. It hurt bad enough I had to walk slow and even take some rest breaks.

I was sure glad I had that duck tape with me. I made a note in my brain: From now on I'm always gonna keep a roll of it in my backpack.

Even with four aspirins, my gunshot wound hurt about as bad as anything I ever had before so I didn't get much sleep. On the other hand, my plan had come off brilliant. Them gang guys hadn't seen Holly and the police had probably picked them up for shooting their guns, so we was out of the woods on that for a while. And I was pretty sure their noses was broke so they wouldn't be in the mood to do much fist fighting. And I got their guns and knives, so they'd have to save up for a while to buy new ones. Maybe they'd even get jobs to do that and find out they liked the job better than being gang guys.

OK, so that was the quiet voice in me saying that and it didn't sound real confident. The opera voice was saying they was still a problem that needs a plan, but none come to me right off. They'd probably feel a lot better if I just give them my wallet with the ten bucks and let 'em beat me up, but with my side already hurting that idea went out the window.

Every time I moved I felt like I was getting stabbed so all the next day I mostly stayed on the couch, which is where I sleep anyway. But my forehead didn't feel hot, like I had a infection, so I wasn't too worried. No blood leaked out from the duck tape and some people say it will cure warts, so I just left it alone.

The only time I got up that was interesting was when I remembered Bart in his box. It was mean to leave him in there and there wasn't much chance of him making a getaway, so I turned him loose in the apartment. That was about as much effort as I could make. He was sure to poop on my floor, but I'd cleaned up worse in other apartments.

"Do your worst, Bart," I told him. "I'll deal with it tomorrow." I didn't

113

have any food I thought he might like so I felt bad about that, but there wasn't much to do about it. "We'll go grasshopper hunting in a couple days," I told him and he seemed to accept that.

Bart made pretty good company. Once he understood he wasn't in a box any more he went exploring the apartment. Every time he come to a wall he tried to climb over it but he never made much progress. It didn't bother him much, he just kept trying until he got the idea. When it started to get dark, he sat on the floor by the refrigerator, which was a smart way to tell me he was hungry. He could sit still for a long time, which was interesting, so watching him took my mind off the gunshot wound.

"I'm hungry too," I told him, but beside the pain of getting up, it didn't seem right to get a can of soup out and eat in front of him. I wished I still had some of that cantaloupe cause that might taste good to him, but I didn't.

Then I seen him get more alert. Not like he moved or anything, but you could tell he was hatching a new idea. At first I guessed his idea was pooping on my floor, but then I seen a cockroach come out from under the refrigerator.

"Forget it, Bart," I said. "He's too fast for you."

Bart didn't move and the bug run out a little farther. I keep my apartment clean, but if anyone's got cockroaches in a building, everyone's got them. They didn't bug me much, unless one ran over my face while I was sleeping, but I ain't crazy about them either. The bug ran around, mostly staying by the wall, but then he must of smelt the raspberry juice on Bart, so he ran over to him. The turtle didn't move, even when the roach ran up his leg and around on his shell. When the bug run down onto his head I thought for sure Bart would shake him off, or try and eat him, but he didn't even blink. After a while the bug climbed down and sat on the floor in front of him.

He was only about two inches from Bart's nose, so if it was me I would of made a quick grab. But you just about can't move quick enough to get a roach and Bart must of known that. I never seen anything move as slow as Bart's head did, moving toward that bug. He opened his mouth, but he must have been holding his breath because the bug still didn't move.

The next thing you know, Bart had him in his mouth and was chewing him up. I never even seen the grab but it must of been quick. From the enthusiastic way he was finishing off his meal it must of tasted like a steak dinner. I decided it would be OK for me to eat in front of him now, so I got

114

up off the couch and got a can of soup. I was down to some cans of tomato soup and one cream of broccoli, which normally I'd rank pretty far below minestrone, but compared to tomato it sounded OK to me. I opened the cream of broccoli and took it back to the couch to eat. I didn't feel up to washing the spoon, but it was only dirty from yesterday so there probably wasn't many germs on it yet.

For a day of laying around with a gunshot wound it had turned out pretty good. I hadn't got shot at, for one thing. There was one less cockroach in my apartment. Bart and me had got good dinners without working too hard for them, and I'd had somebody to keep me company.

You really can't complain about a day like that.

CHAPTER ELEVEN

If you got a turtle, you gotta feed it. And if an Officer wants to talk, you pretty much gotta talk to him, even if his questions make you nervous. And you can't miss your art therapy lessons. But that don't mean you don't start the next part of your plan. Which all happens in this chapter.

The next day went about the same only I ate tomato soup for lunch and dinner. By the day after that my gunshot wound started to feel better and I could walk around pretty good unless I moved funny. I wasn't in the mood to eat another can of tomato soup so I walked to the grocery store and got some supplies. They had a good deal on cantaloupes, so I got one of them too.

On the way home it started to rain. I had mixed feelings about that. First, it don't rain that much in Denver, so everybody likes it when it rains. It makes everything smell good and cleans up stuff that don't get washed otherwise, like streets and buildings and trees. Plus it ain't that ordinary in Colorado, so we like rainy days the way people in Oregon like sunny days. Only it seemed like recently we was getting rain every week, so them guys who talk about global warming must be nuts. We could use some global warming to dry things out. People can get used to anything and then they think it's ordinary. People in New York probably enjoy real quiet days when nobody's honking, but people in Nebraska are used to quiet so they might like honking, and fireworks and loud stuff like that.

I also like rain because it makes the ground soft, which is excellent for training. But even if my side felt good enough to walk to the store kind of slow, it didn't feel so good I wanted to jump out of a tree. So I felt bad there was going to be some extra soft grass that wasn't going to get jumped on.

But if you see the bad side of something and not the good one, you probably just ain't looking hard enough. About the best part of rain is that it makes earthworms crawl out onto the sidewalk, and worms seem like good turtle food. So I watched the sidewalk for worms and when I seen a good one, I got him. He wiggled around in my hand, so I knew he was still fresh. It tickled, but not so much I had to laugh.

When I got to my building, I seen the rest of Bart's dinner walk onto the sidewalk. It was a fat cricket, shiny black and looking a little confused by the rain. Since I had my grocery sack in one hand and the earthworm in

116

the other I was at a disadvantage for catching him, so I put the worm in my shirt pocket and caught the cricket pretty easy. He wiggled even more than the worm, but I didn't let him make a getaway. It was tricky unlocking my door, but I figured that out. It might seem boring to you if I talked about setting the sack on the floor and moving the cricket to my left hand so I could get at my key with my right hand, since that's the pocket it was in, so I won't bother telling you about it.

Bart went for the worm right away and it looked like about his favorite food in the world, so I made a note of that. The cricket was a lot smarter. He made a beeline for the refrigerator and went under it before Bart even figured out he was food. That one was my mistake. Sometimes you go to a restaurant with a table cloth, like on a date, and they bring you salad with stuff you ain't seen before and you look at it a while to make sure it's something you're supposed to eat until you see other people eating it. Other times they put leafs on your plate that are just decoration and if you eat them your date will think you're uneducated. I figured that one out the hard way. So if Bart never ate a cricket before, you can't hold it against him for being cautious. If I seen a cricket on my plate at a restaurant I wouldn't choose him as the first thing I ate either.

One thing I forgot to say is that while I was walking to the grocery store I run into Officer Mike.

"Good afternoon, Jumper," he said. "Looks like we might get a little rain." So now that you know it rained later, you see he was right about that, and I probably should of put this part earlier. But there ain't nothing to do about it now.

"Yes sir," I said.

"Well, we could sure use the moisture."

"Yes sir. I like the rain."

"We had another interesting incident," he said, nodding slowly and rubbing his chin with his hand. He was thinking his hardest. "Very interesting incident. Down by the hospital."

I had a pretty good idea what direction this conversation wanted to go.

"I bet your job is pretty interesting, " I said. "Incidents, and talking to people, and filling out forms and stuff." Sometimes if you get people talking about one thing they forget about the thing they wanted to talk about. But Officer Mike didn't fall for it.

"Remember that thing that happened down by the river? Where the guy got his feet broken?"

"I kind of remember you mentioning it to me."

"A gang called The Bones from Chicago..."

"I might not get an A on a pop quiz but yeah, it rings a bell in my brain that you said something like that."

"Well, his two friends were involved in a shooting the other night."

"Was anybody hurt?" I asked.

"Couple broken noses. Nothing serious."

"Always good when nobody gets hurt serious. Couple broken noses seems like a perfect end to a shooting. You see enough violence on TV and in the movies, don't really need more of it in everyday life. People getting hurt. I never cared too much for that. Except like Terminator movies where you can tell it's all pretend. You think they'll come up with another of them?"

Officer Mike pretended he didn't even hear that question. He was pretty stubborn about keeping a conversation going the way he wanted.

"Strange thing about it was they didn't find any guns. They said that was because this other guy shot at them. Same guy as broke their friend's feet. And jumped off the bridge."

I didn't say nothing. Officer Mike looked up and watched the clouds like he had his own weather show.

"They were tied up with duct tape," Officer Mike said after a minute. Now he started looking at his feet like he never seen them before and was wondering what them things was somebody stuck on the end of his legs. His comment made me nervous because I had a big roll of duck tape in my backpack.

"Lots of people use duck tape," I said. "That's just circumstantial."

"So you don't think their story sounds right?"

"You mean if I was to imagine it? I'd say not exactly right, now that I think about it. If some other guy wanted to shoot 'em, they'd be easy targets, all duck taped by the bench like that. So he would of just shot 'em. Plus, being gang guys like you said, you'd think they would of had weapons. So that part don't sound kosher either."

"We couldn't hold them," he said. "Didn't find any guns."

"Well, somebody could of picked 'em up for safekeeping."

"I was thinking that myself," he said. "Picked 'em up just to keep kids from finding them. I hope whoever did remembers to take the bullets out. Dangerous to have loaded guns laying around."

"That's a pretty smart idea."

"Well, you better get on home before it rains."

"I gotta get groceries."

"OK, then, have a good day young man."

So after I watched Bart eat his dinner, I took the bullets out of the guns. I put the guns in the back of my freezer. I don't have kids as visitors all that often, but if I ever did, they wouldn't accidentally find them there. After I ate dinner, I put the bullets in the Dinty Moore can and filled it with water. Everyone knows bullets don't shoot if they're wet, so that seemed about the safest thing to do with them.

So them gang guys was still a problem that needed a plan. But you can't just sit around thinking about problems or you'll get bored real fast. I was nervous about them finding Holly, but when I went back over the incident in my brain, I remembered she had her back to them in the cafeteria and also when they followed us, so they probably never got much of a look at her face. They might remember her ponytail, but they was probably watching me more close, so maybe not too. You can't tell much about a person by seeing them in a uniform so there was a good shot they wouldn't recognize her for sure even if they seen her.

The only other interesting thing that happened that night is that about the time I was going to sleep that cricket under my refrigerator figured out Bart couldn't get him there, so he started chirping. He was pretty proud of himself for his getaway and he had a opera star voice for a cricket.

"Yeah, you're pretty smart, Jiminy," I said to him. "I gotta admit that. You eat some cockroaches under there and stay off my face and we'll get along fine."

Actually, having a cricket chirping in your kitchen ain't that ordinary, so even if he was loud it didn't bother me. Rich people take vacations out in the country so they can hear crickets and stuff, and he hadn't cost me a dime. So I just pretended I was on a expensive vacation and had me a good night's sleep.

119

Them gang guys wasn't going to give up on me all that easy, that was obvious. If you looked at if from their side they had a good case. I didn't need to break the guy's feet in the first place. That was just being mean. Plus I made them other two run when they wasn't in the mood, so if I'd had a car they would of egged it just for that. Then I broke their noses and swiped their knives and guns, so they couldn't feel good about that either. They probably thought I was as mean as they was. It might of been embarrassing to get found by the police all duck taped and nobody likes to get embarrassed. So even if I hadn't started out to be mean to them, they might of saw it that way.

On the other side, they had to take some of the blame themselves, for trying to make an insurance claim on me in the first place. There ain't a law says you gotta give somebody your money just cause they'd prefer you did, unless it's the government. That first part was on them, but they might of forgot that. After that it was mostly my own fault and giving them ten bucks now wouldn't seem a good enough payment.

So I'd made myself a little pickle and there wasn't much alternatives except to fix it. I thought about finding them and explaining I was sorry for the problems I give 'em, but both the quiet voice and the opera voice wasn't buying that as a fix. If they got me alone in some place they felt comfortable, they'd think up ways to be mean they ain't thought of before. By anybody's count, they had me outnumbered so even if I resisted and fought back, it was a low percentage deal.

Officer Mike had said The Bones was a bad news gang, so you had to figure they didn't follow law rules all that careful. Maybe the smart thing was to watch them until they was in the middle of a crime and then turn them in. Nobody likes a guy who turns people in, but I didn't see much alternatives. They outnumbered me, but the cops outnumbered them, and if they got sent to the pokey for something they was already doing they couldn't really blame me.

Now that I had a plan, the whole thing didn't bother me too much. My side was getting better and better, and I was thinking about going down to the hospital to see Michelangelo on Tuesday and maybe have another cup of coffee with Holly. I didn't do any new drawings, but I figured Linda would of, so we could talk about them and feed a earthworm to Bart. I already decided that I'd give her my extra shaving mirror. I didn't need two, so it was being greedy keeping that spare, and it would kind of make up for me not doing any new pictures. No need to tell her about my gunshot wound, even if it might seem cool. It might make her feel sorry for me, and nobody likes that. Even if she used the mirror to do some pictures in the hospital, the nurses wouldn't report her to the art magazines. They'd just think it was cute and not pay too much attention to it.

It didn't make much sense to start tracking the gang guys until my side was healed a little better. I wouldn't be much good for running away if it come to that, and one punch in the wrong spot would ruin the whole experience for me in a hurry. Once you decide that doing nothing for a while is the hot plan, doing it is a no brainer.

Linda looked a lot better on Tuesday and she surprised me by wanting to give Bart his worm. I'd carried Bart in my Nike bag, which seemed more ordinary that a big box. I'd thought a girl wouldn't want to pick up a earthworm, but she did. She'd did a bunch of new drawings and they was all pretty funny. I give her the mirror and she liked it a lot. She looked at her face in it for a while.

"It makes me look so big," she said.

"That's so you can see your whiskers better," I said.

"Look! I got some whiskers."

I laughed at that.

"No, really, look!" She pointed under the cap above her ear. She had little hairs sprouting up.

"That's gotta be a good sign," I said.

"Are you a doctor now?"

"Don't need to be a doctor to know a good sign," I said. "If it ain't a good sign, you're gonna need to start shaving."

"Girls don't shave."

"Well, then it's a good sign."

"OK. Maybe."

I showed her how to use the mirror to do pictures and then Holly come in and we had a nice cup of coffee in the cafeteria.

"So, did Linda make you fifty bucks?" she asked.

"Shoot, I forgot all about the bird drawing," I said. "We got interested in other stuff."

"She's a feisty one. If she's not drawing she's talking about taking Bartholomew to the park."

121

"She's got some new hairs coming in."

"Really? I hadn't noticed that."

"They're pretty small. That's a good sign ain't it?"

"It could be. But hair starts growing back after chemo, so not necessarily. You shouldn't get your hopes up."

"My hopes is pretty much always up. I told her it seemed like a good sign to me."

She didn't say anything for a minute, but just sipped on her coffee. Then she started talking about other stuff, one after another, like to change the subject.

"Have you heard that cricket at our building?" she said. "Sound like he's in the walls or something."

I never thought about other tenants hearing Jiminy. He wasn't a pet, he was dinner that escaped, but if he was bothering people he was still my responsibility and I might have to take some consequences. But only if someone complained. Just saying they heard a cricket ain't the same as complaining.

"I might of heard him. You can't tell where a cricket is by the sound some of the time."

"I think he's in the building. Did you hear about the shooting we had last week? It was right when I was leaving."

"Officer Mike told me about it. Don't sound like it was a big deal."

"Well, it sure scared me at the time. I always thought this was a safe area. Now I get the creeps just walking to the bus stop. I feel like someone's watching me."

"Ain't nothing gonna happen to you walking to the bus stop."

She kind of laughed but, just as fast as I said it, I made up my mind it was true. You feel like somebody's watching you and they probably are. I knew who it was, and I knew it was my fault. So from now on there was going to be somebody else watching her too, and if them guys tried to pull a fast one they'd get themselves duck taped like they ain't ever been duck taped before.

"Ain't nothing gonna happen to you walking to the bus stop," I said one more time. She looked at me like she was about to cross examine, but then she didn't.

122

"I believe you, Jumper," she said.

OK, so my gunshot wound wasn't all the way healed but it was time to start tracking these guys anyway. When Holly went back to her floor I went outside and found me a dark shadow by a bush. I didn't have no trouble with noticing stuff and getting distracted either. I just made sure I noticed stuff that might be clues about them gang guys and that was all I had time to notice.

They didn't show that night. The bus stop was only a block away, so when Holly come out I didn't have to move much to keep my eye on her. When she was on board, I walked home.

My gunshot wound was sore, but it wasn't like stabbing me. I turned Bart loose out of the Nike bag onto the apartment floor, ate four aspirins and went to bed.

The next night I walked over to the hospital about one and done the same thing. I tried not to watch Holly too close, so she'd feel even more like somebody was watching her. Anyway, I wasn't really, I was mostly watching for suspicious guys in the area. Nobody was all that suspicious so, after the bus took off, I went back home.

The next night I done about the same routine, only I was feeling better by then so I jogged partway home. Buses don't ever take the straight way home, so I wound up getting there the same time as the bus. That meant I could stay back in the shadows and watch Holly walk from the bus stop to our building, so she was even safer. Part of me wanted to watch her more than the other part said was appropriate, and it made the suggestion that even if I watched her my hardest she might not notice, but I put my foot down on that idea. When you're doing your best job you usually can't do things exactly the way you'd prefer.

Since I hadn't done much training for a while, I could tell I wasn't in that good of shape for jogging. After about ten minutes I was already breathing a little fast, and could feel myself sweating. But it don't take long to build back up, so it was probably good for me.

That piece of duck tape on my wound wasn't all that fresh any more, but it was still sticking pretty good. It was rolled up some on the edges and you could tell the sweating under it made it looser. This seemed like a good time to change my dressing, like they say on TV. I pulled it off as slow as I could, but it still pulled some of the scab off with it and I started to bleed all over. So it would have been better if I had a big band-aid on there that didn't stick to the cut part. It wasn't bleeding all that much, so I took

123

a long shower and washed it clean. I didn't have a band-aid big enough, which would of taken about six to cover it and part of them would stick to it anyway. But I still had some clean socks from the last time I done laundry. I put a sock over the cut to soak up blood and held it on with several pieces of duck tape. It didn't look pretty, but it felt better than before, so I wished I would of thought of that sooner. If I ever had another gunshot wound I'd do it like that right off.

Before I went to bed I threw a clean sock in my backpack, right by the roll of duck tape. I never was a Boy Scout, but I always liked their saying of be prepared.

From then on, every night Holly was working I jogged over to the hospital and watched her get on the bus, then jogged home to watch her get off. That sock must of had some medicinal qualities because my cut started healing lots faster. I started training again, mostly about midnight when Holly was at work, before I went to watch her. I had two sacks full of trash, so I started practicing throwing it in the dumpster. At first it made my side hurt, but pretty soon I could land the trash sack on my first try so it wasn't much of a problem. In the daytime I started going over to the Platte River to see if I could track down them gang guys, but I never seen 'em there or at the hospital, so I started to think maybe they got jobs after all.

Linda was looking better and better every Tuesday and her hair was getting real noticeable. She was using that mirror to make drawings like a madman, which was looking more and more like photographs instead of drawings. Hers didn't look tall and skinny like mine still did at first until I got used to them. She set up her paper under a cover so it would be dark, with like a tunnel opening out in the room. She almost never did just one line for an arm or whatever any more, or a dot for an eye. It was like once she seen how to draw something one time with the mirror, she got how to do it in her head after that and didn't really need the mirror. So it was an interesting process she had.

Bart always ate a earthworm or something for her. We started taking him on walks around her room. At first Linda was real weak, but she was tough and she wouldn't let you help her. Pretty soon she was keeping up with the turtle easy, unless he got real enthusiastic and tried to make a getaway. So that was good news.

When I went home, Jiminy was chirping up a storm under my refrigerator, which I'd got used to so much it seemed ordinary. I always slid a little piece of fruit or bread under there for him. It wasn't his idea to come

124

to my apartment, so he'd kind of switched from being "a dinner that escaped" to "a guest under the refrigerator." But he still wasn't really a pet, since I didn't play with him or buy him toys. Even if I thought of a cricket toy, I wasn't going to buy it for him and blow my loophole on the apartment rules. One thing was weird: I got used to his chirping and didn't even notice it much except when he first started. Then I thought it was nice.

I wonder if rich people get so used to crickets and birds at their mansions that when they go on vacations they don't even notice them anymore? That would be a big disadvantage of being a rich guy, if you think about it, since cool stuff might not seem cool to you any more once it was ordinary. I never thought a cricket would seem ordinary to me, for one example, but it got that way, so if that could happen to me it could happen to anybody and you can't hold it against them. You gotta concentrate your whole brain on not letting cool stuff go ordinary on you, or else you might as well be poor. I didn't want to be poor, cause it would be a pain in the neck. But there wasn't much chance of me getting poor, being a renaissance guy and all.

So things was about back to how they're supposed to be. I was jumping off my balcony most nights and eating a can of soup for dinner, taking care of my turtle and enjoying my cricket. Most nights I jogged over to the hospital to watch Holly walk to the bus stop. You might do different stuff in your life, but I wouldn't trade you. The cockroaches wasn't too bad, my side only ached sometimes, and I was having coffee breaks with a pretty nurse on Tuesday nights if they wasn't short handed or having incidents with patients. There ain't much wrong with a life like that.

CHAPTER TWELVE

I got to stop the Bones from following Holly if I can, and they get to understand cowboys a little better.

About 1:32 one night while I was hiding in the bushes by the hospital I noticed a car with dark windows going by for the third time. Even with the windows up I heard that thumping bass of rap music coming from it, so that seemed suspicious. It turned into the parking lot that said "doctors" and pulled into a empty spot. Well, a doctor might enjoy rap music like anybody else, so that was circumstantial. But the engine kept running and that rap music was still playing, so that seemed like more clues. I moved around in the shadows to get a better lookout on it. The window on the passenger side come down about halfway and I seen a ethical guy's forehead and eyes, with dark tan skin and black hair. So it still could be doctors talking bout an interesting case before they went in to work. No rule says ethical guys can't be doctors. I kept behind the other parked cars and got closer. One guy got out and took a leak on the tire of another car. The white band-aid on his nose was obvious and I recognized him right off as one of the guys I was looking for. Then the back door opened and a black guy got out on crutches.

Seeing his buddy pee must of got him in the mood too, because he pissed on another car's tires. It was clumsy for him, on account of the crutches and he had a cast on his right hand. Then they both got back in.

This was a situation that needed some extra good planning, which is my specialty. They was waiting in the hospital parking lot for some reason, and my money was on the idea that they wanted to follow Holly. Well, there was no way I was gonna let that happen, no matter what it took, but I had some strategy issues to resolve. It's pretty hard to outrun guys in a car and if they'd saved up and got new guns they wouldn't have to get that close to me. I wasn't crazy about getting a new gunshot wound, except as a last resort. Plus I was outnumbered, and they had some good motives to discriminate against me if they got the chance. So I wasn't going to be able to joke my way out of a fight if it come to that.

On the good side, with the dark windows and that loud music, I wouldn't have to be that stealthy to sneak up on 'em. But once I did, even if I distracted them, they'd just jump out and start shooting. So this was

126

more complicated than that last time. Then I thought maybe I could duck tape their car doors and then if I distracted them they couldn't jump out.

But they'd be able to push the doors open unless I had something good to put the other end of the tape to. The door handle would be the best spot to hook one end of the tape to, since I could wrap around it if I stayed low below their windows. Maybe if I used a long piece I could go all the way under the car and hook the other end to the door handle on the other side. That way, they'd be pulling against each other.

I couldn't see any reason that plan wouldn't work. I pulled a pretty long piece of duck tape off the roll and crawled up beside their car. Laying on the ground next to the car that music was loud, so I didn't worry about making noise. But I had to stay low so they didn't see me. It was easy to loop the tape around the first door handle and run it down the side of the door. But the car was too low to crawl all the way under. My plan didn't seem so hot about then. I reached under the car and felt around. There wasn't much under there to hook the tape to, but I felt some little pipes up by the front tire. They wasn't big enough to put much trust in, but they was what I could reach, so I looped the tape around them a couple times. Then I snuck to the other side and did about the same thing. That left the guy on crutches in the back seat who could still get out easy, but if he could catch me on crutches I deserved to get caught. OK, maybe he could shoot me easy enough, but his knife hand still had a cast on it and that was probably also his gun hand. It didn't seem fair to give him more disadvantages, so I didn't tape his door.

I still had the problem of a good distraction. Otherwise they'd just sit there not knowing their doors was taped and follow Holly to the bus stop. Then they'd follow the bus in their car until they seen her get off.

This was one of them times when I'd thought up the first part of a plan pretty good, but hadn't paid enough attention to the end part. There was still about ten minutes till Holly got off, so I had plenty of time, but I decided I should use my whole brain on it. I moved a little bit away from where they was parked and sat in a empty parking spot.

There was a big oil spot on the pavement and for a minute I started thinking about how some doctor had a oil leak in his Mercedes and I ought to notify somebody so they could tell him, but I put my foot down on that idea on account of my time limits. But that idea give me another idea. There was some pages from a newspaper under a car and I took a big one and pushed it around in that oil spot till it was greasy. At about 1:58 I went

127

around to the driver's side of their car. They must of been watching the hospital door because I got right up to them before they seen me. I started acting like I was washing their windshield like some guys do to make money. They yelled at me to get away from their car but by then I'd washed the whole windshield with my greasy newspaper. They honked the horn a bunch of times. I knew they couldn't see me that good in the dark, with that grease on their windshield so I walked toward the street pretty casual and started jogging away. They turned the headlights on, which caught me dead square, so I waved at them over my shoulder. But I didn't turn and look right at the headlights, since that screws it up to see anything else at night. Plus there wasn't much advantage to their recognizing me. When I was out of their headlights I turned and seen their windshield wipers going full speed, and washer fluid squirting up, but it ain't much good on grease. They was gonna have to wash that off the old fashioned way, and by then Holly would be on the bus.

That's when they tried to open their doors. When they noticed they was stuck they started using real impolite words, which they had to shout over the rap music, "What the fluff did you do to this fluffing door?" But they kept pushing and pretty soon them doors flew open. By now I had a little head start so they jumped back in the car. They hit the gas and started following me so I started jogging away from home pretty fast. They turned left on Colorado Blvd. out of the parking lot and some cars honked at them for not taking their turn. They was driving on the right side of the road like they was supposed to and I was jogging on the left, just so you can picture it. They swerved around some, from not being able to see the road too good, because they hadn't washed off the grease yet. Even swerving, they caught up pretty fast and I seen the guy in the back aiming a gun at me out his window. I started running a lot faster. I come to a stoplight that was yellow and about to go red when I heard a gunshot and some bark flew off a tree right beside me. I didn't slow down but ran about as fast as I could across that street, even if it had turned red. Cars was already starting to go so I thought I was safe. But the guys who was after me didn't slow down either. Cars honked and a big red pickup truck slammed into the front corner of their car with a loud crunching sound.

I stopped and moved into the shadow of a tree to watch. After a minute the doors opened and they got out but they was moving slow and you could see a couple of them was bleeding, but not too bad. Other drivers was around them by now and all the traffic was stopped from both directions.

128

Obviously they should of stopped at that red light, so it was their fault. And it wasn't safe to drive with your windshield greased up either, so that was on them too. I might of greased it, but I didn't make 'em drive it that way. They could of just done the correct thing, which was decide to shoot me a different time when their vehicle was safer. So I wasn't taking no blame on that. After a minute they didn't seem so dazed, they just seemed mad. They should have been apologizing, but they wasn't. Instead they was yelling about the brakes not working, and crap like that.

The guy in the pickup truck wasn't happy either, but he was a lot quieter. At first he just seemed annoyed that his new pickup bumper got bent up a little. He had on new jeans and cowboy boots and a cowboy hat. Sometimes in Denver you see guys dressed like that who have regular jobs and just dress like a cowboy to go to a country bar. But this guy had bales of hay in his truck, so his hat and boots wasn't a disguise. There's lots of farms and ranches in Colorado, and the guys who work on them come into Denver to do business. They tend to be quieter than city guys so you think they're harmless, but they're used to dealing with cows who weigh about as much as a car. When you do business with big dumb animals all day long your whole life, you see things in a simple way that don't involve subtle negotiations. Cowboys don't take much crap from a cow or a horse so, if you ain't bigger than a cow, you need to keep that in mind when you deal with them.

The tan guy who was driving the car was from Chicago, so he didn't understand cowboys. Guys who carry knives and guns think they got the only opinion, so you can see we had the makings of a misunderstanding. He went right over to the cowboy and started yelling at him and calling him names. He said something like, "fluff you, you mother fluffing pile of sticks" quite a few times, and variations on that idea. The cowboy looked at him pretty calm and didn't say a word, like the gang guy was one of them little yappy dogs who make a lot of noise but you don't get scared of. The gang guy poked his finger in the cowboy's chest, which I would not have did, but the cowboy just stood there listening politely. The gang guy seemed like he was talking mean to cheer lead himself into doing something bad. I felt sorry for the gang guy, cause he just didn't know any better. After about the third time he called the cowboy a fluffing something, the gang guy reached into his jeans and pulled out a gun. That was the last straw for the cowboy. Before the gun got pointed at him, the cowboy got tired of it and punched the gang guy in the face. Only he punched him about as hard as you'd punch a cow who had pissed you off and you wanted to make sure

129

you got his attention. The gang guy's whole body straightened up, then it lifted off the ground and went backward and he fell down on his back and didn't move. The crowd of drivers held the other gang guys back. It went from being noisy with yelling to even quieter than Nebraska in about a second, with nobody talking at all. Everybody just stared at the guy on the ground. The cowboy looked at the guy on the ground for a minute too, then got some chew out of his shirt pocket and stuck a wad in his mouth. Then he went back to his truck, pulled a rifle out from under the seat and held it casual across his lap so the other gang guys knew not to try to get fancy on him. He turned up the country western station on his radio super loud, like the way gang guys like to listen to rap, to remind them who was the boss in the current situation and then just sat there waiting for the cops.

Everything seemed in control, so I run home. It felt good to run, so I went pretty fast and got to the bus stop about the same time Holly was getting off. It was more habit than that I was worried about her tonight. Them gang guys was occupied for a while. I stayed in the shadows and watched her a little closer than usual. Her ponytail bounced from side to side and the streetlights made nice shadows on her uniform. She had a pretty way of walking like some girls do, which I enjoyed watching.

After she went in our building I stood leaning against a tree, noticing the way the bark felt on my back and trying to memorize the way she looked walking so I could think it up again whenever I wanted. Whenever you notice stuff that makes you feel cheerful you ought to memorize it in case you need to remember it later. You can't ever tell. Someday you might be old and can't jump, or run, or even lean against a tree and you'll want to think about watching a pretty girl walk in the moonlight. But if you ain't bothered to memorize it now, you'll be stuck thinking about a hospital ceiling or politics or whatever's on the TV in your room. Then you'll wish you was me, in the bed next to yours with a big grin on my face.

CHAPTER THIRTEEN

Officer Mike asks a bunch of questions, and my plan gets a lot thicker, and I have to go all Rockford at the Thrift Store

The next day I thought about the incident. Most people don't go to the pokey for a traffic accident. Pulling the gun might be aggravating circumstances, but the jails is so full they can't keep you there very long unless you get caught smoking weed. If you wanted to be a murderer, the smart thing would be to make sure a bunch of guys got caught smoking weed before you done your murder. That way, even if they caught you, they wouldn't have no jail cells to put you in and they'd have to let you go. With as much weed smoking as I've seen guys do, I know the jails is full, so the Bones was going to be back out on the streets pretty soon and still a problem for me. The good news is their car looked about totaled, so we'd be more even again. Between getting themselves out of jail and shopping for cars, I figured I had at least a week of vacation time from them.

I decided it was time to do some more drawings, but I was running low on paper. The grocery store sells computer paper pretty cheap for 500 sheets. It looks about like any other paper, once you drawn on it, so I walked down there.

As I was walking home, Officer Mike stepped out of a doorway right in front of me. I'd been watching out for him so I could avoid him. You get enough circumstantial stuff against you and it don't matter if somebody picks you out of a line-up or not. I'd just as soon not talk to him too much in case I give away clues about the bridge incident, plus the incident last night. But he stepped out of the doorway right in front of me like he'd been waiting. So I couldn't avoid talking to him and had to concentrate on not acting suspicious.

"Hello, Jumper," he said. "Just the man I was looking for. Lovely morning, don't you think?"

"Yes sir," I said. "A real good morning."

"You been shopping?" he said, looking at my bag.

"Just paper. Anybody could buy paper."

"You bet," he said. "I've bought it myself."

131

"And a new pencil. Just for drawing, not as a weapon or anything."

"No law against pencils," he said. "As long as you got a permit."

I knew he was joking on me so I didn't say nothing.

"Those guys from Chicago got in more trouble last night," he said. That was exactly what I didn't want to talk about. But being a cop and all you could see why it would be on his mind. "I was hoping you could give me some more advice about them."

"Oh yeah?" I said. "They rob a bank or something?" I tried to think up something they probably didn't do to keep him off the track.

"Nah, nothing that big. Car accident."

"Well, they're probably more used to driving in Chicago. Maybe the yellow lights last longer up there."

"That could be part of it at that," he said. "But the other part is that their brake line broke."

"That's the problem with cars," I said. "Stuff breaks and you fix it and then something else breaks. I had me a Pinto once and stuff broke all the time."

"Their brake line had a little help. Someone ran duct tape from the door to it. When they opened the door the duct tape broke the brake line."

"I didn't know that."

"Well, you couldn't have known. They didn't mention it on the news. Didn't report any of it."

"Right."

"They haven't been lucky around duct tape, have they?"

"It could be a coincidence. You can't overlook coincidences. They happen all the time. If one day they didn't, that day would be the biggest coincidence ever."

"Right," he said. "A coincidence."

"How bad was they hurt?"

"Not bad. Passenger dislocated his shoulder trying to catch himself. Driver got bruised ribs from the steering wheel. Plus he got his jaw broken arguing with the other driver."

"Can't arrest them for a accident though, right?"

"Not for the accident. A witness saw the guy in the back seat take a shot at a jogger though. So we charged him with discharging a firearm in the city. He already made bail."

"So, if they shot at a guy, you could think of it like they got what they deserved."

"The Bones deserve a lot worse than that. In Chicago the police thought they were selling drugs to school kids. And they suspect them of two murders. Like I say, these guys are bad news. But they couldn't convict them. Nobody'd testify against them."

"It ain't right to sell drugs to school kids."

"That's the truth. But it wouldn't be smart to piss 'em off either."

"They sound like guys who get pissed off pretty easy even if they ought to take some of the blame themselves."

"Yeah, I think they do get pissed off easy."

"It's too bad they didn't catch them smoking weed so they could hold them in jail longer."

"Probably some truth in that," he said.

"Did they say who duck taped their car?"

"Nah, they said the doors were rattling and they put it on themselves to quiet it down. Just an accident it got tangled in the brake line. Didn't sound quite right to me."

"I don't know, it sounds like a good explanation. My Pinto's doors rattled like heck."

"Hard to tape the outside of a door from the inside."

"Maybe they're real limber."

"They're not too limber today. We didn't find a roll of tape in their car."

"That's too complicated for me. That's like a Colombo deal, where you never know who done it till the end. But you're probably good at mysteries like that, being a cop and all."

"Yes, it's a mystery. But if there's a guy out there chasing them with a roll of duct tape, he ought to be careful. He's been lucky so far. But luck has a way of running out on a guy."

"Yeah, it runs out like an Olympic sprinter. Or like that new punt returner the Broncos drafted. You seen him? Fastest guy I ever seen."

"I saw him. But even the fastest guy gets tackled sooner or later."

"OK, well, I better get this paper home."

"You have a nice day, young man."

I felt lucky Officer Mike hadn't asked me a bunch of hard questions, like my whereabouts on the night in question. If he did, I'd just have to come clean. If my tape had broke their brakes then that accident was on me. You can't lie to a cop without purging yourself, and the cowboy wouldn't be that happy with me either. But I didn't have the intent to cause an accident, so that might go in my favor. You just about can't do anything without breaking some law, which is what makes America great, but they don't count it against you so much if your intent wasn't there.

On the good side, Officer Mike had give me a clue about how them guys operate. Their modes of Opera Andy, which means the way they mostly like to work, was to sell drugs to school kids and a guy don't change his mode too easy. If I moved to Chicago, for one example, I'd find where to sell cans to, and where you give blood, and be in drug studies. You can change where you live easier than what you do. But there's lots of schools in Denver, and lots of video arcades and other places kids might hang out, and I confess I don't know where all the schools is.

Up to now I'd been playing a prevent defense, waiting till they come to me. Officer Mike was right, I'd been lucky even if he didn't know I was the guy that was lucky, but you can't count on luck as your whole game plan. The Broncos tried that for a lot of years with results everybody likes to forget about. I needed to go back to my first plan of catching them in the act. Obviously, the best thing would be catching them smoking some weed so they'd go to jail for a long time, but after that the best thing would be to catch them selling heroin or crack to kids. I'd just follow them around 'til they smoked some weed or sold some drugs and then I'd turn them in to the cops. Even if there was three of 'em, they was pretty banged up so it didn't seem too dangerous. I didn't see any big problem with my plan.

OK, so I didn't know right where they was, that was one problem, but about as quick as I thought of it I got an idea how to solve it. There was lots of gang guys on Colfax, and some of 'em had made insurance claims on me so they knew I wasn't a cop. They wouldn't like competition coming in from out of town, so they'd keep track on 'em. I just had to find some gang guys and ask them.

I thought about that plan to see if there was hidden flaws in it, but I couldn't think of none. The first night Holly was off work at home so I

134

didn't have to watch her, I put fifteen bucks in my old wallet and walked down to Colfax. Asking a favor is worth more than just a mugging so I wanted to be fair about that.

I'd only walked about two blocks on Colfax when I seen a bunch of gang guys hanging out. They was across the street from me so I crossed over. I was lucky about finding this particular gang, cause they'd made one insurance claim on me, but they hadn't beat me up, so you had to like that. They had mostly black guys, but also a couple Hispanics and other ethical groups, so they was more open minded and civilized than some in their business.

I walked up to them. There was six of them, but one big guy seemed the main one.

"Hey Rubin, check this out," one of 'em said and the biggest black guy stepped toward me. He was the one I already decided was the main one.

"Nice evening, Mr. Rubin," I said.

"You got a death wish, Snowflake?" he said to me.

"Everyone calls me Jumper," I said. He smiled at that, but not a real friendly smile.

"We got a party fund, started, Snowflake. You come to contribute?"

"I come to ask a favor," I said. "But I don't mind settling the business part first." I pulled out my wallet and give it to him. He took out the money and stuck it in his shirt pocket.

"Fifteen fluffing bucks! That ain't enough to even keep you alive the next five minutes."

"It ain't much for a rich guy, but I ain't all that rich," I said. "Plus, it was pretty easy for you. If you don't need a wallet, I could use it back. Cost me fifty cents down at the thrift store."

Rubin stared and me and then started laughing and give me back the wallet. The other guys laughed too.

"What's this favor you want?"

"Well, everybody knows you guys is the number one gang." OK, I made that part up just to make 'em feel good. But they probably seen themselves that way, so to them, it was the whole truth. "I got some issues with some of your competition."

"We ain't got no competition."

135

"Yeah, I can see that. I probably said that bad. It's these three guys from Chicago."

"You mean the Bones?"

"I ain't been formally introduced but I heard that name used. But they tried to cut me, and they shot me once, so I ain't feeling friendly toward them like I do you guys." I pulled up my shirt to show 'em the duck tape on my gunshot wound. "That's where they shot me." They all stared at it. Then Rubin looked at my face, studying me like he was going to do a drawing of me.

"You're the duck tape guy?"

"I didn't have no band aids," I said. "And some people say it's got medicinal qualities."

"And you call yourself Jumper?"

"Yes, sir."

He gave a little whistle and stared at me some more.

"The Bones is some fluffing bad sass dudes," he said, talking soft, like someone might overhear him.

"They been kind of unlucky. But they try pretty hard, so you gotta give 'em points for that. Only they sell drugs to kids, which ain't right, and now they started following this girl who didn't do nothing to 'em. So that pissed me off and I think they need to get a little unluckier."

"You want us to take down the Bones for fifteen fluffing dollars?"

"No sir, Mr. Rubin. They ain't your problem. They're my problem. I just want to find them, and make them take their consequences, but I don't know where to find them. I figure you guys might of heard something could help me. Being the number one gang and all."

The other guys started whispering.

"Shut the fluff up!" Rubin shouted and they got real quiet in a instant. He shook his head at me.

"You one crazy motherfluff," he said.

I couldn't think of a good answer to that so I didn't say nothing. Most people would take his comment like an insult, but gang guys use words a little unusual so it sounded more like a compliment. His friends stayed quiet while he stared at me and thought for a while. I think he was being smart, thinking about what would happen if he just turned the Bones in to me, and if there was hidden flaws in doing that. You could tell by him doing that that he had some experience. Even the President don't always think before he decides something. Finally he reached into his shirt pocket and pulled out my fifteen bucks.

"Give old Snowflake here his props," he said. "Ain't none of you girls gone looking for the Bones and they done shot him once already. Here, boy, you buy yourself another roll of duct tape. You might need it messing with the big boys. They staying down at the Marybeth. Anyone finds out who told you and you'll be eating that roll of duct tape the hard way, you hear what I'm say?"

He held out the money.

"No sir, Mr. Rubin. A deal's a deal. You need that money for your party fund. Thanks." As I walked back across the street I heard them laughing. I felt pretty good. I hadn't got beat up and I had me a good clue. It started to get dark while I walked down Colfax toward the Bones suspected whereabouts.

Like I said, Colfax is an old street, so it's got some old buildings and the Marybeth Motel was one of them. It was three stories with a cracked up parking lot and some of the windows was boarded up. There was some plastic flowers in front of the office door on the dirt where grass maybe used to be. It wasn't all that close to my neighborhood, but I heard about it sometimes. The rent was cheap so hookers liked it. About every year the police decided to make a example of it and sent lady cops down there to pretend to be hookers and arrest the customers. That was bad for the motel business, but after they showed it on the news the cops moved on to make a example of someplace else and business picked up again. Once the cops left you could figure you'd be unobstructed for about a year, which was convenient for business planning. Since the lady cops was a lot prettier than the hookers, anybody with a brain knew when it was a good time to stay away from there. They mostly caught guys in town for the stock show, or a convention, who paid their fines and went home feeling they escaped a close call.

I walked over there and seen three ladies in short skirts hanging out in front who was obviously not lady cops, of if they was, they were about ready to retire. There was stairs up to a little walkway on each floor above the parking lot. You always want to do the easy obvious stuff first, in case that's all you have to do. The easiest thing was just to listen to each door in case you heard a familiar vice. But you had to act casual or someone would notice you. I'm pretty good at being casual. I mostly just walk slow and act

137

like I'm thinking real hard. If you're thinking real hard you're probably an important person and nobody messes with important people.

I walked past all the doors on the main level by the cars. You could hear some TVs on, and some sounds that indicated business was being transacted by hookers, but nothing suspicious. So I went up to the second floor. The last door had loud rap music coming from it, so I made a note of that. Nothing suspicious on the third floor. So room 219 seemed the best bet.

At first I thought I'd just go to a pay phone and call the motel, then ask for room 219. Only you don't see that many pay phones any more since everyone has cells. Then I thought about asking one of them veteran hookers if they knew the guys in there, but they could already be buddies with them.

So finally I just walked into the lobby. It was about the size of a bathroom and smelled like that too. There was a window in one wall with chain link across most of it and a skinny guy back there with long black hair. He was real pale and didn't look that alert, like maybe he'd been sleeping.

"Twenty-nine bucks," he said. "Cash."

"That's a good deal," I said. "But I don't need a room. Let's say I had an appointment to pick up a package from three guys from Chicago, a black guy on crutches and two ethical guys that might be Hispanics or Native Arabians. I think it was suite 219 but I ain't sure, and I forgot to write it down. I don't want to bother any honeymooners."

"Yeah, we get a lot of honeymooners," he said in a way that suggested the opposite of what the words meant. "You remembered right. 219's up those stairs and down at the end."

"Thanks," I said and walked out.

I wasn't prepared to start my surveillance of them, since I hadn't finished my plan. Like, I didn't know how I'd call the cops when I caught them in the act and I hadn't decided on a good place to watch them from. I didn't happen to have a cell phone and I didn't think the motel manager would let me use his phone to bring a bunch of cops to his place. I also wasn't too familiar with the area and if we got into another running situation it would be handy to know if there was dead ends. Or, if it was a hiding situation, I ought to find some good spots ahead of time. So I did me some exploring.

For an old building, the Marybeth still had some good gutters, but the down spout didn't look too secure. That was always good to know, in case you needed to climb up on a roof. One looked pretty good, way in the back by the dumpster, but I decided to wait to try it until I finished exploring. There was a bunch of cans by the dumpster, which was like free money laying there. That give me the idea that if I needed a cover story I'd bring a trash sack with me so if somebody thought I looked suspicious I'd have a good reason for being there. Plus I could make some extra income.

There wasn't any dead ends and there was plenty of good hiding spots. The first one was a tree at the end of the alley. Whoever owned it hadn't been professional with their trimming, so for a big tree it had lots of spots in easy reach where they hadn't cut branches flush but left a inch or two of stump. Even if I wasn't done exploring you can't blame me for not resisting that. Them stumps was like a little ladder and you could climb it as easy as walking up stairs. In about ten seconds I was twenty feet up sitting in a nice fork of big branches. I could of slept up there, it was so comfortable. But I had to keep exploring, I knew that. James Bond never climbed a tree and then took a nap. It was dark so you couldn't see me from the ground. I made a note of that and started back down. Of course, it would have been quicker to jump, but I hadn't checked out the ground first so that would of been reckless. I climbed down regular. On the ground I walked around the tree. There was some beer bottles, which I picked up and threw in someone's trash. Now if a guy was in that tree and had to, he could jump and land wherever he wanted without landing on something.

Of course, if it was an emergency I ought to climb up there faster and the only way to do that was practice. Plus it wouldn't hurt if I did a test jump, like an experiment.

Now that I knew where the foot holds was, I made it up the tree a lot faster. And sure enough, the ground was good for landing. The third time I about run up the tree and my landing was kind of elegant when I jumped. I did two more jumps as practice but even if I wasn't tired I knew I was playing instead of working. That wasn't grown up of me, so I went off to do more exploring.

After I noticed everything for two or three blocks around the Marybeth I decided to try that downspout. It was even more secure than it looked so I got up to the roof with no incidents. From up there I could see the walkway in front of the doors. It was a good place for a stakeout. I lay down on the roof and watched for a while. Nothing interesting happened and I knew if

I stayed up there I'd just fall asleep so I moved a little ways away from 219 and jumped down to the walkway and then went down the stairs and went home.

The first part of my plan was pretty good. I'd found my suspects, explored the area and had a good spot for surveillance. Now I just had to come up with the end part of my plan.

There's lots of good detectives, like Colombo and James Bond and Rockford, so I thought what would they do? James Bond would drink shook-not-stirred martinis with a pretty lady and use some cool gadgets, which didn't seem too promising a plan to me since I didn't have martinis, or gadgets or a pretty spy lady. Colombo would look around, scratch his head, smoke a cigar, take notes and ask questions. The taking notes was a good idea so I decided to buy a little pad of paper I could keep in my pocket. Rockford would dress up like a rich Oklahoma oil guy and get beat up, but then he was getting $200 a day plus expenses so it was worth it to him. Lots of guys stake out their suspect and just wait till they're in the act, so that still seemed like a sound plan. A disguise might not be bad either, like Rockford done, but I didn't have that big a wardrobe. And I didn't know all Rockford's rich oil guy talk, so that would be hard to pull off. So maybe a different disguise.

The next day I went to the thrift store.

"Hey Jim, I need a disguise," I said. I didn't want him to think I was weird if I bought stuff that was unusual.

"Little early for Halloween," he said.

"Like the Boy Scouts say, be prepared."

"What do you have in mind?"

"I'm thinking about going as a homeless person. What do you think?"

"I think you could pull that one off."

"Cool," I said. "Maybe I'll just look around for a minute."

So by now you know Jim was a friend of mine, but I ain't said much about him because I don't know too much. Even if I didn't have actual evidence about him, Jim was a guy who had give me clues, which I could tell you about while you're imagining me walking down the aisle to look at stuff in the thrift store. I looked at the old records, and the broken lamps, and some of the toasters, which won't be that interesting to you if you wasn't there, so you got some extra time until I do something again.

140

People are all the time giving you clues to theirselves. Sometimes on purpose to see if you're paying attention, which is what girls do all the time. And sometimes they say stuff accidentally, like, "When I was in prison they give us potatoes every day." If you're paying attention you figure out they was in prison one time, and if you're Sherlock Holmes or Columbo you figure out they probably got sick of potatoes.

Most people ain't that good of detectives and even some real smart people don't pay good attention and so they miss clues. Like a guy might wonder why his wife seems pissed when it's her birthday and he didn't remember it. The red pen note on the calendar his wife made would of solved that mystery for him if he'd looked at it. Sherlock Holmes would of figured out it from last year when the same thing happened and probably made an extra big red mark ahead of time this year before his wife even had the chance. But a lot of guys see a big red BD on the calendar and say, hey, that's kind of interesting, I wonder what that means? Sooner or later them guys wind up in a bar, drunk as a worm in a tequila bottle, complaining to a stranger that they just don't understand women. You and me both seen it a lot of times.

I got some clues about Jim by just paying attention. He mostly wore a leather jacket that had a NASCAR symbol on the back. By itself, that could of meant he got a deal on the coat, cause it was pretty old and not that neat anymore. But it could be a clue to a different thing so you take one clue like that and you write it in your notebook, but you don't decide nothing.

Then, when racing season was going and I come into the thrift store, he'd have a newspaper on the counter and he'd read all the race stories for a long time, like he was reading every word of them. So that was another clue.

Then, every now and then he'd give me a ride someplace in his old Mustang, which wasn't a convertible but was fast. He told me the number of the engine, and he said the number meant it was big, but I don't remember it. Jim liked to drive faster than anybody and he always had a grin on his face when he did. He was the best driver I ever rode with.

But here's the main clue. Jim only had one leg and the Mustang was a stick shift. I ain't never seen nothing like it. He'd use his foot on the gas pedal until it was going just the right speed then quick as you could see, he'd use that same foot on the clutch and shift gears, then get it back on the gas pedal. The car never jerked, he just knew how to do it. Sometimes he'd shift without even clutching, which he admitted was just showing off.

141

I tried that trick once on a car I borrowed and you could tell I was about going to explode the gears, so I never tried it again.

It didn't take much brains to figure out that Jim used to race cars, and maybe even made money at it, and it was his number one thing. Then he lost his leg, maybe in a car wreck, or maybe in the Army, and he couldn't do his number one thing anymore. Even if you can shift better than most people using only one leg, you couldn't keep up with guys as good as you but with two legs. Plus, they might have rules about how many legs race drivers got to have.

It didn't seem polite to ask him about that so I never did. But I was pretty sure.

You can tell about a guy when he loses his number one thing. Jim never complained, he just moved on, got him the job at the thrift store and he was the best one working there. Him being too skinny made me worry about him in case he had health issues which wasn't getting solved, but except for that I liked everything about Jim. I figured that, in his brain anyway, race cars was still his number one thing.

In case you forgot, while we was talking about noticing clues I was walking around the thrift store looking at stuff to find a good disguise.

The first thing I seen was a box of sunglasses. James Bond wore them a lot, and Rockford did sometimes, so you had to figure they was a good bet. I liked a big pair with bright blue lenses, so I kept them with me. They had a good deal on some Hawaiian shirts, so I took a dark blue one with big pink flowers on it. The blue shirt and blue sunglasses looked awesome together, giving me kind of a designer look. I already looked so different from ordinary I hardly recognized myself in the mirror. But that shirt was bright, so it would be easy to spot at night. For a minute I thought about getting a two-dollar sports coat to put over it, but that made me look like a businessman, which wasn't the look I was going for. Then I seen some big robes. Lots of times you see homeless people talking to people who ain't there or preaching to the cars going by and sometimes they wear robes, so that seemed a natural. The darkest one they had was green, and some people might say it was big for me, but it finished off the look pretty good. Some people say blue and green ain't the best combo, but the sky is blue and grass is green, and that works out OK, so I wasn't worried about that.

The last thing I wanted was a hat, but there wasn't any obvious ones. I looked over at Jim. Sometimes the easiest way to make a guy feel good is to let him help you. If he ain't got money to contribute to a church or politi-

142

cal party he might feel poor. But nobody feels all the way poor if they can help somebody else. Plus, then the guy who asks get something he needed too, so it's a win-win deal. I went up to Jim to ask his advice. Advice is the cheapest thing someone can give you, so it's usually the way they prefer to help.

"What kind of hats might be popular with homeless people these days," I asked him.

He kind of laughed. "A lot of them make hats out of aluminum foil. It keeps the spacemen from reading their thoughts."

"How does it do that?"

"Maybe if the homeless guy thinks they can't read his mind, he doesn't worry about what he's thinking so much."

"And if he ain't worried, then they can't read his mind?"

"I don't know, maybe something like that."

"I ain't too worried about spacemen, and I don't need a hat for calming purposes," I said. "But I already got some foil so, if that's the current fashion on the street, maybe I'll try it." I paid him for my stuff and took it home.

The good thing about a disguise is you can go anyplace and nobody notices you. OK, so maybe I got carried away with the hat, but I had three boxes of foil from apartments I cleaned and I don't use it that much. I started it with some cardboard so it would hold its shape, and duck taped that real secure. Before I covered it with foil it looked like an Abe Lincoln hat, but a little taller and the brim stuck out more. After I put the foil on, it didn't seem that artistic to me, so I added a couple touches, like some extra spoons I never use stuck in like feathers and a roll of cardboard from toilet paper on top. That one was hard to stick on, but I duck taped it good and then put more foil on it, since my suspects might be sensitive about duck tape. When I was done it was a cool hat, and not that ordinary. What was also interesting is that even if I never thought much about spacemen, with that hat on I felt all the way safe from them reading my brain.

When I put the whole disguise on, I was proud of my work, and glad I took the extra time to make a good hat. A regular wool cap is probably the best bet for a homeless guy since they keep you warm even if they get wet. But there ain't much art in that, plus they wouldn't help much if you had spacemen concerns. Plus it was the advice Jim give me, and he wouldn't feel as useful if I didn't listen to his advice. Anyway, the whole

143

outfit worked as good as what you see people wear at the Oscars, if the dress designers got my same assignment, which I think some of them did. I could of passed for a homeless guy easy and nobody notices them, so it was as good as being invisible.

The next day I put on my disguise and walked over to the Marybeth Motel about noon and sat down on the sidewalk across the street. In about five minutes the guy from the dry cleaner store come out and told me he didn't want me loitering there so I'd have to move along. Right then I figured out a problem with my disguise. If I'd gone for the businessman look they would of called it "sitting on the sidewalk" which there ain't a law against. But you dress like a homeless guy they call it "loitering" and throw you in the pokey. So they got different laws based on how you dress. I moved about ten feet down the sidewalk so I was in front of an adult arcade. Nobody come out to make me move away, so it also depends on where you sit on the sidewalk. The reason I sat there was that I could still see room 219 enough to watch when people came and left it. In the daylight somebody might notice me up on the roof, especially with my hat, so I decided to save that spot for nights. Plus, if they had customers that looked like potential known associates, I could follow them easier if I started on the ground.

They had about eleven customers that afternoon, most of them teenage boys. I followed one of them back to a junior high school. I was careful to stay inconspicuous, a block or so behind them. The kid never did go into the school, but just hung around outside. Every now and then someone would come up to him and hand him some money, so you could guess what was going on.

Well, he would of been easy to turn in cause you could just stand there and watch him. But that didn't seem right. He was being dumb, but he was just a kid and kids do dumb stuff. Even I did a dumb thing or two when I was young. The Bones stayed inside their room, so even if I'd had a camera I couldn't of got a picture of them in the act. I still didn't have a good plan for that.

CHAPTER FOURTEEN

OK, so detective work is harder than they make it look on TV. Besides all the detective work, in this chapter The Bones do something really bad and you should not read it if you're a little kid

While I was trying to think up the end part of my plan, I maintained my surveillance every day, sitting on the sidewalk during the day and from the roof at night. I made some notes on my little pad of paper, like what time people come and left, and who delivered pizza to them, and what license plates were on the cars in the parking lot. Sometimes they'd all leave and get into a bright red Camaro. Its muffler wasn't that good so I could jog along a block or so behind them to whatever bar they went to and if they turned I'd hear 'em even if I hadn't seen it. With the traffic and stoplights they never got up much speed, so it wasn't that hard to keep up. I took notes of where they went and all the license plates in the bar's parking lots in case we needed a list of known associates.

I done that for two weeks except for Tuesday nights when I went to visit Linda. I wasn't too worried about watching Holly, since I was already watching the Bones.

Linda was looking better and better every time I seen her. Her hair was getting longer and she was in a chair in her room most of the time, instead of her bed.

"Hey, Michelangelo," I said when I walked in her room.

"Hey, Mr. Jumper."

"You look about ready to go home."

"I'm all the way ready," she said. "My tests have been real good."

"Cool. I was never that good at tests."

"Not school tests, silly. Hospital tests."

"It's probably the Jell-O. I think it's got medicinal qualities, since they make it so much in hospitals."

"Look," she said, and turned her head around. She had her hair in a pony tail with one of them fancy pink rubber bands with all the frilly stuff. There was about a inch of hair sticking out from it. "See? Just like nurse Holly."

"I like pony tails," I said. "It makes you look pretty grown up. You too grown up to feed your turtle?"

"Course not. He's like my patient. And worms are kind of like turtle Jell-O, right?"

"You been eating Bart's dinner when I ain't looking?"

She giggled. "Ick!" she said and made a face.

I pulled a earthworm out of my shirt pocket and dangled it over my mouth.

"Looks like a skinny piece of Jell-O to me."

"Gross!" she said. "Give that to me before you drop it accidentally and have to eat it."

I give her the worm and she fed it to Bart.

"I finished the bird drawing," she said when he was done. She got into her drawer and pulled it out.

"Wow!" I said. "I can about hear him singing. That's a fine drawing. You got natural talent."

"Well, you did the hard parts. I just filled in the blanks."

"It's way better than I could of done. We could sell that easy."

"Let's put it on the wall until I leave. Then when we sell it you can come over to my house and we'll have ice cream to celebrate.

"I like that idea. I bet Holly can get some of that tape they use to put stuff on the walls."

We talked some more, but it was pretty much like the other times we talked, so I don't need to tell you every word we said, or which parts we laughed at, or that I put Bart into his Nike bag at the end. It always made me cheerful to talk to Linda, even if she was just a little girl. She knew a lot of stuff that even I ain't learned about, so in some ways she was just as old as me and it felt like it was OK to be her buddy, and not something that other guys would tease you about if they heard it. But maybe they would, so I didn't talk about it much to anyone else I knew.

As I was walking home I had an idea about the Bones. It's funny how when you need a idea they seem hard to get, but when you're doing one thing, some idea about a whole other thing jumps into your brain. So if you want a idea, you probably should think about something else. Anyway, the idea I had was that maybe I was having trouble catching them in the act,

146

but the police could do it easy. They could just send a real young looking cop up to their room to try and buy some drugs, and then when they sold some, the cops could arrest them on the spot. I'd got so caught up in trying to figure out a plan for me to do it I'd forgot about doing it the easy way. This was a no brainer.

The next day I went looking for Officer Mike. He wasn't that hard to find.

"Hello there, Jumper," he said. "Haven't seen you around in a while. You been on vacation?"

"No sir. I ain't got no vacation days coming."

"Your whole life's a vacation."

"Yes sir, I guess it pretty much is. I was having a conversation with a guy and we had some police questions."

"Really? Police questions? That sounds serious. Anything I can help you with?"

"Well, maybe. Say you knew some hypothetical stuff the cops might like to know. We was wondering how to get hypothetical stuff to them."

"Yeah, I can see how that would be a question. That hypothetical stuff is tricky. Maybe you could imagine an example for me."

"OK. Well, say a guy knew the hypothetical location and modes of Opera Andy of some guys selling drugs to school kids. And some leads on known associates. Only he ain't been able to catch them in the act."

"That sounds like your friend has been taking some foolish risks."

"Well, they was mainly hypothetical risks."

"We'd have to have probable cause. You know, some details."

"We wrote down some examples," I said and took out my little pad of paper. "Just for one example, we was imagining what if some guys called the Bones was staying in room 219 at the Marybeth Motel. You know, the one with the hookers? And every Monday afternoon at about one o'clock they sell some drugs to a kid from Carter Junior High. His friends call him Mango, but it might show something different on his permanent record. Then he sells them to the other kids at his school. They drive a red Camaro, with this license number, and these are the bars they go to. They mostly like Alfredo's Pizza, with pepperoni, mushrooms and sun-dried tomatoes, which is expensive but a good choice. And they like Budweiser. Hypothetically, of course."

147

"Of course. Where do they get the drugs to sell?"

"We didn't think up that one."

"Probably from a known associate."

"We ain't got names for them. Just license numbers of guys at the bars they go to."

"Sure be nice to catch the guy sells them the drugs. But license numbers of guys at a bar don't qualify as known associates. Kind of suspected associates."

"Yeah, that's a point. We didn't think of that. What would you tell my friend?"

"I'd tell him to stay away from these guys in the first place. I'll pass your hypothetical information along to the drug enforcement guys. I bet they'll be real interested."

"Thanks."

"Do you remember what I told you?"

I thought for a minute.

"Be prepared?"

"Not that. The thing I told you to tell your hypothetical friend. About five seconds ago."

"Oh yeah. Stay away from these guys."

"Right. You want me to write it down for you?"

"Nah, thanks. I remember stuff pretty good."

"Remembering and doing are two different things."

"That's really true," I said. "Otherwise the Broncos could just tell their receivers 'remember to catch the ball.'" Cause a lot of times that's the first thing they forget to do

"Exactly. Will you promise to tell your friend to stay away?"

For a minute I thought he'd backed me into a corner with that one. But then, since he didn't say which friend I had to say it to, I seen a loophole.

"You bet. I'll tell Benson to stay away from them."

"Good. You have a good day, young man."

"Yes sir."

148

Back at my apartment I looked over all my notes. I'd nearly used up that little notebook with license plate numbers but I didn't have even one known associate except for Mango the kid. He was buying from them not selling to them, so that wasn't much use. Officer Mike was right though, you keep selling something and pretty soon you run out of it and got to buy more. It don't take a rock star to figure that out.

Then I thought this: when they went to different bars there'd be mostly different guys in there. But if somebody was there lots of the same times, they could be a known associate.

So many license plate numbers made it confusing until I remembered a trick that lady detective on the Remington Steele TV show had did. She put all her facts on 3 by 5 cards and spread them out on a table. I owned four packages of 3 by 5 cards which I don't use that often except for grocery lists, so I thought what the heck? I wrote every license number on a 3 by 5 card, plus what kind of car it was and where I seen it, and on what night. That took me the rest of the day, but sometimes the organizing part of a job is just as important as the part you get paid for. Well, I wasn't getting paid so that ain't exactly what I mean, but you get the idea. Then I spread them out on my table, but there was way too many, so I moved the operation to the floor. I had to hope Bart didn't take a interest in 3 by 5 cards or this was gonna be a lot harder. But if he screwed up the cards, I'd just put him in his box until I was done. I pictured James Bond putting his turtle in a box if he had to get organizing work done, which was easy to picture, so that made it seem more official. Rockford had a trailer, so he had more room than me, and a turtle wouldn't of bothered him that much.

I made it like a game, which you always want to do if you got work that seems boring to you. I thought of it like a puzzle. If I ever seen the same license number on different cards, I put them next to each other. Like if I'd wrote down a license number I seen at the Marybeth, and then later I wrote that number down from the parking lot at one of the bars.

One hidden flaw in that plan was that the bartenders and waitresses was always there, so I had several cards with their numbers on it, from different nights. Plus some guys find a bar they like and go back pretty regular. Of the five bars they went to, I had five groups with a bunch of the same numbers on different nights. Then I had a little mess of cards that didn't match anywhere. Those places the bartenders must take the bus, or else they'd have at least two cards with their plates on them. I put all them in their own pile to think about later, since they didn't seem that useful.

149

I stacked the grouped ones like little decks of cards. One stack was from the Marybeth, the other stacks from the bars. Then I looked at the top card of one stack to see if any of those numbers was on top of the other stacks. When it wasn't, I took the top card off each of them other stacks and did the same thing. After I got finished checking all the other stacks against that first card, I turned it over and did the same with the second card of the first stack.

Now that sounds pretty complicated and boring as a Shakespeare play, but really it was about like playing solitaire. I just played one card at a time from the first pile against all the other stacks. When I was done I done the same thing with stack number two. It was sort of fun and I got to day-dreaming about how you could invent a new kind of solitaire out of it and how it would be better with different colors. But it was also kind of boring because you didn't hit a jackpot that often.

Then I hit a jackpot. A Mercedes with a Illinois license plate number had been at the "College Girls" bar one night the Bones was there, and had also been at "Bikini Bar" when they was there. OK, so that was circum-stantial. But it give me some enthusiasm that a solitaire game might have upside potential because I lit up pretty good when I noticed the match. If I lit up, other people might enjoy the game too. Of course, I'd have to have a good name for it, and maybe a TV commercial. There's a used car place on Federal which has good commercials with a pretty girl. I probably couldn't afford to hire her. On the other hand, if she really liked the game she might do it for half the profits and there wasn't any rule against asking her.

When the same Mercedes was a match at "The Shady Lady" I felt like I'd scored a winning field goal.

"Parcheesi!" I said, though I already decided I'd have to come up with a better word for when you win. The best ones, like "Bingo" and "gin" had already been took, and Parcheesi is a whole different game which I never learned. But for its current purposes it worked fine.

It seemed a strong coincidence that Mr. Mercedes was at the same bars the same nights as the Bones, but I had to admit it was circumstantial. Of-ficer Mike made it sound like they had strict rules to qualifying as a known associate. So even if he didn't want me watching them, I wasn't done with my surveillance. He didn't actually give me a court order to stay away, it was more like advice, which ain't as binding. Besides, he wasn't the one they was shooting at so it wasn't as personal to him. Anybody's got the right to self-defense, plus the cops was already pretty busy, what with traffic tickets and loiterers and convention guys giving money to pretty lady cops. And that don't even count their main job, which is busting guys for smoking weed. Really, you could think of it like I was saving them time. When I caught 'em in the act the cops was sure to see it that way.

I decided I'd have to backburner my new solitaire game and use my whole brain on catching them in the act. The next step was firming up the identity of Mr. Mercedes from Chicago in case he could graduate from "suspected known associate" to "known associate period." I thought about asking officer Mike to run his plates like Rockford always done, but if I was wrong he'd think of me like Rockford's buddy Angel, who guessed wrong a lot. Then I come up with a foolproof plan for finding the Mercedes guy without running plates.

The times the Bones mostly went to the same bar as the Mercedes guy was Thursdays. So when I was watching them early on a Monday night and seen them get into their Camaro, I figured they was just going out for fun and not business. I'd planned this all up ahead of time, so I already had a note made out which said "Send me one of the pepperoni, mushroom and sun dried tomato pizzas. Forgot where you get them." I signed it Mercedes. It took me a couple times to get the note right. At first I said "please send" and ended it with "thanks." Then I decided that sounded too nice for a suspected known associate, so I threw that one away and started over. I didn't know the guys' name to sign it, but then he probably wouldn't sign a pizza note with his name and Social Security number either, in case the cops found it. When I seen them leave #219, I walked casually up to the door. I taped the note on their door with some Scotch tape. Duck tape would of been a giveaway. I wasn't too worried that other motel customers would recognize me because I was in my homeless guy disguise, with the aluminum foil hat and the blue sunglasses and green robe. Plus, like I said, I walked casual so nobody'd notice me.

Then I walked across the street and sat on the sidewalk in front of the adult business to watch for them. About two hours later they come back. You could tell they been drinking, so that was an advantage in case they might recognize the guy's handwriting. As soon as they got out of their Camaro I started jogging down to Alfredo's Pizza, which was only about two blocks away and went in. I was the only customer, but they wasn't all that friendly anyway. The kid behind the counter looked at my hat.

"We don't serve aliens," he said.

"That ain't legal," I said. "Plus I ain't a alien."

"You just listen to them through your hat, right?" I give him the benefit of the doubt that he was joking on me in a friendly way.

"They ain't broadcasting right now. I just want a pizza."

"You got money? This ain't the shelter."

"Sure." I pulled a twenty out of the pocket on my Hawaiian shirt and showed him.

"So, what'll it be?"

Before that I could understand him being testy because maybe I didn't have money and was conspiring to loiter. But when he could see I had cash, he should of turned nicer on me. Instead he still sounded pissed that I was bothering him by wanting pizza. That'd be like me being pissed an apartment was dirty when my job was to clean it, which don't make sense. So he must have had a fight with his girlfriend, or maybe his dog died. You gotta cut a guy some slack if his dog died, and something like that could of happened, so I kept on being polite to him.

"You got so many choices," I said. "I need to think a minute. You got anchovies?"

"We got everything your home planet's got." Right then I knew his dog didn't die. He was making a joke on me he thought I was too dumb to get, which is just mean unless you're a Senator and get paid to say mean things.

"OK, so maybe I'll have anchovy. Just give me a minute to decide, OK?"

"Make it quick," he said. "You're making our customers nervous."

"You got a bunch of invisible customers?"

"Ain't nobody gonna step through that door until you get beamed back to the mother ship."

"OK, that's a good point. Just give me a minute." About then I decided to have my own little joke on him, which he had earned. "Uh-oh, they're transmitting again. You better pick up the phone. They like them sun dried tomatoes. And pepperonis and mushrooms."

He started to say something but right then the phone rang. The kid looked at my hat again, shook his head, and answered the phone.

"Alfredo's Pizza," he said. I stared at their menu choices but was noticing his telephone conversation at the same time. "Pepperoni, mushroom

152

and sun dried tomatoes. And where should we deliver it?" There was a pause. "Brown Palace, suite 421. That will be about thirty minutes. Thank you for thinking of Alfredo's."

That last part, the thanking part, didn't sound too sincere, so I bet it was something they made him say. He wrote down the order. Before he remembered I was standing there I left.

If ordering a pizza for somebody don't make them a known associate, then I don't know what would. Plus, if you think about it, the Bones was from Chicago and this guy had Illinois plates on his Mercedes, which is Chicago's state. That was a good clue right there. It didn't prove he was selling them drugs, but the Brown Palace is a expensive place and the Bones didn't seem like they'd have a lot of doctor friends, so that was another clue.

I wanted to tell Officer Mike my information but doing that would put me in a new pickle. He'd figure out right away I hadn't told my friend to stay away from the Bones like he wanted. So he'd probably tell me again in a way that didn't have a loophole.

While I was thinking of that, my brain went a whole different direction, and thought up a hidden flaw in my pizza idea. What if the Mercedes guy don't like pepperoni, mushroom, and sun-dried tomato pizza? He wouldn't want to pay for it, that was for sure. And he'd ask how come it got sent to him and if he asked the Bones they'd say they didn't do it but that was sure their favorite pizza. So all of 'em would start wondering about that coincidence. I gotta admit my pizza idea wasn't Mission Impossible complicated, so the cops probably use it all the time, let alone the FBI. If the Bones started thinking the FBI was on to them, they'd move to new motels and I'd have to start over.

I didn't see much alternatives but to jog down to the Brown Palace and catch the pizza guy before he went in. A half hour was plenty of time.

My homeless guy disguise wasn't the best jogging outfit. The hat was noisy, for one thing. Aluminum foil moves around a lot and it sounded like I had tin cans on my head. Some people noticed me and some cars honked, but it was also kind of cool. I ain't ever heard drums that sounded quite like that, but it reminded me of them. I got to thinking about that song It's a Wonderful Night For a Moondance and if I jogged steady my hat played right along with the way the song was going in my brain. The robe blowed around behind me like Batman's cape. I could even dance around a little bit in time to the song while I was jogging, which was pretty cool. I felt like Mick Jagger or somebody.

When I got to the Brown Palace, which is right downtown, I stood a little ways away from the front door. If a dry cleaner didn't want homeless guys loitering, then a fancy downtown hotel wouldn't either. When I seen a car drive up with an Alfredo's pizza sign on top, I walked over to it. The driver was another kid, probably still in high school. He took out the pizza box and slammed his door.

"Hey, Alfredo," I said. "Glad I caught you. I think that's my pizza."

"I doubt it," he said, looking at my disguise.

"You ever hear of a costume party?" I said. "It's where people dress like stuff they ain't. Room 421, pepperoni, mushroom and sun-dried tomatoes. What do I owe you?"

"Sixteen bucks," he said, but you could tell he wasn't sure.

"We're moving the party," I said. "Here's twenty. Keep the change."

Nobody's gonna argue too much with a four dollar tip so he stuffed my money in his shirt pocket. When he drove away, I carried the box to the next block, which had a parking lot with a little concrete wall around it about as tall as a chair. I sat on the wall and started eating pizza.

I gotta admit, the Bones had good taste in pizza. I don't order it that often, unless I'm on a date or something, but after thinking about pepperonis all day while I wrote the note, I was in the mood. There wasn't many cars in the parking lot, so every time one came in or went out it was sort of interesting and that made the time go by.

I was on my third slice and feeling lucky when a silver Mercedes pulled in and parked. It looked like the one I'd seen at those other bars, but I couldn't see the license, and all them Mercedes look the same. A big black guy got out and started walking toward the sidewalk. He was so big he could of been a Denver Bronco, and he was dressed in a suit that fit real well, only I recognize most of the Broncos and I didn't know him. But they're always doing trades so he could be new. When he got up to me he stopped.

"That looks like a pretty good pizza," he said.

"Yes sir. Pepperoni mushroom and sun-dried tomato. You want a slice?" I opened up the box and held it out to him.

"Yeah, I want a slice."

He took the box with one hand and with his other hand he pushed me in the middle of my chest real hard. I fell backward off the wall I was sitting on. I probably would of conked my head except my hat was sturdy and took most of the fall. It smashed up some, but I didn't get hurt.

"Thanks," he said and laughed. By the time I got untangled from my robe he was a block away with my pizza. You might think I'd of been pissed off, and I was, but not so bad I felt like running after him to argue about it, what with him weighing about three hundred pounds and all.

The bad part was someone swiped my pizza. On the good side, I hadn't got hurt, which I could of easy. I'd had some slices of pizza myself, which I had enjoyed. No sense letting that one little incident ruin my evening. I had a new opportunity to investigate a clue, so I walked over to the silver Mercedes and looked at its license plate. It was the same one I'd been watching for. The whole deal had turned out a lot better than my first plan. I was a eyewitness to the Bones known associate but he wouldn't remember me at all without my hat. I even knew where he parked his car.

I had his face in my brain real good, so if I had a different art process I could of drew him easy. But even when I drew stuff perfect with my camera of squirrels some people couldn't get what it was a picture of.

That give me an idea. I bet little Linda could draw him if I told her what he looked like, just like she did that bird. You seen it on TV a hundred times, how they use a sketch artist. If I give Officer Mike his license number, and where he was staying and a picture the cops might take time away from arresting convention guys to catch him in the act.

I was trying to think of any hidden flaws with that plan and getting ready to walk home when a red Camaro pulled into the parking lot. I ducked down behind the wall. But then I couldn't see much, so I took off my hat and raised my head up over the wall a little. It was the Bones all right, but they didn't get out of their car. They just sat there. That was pretty interesting, so I watched them sitting there.

In a few minutes a black Lexus pulled in and parked a few spaces away. I climbed over the wall so I could see better. Only there was too many cars in the way, so I snuck a little closer. A big four wheel drive truck was the only thing between us now, so I crawled under it and stayed behind one of the tires so I was hid if they looked over. A white guy got out of the Lexus. He was dressed nice, but not fancy. He didn't have a suit coat on, for one example. He carried a Nike bag like mine, only the zipper worked. The Bones got out of their car and started talking to him. I couldn't hear what they was saying.

155

Then they all stopped talking and looked behind them. The Mercedes guy had showed up too and he seemed pissed. He come up to them with his hands behind his back, like a principal who's gonna give you a lecture about citizenship issues. Everybody seemed interested in what he was saying, but he talked soft. Not like he was afraid, but like your mom might when she knew she had your attention for whatever dumb thing you done that time so she didn't have to yell but you'd get the idea anyway. Plus the other guys tended to talk at the same time. Anyway, I wasn't that far away, but I couldn't figure out the conversation. Mostly the words I heard was cussing, but I got the impression the Mercedes guy thought the white guy had engaged in some unfair business practices.

The Mercedes guy brought his hands out in front of him and I seen he had a gun. The white guy dropped his Nike bag, put his hands up in the air and stepped back.

"Take it," he said. "It's just a misunderstanding. I'll make it right."

"Yeah, you'll make it right," Mercedes said. Then he shot him three times and the white guy fell down.

I ain't never seen a murder before except on TV or in the movies, but it looked about like that. The gun wasn't as loud as you might think, so maybe it had a silencer on it. The white guy didn't move and you could tell by the way his head was crooked that he was dead. My first instinct was to crawl out from under the truck and start running light speed away, but I made myself be still. It happened so fast I didn't have time to make up another plan. The Mercedes guy looked at the dead guy for a minute, then picked up the Nike bag and said something to the Bones. Then he threw the bag into the trunk of his car and drove away. One of the Bones took the dead guy's wallet out of his pocket, then they got into their Camaro and drove away too.

I waited a minute, then crawled out and felt the dead guy's neck several places, but there wasn't a pulse. His skin was warm, not like you think of a dead guy's but just like anybody. He looked so much the same as he did two minutes ago you wanted to say, hey, get up, let's get out of here before them guys come back. But being dead changed him in some way you couldn't say in words. That guy who was there a minute ago arguing with the Bones had left and gone someplace and this thing he left behind was just his disguise. It wasn't him, like my aluminum foil hat wasn't me. Which was lucky cause my hat got kind of banged up when Mercedes guy pushed me over. I stood over him trying to think what I should do. There wasn't something

I could do for the dead guy, that one was obvious. And if I hung around I'd be the number one suspect. But you can't just do nothing if you seen something like that. I kept hearing my mom's voice, and my dad's voice in my head, which had not happened in a long time. It was nice to hear them and all, but under the circumstances I didn't know what voice to listen to. Somebody said something about being fair, and about unfinished business. The guy who left his body behind obviously got the short end of that stick, which wasn't fair. Just his body laying there was unfinished business with nobody else to finish it but me. If you want to be great, you got to be fair. Plus you gotta help people less fortunate than ourselves, which this guy was. Man, I wanted to run away about light speed times two. But you can't be great if you run away. And what separates men from boys is that men do hard stuff.

I started shivering even if it didn't seem cold out. The Bones was sure to find out who reported the incident, but I couldn't prevent that. I put my fancy aluminum foil hat back on and run over to the Brown Palace. They got an old guy in a uniform standing out front to open the door for people, so I went up to him.

"There's been a shooting," I said. He stared at my hat and didn't say nothing. I grabbed his shoulder to get his attention and he pulled back.

"There's been a shooting," I said again. "I think the guy with the Lexus is dead. That parking lot two blocks down." I pointed. "You gotta call 911."

He still just stared at me. Then he said, "I think you should just move along."

Well, I never seen that one coming. He thought I was conspiring to loiter. I couldn't hold it against him since my disguise was so good. But this was a perfect situation to have a disguise in case I was the number one suspect and there wasn't a number two suspect. So my choice was not to take off the hat and robe, but I still had unfinished business to take care of.

"OK, you don't believe me. I don't blame you. Only thing to do is let me just drag the body down here and leave it in front of your hotel door here. Then you can call the cops, or just let your customers step over him. Maybe your boss will have an opinion on the correct choice for you once he sees the body in question. At least it won't be on me any more. You wait here, I'll be back in about two minutes." I turned and started to jog away.

That seemed to get his attention.

"No, no, we don't want any trouble."

"Then you better call 911 right now."

"Of course, sir. And who shall I say reported the incident?"

"I'd give 'em your real name. You don't want to lie to the cops."

"I mean your name."

"I guess I'll go get that body now."

"No, no, that won't be necessary. I'll call right now." He went inside and I started jogging away. After three blocks I cut down an alley and threw my disguise in a dumpster. If Mr. Mercedes thought back to the pizza incident he'd start to wonder if I might of hung around there and been a witness. He'd mostly look for my hat, so that was the first thing I threw away. Plus the Brown Palace guy would tell the cops about me and they'd want to ask me a bunch of questions. Even if I had a good loophole, Officer Mike might think I violated his intent since I didn't stay away from The Bones so I couldn't go to him either.

As I was jogging home in my T-shirt and jeans, I realized that I'd blown a good chance. I'd caught them in the act but when it come to the part about turning them in, I'd forgot all about it. That was a no brainer on my part. The way I'd done it backed me into a corner.

I ain't ever been in trouble with the cops, except for occasional loitering and a few unavoidable traffic tickets when I didn't know a cop was behind me. Unless Officer Mike had seen me violating private property by jumping off that garage. He would of brought that up by now if he intended to prosecute, but it could go against me in a circumstantial way. If they found that pizza box, my fingerprints was on it, plus I'd touched the dead guy's neck, so I could of left fingerprints there. My fingerprints was all over the place on that concrete wall and any cars I might of touched. If the Mercedes guy said I done it, it was my word against a guy who drove a Mercedes and wore expensive suits and stayed at the Brown Palace, so I was at a disadvantage right there.

So, instead of me catching them in the act, they could make it look like they caught me in the act. I could hear Perry Mason asking how come I didn't call the cops myself, being so innocent and all. I couldn't afford to hire Perry Mason myself, or even Johnny Cochran if it come to that.

This was about the biggest pickle I was ever in. I didn't see much alternatives to that.

158

Chapter Fifteen

A new disguise, and a known associate becomes an accomplice. Or a sidekick, depending on how you look at it.

I'm a pretty fast thinker on a ordinary day, but the day after the shooting my whole brain was going fast as a Vulcan space ship. I went over the night about fifty times, starting with the note I left, and ordering the pizza, and listening to my hat jogging over to the Brown Palace, and buying the pizza and then getting knocked off the wall and crawling under the truck, and the shooting, and the door guy, and throwing away my disguise. None of the details changed any time I thought of it. That was good if you was on a witness stand. I still seen the Mercedes guy as clear as if I drew him. I could still feel the dead guy's warm neck, and every time I did I started shivering all over again.

The best thing to do if you got a complicated problem is to cut it into smaller pieces and then solve them one at a time. When you do a puzzle, you might put all the blue-sky pieces in one spot, for one example, because solving them is a smaller puzzle. Then, in the blue pieces, you might start with all the ones with straight edges because lots of them are going to be on the border. A thousand-piecer might only have forty blue skies, of which maybe ten got straight edges. A ten piece puzzle is easier than a thousand-piecer.

The first thing is I needed a new disguise, that one is obvious. Going for the homeless look wasn't going to fool them a second time. You could tell the Bones wasn't too educated from how they talked, but they might not be flat stupid. A businessman look would fool Mercedes, but businessmen don't wear hats that much, so the rest of them might recognize my face and hair. I could of got a shorter haircut, but I liked my hair the way it was and it might seem weird to Linda or Holly. Cowboys wear hats, but the Bones might not be too fond of cowboys after the incident with the guy in the pickup truck. Baseball caps are pretty ordinary and, since I'm a football fan, nobody's think of looking for me in a baseball cap. I went through all my ideas like that, thinking of the advantages and disadvantages. You gotta do that with ideas.

Since it was Tuesday, I was already on schedule to bring Bart down to the hospital to visit Linda. The idea of having her draw Mr. Mercedes still seemed foolproof. If we couldn't draw him good enough, I just wouldn't show it to Officer Mike. Even then, she might have fun doing it, but I wouldn't fill her in on the details. She had enough hard stuff in her life without thinking about murders. But if she did a drawing that anyone could tell was Mr. Mercedes, that would make my whole story better. That's if I could figure out a way to tell it to Officer Mike.

So that night I put Bart in the Nike bag and went over to the hospital.

"Hey, Michelangelo," I said.

"Hey, Mr. Jumper," Linda said back. She was looking like a girl who wasn't sick any more and her ponytail had grown a lot.

"You're looking pretty good."

"Thanks. They say I can go home next week."

"Cool!" I said. "We're gonna have to schedule a turtle release party."

"What did you bring for Bart? This might be the last time I get to feed him."

"I made him a salad," I said. "It's got spinach and strawberries and onion and cabbage all chopped up together." I didn't tell her it was stuff I got from a restaurant's dumpster. A turtle wouldn't care about that, but if she mentioned to her parents I was a guy who swiped stuff from dumpsters they might have second thoughts about her being my known associate. Linda made a face.

"OK, then, but you can have the leftovers."

I'd brung an old newspaper, which I put on the floor. Linda put Bart on the paper and poured the salad out of the baggie I brung it in. Bart didn't waste no time.

"Would you like to play a different drawing game tonight?" I asked while we watched him.

"Sure," she said. "How does it go?"

"Well, you seen police sketch artists on TV?"

"Lots of times."

"I seen this guy I thought would be a good picture. Kind of mean looking, like a criminal. Only I ain't so good at drawing stuff out of my head,

160

while that's your specialty. I was thinking it might be fun if I told you what he looked like and you drew him. What do you think?"

"We could do it easy," she said. She got out some paper and a pencil.

"OK, so first, he's a big black guy, looks a little like the Broncos new defensive tackle."

"That guy we got from the Jets?"

"Yeah, him. So maybe if you started by drawing him real light we could erase the parts that was different and change them."

She must of seen several pictures of the new Bronco, because she drew him perfect.

"Wow," I said. "You been practicing."

"Thanks," she said. "Now what do we have to change?"

"Well, his eyes to start. They're a little farther apart and he keeps them open a little wider."

"That's easy," she said and erased real careful. Then she drew new eyes.

"That's good. OK, his right eyelid don't close as much as his left one. But it's just a little bit."

She changed that and Mr. Mercedes eyes was looking at us.

"This is fun. What else?"

"His nose is a little longer. Not quite so much a black guy's nose and a little more like a white guy's."

She fixed that.

"OK, and his face is skinnier, so his cheekbones show more." She kept drawing real light and erasing. It looked more and more like Mr. Mercedes. Pretty soon it was exact.

"That's him," I said. "You done a perfect job."

"Can I make the lines darker now?"

"Sure," I said. As she made the lines darker it looked even more like him. The eyes was especially good and when she made them darker it was like he was staring right at me.

"What's the matter, Mr. Jumper? You're shivering."

"I must of got a chill," I said and looked away from the drawing. In a minute I stopped shivering.

"What are you two up to tonight?" Holly said, walking in the room.

"We're playing sketch artist," Linda said and held up her drawing.

"Who is that?"

"Just a guy I seen," I said.

"I've seen him too," Holly said. "A big guy. I think he was visiting a patient."

"It was just a game," I said. "Can I take it with me?" I said to Linda. "There's someone I want to show it to."

"Sure," she said and give it to me. "But if you sell if for a hundred bucks, I get half."

"That's a good deal for me, since you done all the drawing." I put it in my backpack, put Bart back in the Nike bag, and threw away the newspaper.

"Time for Linda to go to sleep," Holly said. "You got time for a cup of coffee?"

"Let me check my schedule," I said. I looked at the ceiling for a minute." Yup, looks pretty open." So we walked down to the cafeteria.

"We're going to have to put you on staff," Holly said, drinking her coffee. "You keep healing my patients. Linda's made a remarkable recovery."

"Maybe turtles got medicinal qualities,"

Holly laughed, which always distracted me.

"So, who's the guy in the picture?"

"Just a guy I seen. Thought he'd make a good picture." I felt my face getting hot.

"Right," she said. "Just a guy you seen. So who is it you need to show the picture to?"

"Just another guy."

"You've been acting mysterious lately. Does this guy have anything to do with that?"

If I'd known she was going to go Perry Mason on me I might of skipped the coffee.

"Your ponytail looks nice tonight. You wearing it longer?"

"I haven't changed my hair in a year. I notice you're staying out later recently. I hear you come in upstairs. Do you have a new girlfriend?"

"No ma'am, I can't afford a girlfriend right now."

"So you've been hanging out with the guy in the picture."

"No ma'am. We ain't never even been introduced. Plus he ain't my type."

"Well, you're up to something. Do I need to pretend I'm a movie star from the forties and use my feminine wiles to get it out of you?"

"No ma'am. That is, no I ain't up to nothing. Nothing that would be worth using your wiles on." I gotta admit I'd heard about feminine wiles but nobody ever explained exactly what they was. I had a couple of ideas but if I was wrong it would be worse than keeping my mouth shut. This was a case where you had to think like the President and not exactly answer but say something to make them feel good while you wasn't answering. "Course, if you need to use your wiles just to keep in practice, I bet you got good ones."

She laughed again and her ponytail looked like it was dancing.

"So what is your type?"

"Excuse me?"

"Your type of girl. What do you like in girls?"

My face was all the way hot now. I tried to think of what James Bond would say, but he wasn't in the mood to help me. So I was stuck with the truth.

"I like girls that are pretty much like you."

She laughed again, but I seen her cheeks get a little red.

"Why Jumper, that's about the nicest thing anyone ever said to me. You're a smooth one."

"I ain't trying to be smooth. Nobody ever called me that."

"Then they just haven't looked at you right." She smiled at me, but even being smooth I couldn't think of nothing to say. She picked up her coffee. "So will the Broncos go to the Super Bowl?" she said.

"You bet," I said and felt like I escaped a close call only I didn't know exactly what it was. "Guaranteed. They finally got some good defensive draft picks."

"Well, summer's the best time to be a Bronco fan."

"Yeah, before they start playing games. Last year we was just a couple players short but I think them draft picks will fix the holes."

We talked about the Broncos for a while, which wasn't that ordinary since I never knew Holly was a fan. But she knew a lot about them.

That night I watched her walk to the bus after she got off work. By now I'd memorized her walk pretty good, but it was always better seeing her in person. She walked a little quicker than usual, a kind of happy walk. After she got on the bus I jogged home a shorter way and watched her go in the building. Then I tiptoed up the stairs and was extra quiet in my apartment.

Chapter Sixteen

In which Officer Mike goes all Perry Mason on me and I get a new disguise

The next morning I gathered all my stuff about the Bones together. The pile of papers wasn't that neat, but the card stacks was OK. It seemed too much stuff to give Officer Mike real casual, and they always take points off for neatness, which had cost me about a truckload of points in school. If I had back all them neatness points I'd be a lawyer right now, or at least a doctor. I always felt I had the knack for them two things, and they might have been OK careers if I was a career kind of guy, but you can't get the job if you get points took off for neatness all the time.

I took out a fresh piece of paper and wrote down on it just the most important stuff: The Camaro license number, the Mercedes license number, the Lexus number. Then I wrote out what I seen in the parking lot, with the Nike bag and the shooting. Then I added extra stuff I forgot to write down the first time, like room 219 at the Marybeth, and room 421 at the Brown Palace. It all fit on one sheet of paper, which was wasn't tore or folded and wouldn't cost me no neatness points. I put the paper in a big brown envelope some junk mail had come in, and put Linda's sketch-artist picture in there too. Then I remembered the door guy at the Brown Palace and almost got out the paper to add that, even if it would have been sideways to fit and that wouldn't be so neat. I decided against it, but not just because of getting points taken off. People believe stuff more if they figure out some of it themselves. The cops would of got a statement from the door guy and he would of mentioned the homeless guy who reported the incident to him. They'd already know that part so they'd feel like they done some good detective work there. But they wasn't gonna find that homeless guy in a million years. He was just my disguise and I already threw him away.

"Well, if it isn't the King of Colfax," Officer Mike said when I finally found him. "How is King Jumper today?" A lot of times he joked on me that way, calling me a king, or an ambassador which was about my favorite since they got immunity and can loiter wherever they want.

"I'm feeling pretty royal. But then us kings feel like that every day."

"I'm sure you do. What kind of royal trouble have you been getting into?"

165

"Kings don't get in trouble. Anything they do, that's the right thing, since they're the king. We just change the rule to make it legal. Just like some Presidents done. You had any more interesting incidents?"

"Not really. Except for counting the days till I retire."

"Nothing at all?" I hadn't planned on that. I had hoped he'd steer the conversation to the Bones like he usually wanted to do, and I could just ride along like it was a accident. It wouldn't seem so casual if I had to steer us over there.

"Not on my beat. Stuff goes on around town, but our neighborhood's been quiet. Why, did you hear something?"

"I told my friend not to go near the Bones. So you can feel OK about that."

He was looking at me kind of interested so I got nervous I said something wrong. But I went back over what I said and it seemed OK

"You probably hear a lot of things, though, don't you, being a king and all?"

"Sure. Jim down at the thrift store has new jokes all the time, for one example."

"Yeah, Jim's a good guy. If I had an extra leg I'd give it to him. Who else you been talking to?"

"Well, I'm pretty friendly. Folks just tell me stuff."

"So what did someone tell you?"

I probably should of thought up how I was going to start up this part of the conversation. It was already feeling like a courtroom situation. But once a conversation is started up, you just got to go where you're gonna go.

"One guy was kind of interesting. A homeless guy. I don't think he's from around here and I didn't catch his name. Lots of those guys got some problems so you don't know how much to believe. So it was probably just a story. I think he left town so I can't collaborate what he said."

"What did he say?"

"It probably ain't nothing. He said he seen a murder. He was probably drunk and seen it on TV and forgot it was just a show."

"A murder. Really." Officer Mike started looking up at the sky, even though it was perfect blue so you could see it pretty quick. He studied it like he never seen blue before. "What did this homeless guy look like?"

166

"I didn't pay that much attention. I think he was wearing blue sunglasses and a green robe and a Hawaiian shirt with pink flowers on it. And a big tinfoil hat."

"Interesting," Officer Mike said to the sky. "Don't think I've seen him around. So what else did he say?"

"He seen this black guy in a silver Mercedes shoot a white guy in parking lot over by the Brown Palace. He was under a truck and they didn't see him. I wrote it all down just like he told me. Then he drew a picture of the guy that done the shooting. It's all in here." I give him the envelope and he looked at the papers.

"He needs to come forward. He needs to make a statement to the police."

"I think he don't want to get involved. Maybe he's had legal issues of his own."

"Like what?"

"Oh, shoot, I don't know, I'd just be expectorating. Maybe loitering and traffic tickets."

"This says the Bones were there too."

"Yeah, but they was just arguing with the guy about his Nike bag. The guy in the picture done the murder. One interesting thing is that I checked my notes and that silver Mercedes was at the same bars as the Bones three times. Plus they ordered him a pizza. Room 421 at the Brown Palace. Alfred's pepperoni, mushroom and sun-dried tomatoes. So I think he's a probably known associate."

"Or at least an alleged known associate."

"Yeah, that could be. I get them confused."

"The Bones checked out of the Marybeth last night."

"Stick," I said, maybe stronger than I should of. It was going to be harder watching them if I didn't know where they was.

"Yeah, that was a tough break. But your friend's information was good."

"My friend?"

"I think you called him Benson. The guy who told us where they were staying."

"Oh, yeah. I just didn't understand for a second."

He looked at the paper.

167

"This doesn't say anything about a Nike bag."

"Uh-oh," I said. "Well, I must of forgot to write that part down when the homeless guy said it. It looked just like mine, only the zipper worked."

"Oh yes, here it is. You wrote it down, I just missed it. How do you know the zipper worked?"

"Let me think about that one for a minute. Maybe the homeless guy said it and I forgot to write it down, or maybe I wrote it down and you ain't seen it yet, or maybe it was on a three by five card I didn't bring on account of neatness. The bag was closed, so I could of assumed that part about the zipper working. You don't need to write that down. If the zipper was broke they would of thrown it away, right? So since they didn't throw it away I bet the zipper worked."

"Yeah, I think that's a good assumption. But you're right, I don't need to write it down. Where did he get the picture?"

"He didn't say." I hadn't thought about that part. "Maybe somebody drew it for him. You know, like a sketch artist."

"A homeless sketch artist?"

"Anybody could be homeless. If a sketch artist lost his job, for one example. He could get unemployed as easy as any other artist. If you ain't got a job, pretty soon you ain't got a home."

"It's a good drawing. Whoever did it has real talent."

That made me feel proud for Linda. "Yeah, she really does." Then I thought that might have been a giveaway. "Whoever they are," I said quick so he wouldn't notice.

Officer Mike didn't catch my little slip on saying "she" so I felt relieved at that. He was back to investigating the sky.

"Pepperoni, mushroom and sun-dried tomatoes."

"Yeah, it's real good. Alfredo's makes it." Then I stopped, wondering if that was knowing more than a homeless guy seeing a murder might know. "I had some once. So that's how I know it's good."

"Alfredo's down on Colfax? It sounds good. I might have to try it."

"Well, I got appointments and stuff, so I better go."

"Did the Bones see this homeless guy?"

"He was under a truck. If they would of seen him they would of shot him as a witness."

"Well, you got to figure they might have seen him later. Or they might hear something about him. I think you have to assume they're looking for him. And the sketch artist."

"How would they know about her?" That idea got my attention in a hurry.

"They probably don't. Don't get all upset. There's a time to be smart and this is it. They might have even seen you talking to the homeless guy. You know, when he told you his story so you could write it down. So you should assume they're looking for you too. You should lay low. You and everyone you know. Do you understand?"

"I don't think they seen me talking to the homeless guy."

Now he got kind of firm, like a principal or a judge. He took hold of my shoulders and looked at my face hard. "Stay away from them," he said. "Even if they didn't see you. Do not go near the Bones. Do not let your friends go near them. Do not watch them from a distance. Is there any part of that you don't understand?"

"That sounds smart all right."

"OK then. You have a nice day."

"You too." I started to walk away and he said one more thing.

"Tell your friend thanks for the information."

"Yes sir." It made me feel good, him thanking me. Thanking always makes you feel good and it don't cost nothing, so you'd think more people would do it. They mostly don't but you can't hold it against them if they just ain't educated that way. Officer Mike thanking me felt like getting paid for what I done even if I didn't expect to get paid. That made me want to help the investigation some more. I didn't see much loopholes in the deal this time, except I didn't officially promise. Instead of saying "I promise" I just done like the President and said, "that sounds smart." Not "OK, I'll stay away." Still, you couldn't say I didn't understand so even if I never promised there was a pretty strong case against me for disobeying. I needed a whole new loophole and I ain't seen it yet, but it wouldn't hurt me to do some planning so when that loophole showed up I'd be ready for it.

Whatever my new plan was, I'd need a new disguise and I come up with a good idea for finding one. I looked in the yellow pages phone book and found a costume shop. It was way up in North Denver, so I took a bus to it. I didn't know exactly what look I was going for, but maybe seeing different things would give me an idea. And Officer Mike never said he

169

didn't want me getting a disguise. Anybody could get one, plus I wasn't looking at disguises, I was looking at costumes. It was a foolproof way to get started.

They had a bunch of things that would of been good for Halloween, like Dracula and Wolfman and Elvira. I admit I tried on some wigs that was cool, but I had to rule them out. The idea was for someone not to notice me and you'd notice Dracula or Elvis. Plus they was expensive and to rent them you needed credit cards. I'd about decided I'd wasted my time when I seen a bald-guy wig. When you think of wigs you usually think of something with a bunch of hair, but this wasn't like that. It just had some white patches of hair around your ears, but mostly it looked like skin. When I put it on I looked old and bald so I almost laughed out loud. It was fifteen bucks, which seems like a lot on a per-hair basis, but not that bad if you compare it to getting shot. Plus if I wore it I could go back to my idea of a businessman look, which ain't the first thing you'd think of me as, but would let me sit on a sidewalk if I wanted to without loitering. So I bought it, put it in my backpack and went back to the thrift store.

"Hey Jim," I said when I walked in.

"Hey Jumper. Haven't seen you in a while."

"Yeah, I had lots of appointments and stuff. You got any suits like an old businessman might wear?"

"You in a movie or something?"

"Yeah, Tom Cruise couldn't make it so they asked me."

"Aisle 15 we got some suits that aren't in current fashion. They told me to mark down some of them to get rid of, so you find one you like and we'll see if it's on the list."

Aisle fifteen was on the other end of the store. When I found a nice gray suit that fit me without being tight, I put it on, then put on my bald wig, and looked in the mirror. Right away I looked like somebody's grandfather. I took off the wig and walked up to Jim. "How about this one?" I asked.

"You look like an insurance salesman," he said.

"Well, it is kind of about insurance, so that's good."

He looked at the tag. "You're in luck," he said. "Four bucks for the suit. Only you ought to wear a white shirt and tie with it. I never saw an insurance man without a tie."

170

Once I come to think of it I had to admit my Grateful Dead T-shirt wasn't quite right. So Jim had a good point, but there was one problem.

"I ain't sure where my tie is," I said.

"We got a bunch. Next aisle over from the suits."

The ones I liked all had bright pictures on them, like of Donald Duck or forest fires. Jim said they was cool and all, but they wasn't conservative enough for the suit. He said I should get the one with black and gray patterns with some blue specs. It seemed boring, but then maybe insurance guys don't have that much taste, so it was smart to pretend I was like them. He also found a white shirt that was five bucks but was supposed to be marked down to fifty cents. The finishing touch was some big glasses, with black frames like Clark Kent wore. I couldn't see that good through them, but if I put them down low on my nose I could see over the top. Jim reminded me how to tie a tie, which I knew how to do when I was a kid but hadn't kept in practice on.

When I was all put together I looked like a guy who might be sitting on a sidewalk instead of a guy loitering.

"So this suit is insurance," Jim said. "Like that extra wallet you carry around. Are you in trouble?"

Jim don't ask questions in a Perry Mason way, but that almost makes it harder to find loopholes.

"I guess you could say I was in potential trouble. I seen some guys do something they wish nobody seen. I'm just going for a new look so they don't notice me so easy."

"You should tell Mike."

"I already done that. It ain't a big deal."

"Jumper wearing a suit and tie sounds like a big deal to me. What if they notice your hair?"

"I already thought of that," I said and put on the bald wig. "What do you think?"

He whistled. "Jumper, if you walked in off the street like that I'd charge you double. Or buy a policy off you. You ain't thinking of doing some insider trading are you?"

"Nah, I do most of my trading outside. Specially when the weather's nice like this. What do I owe you?"

"OK, let's see. Suit coat and pants, shirt, tie, and glasses. How about six bucks?"

"That sounds like a insider deal to me. Here, take my money before you change your mind." I give him a ten and he got my change.

"You ever tried them new Britney Chocolate Bars?" I asked him. "Melt in your mouth."

"Heard about them, but haven't gotten around to eating one. Are they good?"

"Some people say so. They're too dang sweet for me. Here, I got a extra. Maybe you'll like it better." I put the bar down on the counter.

"You don't like these?"

"Too sweet. Don't seem natural."

"Thanks," he said.

I walked home in my new disguise. The backpack under the suit coat made it look like I had a hump on my back, but since the coat was a little big it seemed pretty ordinary. I hadn't noticed it being too big in the store, but it turned out lucky it was. I ain't a fan of really tight suits where you can't move too easy in them. I walked past Officer Mike and he said "hello sir" and kept on walking. That made me think it was a pretty good disguise.

CHAPTER SEVENTEEN

Trailing Mango

If you're going to catch somebody in the act, you gotta try to pretend you're them and think of what they'd do. So I pretended I was the Bones. I'd guessed right about them moving locations so that was a good start. If it was me, I'd get rid of the red Camaro too, and stop ordering Alfred's pizzas. But like I said, it's harder to change what you do than where you are. So I tried to remember the stuff I knew they liked to do.

They met at bars, I knew that, and mostly bars that had girl dancers. They mostly met on Thursdays. Maybe that was a coincidence, but maybe that was a night that didn't have their favorite shows on TV, so they might stick to that. They was probably extra careful after the shooting. On the other hand, they didn't know there was a witness, unless it had been in the papers, so maybe that didn't make them too careful after all.

What they probably wouldn't change is their way of making money. They wouldn't want no other gang guys to step into their supply chain and start selling drugs to Mango. So I could probably find them by following him. That was a no brainer, so the cops was probably already doing it. Cops is pretty smart about doing the no brainer stuff. If they had Mango under surveillance, I could just wait for them to make their move. But I ought to make sure the cops was on the case.

You're probably thinking I had some good reasons to lay low like Officer Mike suggested. The big one is getting shot, but there was also getting beat up, or interfering with a police investigation. But that was all being said by the quiet voice in my brain, which can be real smart but not that good a salesman. The voice that was singing Oklahoma in my brain and offering free hot dogs just for taking a test drive was saying the Bones is looking for the sketch artist. It's one thing to make an insurance claim against a guy, or swipe his pizza. You could even understand them being irritated by the duck tape incidents if you look at it from their side. But thinking about them going after Holly or little Michelangelo made it personal. I shivered when I thought it and my face got hot at the same time and I started to hear that buzzing sound that has got me in trouble several times, and I knew I wasn't done with them yet. They wasn't getting close to Holly or Michelangelo on my watch, even if I had to get inappropriate with them.

173

Then I had a thought that Mr. Vinci would of been proud of. Officer Mike had told me to keep away from the Bones, but he hadn't said nothing about Mango. That was a loophole right there. I'd stay away from the Bones but just watch the kid. If he happened to go wherever the Bones was, you could look at that as circumstantial.

There was a bus stop about a half block away from Carter Junior High, so that's where I aimed. I put on my "bald guy in a suit" costume and walked to the school in question. As part of my costume, I got yesterday's newspaper out of a dumpster and brung it with me.

Newspapers is funny. After a day or two there ain't much market for them, even if the news in 'em ain't changed that much. If a Bronco tore his ACL, which is your knee and what they mostly tear, a day or two later it's still gonna be tore. If a Senator said something last week, he'd still be saying it. So I never got people's enthusiasm for fresh papers. For my purposes it didn't matter if it was written in Brazilian, since I was using it as part of my disguise. Nobody notices a guy reading a paper, they just figure he ain't got something better to do.

The problem with following Mango is that I knew where he ended up, which was at the school, but what I wanted to know is where he come from, which is the Bones. I told Officer Mike he mostly visited them on Mondays, which was true because he was there every single Monday, but he also came on most of the other days. But he missed a Tuesday once, so I couldn't say he come on Tuesdays, since that would be stretching things.

My idea was to wait for Mango and watch where he come from. That would give me clues as to which direction the Bones was, if he was walking away from them. I didn't need to get all my clues the first day. This is complicated to explain, so I'll give you an example. Say I start watching him on Tenth Street, and when I see him, he's coming from Ninth Street. So the next day I'd start watching from Ninth Street, and if I see him coming from Eighth Street, that's where I'd start the next day. Maybe one day I'd see him coming up Maple Street, so that's where I'd start watching him. Pretty soon, I'd be starting the same spot as him, and I'd know where the Bones was.

I got to the bus bench about 12:34 and he wasn't there yet, so I sat down and started looking at the paper. Sure enough, a Senator had said some stuff and a Bronco had tore his ACL. Luckily, it ain't that easy to get interested in reading, so I was able to watch out for Mango at the same time. When I seen him, I made a note of what street he come down and

174

then started watching for cops following him. I never seen a single cop. I watched all the people dressed ordinary to see if they might be plain clothes cops watching him undercover but nobody looked suspicious.

I'd already done my job for that day, so to keep up my cover as an old guy waiting for a bus, when a bus come along I got on it and rode a few blocks before I got off.

The next day I skipped the bus bench and took my newspaper to the street Mango come down yesterday. I started walking down it till I seen him walking toward me. I made a note of where he was coming from and when he was still a ways ahead of me I turned up the sidewalk to somebody's house and acted like I was looking in my pockets for keys until he went past. There still wasn't anybody that might of been cops so either they was pretty stealthy or they hadn't come up with this idea yet.

On the fourth day of following Mango backward I seen him coming out of a old brick apartment building. It was like mine, with one main door and little balconies but it wasn't as kept-up as mine. It had three stories and good downspouts. Some of the windows was boarded up.

OK, so that could either be where he lived or where the Bones was staying. Plus there might of been thirty or forty apartments in it, so that wasn't close enough.

The next day I got to that building about an hour before Mango left it yesterday. After a while I seen him walking down the street so I started walking toward the apartment. I walked real slow, like you see old guys walk. After he went in I run up to the door and caught it before it closed all the way. Some little kids playing in the dirt out front looked at me funny, like they never seen an old insurance guy run before, but I figured they wouldn't say nothing. There was stairs right inside the door and I heard Mango going up them, so I followed behind. He was clumping up them in his boots so I could of caught him easy, but instead I was real quiet and stayed behind so he wouldn't notice.

The trick to being stealthy on steps is this: it's the nails that creak. The nails in the middle get loose first, since that's where everybody walks. If you keep a foot on each edge by the wall, instead of the middle, they don't squeak near as much. It looks weird, going up stairs with your feet wide apart, but you can be quiet that way. But then everybody knows that trick so that's why you never see James Bond do it. You probably done it yourself. You don't pay to go to a movie to watch James Bond walk up steps like a goofy penguin since you do it yourself when you're being stealthy.

175

But since Americans don't blow up cars that much except for terrorists who ain't usually Americans and don't go to movies because their religion says it's a sin, then blowing up cars is a good thing for James Bond to do. That's how you can tell a good movie. They gotta do stuff you'd never believe if you seen it in real life.

Mango took the door to the third floor, that was obvious from his boots not clumping any more. So I took that floor too.

Only Mango was standing right there and he looked straight at me.

"You lost, honky?" he said. He looked about thirteen years old up close. I was thinking at light speed.

"Mr. Jefferson?" I asked him.

"No," he said.

"I have an appointment to discuss some insurance needs with a Mr. Jefferson."

"I ain't no Mr. Jefferson."

"Well, it ain't ever too soon to start thinking about insurance needs. I bet we got a policy just right for you."

"Fluff you," he said, and then he walked down the hall.

"You have a nice day too, young man," I said as he knocked three times on a door. I followed him, but walking in my real slow old guy walk. "Seems like just yesterday I was young and feisty like you. Never too soon to think about insurance needs." The door opened, he made a rude gesture at me and went inside. I listened at the door for a minute but couldn't be sure it was the Bone's voices. So I went back outside.

The name of the building was the Gentle Arms Apartments, so I made a note of that. I could tell which apartment they was in easy from outside. The rainspout next to their balcony looked good, so I made a note of that too and went home.

CHAPTER EIGHTEEN

Planning a turtle release party

By now you're probably thinking I'm secretly rich, the way I been spending money on disguises and pizza. But I ain't. My money was getting low, but I didn't want to go can-hunting dressed as an insurance guy, even if it was my best disguise and I hadn't thought up a new one, so I was stuck with it when I went places. To sell blood I'd have to take off the coat and even if I ain't Conan the Barbarian, my arms is too big for an old guy. So them folks would notice me for that, and the whole idea was not to get noticed. I wasn't broke, exactly, but I couldn't keep spending money like a preacher in Las Vegas forever either. It didn't bother me much, but I didn't want you to get the wrong impression. Everybody gets nervous when their cash reserves get low. It's just a different amount for everyone. Even if they got a thousand dollars, which I didn't, some people might get nervous if they thought it should be more. I was OK until next month's rent come due, so I had a couple weeks. I'd have more time for making money once the Bones was dealt with, so I had a practical reason for hurrying that up a little.

I seen Holly in the laundry room and she said they was releasing Linda on Wednesday so I could visit her one more time on Tuesday night.

On Tuesday night I walked to the hospital with Bart in my Nike bag. He was getting pretty used to it by now and mostly didn't try to make no getaway. I felt weird that this was the last time I'd see Linda in the hospital, but good she was getting out. It would probably be better for her at her own house, and she could go back to school if she wanted and everything. But even if it was good for her, it made me feel kind of odd. I had a guess that she'd get busy with her kid life and I wouldn't see her so often any more. But that was a silly idea. I'd still see her sometimes, and mostly I was glad she was feeling better. When I thought about how it wasn't as good for me if she was healthy and back home, I gave myself a good talking to and said to throw that idea out the window. Friends want their buddies to feel good, that was a no brainer.

I brung earthworms for Bart and Linda fed them to him.

"I'm getting out tomorrow," she said.

177

"That's all the way cool," I said. I was glad Linda was going home for more reasons that the obvious one of her health. The Bones probably come to the hospital sometimes, either looking for me or Holly or to see doctors about their different health issues. I didn't wear my disguise when I visited her because she would of thought that was weird. So if they seen me in her room, with her drawings, at the same time they was thinking about sketch artists they might put two and two together. After she was gone she was safer from them even if she didn't know it.

"Can we release Bart tomorrow too?" she asked.

"I don't know. What do your mommy and daddy say?"

"They say I need to stay at home for a while before I can go to the park. But I bet if I pout and cry they'd let me do it tomorrow."

"You don't seem like a kind of girl who'd need to do much pouting or crying. You seem more like a girl who outsmarts people into doing what she wants."

"I know. I just bet Bart is ready to be free as much as I am."

"Are you trying to say I ain't good enough company for a turtle?"

"No, silly! I'm sure he likes living with you just fine."

"Well, then, letting him be an all-expense-paid guest at Hotel Jumper don't seem like the worst thing in the world for old Bart. And if you do what your folks want, you'll get bonus points with them. "

We watched Bart eat a worm like it was spaghetti at a restaurant.

"I'm gonna miss him though," I said.

"Me too. But maybe when we go to the park he'll recognize us."

"Turtles ain't got the best memories for faces. But maybe sometimes he will. Anyway, we wasn't friends to him just so he'd be friends back. That ain't the way being friends works."

"I bet if we bring him earthworms he will. Will you come visit me at my house? Mommy says you can."

"Sure. I'd like to meet your mommy and daddy."

"They want to meet you too. Holly told them you were real nice."

"She says nice things about most people."

"Not that nice," Linda said and giggled.

"Well, she's nice too." I noticed they was keeping the hospital room hotter than usual.

"I bet she'd like to watch us release Bart. She calls him Bartholomew." She winked at me. "Only Daddy doesn't get off work until eight-thirty at night. He travels a lot for business too, so it's hard to find a time in the daytime when he can be there. Holly has to work nights, so that makes it even harder. But she's off most Sundays, Daddy's in town on some Sundays but has to work until 8:30. So I was wondering if nine o'clock a on a Sunday in two or three weeks would work for you."

"Ain't that a little late for you? What with bed time and all. Plus, it'll be dark."

"I never go to sleep before 10:30. At first Mommy tried to make me. She'd make me lay there in bed for hours with the lights off. Finally she figured out it's just how I am. I don't go to sleep early. Everybody's a little different, aren't they? And being different is OK, right?"

"It's one of the best things," I said.

"Plus, mommy knows this is special. I told her it was more a celebration of getting out of the hospital, which she couldn't really argue with. How can you object to a little girl who's had cancer celebrating being healthy again?" She tilted her head sideways, and opened her eyes real wide, like a little puppy, and blinked them at me in about the cutest way you could.

"See, I knew you was better at lawyering people into doing stuff than pouting them into it. But don't you use them puppy dog eyes on me unless it's a last resort."

"Can you do it?"

"Well, I'd have to check my schedule..."

"Pooh!" she said. "You got as much schedule as I do. And don't forget Bart." She shook her finger at me like a school teacher.

"Oh yeah, the guest of honor. I'll have him check his schedule too. Maybe his people can call your people." She rolled her eyes at that, but she giggled a little too."

"Well, I guess I could move some appointments around."

"Cool. There's a spot by the lake with some weeds. I thought Bart would like that. Lots of bugs and nobody'll see him in there."

179

"I know the spot."

Just then Holly walked into the room.

What spot?" she said.

"A turtle release spot," I said. "Just as soon as Michelangelo's mommy and daddy say it's cool we're going to have a turtle release party down at City Park."

"That sounds fun," Holly said.

"You're invited too, of course," Linda said. "After all, you're the one who let Bartholomew come and visit me. We can't have it without you. You'll come, won't you? Please?"

I about cracked up because Linda was using her puppy dog eyes on Holly. Holly kind of smiled like she knew she was getting conned, but there wasn't any way she could say no to that kid who was smiling like a cocker spaniel at her.

"I wouldn't miss it," she said.

"Oh good!" Linda said, and clapped her little hands together. "It will probably be on Sunday night at about nine. That's when my dad can be there too. How about if I have my mom call you, Holly, when they think I'm strong enough and then you can tell Mr. Jumper."

"That sounds like a fine plan," Holly said.

"You're really messing up my Tuesday nights," I said to Linda. "I guess I'm going to have to stay home and watch TV reruns."

"I wanted to talk to you about that," Holly said. "And to you too, Linda. I've got another patient that could use some art lessons. He's a little older than you, Linda. Besides his other problems, he broke both his legs so he can't get out of bed and he's feeling kind of down. I was thinking he might like it if Mr. Jumper visited him on Tuesday nights, now that you're going home. What would you think about that?"

You would of thought she'd be asking me that question, but she was looking right at Linda and asking her.

Linda stared up at the ceiling, thinking about advantages and disadvantages to that plan like smart people do. She didn't look upset or nothing. It was the look you get when you're choosing what size french fries to get with your hamburger. Then she nodded.

"I think that's a good idea. If you're selfish with your friends, you aren't being a very good friend yourself. Anyway, Mr. Jumper's a pretty good art teacher, for an old guy."

"Hey!" I shouted and she started giggling pretty hard.

"You won't forget to let us know when the turtle release party is, will you?" Holly asked.

"I'd forget my own name first," she said.

"OK," I said. "Well, we'll see you in two or three weeks then. You hurry and get strong so I don't have to keep digging up worms for our turtle." I turned to go out the door, but little Linda was too quick even for me.

"You ain't getting away that easy," she said and before I knew it she'd run right at me and jumped up and grabbed both arms around my neck like a python and give me a big bear hug. There wasn't much I could do but give her a big hug back. I ain't ever give a little girl a hug before so I was careful not to squeeze her too hard. She felt so little and light and warm it surprised me. Before that second, I never thought about what it would feel like to hug a little kid. It made me feel like I was this huge, strong guy, like a superhero. The weirdest thing was the way my throat felt. It felt like I had a walnut stuck in there and my face got hot and I couldn't talk at all. So when she finally let me lower her back to the ground I didn't even try to say something. I just messed up her hair a little bit and walked out the door, waving to her over my shoulder.

Holly give her a hug too and then followed me out to the hallway. It looked like she was going to ask me a question. Then she looked at my face in that careful way some people do, where they look at one of your eyes and then the other one and then back to the first one. She nodded and changed her mind about whatever she was going to ask me. We started walking.

"Listen," she said. "Maybe I should tell you a little about Greg before you decide if you want to visit him. He has a lot of problems and they aren't all physical." She kept looking straight ahead while we was walking. I just nodded like I was listening hard, but mostly I knew that if I said something my voice would sound goofy because of that walnut thing. I got lucky on that one and she didn't ask me nothing.

"He wouldn't normally be on this floor because... well, because he's not that sick. But he needs us to keep an eye on him as if he were, and right now we're set up the best to do that. You know what emotional problems are, don't you?"

181

I nodded like I did. I was having a little emotional problem of my own on account of feeling strange from Linda giving me that big old bear hug. Feelings is weird. I was happy that little girl was healed up enough to go home, that one's easy. And her giving me a hug was a way of saying she liked me which was also good. And I'd be seeing her again at our turtle release party, and parties is always fun. Every single thing was good except that I wouldn't be seeing her on Tuesday nights which I had got used to. So I should have been feeling a hundred and ten percent, but instead I felt like I was going to cry. I bit down on the inside of my cheek, because sometimes that makes me forget how I feel, and tried my hardest to listen to Holly.

"Sometimes emotional problems are like a kind of sickness," she said. "They make people do strange things and say things they don't really mean. This kid Greg is like that. He says things that sound mean and he does stupid things, so not too many people want to be with him. He chases them away. But I think he's a good kid underneath all that. He just needs..." She stopped and turned toward me like she was trying to think of the best word. She put her hand on my arm. "He just needs someone like you in his life." She looked at my left eye and then at my right eye. I never noticed before she was one of them people who do that. Obviously I had to say something even if I didn't have a good idea what it was.

"I don't scare too easy," I said. She laughed at that even if it wasn't really a joke. The sound of her laugh made me feel a lot better.

"No, I don't think he's going to scare you. Actually, just the fact that he can't frighten you off might make you seem scary to him. Does that make sense?"

"I won't make faces at him or anything like that."

She smiled and nodded. "Would you like to meet him?"

"Ain't visiting hours over?"

"He's not very concerned with rules."

"Cool. And he likes to draw?"

"Well, I guess I can't say that." She said. "Greg doesn't like much of anything."

"So what am I supposed to do?"

She stopped because we was outside a hospital door which I figured was the room we was going to. "That's a good question." She said. She stared at the floor for a minute. I started to feel bad that I stumped her on a ques-

182

tion I figured she knew the answer to. Nobody likes to get stumped. So I thought real quick and come up with an idea so she wouldn't feel bad for being stumped.

"Oh, I get it!" I said. "It's like playing Dr. Hudson where I'm supposed to figure out something to give him without him guessing I'm doing it. I always liked playing Dr. Hudson. Only you ain't supposed to give me too much hints."

"I never heard of the Dr. Hudson game, but yeah, it's something like that. Greg has spent a lot of time with jerks and losers. He's made a lot of bad choices. I just think it would help him if he spent some time with..." She stopped for a minute. "I think he should spend some time with a good man. You know, someone like you."

I about fell over when she said that.

"Nobody ever called me a good man before," I said.

She laughed like I was making a joke on her. "Of course you're a good man," she said. "Anyone can see that. This is his room. Are you ready?"

"Sure."

"Good. Just pretend you're Greg's big brother. Don't let him irritate you too much. That's his best skill."

"Maybe he wants to be an attorney."

"I don't think so." She pushed open the door and I followed her in. "This is Greg."

CHAPTER NINETEEN

I get me a new art therapy client and meet another jumper

The kid in the bed had pale skin and long black hair except for the middle part which was purple. He had a ring in his nose. Both his legs were in big casts which was held up off the bed by some straps. He turned his head slowly to look at me and his face didn't change at all. He just looked in a pretty bad mood, which you couldn't hold against a guy with two broken legs. Then he looked away again.

"Greg, you have a visitor."

For just a second he looked back at us, then he looked away again like he was really bored.

"I'll leave you two alone," Holly said and then she left. His room was dark except for one light on the table by his bed. It made the room cozy.

"Too bad about your legs," I said. "Does it hurt?"

"What are you, the doctor of stupid?" he said without moving his head a inch or looking at me.

"Nah, I ain't a doctor. I'm just a friend of nurse Holly."

"Bull shirt," he said in an angry way. Well, that ain't exactly what he said. It was funny and interesting that he could gear himself up to be mad without moving at all. "Women who look like Nurse Slut don't have friends like you. What are you, the janitor? Did she lose a bet? Get the fluff out of my room."

I had to laugh at how easy Greg got pissed at a guy he didn't even know for one minute yet. Guys like that ain't mad at you, they're just mad in general and you can't hold it against them.

"Well, yeah, I done some janitoring," I said. "Mostly apartments. How about you?" I sat down in the chair next to his bed.

"I said get the fluff out of my room, you mother bluffing son of a clock slushee horn!"

OK, so you probably get the flavor of how this kid talked, which meant he'd watched way too much cable TV and listened to too much rap

184

and didn't ever learn enough regular words to get through a adult conversation. I won't try to keep up with his style of talking. I think you got the picture. It's pretty much how he always talked.

"Man, you're gonna embarrass Bart Simpson here," I said.

He didn't say nothing. I pulled the turtle out of his Nike bag and held him on my knee. "He ain't much of a rapper. Look, you made his ears turn red."

"Turtles don't have ears you stupid mother fluff."

"Sure they do. Watch this."

Bart was pretty used to me, so sitting on my knee he had been starting to poke his head out. I snapped my fingers. And he ducked his head back in at the sound. "How'd he do that if he ain't got ears?"

"Well then he's way ahead of you, you shirt eater. Hey turtle, tell your pet human to get the fluff out of my room. He don't seem to hear very well."

I had to laugh at that one too. "That's pretty funny," I said. "You calling me his pet human. I gotta admit, it kind of feels like that sometimes. He don't do much tricks for me, but he gets me to catch crickets and worms for him all the time. How'd you train me so good, Bart?"

Greg rolled his eyes and looked away like he didn't even want to try to talk any more, which in some ways was a improvement.

"Bart's gonna have to find himself a new pet pretty soon. I'm turning him loose at City Park. Only reason I got him with me is because a little girl down the hall likes him and so he comes to visit her. But she's going home, so we're going to have a turtle release party as soon as she's strong enough."

I figured that was enough talking about me and my turtle for a while, so I just held Bart on my knee. I could see out the window from my chair, but only sky. Since it was night there wasn't much happening in the sky except stars and sometimes a cloud which was lit up more on the bottom from the city lights than from the top like daytime clouds is.

My dad had told me that the stars was so far away that the light I was seeing from them started flying toward me before I was born and took that long to get here. He said the night I was born he went outside and shined a flashlight up at the stars. He said the light from that flashlight would keep traveling out there for a million years telling them space guys that his

185

kid was born that night. It always made me proud that he'd tell the whole universe about me. Sometimes when I look at the sky I wonder if maybe some space guy held a mirror up at exactly the right second and one of them lights I was seeing was my dad's flashlight reflected back to me. I ain't enough of a scientist to know for sure it would work like that but it don't hurt to wonder stuff or pretend stuff or believe stuff. Maybe it's like karma: you might have a better life if you believe something, even if you're wrong.

I can sit and look at stars for pretty long. I can also sit in the same room as someone else and not talk. It makes some people nervous but I like it. Most of the time whatever you say is just an excuse to sit together anyways, and when you talk you got the chance you'll say something to piss someone off or make them feel bad. And if the other person talks, there's a pretty good chance they'll ask you something you don't know or give you a assignment, or tell you, hey, you ain't supposed to be here. Most of the time sitting together not talking is best.

I admit I was enjoying sitting and looking at the stars out the window better than when Greg was talking. But it seemed impolite to bring your turtle into a guy's hospital room and then just sit there. Anyway, I was curious about Greg.

"So, what happened to your legs? I asked.

He turned to look at me and you could tell he was about to say something pretty rude, but then he decided it wasn't worth the effort. He'd figured out I wasn't real easy to chase off with bad words. Instead, he shrugged.

"Broke them."

"I kind of guessed that on account of the casts. Does it hurt?"

"My days as a ballerina are over. My fluffing life is ruined."

"Wow, that's too bad. I never met a ballerina. I bet that's a good way to meet girls though. Maybe you'll heal up good enough to do it again." I was pretty sure he was joking about being a ballerina so I was joking back at him, but it wasn't a big deal either way. "How did you break them?"

He looked at me straight on, watching my face like he was going to say something I'd react to. I seen it lots of times. Perry Mason, for one, done it all the time. Cops do it when they're gonna say something a guilty guy would react to. Just to be on the safe side, I've practiced keeping my face real still when someone uses that look on me. But there was no way I could keep my face still at what this kid said:

186

"I'm what the police like to call a jumper."

It's a good thing I wasn't drinking Fresca at the time, because it would of all come out my nose at that.

"You're kidding!" I said. My whole life I was the only jumper I ever knew and even if I suspected there must be a bunch of us out there, I ain't never met a single other one.

"Do those look like I'm kidding?" he said.

"No," I said, looking at the casts in a whole new way. "Obviously you're a jumper I didn't mean you was making a joke. It's just I never met...I mean, I figured lots of people must be jumpers... I mean, I never got to talk to..." I could tell I sounded like a idiot so I stopped and took some deep breaths. Greg was watching me pretty careful and was obviously as amused as he ever got. My getting all jumbled up was the funniest thing he seen all day. I took some more deep breaths and carefully put Bart back in his Nike bag. Then I stood up and went closer to the window and looked out. You can't see stars very good from inside, but you can see them better if you're close to the window. If my dad's flashlight was getting reflected back this very minute, of all the minutes, I sure didn't want to miss it. Greg was a jumper just like me!

It was like finding someone in my own family I never knew about. I felt my insides getting warm, like I was drinking hot chocolate and it was spreading around inside me. It was like walking down the street not feeling hungry and then you go past a restaurant and smell hamburgers and French fries and all of a sudden you realize you could eat an elephant, you're so hungry. I hadn't even known how much I wished I'd meet just one other jumper in my life. And now I was in the same room as one.

Between the clouds was lots of stars and most of them looked like space guys holding mirrors. After I took some more deep breaths I went back and sat next to Greg again. He looked like a whole different person. I put one hand on a cast for a second. It felt cold and hard. I took my hand back and folded it with the other one.

"So what happened?" I asked.

"I don't want to talk about it."

I nodded. I knew just how he felt.

"Yeah," I said. "People don't understand."

187

"Right. Even people. Let alone turtle pets."

"You can't hold it against them if they never jumped. Your jump just didn't turn out like you planned it. Now it makes sense why you're pissed."

"You could say that. If we were talking about it. Which we are not." Greg still seemed pretty pissed, but it was understandable. I train every day and worked up to my height jumps and I was a careful guy to start with. And even I had times when I could of broke my legs. Lots of times I just got lucky, which is as good as being smart most of the time, but you don't get points for it. That could be me in that hospital bed wondering if I'd ever heal good enough to jump again. Let alone do ballerina dancing. If that was me, I'd be just as pissed as Greg.

"It's OK," I said, trying to cheer him up. "I bet you get to jump again. And this time you'll get it right."

"Are you trying to be funny? You're dang right I'll jump again! I'd jump right now if they didn't have me strapped in here like a prisoner. I hate my fluffing life."

"One good jump will fix that for you."

"You're dang right it will."

"That's the spirit," I said. "But they won't ever unstrap you if you keep acting crazy. They already think jumpers is strange. But they think crazy jumpers is somehow their fault so they keep us strapped in, or locked up, so it don't go on their own permanent record. It don't take brains the size of Bart's to figure that out. Sooner you start acting like you ain't crazy the sooner you'll be flying through the air again."

He was staring at me different now, with a lot more of a Perry Mason look than before.

"What do you mean us?

"Huh?"

"You said they keep 'us' strapped in. What did you mean by that?"

"I didn't mean nothing."

"You jumped too, didn't you!"

"I might of jumped a time or two..."

"A time or two!"

188

"I don't want to talk about it," I said. That only seemed fair. He didn't want to talk about it. I could play that same game. He stared at me a minute but I didn't say nothing.

"You're a fluffing liar," he said. "You never jumped even once."

OK, so him saying that cracked me up pretty good. I tried to hold it in but you already know how that goes. I didn't want him to think I was laughing at him in a mean way or making fun of him, but I started laughing a little bit and it kind of got out of control. I got laughing harder and harder and the more I tried to stop the worse it got. Pretty soon I was laughing as loud as a donkey. What was funny was this: I spent my whole life explaining how come I jumped, or pretending I didn't and training at night so no one would see me and think I was weird and now this kid didn't believe I was a jumper at all. First guy in my life who had my same sport and he didn't believe me. It made it even funnier that he had casts on his legs, even if that was mean of me, but it did. And it made it funnier that he was so pissed at me and everything else in the world. I just couldn't help it. I had to bend over and hold my stomach from laughing so hard.

He just stared at me like I was from Mars and didn't even crack a smile. Some guys ain't easy laughers like me, which is OK. It makes me feel better to laugh, but if you ain't like that, that's cool. It makes some guys happy to see what's bad about something which is probably pretty handy if a lot of bad stuff happens to you. Breaking two legs is pretty bad, so Greg was lucky he liked seeing the bad side of stuff. Plus, obviously, he didn't get what was funny. From his side maybe I wasn't a jumper so there wouldn't be much of a joke.

"I'm sorry, man," I said when I mostly got it out of my system. "There's no way you could know how come that was funny. The good news is," I patted his cast with my hand, "it looks like you're going to be in here a while."

"How in the hell is that good news?"

"Well, not so good for you, of course. I didn't mean that. It just means I'll get some time to visit with you, which will be good for me."

"Don't bother."

"It ain't no bother. Nurse Holly asked me to come visit and neither of us want to get her pissed at us, so I'll be coming to visit. That's about the end of that conversation. We just got to figure out how to spend some time until they let you out. Do you like to draw?"

189

"No."

"Well, then you never done it enough. Everybody likes to draw. Anyway, if you got a paper and pencil in your hand, people pretty much leave you alone. And since that seems like the main thing you want, it sounds about perfect. Next week I'll sit here and draw, and you can sit there with a pencil pretending to draw and nobody'll bother us."

"That's the most idiotic thing I ever heard."

"That's just because you ain't heard some of my other plans."

He didn't say nothing for a minute. Then he kind of smiled.

"You don't have a shot with Nurse Holly. You know that, don't you?" he said.

It surprised me him saying that.

"What do you mean?"

"Well, in the first place, she's hot for an old woman in her twenties. In the second place, you're an idiot. In the third place, I've seen Dr. Anderson follow her in here. I've seen the way he stands close to her and puts his hand on her shoulder. He's a fluffing doctor, bologna brain. He makes more in a week than you do in a year. Plus he's smart. You don't have a shot and you're such an idiot you don't even know you don't have a shot. That's what I mean."

I could feel my face getting hot and the mood to laugh was all the way gone.

"She's just my friend, and she asked me to visit you. Friends do things for each other. It don't mean you're going steady or something. Ain't you ever had a friend that was a girl?"

"We ain't talking about me. I'm just saying you don't have a shot. Sounds like you're cool with that. But you don't need to come here and pretend to be interested in me for her. Trust me, she don't give a shirt about either of us."

OK, so maybe he had me figured out better than I had myself figured out about Holly. Once he told me she had a boyfriend who was a doctor I might of decided it wasn't so fun to come back to the hospital. But the part I figured out better than him is that him and me was just like each other. We was both jumpers and neither one of us knew another person who done that. Nobody else understood what it was like to fly in slow motion through the air and land on soft grass and then climb back up the tree to

190

do it again. There wasn't nobody to high-five after a real good jump and nobody to talk to when you wondered how come your roll-out didn't work the way you expected. Anyway, you can like somebody pretty much who ain't your girlfriend, and I still liked Holly and I told her I'd do this. I remember what Linda said to me earlier tonight and I stole her line.

"Sorry, buddy. You're my new friend. You ain't getting rid of me that easy. I'll see you next Tuesday."

I walked out of his room. I gotta admit my feelings was mixed. On the one hand, I finally met another jumper, which made me feel so good I must have been lonesome for one my whole life without knowing it. On the other hand, the one I met wasn't exactly a barrel of dancing monkeys as far as being a fun guy. On the still other hand, it sounded like Holly had a boyfriend, which was mixed all by itself. You gotta be happy for your friend when nice things happen to them. But I gotta admit it didn't make me as happy for her as it would of if I was a better person.

As I was walking down the hall I had another idea that cheered me up a little. Maybe Greg was joking on me about Dr. Anderson. He had some stuff figured out about me pretty quick, so he probably seen right off that I liked Holly and that would make an easy joke on me. Plus, he was only a kid and he might not understand grown up stuff like love, so he might think Dr. Anderson and Holly was in love when they was really just buddies. He obviously made some mistakes jumping, so he might make other mistakes too.

The only solution was for me to do my own detecting. But that was going to have to wait until I finished up with my previous case, which was the Bones. Since I had the incriminating evidence on them, which was where their current whereabouts was, all I had to do was tell the cops.

191

CHAPTER TWENTY

It was a good plan, but there was some unexpected flaws in it. Like a new cop. So I come up with a new plan, which I don't see any way it could fail.

The next day I went looking for Officer Mike to tell him where the Bones was staying, in case the cops hadn't figured that out yet. But instead of him, I run into a different cop, a young guy.

"Where's Officer Mike?" I asked him.

"He retired," the guy said. "Is there something I can do for you?" the guy looked about college age and had real short hair like a Marine, but he was skinny. This was a whole new wrinkle. But a cop's a cop, so I decided to give him a try.

"I was wondering a question. Say a guy had some information he wanted to give the cops. How would he do that?"

"He'd go down to the station and fill out a report."

"OK, so that's one way. But say he had appointments or something. Is there another way?"

"If he's too busy to be a good citizen I'd say his information's probably not worth much."

"Well, you never can tell about information, how valuable it might be."

"You can tell by the source. Someone who isn't willing to fill out a form probably isn't a very reliable source."

"Yeah, that's a point."

"I think you better move along."

"Talking to a cop ain't loitering. I was just wondering..."

"It is if I say it is. You move along now before I haul you downtown."

So that didn't work out as smooth as I imagined it. I walked away. There didn't seem much choice but to go down to the police station and fill out one of their forms. I went over the clues in my head, which I had wrote down on a 3 by 5 card too, and for all the time it had took me to get it, it didn't sound that reliable. All I really knew was that this kid Mango went to one apartment in the Gentle Arms and then went to Carter Junior High and hung out. It looked like he was selling drugs, but it could of been cigarettes or real small Bibles for all I really knew. That put a twist on it. Say it wasn't the Bones in the Gentle Arms at all, but a Bible guy. The cops wouldn't think it was that funny if they busted down the door and Billy Graham or the Pope was in there praying and handing out little Bibles to his missionaries, which is what they call their salesmen. They might decide the guy who give 'em the information was both a criminal and a suspected sinner, which wouldn't do me no good on them loitering tickets. So that young cop was right. I ain't that reliable a source.

I already decided there was hidden flaws in my plan to catch them in the act. I still hadn't figured out a way to get a cell phone to call the cops, that was the big flaw. But there was also the part about the Bones catching me while I was catching them, which seemed about as likely. Now I seen the hidden flaw in filling out a form. I couldn't swear I knew what was going on. That bugged me since I usually know what's going on all the time.

I wasn't crazy about waltzing into the police station with my suspected information for another reason. Me and the cops had some loitering misunderstandings that wasn't worth their time to follow up on if it was hard. But if I was just standing there in their precinct and my name come up on their computer screen and they had some jail vacancies available, I'd be their guest for sure. They probably got bonus points for stuff like that. Officer Mike didn't care about bonus points, but they ain't all got his common sense.

So then I had me an idea.

Sometimes one idea makes your mind turn down a different road from where it was going, and that new road leads to a whole different idea a little farther down that road which you never would of got to if you hadn't had that first idea which didn't seem like a big deal. This idea was like that. One idea led to a different one.

The second idea, the idea the first one led to, was the one I started to tell you about first thing, when I said some folks said I ain't smart enough to have did what I done. Depending on how fast you read, that could have been a month ago if you're fast, or a year ago if you're a slow reader or had a lot of appointments. So I won't hold it against you if you forgot. I almost forgot myself. The thing I was talking about when I said that was writing this book. A lot of guys ain't wrote a book, and some of them wished they would of. Some of them guys, plus a few others from time to time, told me

193

I ain't smart. Like some of the kids in school, and three of my teachers, and a guy who puts the groceries in my sack down at the store one time. I don't go to that grocery store any more if even the guy was just a sacker shooting off his mouth, and sometimes they have good deals. Then there's been homeless guys who called me stupid for no reason, and the lady at the drivers license place when I filled out my form wrong, and guys in drug studies, especially college guys with computers. And sometimes a girl in a bar will say something rude and call me a name that means stupid, like "stick for brains" or "loser" when all I said was "hello" or "I like the song they're playing." Or sometimes you run into a guy who got evicted for not paying his rent after he blew all his money on drugs and he knows you cleaned up the pig pen he moved out of and made twenty bucks and he starts calling you names that mean he's smarter than you. Them guys probably just feel weird since you know they got evicted so you can't hold it against them. Same with gang guys. They know they ain't making very bright career choices and is probably gonna get screwed, or shot, or addicted, or thrown in jail. Calling other people stupid is their number one thing. It would be depressing to be a gang guy if you took it away from him, plus it's just part of the uniform. You can't take it personal. A gang guy calling somebody stupid is like a McDonald's guy saying "You want fries with that." You put on the uniform, there's stuff they make you say.

Writing this book is the second idea that the first idea led to. The first idea was to write Officer Mike a letter. I thought it was about as good a idea as I ever come up with, about like Mr. Vinci using Mona's shaving mirror. It had a lot of pluses.

First, I wouldn't have to go to the police station and fill out a form and risk taking some unexpected vacation days there. Second, Officer Mike knew me pretty good so he'd know I was more reliable than the new cop thought. Third, he knew procedures so he'd know which guy to tell stuff to without somebody looking my name up in their computer.

If the guys in the Gentle Arms apartment was selling Bibles he could tell them it was just routine and nobody'd get their feelings hurt. Cops do routine stuff all the time.

Writing a letter probably ain't a big deal if you done it much. But I never had anyone I knew who lived far away to write a letter to, so I never practiced up. I didn't know if I was supposed to buy special paper, for one example, and I didn't have no stamps. I had two pencils that still had some use left in them, but it seemed like maybe a letter was more of a pen kind of thing than a pencil kind of thing. I had some pens but I don't like the way

194

they write as good as a pencil. But maybe for a letter I should be formal and use a Bic. Maybe even use two different colors so it didn't look so ordinary.

But then this wasn't like a Christmas letter where you want it to be perfect because of Jesus' birthday and all, so I figured some compromises was OK. If you're God you probably got extra high standards, and since I didn't know what them was I never wrote a Christmas letter. Didn't seem like a smart risk. God likes to smite people who screw up. I ain't exactly sure what that means, but if God does it when he gets pissed I ain't interested in trying it out. Officer Mike never seemed much like the smiting kind. So a pencil letter on some of my extra computer paper I use for drawings was probably fine. If he needed to smite me for it, I'd just take my consequences.

It took me a couple days to decide all that before I got out my pencil and 3 by 5 cards. A couple days would be slow if the job was cleaning a apartment, but us writers got different rules. If you ain't writing the letter you was supposed to be writing, you could call it writers block, which means "I ain't got around to writing something yet." Then it's OK.

In this case, since I was collecting all my 3 by 5 cards and planning out my letter you call it research, which means "I ain't got around to writing something yet." There's lots of reasons writing is a good job for me, but stuff like that is about the best ones.

My first try at a letter didn't go so good. I think I got myself all spooked by thinking of Christmas letters and getting smited. I wrote "Dear Oficer Mike" but it didn't look right. So I erased it and tried writing Mike with two k's, and then without the e on the end. After about six erasings, the paper didn't look that fresh any more. I decided my first try would just be practice, which was easier. When I had it like I wanted it, I could copy it on a new paper and use a pen to be formal. Or a pencil. I didn't have to make that decision until I crossed the bridge it was under. Until then I could do cross-outs and erases as much as I wanted.

It took all morning to write that practice letter which was about six and a half pages long. That's when I realized I didn't know how much pages you could have in a letter for one stamp. If it was too heavy, they wouldn't deliver it. But if I guessed wrong and put extra stamps on it, the post office might think I was a suspected terrorist for being dumb about U.S. mailing rules. There ain't nothing they like as much as finding a suspected terrorist. I talked to a guy about it once and he said if you're a suspected terrorist they send you to Cuba and make you smoke cigars 'til you throw up. If you're a suspected terrorist they can do anything they want to you and the rule book is out the window. Better to tell them you're a murderer. Murderers get out on DNA sometimes, but suspected terrorists is just screwed. I sure didn't want to mess up on post office rules.

I wrote eight practice letters and every one was shorter than the last one. My last practice letter said "My friend thinks the Bones is at the Gentle Arms Apartments, number 315. Turtle release party one week from Sunday at about nine at night at City Park if you want to come. My friend who followed the Bones moved to Darkest Africa where there ain't no phones or mail so he can't fill out a report. Happy retirement, yours truly, Jumper."

That seemed pretty good, so I copied it extra careful on a new paper. I finally used a pencil because it seemed friendlier. I had an envelope I'd been saving for a long time, so that wasn't a big deal. Now I just needed a stamp and an address.

About then I realized I didn't know Officer Mike's last name, so the only way I'd find his address was to call the police station. It don't take a brain scientist to figure they wouldn't give out information on cops. If you called with a suspicious question like "what's a cop's address?" they'd probably trace your call and decide you was a suspected terrorist after all and you'd be screwed worse than if you turned yourself in and said "Hi, I'm Osama. Any messages?" Which, if you're reading this, that ain't my name.

Then I started laughing at myself cause I'd been working on doing something the hard way instead of thinking up the easy way. Officer Mike was probably getting all kinds of cards saying "happy retirement" at the station and they'd make sure he got them. I didn't need to waste a bunch of time trying to find him. Then I figured out I didn't need to waste no stamp either.

I put my letter in the envelope, licked it good, then wrote "to officer Mike, happy retirement" on the outside. Then I put on my bald guy wig, and my shirt and tie and businessman suit, and the big blue sunglasses and walked down to the police station. I wore my regular sneakers, because nobody looks at your feet anyway, and they was pretty comfortable. Plus I didn't have no other shoes.

By the time I got there it was five o'clock and traffic was bad but, when you're walking, bad traffic ain't a problem except for the honking. The police station was a clean brick building with a ramp for wheelchairs and a big US flag. I walked up the ramp, because that seemed like what a bald guy in a business suit would do. Between the suit and tie and bald guy wig,

I looked a lot different from a guy who might have had loitering misunderstandings. The cops who worked there couldn't know all Officer Mike's friends, so my plan was to just walk in and hand the letter to the cop at the information desk and then walk out. If you was leaving a happy retirement note you wouldn't have to fill out forms or say your name. I couldn't see no hidden flaws in that plan, so I walked right up to the desk.

"I just want to leave..." I started to say, but the cop held up his hand and stopped me. The phone was ringing and he picked it up.

"I'll be with you in a minute," he said to me, then he said hello into the phone.

"That would be eloquent," I said. I figured a businessman would use extra good words. The cop raised one eyebrow like Spock on Star Trek while he looked at me and talked on the phone. I smiled to myself. Spock used big words all the time and he was James Bond cool even for a Vulcan. Vulcans is all pretty cool if you ever seen the show, but Spock is about the coolest. Using big words was a good idea, and it just come to me like dust in the air without using anywhere near my whole brain.

The cop on the phone kept watching me in that extra careful way that makes anyone nervous. I looked away as casual as I could and started singing Oklahoma in my head so I'd look like I was thinking about something. I'd just got to the part where it says "and that standard wheat can sure smell sweet when the wind comes whistling down the plane" when a door to my left opened and a cop come out with a teenage boy.

"We're going to let you go with a warning this time, young man," the cop said. I started to say thank you sir, and then figured out he was talking to the kid. "But next time we catch you loitering at the Stop and Shop during school hours we're going to have to call your parents. Do you understand?"

"Yes sir," the kid said. He was facing away from me but the first time they said "loitering" I started listening pretty hard cause I like to keep up on legal issues, and when the kid talked I recognized his voice. It was Mango, the kid I'd followed. He'd seen me at the Gentle Arms in exactly this same disguise. About the last thing I wanted was for him to ID me standing at the police station turning in information about his gang's whereabouts. Luckily, I'm a fast thinker. There was a car magazine sitting on the cop's desk so I picked it up and opened it and held it in front of my face like I was reading it. The cop and Mango walked right in front of me. I watched the cop's shoes beneath the magazine until they got to the front

197

door. I didn't put the magazine down until I heard the door open and close and the cop walked away saying something about "kids these days."

"Can I help you?" the cop at the desk said as he hung up the phone.

"With pleasure," I said. "I wanted to give Officer Mike a happy retirement card. Could you assure that he gets this please?" I handed him the letter.

"Are you from around here?" He asked it like I was a suspect.

"Oklahoma," I said, which ain't true but it was in my brain and come out anyway. "A whole different precinct. Will you give it to him?"

Just then the phone rang again and he got interested in that.

"Sure," he said, while he picked it up. "Got a whole stack of 'em." As he started talking into the phone I turned and left the building.

I had a couple of issues to decide right then. Part of me said I ought to follow Mango again in case I'd get some new information. Even though I didn't see him right away when I went outside, he had to be close, and surveillance is about a detective's number one way to detect. They get paid lots more for surveillance than they do for watching. That idea had the advantage that I was already near him, which was lucky, and if you don't pay attention when you get a lucky break you'll never know you had any.

The disadvantages was two. If he seen me tailing him he'd get suspicious and the whole gang might move out of the Gentle Arms before Officer Mike even got my letter with their whereabouts. The other thing was if he seen me he might act all casual and lead me right into a ambush. Kids has all got cells anymore, and he could call the Bones and set one up while I was surveilling him. If the Bones'd shoot a known associate dead because of a business deal you couldn't count on them being good natured about me.

The quiet voice in me was saying it was too good a chance to miss, and I ought to follow him. At the same time, the opera star singer in my head was yelling for me to walk in the opposite direction of Mango and let the cops do their job. Then the quiet little voice started talking all casual and said, what would James Bond do? That was easy. He'd follow the suspect until the bad guys caught him and tied him up with a pretty girl. Then the opera star voice said, yeah, but if you ain't noticed yet, you ain't James Bond. Go home!

The police station was a block off Colfax and since I didn't see the kid anyway I made the compromise that I'd just walk up there and, if I seen him, I'd decide what to do then.

198

That block of Colfax has three story buildings with businesses on the first story, which all had big windows, and then apartments above that. As soon as I got to Colfax I seen Mango across the street with his back to me just standing and looking in a window. That caught my attention right there because the store was selling drapes and most teenage guys ain't so much into drapes they'd just stop and look at 'em in a store window. You didn't have to be Columbo to figure out he was using the window as a mirror so he could watch behind him without someone knowing. I pretended not to see him and turned left on Colfax and walked away from him without even stopping.

Two people can play at the game of using windows as mirrors. I was on the left side of the road, so the buildings was to the left of the sidewalk. Mango was on the right side of the street and behind me. I wasn't sure he'd seen me, or if he was going to follow me, but I wasn't taking no chances. I stopped and looked in a window to my left and seen him looking right at me a half block back and across the street. He must of seen me in the police station and recognized me even with the magazine in front of my face and now instead of me surveilling him, he was surveilling me. Some guys got a gift for recognizing clothes like that, which ain't one of my gifts.

You can see the pickle that put me in. If I ran away, he'd know I'd seen him, which is just as bad as if I blew my cover while I was tailing him. But I didn't want to just casually lead him back to my building either, because then I was pretty sure the Bones would be making a house call on me and maybe Holly beside. So neither plan A or plan B was much good and I had to keep walking along real casual until I come up with a plan C, which sometimes there ain't one. On the good side, Mango wasn't the brightest bulb in the tulip patch himself, and I was a lot older, so I can't say I was too nervous about the whole deal.

Up ahead there was some guys standing in front of a building and holding signs. The building was made of red bricks, and it was taller and nicer than most of the block. It had a clean look, like they washed it every night, so I figured it was an office building. The guys holding signs wore suits and ties just like me, so it seemed like an opportunity. Maybe I could blend in with them for a minute until Plan C come to me.

As I got close I seen that most of the signs said the same thing. "What does your sign mean?" I asked the closest guy. "Fair wages for calm?"

"It ain't 'calm'" he said, "It's C-A-L-N, the Colorado Association of Labor Negotiators. Here, take a brochure."

"Thanks," I said. "What ain't fair?"

"Wages," he said.

"Man, that's the truth. A guy's gotta do three jobs just to pay rent. What do calm guys do?"

"C-A-L-N. It's a union of the guys who negotiate big contracts for labor unions. Finally got smart and formed their own union a couple years ago, but their deal didn't keep up with inflation. So if the union don't come up with a better deal, they're gonna strike."

"How much do they pay you now?"

"Me? I get minimum wage."

"Shoot, that don't seem fair if you gotta negotiate big contracts. I can see how you'd get pissed."

The guy laughed. "I ain't a member. Them guys get paid hundreds of dollars an hour. They can't afford to stand on a sidewalk holding signs."

"So they pay you guys to do it?"

"Sure. The pay ain't great, but it's easy work."

"Seems like a good deal to the guy that hired you if you ask me," I said. "He gets to act all pissed so he can get more money and don't lose a paycheck himself. That ought to be worth about two times minimum wage. Maybe three."

"Yeah, maybe, but I need the work."

"But I bet he needs you even more. What would he say if you guys all got together and said they could carry their own signs if they didn't pay you fair?"

"You mean strike? Against the Union of Labor Negotiators?"

"Maybe you'd get your pictures on TV."

He looked off across the street like he was thinking. "We'd have to form a union," he said, mostly to himself.

"They couldn't hold that against you," I said. "Being union guys theirselves."

"There'd be some irony, wouldn't there?"

"Nah, just wear wrinkled shirts. It don't have to be formal."

"Right."

The whole time we was talking I was watching Mango by looking over at the window and using it as a mirror. He was pretty obvious, watching me in his own window, but I had the edge because he didn't know I figured out he was tailing me. I'd been waiting for Plan C to come to me, and when I said "wrinkled shirt" it come.

"Is there a public restroom in this building?" I asked.

"Yeah, past the guard and down the hall to your left. It's normally locked to keep the street people out, but the CALN guys left it open for us. Just walk right in like you know what you're doing and they won't say a word. If you wear a coat and tie you can pee wherever you want."

"Thanks, man." I said. "Good luck with the negotiations."

He give me a thumbs up and I moved around in the bunch of men 'til I didn't think Mango could see me and quick went inside the building.

Sometimes Plan C is the one that should of been Plan A if you'd thought of it quicker, and this was one of them times. I nodded at the guard behind his desk and walked down the hall to the restroom. There was a sink and a paper towel dispenser and below that was what I wanted: the trash. I pulled the white trash sack out of its spot. There was only a couple paper towels in there, so I just left them in the sack. Then I took off my bald guy wig and my suit coat and my shirt and put them in the sack. I even took off my sunglasses and put them in there too. I looked in the mirror. Now I was a younger guy with long brown hair that was a little messy, wearing a blue T-shirt and carrying a white trash sack. No way Mango would recognize me and he wouldn't be expecting a disguise. Especially not the disguise of just being who I really was. Nobody expects that.

I walked out the front door and started walking back toward the police station. I watched in the windows for a while but Mango never showed up so I turned down a side street and took the long way home. I wasn't taking no chances. If opportunity knocks, you gotta be smart and say who's there? But if you ain't James Bond, and you get lucky on Plan C, it's dumb to push your luck. You push your luck too many times and it's gonna start pushing back. I went home, opened a can of minestrone and went to bed.

201

CHAPTER TWENTY ONE

In which I take on the new case of Dr. Anderson, even if the old case ain't all the way finished.

The next night I decided I should go ahead and start on my next case, which was detecting on Dr. Anderson, even if the Case of the Bones wasn't all the way over. The hardest part was over and the rest was up to the cops. The Case of Dr. Anderson wasn't a real case, since there wasn't no crime involved, but once you got detecting in your blood you can't help yourself. I bet guys who work for the government can't go buy food unless they got three copies of their grocery list with boxes to check by every item and a number two pencil in their pocket and three spares in another pocket. They got that government style in their blood and they ain't got a choice. Me detecting on Dr. Anderson wasn't so much I was sticking my nose in somebody else's business, or being extra curious about Holly's boyfriend, as just that detective blood in my veins leading me down a road the way railroad tracks lead a train.

The hospital had a building right next to it where doctors had offices. Not all the doctors who worked at the hospital did, but it was a good place to start, so I walked over there.

Well, of course it was closed so I couldn't just walk in the front door. That was OK, because I didn't really have a plan. But you don't always need to have a complete plan before you start something, I learned that lesson about a hundred times. The night was a good temperature and I didn't have appointments, so I figured I'd just look at the doctor building and walk around it and see if any ideas come to me. Most of my best plans come to me by poking around like I was on a field trip instead of like I was doing homework. Acting like I was on vacation had become my number one plan in most situations, and it always worked out pretty good for me so I'd be dumb to change.

Even if the building was closed, lights was on in most of the windows and you could see a few people inside, which was probably janitors and repair guys. I made a note of that and kept walking. The rainspouts was extra strong, you could see that right away. It was a sturdy brick building, five stories tall. It was old but real clean and in perfect shape. If I was a doctor I'd have an office in a building like that.

The back of the building had a loading dock and two dumpsters. A big moving truck was backed up to the loading dock. Workmen was unloading file cabinets from the truck onto the dock and using two-wheel dollies to haul them inside. I always liked using a dolly and file cabinets don't weigh much so they're easy. I didn't even notice when I stopped to watch the workmen. Before you know it I was standing right there on the dock talking to the guys as they come out of the building, got a file cabinet, and wheeled it in. There must have been ten guys and some of them worked for the truck company and some for the janitor company because they didn't know each other very much, but they worked together fine. I think the guys who worked for the building thought I was one of the truck guys and the truck guys thought I was a building guy because nobody asked what I was doing or told me to move along.

The youngest guy had trouble with his file cabinets. He looked about high school age. He was skinny with fluffy brown hair like you get when you blow dried it. A couple of times he about lost his balance and nearly dropped the file cabinet on its side. It was lucky the other guys was inside so they didn't joke on him, and it was also lucky I was there to catch it before it fell over. The minute I did I seen what the problem was. These was full file cabinets, so they was pretty heavy and the stuff inside might not be balanced.,

"OK, that ain't your fault," I told him when we got it straightened up again. "These things ain't packed very good. Them older guys should of showed you some tricks. First off, get under the back of it like this. Make sure you got it right in the middle. Then you want to tighten these straps a lot tighter for a full file than a empty one. Like this, see? That was your problem before. Anybody could make that mistake and they should of told you. OK, you take the handles."

The kid took the dolly.

"Now, I'll help tilt it back slow and easy. Use your foot to keep it from rolling backward while we're tilting. You ready?"

He nodded and I tilted it back to him. I was pretty sure he never used a dolly before and this was probably his first job, so that was the main problem. "Lean it back more and it will be easier to balance. Yeah, like that. OK, now I'll walk beside and help you balance it, since this one is extra tricky. If there's any steps or bumps to go over, I think we ought to go backward over them. It's always safer. You ready?"

203

He nodded again and we started walking. He was doing all the work, I just kept one hand on the file cabinet to keep it steady. Mostly he just needed some confidence from practicing. We went in the loading area, and then up an elevator and down a hall. As we was walking, pushing the file cabinet, a janitor came down the hall toward us pushing a cart with cleaning stuff. He was an old black guy with white hair and looked like he ought to be giving a talk at the United Nations instead of pushing a cleaning cart.

"Hang on a second," I said to the kid, and we stopped.

"Excuse me, sir." I said to the janitor. He stopped and give me the kindest smile I ever seen.

"How can I help you gentlemen?" he asked.

"Do you know where Doctor Anderson's office is?"

"Yes, of course. It's number 230. One floor down, third office from the elevator."

"Could you leave that open for us for a few minutes?" I asked.

"Certainly," he said. "But please be careful. Dr. Anderson is very particular."

"Thank you, " I said. "You have a fine evening."

He nodded. "And you as well," he said. Then we all walked away from each other, me and the kid with the file cabinet and him with his janitor cart.

"You don't meet nicer guys than janitors," I told the kid. We got to the office where they was putting file cabinets, which was one big room about half filled full of other files. I helped the kid ease the dolly straight. "Make sure you keep your foot there so it don't roll on you when you set it up, too." I said. "That's the trick. You think you got the next one by yourself?"

"Yeah," he said which was about the first words he said to me. "Thanks."

"No problem," I said. "See you later."

I walked out the door while he was straightening up the strap on his dolly. We had come up the service elevator which was bigger than a regular elevator but not as nice. I didn't want to meet up with any of the other workers, so I took the stairs down.

Sure enough, room 230 had a sign on it that said Dr. Mark Anderson, and the door was unlocked so I went in. I probably should of felt bad for asking that nice janitor to leave it open. I didn't have no official business in there, and he might of thought I did since I was helping to move a file

204

cabinet. If you looked at it one way you might decide I kind of tricked him. I thought about it to see if I did feel bad, but if I did it wasn't a strong enough feeling to notice. I never actually said I was moving anything into that office, so there wasn't an actual technical lie involved. And janitors go into doctors' offices all the time so I wasn't asking him to break no rules. If I was going in there to steal something or break something or find out government secrets, then I'd have to feel bad. Anybody would. But I just wanted to see where Holly's boyfriend worked, and what kind of pictures he had on his desk, and if he had a fish tank or a bird or something. Guys who keep fish tanks and birds is usually pretty interesting so that would make it obvious why Holly liked him. I was just doing ordinary detecting, which don't hurt nobody.

OK, I gotta admit part of me said I was being an idiot going in there. I never expected to even get inside the building on the first night of thinking about it so I didn't have a plan. If I'd got to think about it more I might of decided it wasn't my business to do any detecting on this guy. Some girls get irritated if you poke your nose where it don't belong. And if Dr. Anderson happened to walk in and catch me there he might not be all that delighted himself.

As I stepped in and closed the office door behind me, I decided maybe this was one of my dumbest ideas ever. A real no brainer. But I was already there. I would just stay about one minute, look around, then get out quick. Even if he had a fish tank with red and blue fish and a crawdad on the bottom I wasn't going to let myself get interested in nothing. I had a crawdad in a fish tank once, and they're about the most interesting thing you ever seen, but I don't need to tell you about that right now.

There was two rooms, a waiting room and the doctor room. The hall door opened into the waiting room, which had a desk with a phone and four chairs for visitors and no window. The doctor room was bigger, with two windows and a big desk and bookshelves full of books and a couch for a visitor to sit on. The wall with the windows was made of old bricks and the rest of the walls had dark wood. The carpet was tan and about thick enough you could sleep on it. Since it was an old building the windows was still the old fashioned kind you can open by lifting them. Lots of times they put new style windows in when they fix up old buildings, but these looked pretty cool and it was good they left them. I unlocked one, lifted it up, and stuck my head out of it. There was a nice lawn down below, which would be perfect for landing on. I couldn't help noticing that. I closed the window but didn't lock it, just in case I needed to make a quick getaway.

205

Dr. Anderson had a big leather chair that turned and tilted. I would of liked to sit in it, but that didn't seem right so I didn't. That wasn't my chair and I didn't want to get the janitor in trouble who let me in.

There was some pictures on the desk. Mostly they was of a guy who looked like a doctor. About 40 years old, skinny, with a doctor tan. His brown and gray hair was cut extra neat. In some pictures he was playing tennis, but in other ones he was with a lady and two little girls which you had to guess was his wife and kids.

That made me feel dumb, as you can see. If this guy had a wife and kids he wasn't Holly's boyfriend. Lots of guys have the name Anderson, so obviously I was in the wrong Dr. Anderson's office. I had to admit I hadn't thought up my plan very good. But sometimes you think you're doing something for one reason when really it's for a whole different reason. Maybe I did all this detecting just to help that kid with the file cabinet. Maybe I'd never know.

It was like fishing. I didn't get too many fishing trips with my dad, but I remember him showing me how to use his fly rod. We was standing in the middle of a cold stream and the sun was going down so the water looked like it had red and yellow food coloring in it swirling around. You could see round rocks on the bottom, some with green slime, but I didn't see no fish. The main fishing line was thick and green and there was thin clear leader line tied to the end of it, and the fly was way at the end of that. When I threw out the line, I seen the knot at the end of the main green line, so I kept watching that. I never seen a trout grab at it, which they wouldn't of, since it was just a knot in green line and not the fly. When my dad figured out what I was doing, he laughed and put his hand on my shoulder and said, "Jumper, when you throw your line out, it goes a lot farther than you think." So then I started watching for fish way out there past the green knot, out where I thought the end of that invisible leader line might be, and caught me a fish. I never seen the fly, but when I seen a fish come to the top of the water way out there, I pulled on the pole and got him. Every Saturday I make a point to remember that day. I don't ever want to lose a day like that.

So maybe I was in that doctor office for a reason that was past the part of the line I could see, and past the knot, and out at the end of that invisible leader line. Or maybe it was just a dumb mistake. Either way, it was even dumber to stay there, so I turned off the light and locked the door behind me when I left.

206

CHAPTER TWENTY TWO

Even doctors got to take their consequences, and the art therapy business goes big time

The next Tuesday night I brought a whole stack of typing paper to Greg's room and four new pencils all sharpened, plus one of them little plastic pencil sharpeners for him to keep. I decided to leave Bart at home, since him and Greg didn't hit it off as good as Linda and him did. I also didn't bring my camera of squirrels. Me giving Greg art lessons was sort of the excuse for me to go there and visit more than I thought I could turn him into Rembrandt or Dali Lama or some other artist you might of heard of. I put the paper and stuff in my backpack and left the Nike bag home too.

I got to the hospital twenty minutes early, since I didn't get distracted on the way. That was happening more times lately. I was interested in the place I was going to so much I didn't notice as much on the way. I was getting a lot better at thinking about important stuff and not so much about my own life, which was kind of fun and saved a lot of time. Obviously it was easier for me than most people, since I was going to a hospital. I was going to draw pencil pictures with a kid who had an interesting way of looking at things and wasn't shy about saying his opinions, but who was also a lot like me since we done the same sport. Plus I might get to have coffee with Holly, who was still my friend even if she had a boyfriend. And there ain't many places as interesting as a hospital, you can't argue that one. I had to rank going to the hospital to see Greg and Holly right up about the same level as going to the zoo on a rainy day or going to traffic court when it was busy, which was two of my favorite places.

Since I was early, I decided to go to Holly's nurse station first to see if this was a good night for coffee later on. Girls like it when they got a plan.

But I stopped in the hall before I got to the nurse station because I seen Holly was talking to Dr. Anderson, the one whose office I went to. I couldn't tell what they was saying, but I didn't want to interrupt hospital business, so I stayed in the hall until they was done. Him being there was a odd coincidence. I'd already decided her boyfriend was a whole different Doctor Anderson, but this was sure the same one who I seen in the tennis pictures. They was talking about some papers Holly was holding and he

207

was standing about as close to her as a boyfriend would to read them. He had a big smile on his face but Holly didn't look too happy. He put his hand on her back, pretty casual, which should not of bothered me but I gotta admit it did. You could see her shoulders go up a little like she was tensing them. He kept smiling and pointing to something on the paper, but while he did the hand he had on her back started moving around in a little circle.

Sometimes you see girls like that kind of thing and sometimes they don't. Holly pulled away from him and you could tell this was a time she didn't like it. That was a good clue, but it could of meant several things. It might of meant that he wasn't paying enough attention to the papers. Even Juliet would of got pissed if Romeo was thinking about getting friendlier when she wanted him to look at papers. Or it could of meant they had a fight and she was just pissed at him in general and she'd be mad even if he was trying to give her a ruby necklace. Any of those was good explanations if they was going steady but having a fight. If they was going steady, then the pictures in his office was probably of him and his sister and her daughters. Or maybe he was divorced, which a lot of people are. But no matter what the deal was, she kept moving away and he kept smiling and moving closer and it wasn't making her happy.

Or me either. If she wanted to go steady with a doctor that was her business. But if a guy don't even know how lucky he is, then he's gonna have to take his consequences even if he was the number one doctor in the world. Since I didn't know what they was fighting about it wasn't my business to help them negotiate a peace treaty. But I could probably interrupt the fight. I walked toward them.

"Holly," I said before I got there and it come out louder than I expected it to. The doctor looked up, surprised at my voice and stepped back from her.

"Jumper!" she said and the way she smiled made me know she was happy to see me. She tossed her pony tail like she was shaking flies out of it. "You're early."

"Thanks," I said. It was nice of her to remember when I was going to visit Greg. "But I don't want to interrupt hospital business."

"Not at all. In fact, I was hoping to talk with you after your appointment."

"My schedule looks pretty open," I said. I looked at the doctor.

"Good," she said. "Jumper, this is Mark Anderson. He's a doctor here, and he was just leaving."

I reached out my hand to shake his. He was watching my face trying to figure out exactly who I was, but Holly beat him to the punch. "Jumper is consulting with some of our patients. He's an art therapy counselor, and has had remarkable success."

"Is that right?" he said, but it wasn't a voice that meant "hey that's cool" but more a voice like he didn't believe her. He reached his hand out too. I gotta admit I wasn't thinking joyful Sunday school thoughts about him, but I didn't let on. Well, maybe I squeezed his hand a little tighter than a normal friendly handshake because his eyes got bigger.

"I wouldn't ever say Nurse Holly was wrong about something," I said. "Would you?"

You could tell he was ready for the handshake to be over before I was, but there wasn't much he could do about it. When you climb trees and downspouts every single day you get pretty strong hands. I didn't crush his hand or nothing, and I was trying to like him since most of the clues was pointing to him being Holly's boyfriend. But part of me wanted to pick him up and throw him out a window.

"Of course not," he said. "Holly is a very special person."

When he said that I remembered I was shaking his hand and let go of it.

"I'm sure you two have art therapy to discuss," he said. He looked at Holly. "We'll continue our conversation tomorrow."

"That conversation is over," she said.

He just smiled and walked away.

"He seems like a nice guy," I said. Sometimes you gotta say white lies about someone's girlfriend or boyfriend.

"No he doesn't," she said. "Coffee in the cafeteria at about ten?"

"You bet."

"Great. I'll stop into Greg's room at five 'till."

Then she walked off.

I went back down the hall toward Greg's room. Part of me was sad that Holly and her boyfriend was having a fight because she was my friend. But another part of me was whistling a happy song for no real good reason.

Greg looked about the same as last time. His legs was still in casts and hung up in the air with straps. He didn't look that happy to see me, but it didn't bother me. I already knew we was going to be friends since we was both jumpers. If you know somebody's going to be your friend, you don't worry too much about some challenges getting there.

"Hey there, Mr. Sunshine," I said as I walked into his room.

"Oh shirt, not the retard," he said. "I'd convinced myself you were just a bad dream."

"That's me all right," I said, playing along with his joke. "I'm just a bad bologna sandwich come back to remind you about lunch. But you know what nurse Holly just called me? A art therapy consultant. Ain't that something?"

"Something. Right. It's another way to say 'bad bologna sandwich.'"

I laughed at that one. "You're pretty funny, Mr. Sunshine. I know you ain't that crazy about me being here, which is cool. But then, you don't seem that crazy about much stuff. Am I right?"

"My life is shirt. I hate my life. I wish I was dead. Do you understand any of those? Do any of those words penetrate your Neanderthal skull?"

"Cool. We agree then. You ain't crazy about a lot of stuff. But did you ever rate the stuff you hate?"

He leaned forward and said the next words real slow, one at a time, like he thought I couldn't hear too good. "I. Hate. My. Life. All of it. Life sucks."

I had to laugh at that one too, and give him a friendly slap on one of his casts.

"Ouch!" he yelled. "Darn it to bell you mother fluffing shirt eating son of a bleach. What the fluff do you think you're doing?"

"Art therapy," I said. "I hope that wasn't rude."

"Rude! You mother fluffing…"

So I slapped his cast again and he yelled again.

"I forgot to mention that I ain't a big fan of the salty talk." He opened his mouth again, I raised my hand, he closed his mouth.

"See, I figure there's lots of things you could be doing in the next hour. You ever talk to a social worker?"

"Biggest losers on…"

"Right. That ain't one of my favorites either. Did you ever have a doctor stick his hand up your butt for an exam? I ain't had that either, but I can already say that one ranks pretty unfavorable." I leaned forward and whispered the next stuff in case anyone was outside the door listening.

"Ever had people ask how come you jump? Did they ever try to cure you?" He just stared at me. I think he was mostly nervous I'd hit his cast again, but I could tell people talked to him about jumping all the time and he didn't like it.

"There you go," I said. "I ain't gonna try to cure you from jumping. I ain't gonna stick my hand up your butt. And as long as I'm in here and we're doing art therapy, no doctor is coming in here, and no social workers."

Then I had a thought.

"You got parents?" I asked.

"Sure. Everybody's got parents. Their whole mission in life is to tell me what to do, tell me how I screwed up. They exist to make me miserable."

I was so surprised at that comment there wasn't nothing I could say. I stared at him for a minute, but his face was just mad and he didn't see how what he said might seem weird to someone else. When I couldn't think of nothing to say I got up and went to the window for a minute.

There was clouds in the sky and I couldn't see no stars, which made me sad all of a sudden. Greg didn't mean nothing by what he said, he was just being a kid. Only never in a million years would I have thought up the idea that somebody could have both their parents alive and not count that as a lucky part of their life. But it wasn't my business and he was still my friend even if he didn't know he was lucky. I just needed to take a minute before I'd be ready for an art lesson. I stood and looked out the window.

Most nights if it's cloudy I know it's just one night and it ain't better or worse than a clear night. I like to look at the clouds. They're extra mysterious at night. But looking out that window, I gotta admit, I kept looking at all the parts of the sky in case the clouds had a hole in them. Then I seen one, a hole where the wind blew the clouds apart. In the middle of that there was a big old star winking at me.

"Hi, dad," I whispered. I felt better so I went back to Greg.

211

"OK, so you got issues with your parents. I bet while you're having art therapy lessons Holly would even keep your parents out. So maybe sitting with a pencil and paper ain't your number one thing. But it ain't as bad as some stuff, so it seems like a pretty good deal."

He was watching me careful. "What if I don't want to draw?

"Nobody likes to draw all the time," I said. "I can't hold that against you. But if you got paper in front of you and you're holding a pencil, then doctors and social workers and parents can't come in and make you do something worse. You can be safe."

"What's in it for you?"

That was a good question, and I hadn't ever thought about it from that side. I sure couldn't tell him about playing Dr. Hudson, because it was against the rules and because he'd think it was dumb. I had to think of some answer that a mad kid might understand. So I said the next idea that come into my brain.

"Well, when we're done, nurse Holly said we could have coffee together in the cafeteria..."

He looked at me for a second and then he busted out laughing. That surprised me, cause he didn't seem like the laughing kind of guy, but he thought something was a pretty good joke.

"You do like her!" he said between laughs. "Dr. Bad Bologna thinks he's got a shot with the hot nurse!"

Well, that wasn't how I'd been thinking of it, but if somebody figures out an answer they like they don't keep asking more questions so I let him think he was right.

"I guess you got me there, Sunshine. Maybe you got me figured out better than I thought."

"Dr. Bologna putting the moves on the hot nurse— watching that train wreck would be worth the price of the ticket. Hand me some paper, oh great art therapy master counselor."

I handed him a clipboard with about 20 sheets of clean paper and two sharp pencils. I had a clipboard and paper and pencil myself in case I had an idea to draw something.

"OK, everybody's got their own process," I said. "And I ain't gonna tell you what to do. It would be better art therapy if you drew something, but

212

it's up to you. You just keep the paper in front of you in case someone comes in." He put the clipboard in one hand and held the pencil in the other.

"I don't feel inspired," he said.

"Inspiration is for sissies," I said.

"I don't know what to draw," he said. He put down the clipboard and pencil and reached for his video game. But I was quicker and took it away before he got it. Then I sat back down.

"Well, that ain't my problem. I ain't gonna tell you what to draw, and I ain't gonna sprinkle magic inspiration powder on you and I ain't gonna pay you a million dollars for something my turtle could draw. You're on your own, Pinocchio. It's up to you if you want to be a real boy instead of a wooden one. I got my own drawings to do." I thought for a minute about what to draw. "I think I'm gonna draw me a pair of sneakers."

"Sneakers?"

"Yeah, I think so. But they'd be tricky to do from memory. I had some brand new sneakers once and they felt so good I never even noticed I was wearing them. Then these gang guys beat me up and swiped them right off my feet. I had to walk home barefooted. I never noticed how good them shoes felt, but I sure noticed how bad it felt not to have them. I'm going to draw sneakers."

He stared at me like I was crazy.

"It's OK," I said. "You go ahead and draw a blank sheet of paper. I ain't gonna give you grades." He just turned his head away, so I gave his cast one more good whack. He yelled, but when I lifted my hand again he picked up the clipboard and pencil like he was going to draw.

I gotta admit I felt better after I give him that last whack. We didn't say nothing else for an hour. And I drew my favorite pair of sneakers from memory.

I didn't pay much attention to time and the next thing I knew Holly was coming in the door. She stared at Greg for a minute before she said anything. He was busy drawing and didn't even notice. She turned to me.

"Are you ready?" she asked.

"You bet," I said. "That was an excellent session, Mr. Sunshine."

"Whatever." He didn't even look up. But it sure looked like he was drawing.

213

"OK, I'm going to leave extra paper here on your table in case you want to do homework art assignments. But if you do more pencil drawings, you don't need to show them to anybody if you don't want. You can tell your parents that was part of the rules. I'll see you next Tuesday."

He didn't even say "whatever" so Holly and me walked out the door and went to the elevator. Neither one of us said nothing, which I already explained don't bother me much. Once inside the elevator she stared straight ahead.

"What did you do to him?"

"I didn't do nothing," I said, but I was afraid she might be referring to me hitting his cast. Hospitals probably got rules about that one too, and maybe she heard him yell.

"You were in there two hours and neither one of you were screaming by the end. That's a new world record."

"I ain't that much of a screamer..." I said.

"And he was actually drawing!"

"Well, him and me got a lot in common."

"Right."

We didn't say nothing else when we got off the elevator and walked to the cafeteria. Holly had bought my coffee the last time, so I bought hers this time. She tried to pay, but I put my foot down on that idea.

"OK," Holly said when I gave the cafeteria lady my money. "I guess it's OK to let an art therapy counselor buy me coffee." We walked to a table and sat down.

"You bet," I said. "It's about the best job I ever had. The hours are perfect, and you meet interesting clients. Plus, it's got about the most grown up sounding name of any job I ever had."

She laughed. "You didn't mention the pay."

"You can't judge a job by its pay," I said. "That'd be about the last reason to pick a job."

"You're right about that," she said. "But there are only so many hours in a week and everyone needs to use some of them to make money. Would it completely ruin art therapy for you if you got paid to do it?"

I laughed at that joke.

"No, really, I'm serious," she said. "If someone said they'd pay you money to spend two hours a week with Greg doing whatever you wanted, would that make it seem like a chore?"

Now I seen she was serious, so I didn't laugh. Some people like to play a game of questions, like what would you do if you was President, or what three things would you take to a desert island, which I always answered, "I'd take Gilligan and Ginger and Mary Ann." Them games are pretty fun so I played along.

"Well, if there was a lot of rules to the job, I wouldn't like it. Like if I had to teach him to draw the Mona Lisa or something, that wouldn't be my favorite. But if it was just hanging out and drawing with no rules they'd have to pay me a lot of money before I'd let that ruin it into being work."

"How about fifty dollars?"

"Well, that's a whole day working cleaning apartments or maybe three days of picking up cans. So it ain't a fair example."

"It's not an example," she said. She reached into her purse and pulled out a fifty dollar bill. "Greg's parents are rich. They buy him video games, DVD's, computers– whatever he wants. They pay hundreds of dollars a month for medicine and nothing works. I told them about you and they said if you could keep Greg calm for two hours they'd pay you fifty dollars. Every week." She slid the bill across the table in front to me and picked up her coffee cup. She watched me over the top of the cup and her eyes were smiling. I just stared at the bill, then looked up at her, then back down at the bill.

"So, Greg gets his being crazy from his parents," I said. They was obviously lunatics.

Holly laughed. "I guess we all do. What do you say?"

I looked at that fifty dollar bill some more. I ain't never made fifty bucks for two hours work in my life, but something bothered me and I didn't know how to say it without sounding dumb.

"What about hospital rules?"

"Hospital rules? I don't see how it's any of the hospital's business who Greg's parents ask to visit him."

"I don't mean that. I mean like if they have rules about interesting conflicts, or staff associations... you know."

215

She turned her head sideways and looked at my face like I was talking French and she didn't understand. But I didn't know how to say it better. Then her face lit up.

"You mean me? You're worried we'd be breaking some rule if we had coffee together if were both sort of working here?"

"Well, yeah, I guess that would be one way to say it."

She smiled and turned away to look at the floor next to her chair. Then she looked back at me with a kind of teasing look.

"And what if they did?" she asked. "What if you had to choose?"

I put my finger on top of the fifty dollar bill and slid it back across the table to her. "I already got plenty of money," I said.

Holly smiled and her face got red and she bit her lip. Then she put her finger on top of the bill and slid it back to me.

"That's sweet," she said. "And very mature. I wish more men at this hospital were as mature as you. I didn't mean to embarrass you. But there aren't any rules like that. We can have coffee whenever we want to and no one can say a thing about it."

Obviously I wanted to switch the conversation away from that direction before my face got hot.

"OK, but Greg and me wouldn't get very friendly if we got interrupted. He's got this cool gang-guy act he likes to play for grown ups and it takes him a while to forget to play it. So would it be OK if nobody come into his room during our appointments? I mean, no doctors, no parents, or nobody else."

"I'm sure I can arrange that. What else?"

"Well, I ain't very qualified. I ain't got a degree and I ain't practiced up as a artist. It seems like for fifty bucks you could get the best artist in Denver. So how come you're asking me?"

She thought about it for a minute. I liked it that she mostly waited until she knew what she wanted to say before she said it. Lots of people start talking about two minutes before they started thinking of what to say.

"Here's the thing," she said. "Little boys want other people to take care of them. Men want to take care of themselves. Mature men," she stopped and thought of a better way to say it. "Full grown men want to take care of the people they care about. That's just the way they're programmed. They move from child to man to father. But some get stuck along the way. Greg's

216

stuck. Part of him still wants the world to take care of him. But another part knows he should be starting to take care of himself. He just doesn't know how. Those two parts are fighting inside him. He hasn't even started to think about taking care of someone else. He's at an age where he could use an older brother, a man who isn't his father, to guide him through his confusion. You'd be a perfect older brother."

"What about Dr. Anderson?" I asked. I hadn't meant to say that but it's what I was thinking about.

"What about him?"

"Will he mind if we have coffee?" I know some boyfriends are pretty jealous.

She looked off in the distance and her face got blank and her voice got soft. "Dr. Anderson is a harassing pestilence, an abomination of all that is holy on God's green earth. No, he won't say a word."

Well, I never heard her use that much big words at one time before, and they wasn't words I used myself, but it was pretty clear what she meant: she was in love with Dr. Anderson, and if you use that much big words you probably aim at getting married to the guy.

I had some mixed feelings about that. If Holly's boyfriend didn't mind us drinking coffee, that was good and went on the side with reasons to take the money and give art therapy lessons. As a business decision, it would be dumb to miss being friends with the only other jumper I ever met just because his parents wanted to dump a bucket of money on my head. I picked up the fifty and put it in my shirt pocket. The mixed feelings was that, if I had to tell the whole truth, I'd say that some little tiny part of me, a part so small you couldn't even see it if you didn't have a microscope, that little part maybe wanted to keep pretending Holly and me was on a date when we had coffee. Also, I had the thought that her boyfriend might not be as understanding as she thought, so no matter if her opinion was different right now, he could get pissed at her, and then she'd get pissed at me. I seen it lots of times with girls and their boyfriends. They always think they know them better than it turns out they do.

But that was a whole separate issue. I picked up my coffee and took a drink. One thing I like about hospitals is that they got great coffee.

"I guess I'm a art therapy counselor," I said.

"Good," she said. "Now that that's settled, what do you think about the rookies the Broncos drafted?"

217

"I ain't never seen that fast of runners at safety," I said. Right away, I felt myself relax when we started talking about more ordinary stuff. "And we got two of them. If we can just get through the preseason and then the regular season, and then the playoffs, I figure we're going to the Superbowl."

She laughed at that joke, which you would not get if you don't watch football. "Me too," she said. And then we had a nice talk about football until her break was over.

There ain't much wrong with a night like that.

CHAPTER TWENTY THREE

Roses in pencil

The next Tuesday night I got to the hospital early again, but this time I didn't go looking for Holly. Instead I went straight to Greg's room even if I was early. I figured he didn't have a full schedule of events and for fifty bucks I wanted to make sure his parents got their money's worth.

I brought a whole package of typing paper, which is 500 sheets, and some extra pencils. I also had bought a red rose. If you were stuck in a hospital room without stuff to draw it would be a good model, plus people bring flowers to people in hospitals all the time so nobody would think it was weird if Greg had one in there. Roses seemed to last pretty good in water, so it was a no brainer choice. But it was another reason I didn't go looking for Holly first. If she seen me with a rose she might think I was bringing it to her since I knew she liked them, but it would seem weird to her if somebody besides Dr. Anderson give her flowers, so there would be explaining to do. I always get in the most trouble when I have to explain stuff, so to be safe I decided to just skip that part.

"Hello, Mr. Sunshine," I said when I walked into Greg's room. "I brought you some stuff."

"Well, if it ain't Dr. Bad Bologna. I didn't expect to see you again."

I laughed at that. "You ain't getting rid of me that easy. I think I already told you that line. Didn't I tell you we was going to be best friends?"

"I hoped you were lying." He looked at the rose. "I don't care how many flowers you bring me, you'll never defeat my virtue," he said. "You got a better shot with the hot nurse."

That cracked me up again.

"Don't be so sure," I said. "I got lots of hidden charms."

"Very well hidden."

"You're too skinny for me anyway," I said. "Plus, I ain't a big fan of guys with a belt buckle in their nose." I stuck the flower in a plastic water bottle he had by his bed. "They got lots of these, they'll give you another one for drinking. The rose is for drawing."

"Right. You want me to draw a red rose with a pencil. You don't see any problem with that plan, Mr. Art Therapy Counselor?"

I stopped and thought about it for a minute.

"No, it's a pretty good plan. I don't see no hidden flaws."

"I got one clue for you, Dr. Bologna Brain: Color. The rose is red."

"It's a cool color of red, ain't it? I almost went with a yellow one, but I think this one's better."

"Focus with me here, if you understand the word. Roses are red. And pencils are black." He stopped like he was waiting.

"I'm with you so far," I said.

"So nobody but an idiot would use a pencil to draw a rose."

I waited in case he had more to say, but when I seen he was done, I started laughing.

"You should have a TV show," I said. "You're funnier than lots of the guys even on cable stations."

"So you are an idiot."

I seen then that he wasn't joking so I felt bad I laughed at him.

"OK, I see your point," I said. "I gotta admit you're right. You could do a better rose if you had colors. I shouldn't of laughed at your opinion, especially since it's a good one." I sat for a minute trying to think of how I could make it so he was right and I was right too without making him feel dumb, which nobody likes. It seemed an easy problem to me, but he was looking at it some whole different way I never thought of, which is usually how arguments get started. Even if I knew I was right, the point was for me to be like a big brother, not for him to feel bad we had different opinions. It was a tricky problem. Finally I had a idea.

I pulled the rose out of the glass and water dripped off it.

"It's wet," I said.

"Yeah, water will do that."

"But the pencil ain't wet. Even if it was a red pencil that drawing wouldn't be wet, so we couldn't do it. Ain't that the way you'd have to look at it? "

"A little advice, Bologna: I don't think you're a guy who should try to play word games."

I stuck the rose under his nose.

"Smells good, too, don't it?"

He pulled his face away. "It smells like crap. Smells like an old lady's perfume."

"Yeah, I smelled some old ladies before too. By your idea it would be dumb to take a camera picture if it wasn't going to smell."

"Like I said, you're an idiot."

Just then some skinny little guy come right into the room in a green hospital outfit and started emptying the trash. It surprised the heck out of me and also kind of pissed me off.

"Excuse me," I said, as polite as I could. "We're having a art therapy session here."

"I'll be done in a minute," he said in a kind of disrespectful voice. Then he kept on cleaning. He obviously just didn't understand. So I tried again with a different sentence, but still in my politest voice.

"Nobody's supposed to come in here while we're doing a session. It was part of the rules."

"I said I'd be done in a minute!" he said, and this time he sounded pissed, like I was the one breaking rules. He kept on emptying trash and wiping off stuff.

Well, I couldn't believe he was going to break rules right there in front of me. Greg was kind of smiling while he watched, which pissed me off as much as the cleaning kid did. But you got to try to be polite to people even if they're breaking rules, so I used the line people used on me a lot when they thought I was loitering.

"I'm sorry, but I'm going to have to ask you to leave."

He looked right at me and said "Fluff you," and then he just kept picking up stuff. Greg was snickering from the bed, but I wasn't paying much attention to him. My face was getting hot and my ears was buzzing. I sat there for a minute, nodding my head and trying to think about art. But there wasn't much art thoughts in my brain.

Then I stood up. The hospital guy was facing away from me, cleaning stuff off a counter. I walked up behind him. He was small like a girl, and I sure didn't want to hurt anybody, so I put my left hand in my jeans pocket. Then before he knew what was happening, I wrapped my right arm around his waist and picked him up. The way I done it, his right arm was trapped next to his body, but his left arm was free to wave around, which it did a lot. He yelled once too, out of surprise, but I squeezed him tighter and shook him a little and said, "Be quiet. This is a hospital," and he did. He wasn't that heavy, so it was like having a big sack of potatoes under one arm. He tried to punch me, which was only fair, but I ignored that and carried him over to Greg.

"I promised this young man that no one would come in during art classes. You made me break my promise. So now you need to apologize to him."

Greg's mouth had come open and kind of hung there like a fish while he stared at the hospital guy. It was like he never seen somebody get picked up before and thought I was doing some magic trick or something. The hospital guy tried to hit me some more, so I squeezed him again and shook him up and down a couple of times. He wiggled around like a earthworm, or a kid getting tickled, but he finally got the idea that he wasn't getting away and that I was being as gentle on him as I could, but if I decided to throw him out the window there wasn't much he could do about it. And if he squirmed too much I might use both hands on him, even if that didn't seem fair. So after a minute he settled down and just hung there not moving too much.

"I'm... I'm sorry."

"That's good. Now Greg, you got to be a gentleman and accept his apology." Greg just kept staring like a fish. I got a bad itch on the back of my head, so I took my left hand out of my pocket, scratched it then put it back. That seemed to wake up Greg.

"Sure, whatever," he said. I turned to the guy I was holding.

"OK, now you go find nurse Holly and have her explain the rules to you again. Will you do that?"

"Yes. Nurse Holly."

I carried him over to the door. He didn't seem interested in trying to hit me much any more.

"Before I let you go, I'm gonna give you some free advice. Sunshine, this might be useful for you to listen to too. You ever heard the one about don't point a gun at someone unless you're ready to shoot?"

He didn't say nothing, so I shook him a little again to get his attention.

"Yes. Yes, of course I've heard that."

222

"Well, words is kind of like that. In here, people are pretty nice, but outside, if you tell somebody "fluff you" some guys think of it as an invitation. You're pretty lucky you ain't my type, but sometime you might not be so lucky. Before you tell somebody "let's dance," you better be sure you're ready to put on one of them little ballet skirts and spend the weekend dancing. You see what I'm saying?"

He nodded, so I put him down, and he went out the door pretty fast. I went back to my chair and sat down. My face wasn't hot any more. Greg was looking at me harder than usual.

"Anybody could get confused about the rules," I said. "Now where was we?"

Greg didn't say nothing. He just kept looking at me like I beamed in from a Star Trek space ship. Greg staring was maybe better than Greg talking, so I just went on.

"Oh yeah. Drawing roses in pencil." I thought for a minute. Greg would make a joke on pretty much anything somebody said if they stretched the facts to sound smart. My best bet was the truth.

"They're what I got, that's the main answer. I ain't got colored pencils, or crayons, and I ain't never gonna be so rich I could buy paints even if I knew what to do with them. I also ain't got wings or fairy dust, which I notice you ain't got either. What I got is pencils. You make art with what you got.

"But that's just the 'making' part of art. The way you look at it is just as important as what it is. After it's done you can add whatever you want, and if you want your rose to be red when you look at it, I ain't gonna stop you. If you want it to be just a bunch of black lines on a piece of paper, hey, it's your life." I picked up my clipboard and my pencil.

"Now, I'm going to draw me a rose. Mine is going to be orange and purple, and it's gonna smell like a Thanksgiving dinner, and it's gonna be as slippery as wet grass, and it's gonna sound like a choir practicing in a big empty church." I looked into the distance like some fancy artist would when a great idea was coming to him. "Oh yeah. And mine is going to be as warm as a bathtub full of bubbles on a Saturday night. But you can draw yours however you want. Oh, wait, I forgot. You only got a pencil."

I started drawing the rose. It ain't never as easy to draw one without something to trace, like my camera of squirrels made, so I had to expect it wouldn't be as good as my other ones. But maybe it would be even more

223

modern, which some people like, so that was OK too. Even if it didn't turn out good, it was nice to sit there with Greg and do something. Sometimes it's even better to sit with someone and do something than it is to sit with them and do nothing, which I already explained I don't mind either. He just watched me for a while until he figured out I wasn't going to give him a assignment or rules. Then he picked up his clip board and pencil and started drawing too.

We was probably drawing like that for a half hour when he finally said something.

"Maybe you got a shot with the hot nurse after all," he said.

I didn't say nothing back for a while. If it takes a guy a half hour to say something it would be mean to answer right away so he had to think up something again. Anyway, I didn't know exactly what to answer.

Finally I said, "I think she's going to marry Dr. Anderson."

This time he answered right away.

"Bull hockey. Why do you think that?"

"Just something I heard."

"Well, maybe one of them thinks they're going to get married, but I guarantee that both of them don't. Plus, she said she had a job offer in Cleveland and I don't think Dr. Horn Dog Anderson has any plans to move."

"She's moving?" I said. It felt like he punched me in the stomach.

"Maybe. I don't think she's decided yet. She wasn't really talking to me. But I hear more than people think I do."

"She's moving?"

"Ask her yourself. Cleveland's got good hospitals and a good football team."

"No they ain't. They just got the Browns." I wasn't really thinking quite full speed. I looked around the room like I was on a rowboat ready to tie my rope to the dock only the dock had disappeared and there was just water everywhere. Nothing looked familiar and I was paddling in circles. "Why would she move to Cleveland?"

"Why would anybody? Don't go picking up some intern and throwing him out the window, Bologna Brain. All I said was that I heard she got a job offer."

"Do you think Dr. Anderson's moving there too? Is that why she's moving?"

He stared at me for a while.

"Why yes, Sherlock, that must be it. She's fallen head over heels in love with one of the top doctors in the region and he's going to run off with her to live in a mud hut in Cleveland and teach basket weaving to the natives. It's all so obvious."

"It is?"

"No, Bologna. This is a severe case of unrequited lust. I think Cleveland is a last resort."

"Right," I said, but I didn't get exactly what he was saying and there wasn't a way to ask without him making more jokes on it. I was pretty sure there wasn't many resorts in Cleveland because they don't have an ocean. So some of what he was saying was jokes, and maybe all of it was.

"It ain't my business anyway. I ain't her father or something."

"Duh. It doesn't take a DNA test to prove that. She doesn't look at all like a moose."

I had to laugh at that one too, but I wasn't in a mood to laugh real strong. And then we just drew.

When it was 10:00 I went down to Holly's nurse station and told her I was too tired to have coffee. That was a sort of a pink lie, since I wasn't that tired and I didn't fib to make her feel better which would of been a white lie. She give me another fifty dollar bill, and I thanked her of course, and then I left.

The whole truth was it was just confusing to hang out with her when she was in love with Dr. Anderson, but if Greg was right, he didn't love her. Once she figured that out, she'd get her heart broke, which I seen lots of times. Maybe she already figured it out and didn't want to stay working in the same place if he wasn't going to marry her. Or maybe Greg only heard part of the story and Dr. Anderson was the one moving and she was moving out there to be with him. So all the choices was bad from my side. Being heart broke is worse than the flu and lasts a lot longer, and there ain't much you can do once you got it except drink beer in bars and listen to sad country songs. Which I could not see Holly doing on purpose too many times before she just shot herself for relief.

225

My problem was this. Holly said that full grown men do stuff for other people, like a father. And my dad had sure been like that, so I think she was right. I always wanted to be like dad, and I wanted to be full grown, so if there was a way I could keep Holly from getting a broke heart and having to listen to country songs I sure wanted to do that. Anyone would. And the way to do that was to make sure Dr. Anderson loved her back and wanted to marry her, even if it meant she moved to a town whose team was in a whole other division.

On the other hand, I wasn't Dr. Anderson's biggest fan and part of me wished he would just fall in a volcano. But that ain't a mature attitude.

The other problem was that it's pretty hard to convince somebody to get married and you're about as likely to piss them off from trying. If I pissed off Dr. Anderson, then he'd tell Holly and she'd hate me forever, plus be heart broke. I got to admit, I liked Holly pretty much even if I pretended to Greg I didn't. If I screwed this up, I'd lose Holly and I'd probably lose my art therapy gig, and there was probably some beer and country songs at the end of that road for me, too.

But I put my foot down on even thinking about that. The thing that was important was saving Holly from a broke heart and if I screwed it up I'd just have to take my consequences.

I was going to have to pay Dr. Anderson a visit.

CHAPTER TWENTY FOUR

In which I use my negotiating skills to fix things between Holly and Dr. Anderson

I thought about visiting Dr. Anderson every day for six days, but every time I did there was a really good reason it wasn't the right day. For one thing, I had to practice saying something that wouldn't piss him off and my ideas for that kept changing. Then I thought he was probably pretty busy with appointments so maybe I should call his office first, only I didn't know his number and I didn't have a phone.

But the big opera star voice reason? I just didn't want to do it. I could make up stuff all day long as reasons, but if the judge looked me straight in the eye and said, "Young man, is there something else the court should know?" I'd have to say I wished that there was some way I could get out of doing it. The odds was pretty good that Holly was going to get her heart broke no matter what I did. There was three ways it could work out:

One way was for me to do nothing. In that case, her heart got broke but I was just an innocent bystander and she could cry on my shoulder if she wanted to, or I could listen to sad country songs with her until she felt better.

The second way, if I tried to help but screwed it up, she'd get her heart broke anyway, her boyfriend would get pissed off at me, and she'd see me as the reason and hate me forever.

The third way, if I didn't screw up and done my very best diplomat talking, then Dr. Anderson would remember how much he really loved her, she'd marry him and they'd live happily ever after, maybe in Cleveland. And I'd be trying to cheer up Willie Nelson all by myself.

So the best thing for me was to do nothing, which is also the easiest thing. But the best thing for Holly was for me to try and fix it. I couldn't think of no alternatives to that and, when you put it that way, I had to do the grown up thing. I had to convince Dr. Anderson to marry Holly. And it had to seem like his own idea.

So on Monday at noon I walked over to the doctor office building. Doctors love to eat lunch at restaurants, so I figured I could catch him coming out of his building and it would be real casual, like an accident, that I run into him. I could walk along with him to his lunch and while we was walking I could casually mention what a neat woman Holly was, and how lucky he was to know somebody like her, and maybe give him the hint that she liked roses. That way, even if he didn't get the hint, then we'd be buddies and I could accidentally run into him a few days later, maybe at a golf course, and give him more hints. In my brain, it worked pretty smooth and I could see Jim Rockford doing it easy, or even James Bond. There didn't seem to be no hidden flaws no matter how I looked at it, so I stood outside his building and waited for him to come out.

I was thinking so hard about my plan that I didn't see Dr. Anderson come out of the building until he was already a half a block down the sidewalk. As soon as I seen him I started walking after him. My first thought was, OK that plan didn't work so I should just forget the whole deal, which is how some people treat all their plans. But I ain't like that, which is probably how come I'm pretty successful at things. I just needed to walk after him until I caught him and then act like it was an accident and start the plan over from that part. But I needed to come up with a new first line, since I was going to say, "Hey, ain't you Dr. Anderson whom I met at the hospital. Is your office in this building?" only now he wasn't by that building any more, he was on the next block, so I couldn't use the line.

I stayed about twenty-five feet behind him and kept trying out new lines in my head. None of them seemed too good. So then I thought, OK, I'll just go into the same restaurant as him and if he ain't meeting some other doctor I'll say, "Hey, ain't you Dr. Anderson whom I met at the hospital? Can I buy you lunch?" That seemed like a perfect plan. I had my wallet with ten bucks of insurance money in it, plus the fifty Holly had give me in my shirt pocket. Lunches can be expensive at restaurants so I usually make a sandwich, but even elegant places in Denver you could get two lunches for sixty bucks. Doctors like money better than about anything, so a free lunch seemed foolproof. Then if we was eating lunch together I could talk about the Broncos, or apartment cleaning, or anything else that everyone's interested in, and aim the conversation over toward Holly slowly.

He went into a nice restaurant I ain't never been to before that was in a brick building. Besides the tables inside, it had tables and chairs on the sidewalk too, with a little brick wall around them about knee high and a shiny metal railing on top of the wall. The tables had tablecloths and a jar with a flower on every one. The people sitting there had on nice clothes, and some of the men wore ties. Obviously this lunch was gonna use up most of my sixty bucks, but I didn't even let myself think about that part of it. In fact, it might be easier to aim a guy at noticing how much he liked a pretty girl if he was eating a nice, free lunch in a restaurant with table-cloths. Now it seemed like my plan had an extra good chance of working.

I didn't follow him in right away. I wanted him to have a chance to find his buddies if they was meeting for lunch. There wasn't much point of me buying a fancy lunch if he was going to be sitting with his friends and talking about golf or taxes, which is what doctors talk about.

While I was waiting, I leaned up against the wall of the building next to the restaurant and tried to look like I wasn't loitering. The trick to that is to keep looking at your watch like you're waiting for someone. If you're loitering you don't care what time it is, so you don't look at your watch. If you lean against a building for about eight minutes without looking at your watch, the cops pick you up and you ain't got much defenses.

Between looking at my watch I noticed the different people sitting outside at the restaurant. There was several guys in suits who could of been doctors, and two women about old enough to be my mother who was also wearing suits, and one pretty lady in a black dress who was about 35 years old who looked rich. It wasn't that she was wearing fancy jewelry or something but just that she sat real straight and was polite to the waiter but not friendly, like he worked for her or something. She looked at her watch almost the same time I did, but then she looked up and smiled about the biggest smile I ever seen at a man who come out of the restaurant. He leaned over and kissed her and she laughed. He turned toward me for a minute as he sat down in the chair across from her and I almost fell over.

It was Dr. Anderson! I looked away and blinked a couple of times to make sure my eyes was working. The woman was not Holly, and she wasn't the lady in the pictures in his office. That smile she give him and that kiss was not a sister smile or a cousin kiss, or a California kiss like you see movie stars give each other. My eyes was working fine, but my brain wasn't understanding.

I turned and started walking away before they seen me. There was no way I could put all the pieces of this puzzle together. This was a thousand piecer with maybe some extra pieces from a different puzzle thrown in the wrong box besides. Who was that lady? And if Holly and Dr. Anderson was going to get married, how come he was kissing her? And then on top of that, who was the lady in the pictures in his office?

Your brain is probably doing the same thing mine done, which was coming up with stories to make all the parts fit. The first one is obvious: Dr. Anderson has a twin brother and he's the one I followed. And the sec-

229

ond one I come up with could work just as good: aliens was probing my brain and made me think I seen something I didn't see. And the third story was that the woman in the restaurant was actually Holly in a really good disguise.

But then the story come to me that maybe Dr. Anderson didn't really love Holly as much as she loved him and sometimes dated other women. Even if I liked Holly myself, that idea was as sad as waking up in the middle of the night and hearing a train whistle blowing a long ways off and in the rain. If that was the case, I needed to act fast, even if I didn't have all the parts of my plan ready.

I walked back to the doctor office building and rode the elevator up to the second floor. Dr. Anderson's office door was locked, of course, so I went down to the end of the hall and sat on the floor to wait.

Sometimes things ain't near as complicated as they look. I kept reminding myself about that. Lots of times you think you understand something when you guessed wrong about some part and then you feel like a idiot. Otherwise it wouldn't be funny to put salt in the sugar bowl. That one little thing you thought you understood changes everything. So I had to be careful.

The best idea was to use the lawyer trick of asking questions instead of saying my opinion. If you ain't saying what you think the judge can't say you purged yourself, which is probably why lawyers always say things as questions, like on that TV show Jeopardy. You ain't saying anything if you ask a question. Dr. Anderson couldn't get pissed thinking I was accusing him of something if I just asked him questions, especially nice ones. Once I was sure I understood the situation, then I could make him hints about Holly liking roses or whatever.

At one o'clock a lady walked down the hall, unlocked Dr. Anderson's door and went in. She wasn't the lady in the pictures, she wasn't the lady in the restaurant and she wasn't Holly either. Geez, I thought. Dr. Anderson needs 3 x 5 cards to keep track of all the women in his life. This one had gray hair and was skinny and stood up straight. I figured she must be his secretary. She looked pretty strict, like my fifth grade teacher, so I didn't think I had much chances of using charm to get an appointment.

While I was thinking of ideas of what to say to her, she come out of the office again and walked down the hall away from me, then went into the ladies' room. I got up and went to the office door and, sure enough, it wasn't locked. I didn't even think but just went right in. The door to Dr.

230

Anderson's room from the waiting room wasn't locked either, so I went in there. The light wasn't on, but the window made it pretty light. I closed the door behind me.

The first thing I done was check the window again. It wasn't locked. The window was sticky but I opened it once to make sure it worked, then closed it again. You always want to have an extra escape route in your mind. That's just common sense.

I looked at the pictures on the desk and they was just like they had been before. But I didn't disturb nothing. Then I sat down on the couch he had for patients and just waited. I gotta admit I was as nervous as if I was in the principal's office, or in a police car, or a fancy restaurant. I kept thinking of ways to ask questions that would be friendly and nice but would help me understand the situation like Colombo would do. I also looked over at that unlocked window about forty times and pictured how soft that grass was underneath it, and how easy it would be to just leave. Nobody would ever know I'd been there and I could go home and work on a plan that had more details in it. With enough time, I could come up with a plan with as much details as a government plan and them are about the most expensive ones. But every time I almost jumped out that window, I seen Holly in a bar listening to songs with sliding steel guitars and words about a guy's dog that died. This was hard, but I couldn't put her through that.

In a minute I heard the secretary come back. The phone rang several times and she answered it. But she never come into the office, which is good since I didn't have a good story made up yet. I already decided that if she asked me what I was doing there I'd just say it was personal. Sometimes people will let you get away with that one. Sometimes it's better to say a general true thing like "it's personal" instead of some other true thing that's more exact like, "I didn't read them pages of the homework."

At about 1:23 I heard Dr. Anderson come into the front office and talk to his secretary but the door was thick and I couldn't tell what they was saying. Then he come into his office, flipped on the light, closed the door and sat down at his desk. I was on the couch in front of him but he was so busy looking at papers on his desk he didn't notice me. I waited for a minute so he could finish his business, but pretty soon I couldn't wait no longer.

"We got to talk about nurse Holly," I said.

He about jumped off his chair. I probably should of apologized for scaring him but all I could think of was my plan and I didn't want to get off track by adding extra stuff. As you probably figured out, once I get off a track it's hard for me to find it again.

"What are you doing here?" He sounded mad and surprised and scared all at the same time. Plus it was a reasonable question from his side of things, but it was off the track and I sure didn't want our conversation to change into him asking the questions, so I pretended he didn't say nothing and started over with my first line which I already had memorized.

"We got to talk about nurse Holly," I said again.

"Who are you, what are you doing here?" he said again. So he was ignoring what I said, which doctors do a lot, and it was going to confuse me if I wasn't careful. But we couldn't both just keep saying the same thing. I decided the fastest way to get back on track was just to answer him.

"I'm a friend of nurse Holly," I said. "Kind of like a big brother, you could say. But I ain't here to answer of a bunch of questions, since you're a busy man and I don't want to waste your time. So it would be faster if I just asked questions and you answered them. Don't that make more sense?" I tried to sound as polite as I could. He watched me for a while like he was deciding if I was an important person or not. When he decided I couldn't give him a good deal on drugs or Mercedes cars or real estate deals he looked back down at his papers like I wasn't there anymore.

"I'm sorry, you'll have to make an appointment just like anyone else. I'm going to have to ask you to leave."

Well, you already know I had that line used on me about a hundred times. If you think about it, it's more of a warning that pretty soon somebody's going to ask you to leave instead of somebody saying 'get out.' That was a obvious loophole. He was moving his papers around like I would take the hint and leave. But he didn't understand I was trying to help him.

"I know you're busy and all that, but this is personal and I just want to help you and nurse Holly and it will just take one minute. So please, if I could just ask a couple of polite questions…" He slapped both hands down on his desk as hard as if it was a drum.

"Get out!" he shouted and pointed at the door. OK, so he already seen that loophole and closed it. Doctors is pretty smart about loopholes.

"You bet, sir, I'd be happy to get out in one minute just as soon as we had a polite conversation…"

232

"Get the fluff out of my office this fluffing instant!" He stood up and leaned one hand on his desk and pointed to the door with his other hand. "I don't have time for bumbling idiots!" He pointed at the door again.

"OK, so I can see we got off on the wrong foot, which is my fault from not making a appointment. But I said please and it ain't fair to call a guy a idiot before he even took a test, which I ain't gonna hold against..."

"Get out, you fluffing clock shocking son of a wart! I can have security come through that door in two minutes!" he said, pointing to his door, which he would not have had to since it was the only one in the room.

This wasn't going as smooth as it did in my brain and that just made me concentrate even harder. Full grown men do hard things, and this was important, but it was hard to keep track of what I wanted to say with him yelling like that. Plus my brain was starting to make that buzzing sound and my face was getting hot from him calling me names and his crude reference to Mom which had not been called for. It was going to be hard to do my best diplomat talking and try to convince him to fall in love with Holly with that buzzing in my ears. But it was about the most important thing I ever had to do, even if I hated to do it. There was too much stuff in my brain to keep track of. It seemed like maybe we was just too far apart in the room, so I stood up and walked toward him. He stepped back and when he did, he accidentally sat in his chair which rolled back until it ran into the wall behind him.

You could tell it surprised him that I stood up and came toward him after he give me the instruction to get out. Doctors expect people to do whatever they say, like they was gods. It surprises them if you don't think they're a god. Except if they was gods then they would of been able to keep Mom and Dad alive. If they was gods then people wouldn't die in the middle of a treatment without even getting to say goodbye, for one example. And gods wouldn't call people idiots or use salty language. It would be easy to get pissed at doctors without even knowing them. Then if you start to think about how maybe they got special medicines in the back room they only give to rich people, you could start to feel like discriminating against them, but that wouldn't be right. Doctors is as good as you and me and you got to treat them with respect. But sometimes you got to get their attention first.

"I don't do as good when I get interrupted," I said as I walked toward him. "So I'd just as soon we didn't have no security guys come through the door in two minutes."

233

Everything was complicated. Everything was messy. My brain was like an apartment that drug dealers just moved out of.

When stuff is messy you got to start by finding one thing you can straighten up. Sometimes it ain't the big important part of the mess, but it don't matter. You throw away the milk carton or pick up the chair that fell over or close the refrigerator door.

In this mess, the first thing I seen was that he was behind his desk like a doctor and I was in front of it like a patient. He was as mad as if somebody wanted him to look in their ear for free, since he was in doctor mode. But all I was doing was trying to help him live happily ever after in Cleveland with Holly while my face was hot and my ears was buzzing and he was calling me names. I needed to find that first milk carton to throw away and start making everything simpler.

Even if it wasn't the important thing, all I could see was his desk. It was distracting to have it between us, and distracting to think about security guys coming in while we was talking. Maybe I wasn't doing my best diplomat thinking from being nervous and all, but that desk seemed like part of the problem and it seemed a easy problem to fix, like that first milk carton in a messy room you throw away to get you started. It wasn't that big. I picked up the telephone off the desk and set it on the floor. I laid the pictures down flat. Dr. Anderson didn't say nothing while I done that, but looked pretty nervous and confused since I forgot to treat him like a god. I put one hand on each side of the desk and picked it up. Even if it was a small desk, it was heavy, even for me, so I had to work a little bit to carry it over to the door. But when my ears is buzzing and my face is hot, I can pick up pretty heavy stuff. I set the desk down in front of the door and that made me feel a lot better. Nobody could open that door with the desk in front of it.

"There!" I said. "Now we don't have to worry about getting interrupted, and we can have a nice friendly chat without that big old thing between us. That seems better, don't it?" My ears was still buzzing but not as much. I walked back toward him and crossed my arms.

He pushed on the floor with his feet to roll his chair backward but, like I said before, he was already against the wall so he didn't go nowhere.

"What do you want?" he said, but now his voice was quiet and he didn't sound as mean. He wasn't in doctor mode any more. I shook my head and reminded myself that he wasn't the doctor who didn't do his best job with Mom. This was just a man that Holly loved and I had to help him remember that he loved her too without him figuring out that's what I was doing.

"I thought we agreed I'd ask the questions," I said. "Just the same, there ain't much sense in running around the bush. I mostly got one question, so I might as well ask it. I mostly wanted to know when you and Holly was getting married."

"What?"

"OK, if you ain't got one date picked out, that's cool. Have you got a month picked out? Lots of people like June for weddings."

"What makes you think we're getting married?"

"I know you want to keep it quiet, since you work together and all, so I won't say a word. But I seen how you act with her. If that ain't love I don't know what it is."

"Why do you care how I act with her?"

"OK, see, there you're asking me questions again, which we decided would make this take longer. But it ain't a big deal." I was standing in front of him and he was leaning back in his chair. "Like I said, I'm sort of like Holly's big brother. I mean I ain't really, we're just friends. But I feel like her big brother sort of. And I'd sure hate to miss her wedding. Like if I made plans that was in conflict. So if you could just tell me what month it was, I wouldn't make no plans to conflict."

"We... we haven't set a date. Actually, we're not at all sure we even want to get married. We're very modern people."

I nodded and thought about that, since I didn't know exactly what he meant. But it was probably like modern art, and modern music, which meant complicated and hard to understand. While I was thinking, I noticed there was some lint on his shoulder so I leaned over him to take it off his suit coat. His eyes got wide. He probably thought I seen a spider or something on him.

"I ain't a very modern guy," I said, in a kind of whisper since I was so close to him and I didn't want to make him more nervous than he already was by talking loud. I threw the lint in his trash can and moved back away from him. "I think there ain't so many girls like Holly. When you find one, you got to be a gentleman. Don't that make sense to you?"

He nodded. This hadn't been as hard as I thought it was going to be.

"Cool," I said. "That's pretty much all I wanted to say. See, I told you this wouldn't take long. I only got two more questions for you." I walked over to his desk and got the picture of the lady with the two kids and brought it back to him. "This has been bugging me. What's her name?" I handed him the picture.

"Stephanie," he whispered, and held the picture close to his chest.

"That's a pretty name," I said. "And she's a pretty lady. Not as pretty as the lady in the black dress you had lunch with today, but real pretty. Well, that ain't fair. They're pretty in different ways, ain't they? But that ain't none of my business, I was just curious. And them kids is cute too." He stared at me and his eyes got bigger. For a doctor he seemed shy. I tried to relax him by talking about the kids. "I could play with kids like that all day long. I bet there's lots of stuff I could teach them."

"There's been a terrible misunderstanding," he whispered. You don't have to do anything. I understand you completely. Trust me, I'll make it right with Holly."

"That's all I want. For things to be right with Holly. Did you know she likes roses pretty much?"

He shook his head no.

"She does. Lots of girls do. What about her job offer in Cleveland?"

"She doesn't need to move to Cleveland. In fact, I think she probably deserves a promotion right here in Denver."

"Cool. Is that a surprise?"

"Yes. Of course. A surprise."

"Well then, I won't say nothing about it."

By now it seemed like I'd given him enough hints about Holly, and we'd had some small talk like buddies do. I decided I'd put some pieces of the puzzle together wrong anyway, since there was so many of them. Him and me agreed about being gentlemen; that was the main thing. I was glad I hadn't said anything, but had just asked questions. The way I done it, if he hadn't took my hints about Holly, it wouldn't seem weird if I visited him again sometime. Maybe we could even have lunch together.

"OK, so if you and Holly ain't even sure you're getting married, then you don't need to tell her I come by to visit so she gets her hopes up. I must

236

of just not understood something. That could happen to anybody. I better be going now, I'm sure you got appointments. Do you want me to move that desk back for you?"

"Unless you want to jump out the window to leave."

I laughed. Since he was joking on me, I figured we'd hit if off pretty good so I joked back.

"It's tempting," I said. "I'd even let you go first to soften up the ground for me. But I'll save that for our next visit."

I picked up the desk and set it back where it had been, then put the phone back on it. "Unless you cured me, doc, and we don't need more visits. Do you think you cured me?"

He nodded up and down real fast.

"Cool," I said. "You must be a good doctor. I'm glad we had a chance to talk. See you later."

Then I walked out the door and left the building.

CHAPTER TWENTY FIVE

An art therapy lesson with Greg, who ain't that crazy about art therapy

On Tuesday night I went to the hospital to give Greg a art therapy lesson.

"Hey, Sunshine," I said when I went in his room. He was sitting straighter up than last time, which seemed like a good sign.

"Dr. Bologna," he said. "Your pet turtle let you out again?"

"Yeah, he ain't a very strict owner. He lets me go out pretty much whenever I want as long as I bring him back a worm. If you got to have an owner, a turtle is a good choice."

"Are you going to pick up any more interns tonight?"

"Only if they come in here. Which Holly says ain't very likely."

"That's too bad. But I'm not surprised."

"Yeah, I think Holly explained the rules a little better to them."

"I don't think she had to."

I laughed at that. "I probably should of thought of an easier way to explain the rules to that guy last week."

"He transferred to a different floor. Now every time someone wants to clean my room they stick their head in the door and ask if it's OK with me first."

"That only seems polite," I said. He wasn't using swear words near as much as he done before but I didn't want to say something about it and remind him. "I brought different stuff to use as drawing models this week."

"Don't you want to see my homework?" he asked.

"Did you do some?"

"There's not much to do in here. Plus, I decided you had one good thought, which is that they'll never let me out of locked rooms until they decide I'm not crazy. So I'm going to play along with you until they let me out. Then the first chance I get, I'm jumping again."

"Good for you!" I said. "There's nothing crazy about wanting to jump off a building. But it ain't smart to tell people about it. So we just won't

238

mention that part and if they ask me I'll say you're making excellent progress. How's that?"

"Perfect. And I'll follow the main cuckoo bird right out of the cuckoo's nest."

"What?"

"It was a movie. Never mind, it's not important. My drawings are in the top drawer here." He twisted around so he could get them and pulled out a stack about an inch thick.

"Holy macaroni!" I said. "You must of done two hundred pictures!"

"Yeah, something like that. I should probably number them and sign them so I can sell them for more money."

You could tell from his voice he was making a joke on himself, so I laughed. It's a good step when somebody starts making jokes on themselves instead of on everybody else.

"Yeah, lots of popular artists done that. There ain't no rule says you can't make money at something just because it's fun. Let's see what you got."

He handed me the first picture and watched me to see how I'd react. It was so good I about dropped it.

"You didn't do this!" I said before I had a chance to think it might sound like an insult.

"Oh yes I did. Just like you said, with your rose and my pencil."

"You found a picture and traced it, right?"

"Wrong again, pumpkin brain. It's just part of my therapy."

"Wow. You got natural talent like I ain't never seen. You got shadows and everything. How'd you do that part right there? It don't even look like pencil lines."

"I put the pencil sideways and used the side of the lead instead of the point. Made a broad soft line. Very impressionistic don't you think?"

"I ain't so good with the names of different techniques," I said. "But that's pretty cool. I might have to steal that idea off you. Let's see another one."

"Don't you have anything else you want to say about that first one?"

He was right about that. I was getting paid to look at his stuff pretty careful and I only seen a couple things. I looked at it harder.

239

"OK, I like the way you left big white spots on the paper with no pencil marks at all. That's pretty cool."

"If shadows are the absence of light, then white space must be the absence of everything," he said. "Isn't that what life's all about?"

"Nah, white space is just the paper showing through."

I looked back at the picture. "Don't give me no hints." I studied it as careful as I could. "Some of the lines is extra dark, so you probably wanted us to look at them harder." I snuck a look at him, but he didn't look like I guessed the right answer yet, so I looked back at the drawing. Finally I give up. "I ain't sure what you're talking about. It's a great drawing, with lots of pluses. If I was giving grades I'd have to give you an A. I ain't never drew a picture as good as that."

"What about the subject matter?"

"The what?"

"You know. What the picture is about."

"Well, it's a dead woman with a rose stuck through her neck. You mean that?"

"Yes, Dr. Bologna Brain. As my art therapy counselor, shouldn't you be agonizing over the dark implications?"

"Well, like I said, some of it's got pretty dark lines, but it's also got blanks, so they kind of balance out."

"Not the pencil lines. Shouldn't you be worrying about how evil and disturbed I am?"

I laughed. "You crack me up, Sunshine. You ain't any more evil than I am. You're just drawing pictures about stuff you're interested in, which is what everybody does. You're a kid, so you're interested in death, and you're interested in girls, and you ain't that interested in roses but it's what you had, so you made it the murder weapon. Colombo's interested in girls and death and murder weapons too and nobody thinks he's disturbed or evil. They just think he needs to iron his clothes more."

"So you don't find it... interesting that all my drawings depict the most gruesome kinds of death imaginable? That they're full of torture and dismemberment and pain and anguish?"

"Man, where did you learn so many big words? If you had all them good words in your brain how come you was using that crude gang guy talk?"

"I've always been a victim of peer pressure."

I laughed again.

"You mean you do stuff cause everybody else is doing it? I think you're more a guy who does stuff because nobody else is doing it. But that ain't my business. Let me think if your art bothers me."

So then I sat there a while looking at his picture. I tried to picture myself being Greg's dad to see if it would bother me. Then I imagined I was a cop or a priest. No matter how I worked at it, it just seemed like a cool picture.

"OK, maybe if I was a girl I wouldn't like it," I said. "Since a girl got killed in it and all. But to me it's just a neat picture."

"You're crazier than I am."

"Yeah, I think you'd get lots of votes agreeing with that."

"So you don't even care what I draw?"

"It ain't up to me to care. Art is like talking to yourself and whoever else might listen. Right now you want to talk about death because it's scary to you."

"Death is scary to everybody."

"Scary? Nah, I don't think so. It ain't scary, it's just sad, like leaving on a train. People you ain't gonna see again, things you liked that fall apart without you there to take care of them. Everybody's scared of what's behind the door in a spooky movie. Old people ain't scared of death because it's a door they seen behind a few times. They're just sad about it. You're young, so you ain't ever seen behind the door and it seems scary to you. So of course you got to draw it. That's how you make it less scary. I ain't gonna hold that against you."

"Some might call it a fixation."

"I ain't that good with words for stuff. But if you're right, then churches sure got a fixation on killing their best god. They got crosses everywhere. Nobody calls them crazy except other churches. Let's see that next picture."

The next picture had a dead girl on her stomach with about eight roses stuck in her back. I tried to think of some compliment to say about the stuff in the picture instead of just how he used his pencil.

"It's interesting how the girl is deader than a doorbell but them flowers all look pretty healthy. Am I supposed to get some therapy message from that?"

241

"I'm sure you are," he said. "Probably something about beauty springing from pain and death." He was obviously joking.

"That's pretty good." I said. "You ought to write that down and then when you feel good enough to get out of here we'll have somebody type it up, like a book report. People love typed up stuff. I bet they'd give you extra points toward a grade of not crazy. But it would be hard."

"Hard? They're so transparent. Any idiot could guess what they want me to say. Well, most idiots. Maybe not you."

"If you know what they want you to say, why don't you just say it?"

"They'd never believe me."

"I bet they would if you typed it up."

He shook his head and rolled his eyes the way kids do when they think you said something dumb. Then he stopped and stared at me.

"You know, Dr. Bologna, you might be on to something there. If I demonstrated some self awareness, some discipline, I could play them like a cheap video game. If I confess to my depression, they'll forgive my darkness."

"I ain't that interested in going to a church."

"Not a stained glass church. The church of red tape and psychobabble doublespeak."

"Right." I said. It had been easier to understand him when he just swore all the time.

Then I looked at the rest of his pictures, which was all really good and they all had a dead person and a rose. I tried to notice extra good things and say something nice about them. "Man, you see shadows places I never would of thought to look," I said. "You got a gift for that."

Just then Holly knocked on the door and stuck her head in.

"I don't want to interrupt," she said. "I know the rules..."

"Them rules don't apply to you," I said.

She smiled at that. "I just wanted you to know I have to help with a procedure so I'll be a few minutes late meeting you for coffee. Will that be all right?"

"Sure," I said. "Me and Sunshine could talk about art all night long. He's pretty impressionistic. You seem extra cheerful tonight, Holly."

242

"My working conditions seem to have improved suddenly and dramatically."

"Cool. Nobody likes bad working conditions. How come they improved?"

"I have no idea and I'm not asking questions. I'll see you later, Jumper." And then she left.

"OK, where was we?"

"She called you Jumper."

"Yeah, everybody calls me Jumper. Unless they call me Dr. Bologna Brain, which is mostly just you."

"Why?"

"I don't know, you made it up."

"No, Sherlock. Why do they call you Jumper?"

I hadn't thought about nobody calling me by my name in front of Greg before. I kind of figured we had introductions out of the way, but now I seen I was wrong.

"People called me that all my life, except in court."

"Why?"

"Mostly alleged loitering."

"Why do they call you Jumper?"

"It's just a name."

"Then why is your face getting red?"

"Well, I just wasn't ready to talk about it yet and you didn't seem that ready either, so you surprised me. It's just we got the same hobby, but you can't talk about it much or you wind up getting strapped into a hospital bed for being crazy. That was your big mistake, plus breaking your legs. I ain't that interested in getting strapped into a bed."

"A hobby? That's what you call it?"

"Well, I think of it as more a sport than a hobby. Hobbies seem like things you do sitting down, while jumping is mostly a standing up thing. So to me it seems more like a sport."

"Leaping into the black void of death seems a lot different from table tennis or bowling."

243

"Yeah, jumping at night can be tricky. But I don't jump to feel dead. I jump to feel alive."

"Briefly."

"Well, sure. It don't last long. But then you land and that's good too. And then you figure out what you done wrong and climb back up and do it again."

"You what?"

"You can't expect to get it right the first time."

"I sure thought I would."

"Well there's your problem. We ain't so different at what we do, we just think about it different. Maybe that's the whole trick. You want to see what I brung you as drawing models?"

"You're the alpha cuckoo."

I opened up my backpack and took out some magazines.

"These ain't brand new," I said. "But they got good pictures. Since you can't go outside to draw stuff, it seemed like the next best thing would be drawing things somebody took a picture of with a camera. I got a good deal on them at a garage sale." I handed them to him and he looked through them.

"National Geographic, that's predictable," he said. "And Great Autos..." he looked at me. "Great Autos?"

"When I was your age I thought cars was pretty neat. They could take you anywhere in the world and you was the boss if you was driving and they was a good place to be alone with a girl if you wanted to talk or something. I figured teenagers still liked cars so I gambled a quarter on it. If you don't want to draw cars, it ain't a big deal."

"The swimsuit issue?"

"In a million years teenage boys will still like looking at pretty girls. That one was a no brainer. For your drawings you just need to cut the girl in half and poke a rose through her neck. But if you don't want it, I'll take it back." I reached out my hand but he pulled the magazine back.

"No, that's OK. If my art therapy counselor wants me to draw pretty girls, I better do what he says."

"See? Now I can say the patient is making excellent progress."

"Horology Annual?"

"It ain't what you think. It's all pictures of clocks. I ain't ever paid much attention to clocks, so that one was just a lucky guess. What I liked was all the shadows in the pictures. Who would of ever guessed that something as exact as clocks would be mostly shadows when you took a picture of them? Now that I see how shadows is your specialty, that dime seems like a good investment. I like the ones where the words say how cool their chimes sound. I bet those would make the best drawings. But you obviously got a thing for cuckoo clocks and there's some of them in there too. Maybe a cuckoo clock could be the murder weapon in one of your pictures."

He put the magazines down and looked at my face.

"So why do you do this?"

"Do what?"

"This whole absurd art therapy thing. You barge into strangers' hospital rooms and waste an hour of their life drawing stupid pictures and acting goofy. I don't get it."

He didn't look like he was making a joke, so I thought for a minute. Even if the way he said it wasn't as polite as some people, it was the first time he asked me something where it seemed like he cared what the answer was. That's another good step toward a grade of not crazy, so I wanted to answer him like he was a grown up and not with a joke.

"Well, I can't give anybody a pony ride and I can't bake a cake. But that's OK. You don't get as many Dr. Hudson points for obvious stuff."

He stared at me for a minute. "And they let you walk around without a leash," he said.

"OK, I didn't say that good enough. Dr. Hudson is a game my dad and me played when he was alive. You get points if you can do something nice for somebody without them knowing it and without you ever telling anybody. It's a fun game, but it ain't got its own TV show or nothing since you can't talk about it. So I thought maybe if I hung out with you I could figure out some way I could get Dr. Hudson points off you. But you already draw better than me and, now that I told you about the game I can't get no points either. But I still think you're a funny guy to hang out with. You crack me up about every other word you say, which makes me feel good, so maybe you're the one getting Dr. Hudson points off me. And maybe when you feel better I can give you some jumping tips."

"So how do you win this Dr. Hudson game?"

245

"The idea ain't to win it. It ain't that kind of game. The idea is to play it. It's so fun you don't need to have lots of rules, or winner, or losers. I ain't saying you ought to try it. And I'd rather you didn't tell nobody about it either. You tell somebody and then they start playing and having fun, and then they tell somebody else. If everybody played, pretty soon there wouldn't be nobody who needed help and we'd all have to play golf. I'd rather clean toilets than have to play golf. Only reason I told you about it is that you asked."

He didn't say nothing, so I decided to ask him the same thing.

"So how come you do what you do?"

"Did I mention that I hate my life?"

"Yeah, you might of said something. Why?"

"You want a list? Parents, school, stupid people, teachers, cops, the government, TV, doctors, nurses, social worker, waitresses, people who drive cars, pedestrians, stupid nosy kids, old people... do I need to go on?"

"Nah, I think it's better you stop before you get to art therapy counselors."

"Oh yeah. And art therapy counselors."

I laughed at that. "I should of seen that one coming a mile off. At least they ain't number one on your list. How come you hate all that stuff?"

"Because they're stupid. And art therapy counselors are moving toward the top of the list."

"OK, no more question. We're just playing different games. You're playing the I Hate My Life game, which is cool if it makes you happy. Sounds like lots more work than Dr. Hudson. You got ambition, which I ain't got much of."

"It's not a game."

"Well, if it ain't a game then it must be work, which is another reason it probably ain't right for me. Or else you just had a bunch of really bad stuff happen to you, which ain't none of my business."

He thought for a minute.

"Did you ever watch Star Trek?" he said.

"Sure, everybody has. I ain't completely uneducated."

246

"Right. You cling to that illusion. I feel like I got beamed onto a strange planet and into an alien body. All the aliens around me think I'm just like them. But they can't really see me. They don't know who I am. I'm the last member of my species, marooned light years from my home planet and the only way to escape…"

He stopped for a second.

"The only way to escape is to jump."

"Wow! That's the coolest thing I ever heard. I used to feel like that too, but I never said it that good. You got some gifts with words."

"You don't feel like that any more?"

"Well, yeah, I guess I still do. Other people ain't like me in lots of ways. But neither is dogs or turtles or crickets and I got friends in each of them areas."

"So your friends are insects and reptiles and that makes you happy."

"Sure. But mostly I think I'm happy cause I ain't got as many questions as you. You think you can use your brain to make you happy. To me it's more like swimming on your back. If you work too hard, you drink a lot of water and somebody's got to pull you off the bottom of the pool. I learned that lesson about a hundred times."

"That doesn't make sense."

"Maybe, but it's true. I about drowned enough times learning to swim I ain't gonna forget it. Smart guys thrash around. Smarter guys trust the water."

He rolled his eyes, which cracked me up and I laughed.

"Do you know what I'm doing on Sunday night?" I asked.

"Getting a brain implant?"

"Even better. A turtle release party down at City Park. That little girl I used to visit and draw with is strong enough now. Ain't that cool?"

"Yeah, that sounds like the society event of the season."

"I think so too. I wish your legs was better so you could come. Anyway, at the rate you're going, you'll be out of drawing paper in a week, so I'll bring you some more on Tuesday. I better go now."

I stood up and walked to the door.

247

"Thanks for the magazines," he said real quiet, which made me stop in my footprints. I didn't even think he knew the word "thanks." Him saying thanks was worth about a hundred thanks from people who said it all the time and didn't mean it. So I turned back to him.

"You're welcome," I said. "You know, I liked visiting that little girl Linda pretty much. But I think I like visiting you even more."

Then I quick left before my face got hot or he could make a joke on me.

CHAPTER TWENTY SIX

Some serious detective work goes a little bad on me

The rest of the week went by. I done some drawings, and I collected some cans, and I cleaned three apartments but my brain was pretty much full of thinking about the turtle release party. Finally it was the day. The turtle release party was at nine at night, since that's when Linda's dad would be off work, and so would Holly, and even if it was late for a kid, Linda liked to be up at night so it was OK. I took a good long shower and got ready to go over to the park about five-fifteen so I'd have extra time if I noticed something interesting on the way. I put Bart into my Nike bag and combed my hair three times and started walking.

Well, I got to the park just fine but I still had about three hours until Linda and everybody would show up, so maybe I give myself too much extra time. With that much extra time, I decided that before the turtle release party I'd wander over to the Gentle Arms real casual and see if I thought of a plan to get more information so I'd be reliable. As long as I stayed back they wouldn't notice me, but I still thought about it a while in case I was overlooking something. I couldn't think of nothing, so Bart and me started walking.

A couple of things was pretty interesting on the walk, which I don't need to tell you about, except that it took a little longer than I scheduled to get to the Gentle Arms. The sun set while I was walking so by the time I got there it was nearly dark. The building across the street from the Gentle Arms was all boarded up and none of the street lights was working so it was pretty safe standing next to the boarded up building to watch. Nobody was walking around on the street but you could hear kids crying in some buildings, and grown ups yelling at them, and some TVs turned up loud.

The lights was on in the apartment in question and sometimes I seen somebody walk around but I was too far away to make a positive I.D. The balconies was different than mine: they had sliding glass doors which meant you didn't have to climb through a window to get to them. A couple times one of the suspected Bones come out on the balcony, but the light was behind them so I couldn't see them good enough to be sure. About the last thing I wanted was for the cops to bust in wearing their SWAT outfits and find out it was the Pope and his salesmen.

249

I thought a idea would come to me quick, but none did. The problem was I was too far away. If I was on that roof, for one example, I could see them good in the daylight if they come out on the balcony. So maybe tomorrow I'd come down and find stairs to the roof. That way I'd know for sure who they was, but they wouldn't see me, because nobody but Officer Mike looks up very much. I never seen anyone look up as much as Officer Mike, but it don't hurt nobody so it ain't a big deal.

But what if the stairs was locked? I could always climb the downspout up there, so that wasn't a big problem. Of course, in the day somebody'd probably see me. One thing I could do is come back after we released Bart, climb up on the roof and sleep there. That way I'd already be up there when it got to be daylight. I could do surveillance all day and have more answers for Officer Mike in case he thought up some questions.

You probably slept on as many roofs as me, so you know each one is different. Some are flat and easy to sleep on and others is slanted. Sometimes it starts raining and you wish you had some garbage sacks for a raincoat. When that happens, you remember the Boy Scout saying of be prepared and wish you thought of it before you went up there. It was only 8:26 and I could get to City Park by jogging fifteen minutes. So I had plenty of time. The obvious smart thing to do was climb up on that roof right now and check it out. If I got some ideas about stuff to bring with me, I could go home and get it before I went camping. One thing for sure was some garbage sacks.

I felt good about how careful I was being, thinking up everything that might happen before I done it. When I was younger I wasn't always so careful. Sometimes I done stuff that had hidden flaws that wasn't so hidden once you thought about it. I'd learned that lesson about a hundred times.

Bart was a complication. You got to use both hands to climb a downspout three stories and I didn't want to leave him on the ground someplace in my Nike bag. I tried putting the strap in my teeth, but that got in my way. Finally I put the strap over my shoulder and thought of the bag as an extra backpack, which worked fine. About halfway up some screws come out of the bricks and the downspout moved so I thought I'd be making an unscheduled jump, but there was enough more screws holding I didn't have a incident.

I got up to the roof and set the Nike bag down. There wasn't much interesting up there, except beer bottles and empty boxes. One good thing was an old mattress. People in the building must camp up there some-

250

times. That was good because they wouldn't think it weird for someone to do, plus it would be softer than sleeping on the roof, even if it had a lot of stains. When you notice lucky coincidences like that you know you're on the right track.

I laid down on the roof right over the balcony in question and looked down. No one was out on the balcony, but I could see it easy because their light was on in the apartment and it shined out the sliding glass door. There was a little table and a couple chairs on the balcony. The table had some glasses that still had ice in them, so you knew they sat out there sometimes. Maybe they sat out there discussing business deals and if they done that loud enough I could get some good clues.

Then two guys walked out on the balcony. One was a big guy, so it could have been Mercedes but I couldn't tell for sure. The other guy was about my size and could of been one of the Bones. The light was on their backs so I couldn't see their faces.

"It's about time," the big guy said. His voice sounded a lot like Mercedes.

"We cool," the other one said. I didn't recognize his voice but then I hadn't spent that much time chatting with any of them. His voice sounded black, but you couldn't count on that. It's funny how, when gang guys talk to each other, if one of them is black, they both talk like they're black. Or African American if that's what they prefer now. I don't mean to sound prejudiced, it's just they keep changing what they want you to call them and then they get pissed if you don't keep up. So Indians is now Native Americans. Maybe guys from Canada is now Canadian Americans, and airplane pilots might be Captain Americans. I won't get pissed if they don't call me a Jumping American and I hope they feel the same. Saying gang guys talk like black guys if one of them is black ain't prejudiced either. When lawyers get together, they talk like each other too. It ain't a complaint, it's just how people are. They like to talk the same way to each other. Us writers do it too, only if you ain't a writer yourself you probably can't keep up, so I won't make you feel bad by showing off. Nobody likes a writer who shows off.

While I was thinking all that, the guy who might be Mercedes took a cigar out of his pocket. Then he talked again.

"Yeah, you say we cool. I don't care stick about cool. I ain't cleaning up another of your screw-ups. You hear what I'm say?"

"Chill, bro'. Nobody seen that one coming. You come out righteous."

"You got the cargo?"

"Yeah, got it right here in my hand."

"Good. You just do what I said. No business gets done till we inspect all the goods this time. Comprendo?"

"Word, bro'. Smooth as silk."

The big guy bit off the end of his cigar and spit it over the balcony. He yelled into the apartment. "You girls ready yet? This ain't the got ham high school prom." He felt in his pockets for a light. "Feel like a got ham babysitter. You got fire?"

"Dang straight." He got out a lighter. There was a little breeze so he had to cup his hand around the cigar. The lighter kept going out anyway. Finally the big guy cupped both hands around it and the other guy put one hand over the top while he held the lighter with the other.

I was starting to get nervous because time was going by and I had to get to City Park. Finally the cigar lit.

"What's taking you britches so long?" the big guy yelled. "Get in there and kick their lasses," he said to the guy with the lighter. "We gotta leave right frosting now." The lighter guy went in pretty fast, but the big guy stayed out there.

"They deserve this hick town," he said to himself, blowing out smoke. Then he went in. I heard the glass door slide closed. A minute later the light went out.

Time was getting to be an issue, but I didn't want to crawl down the downspout until I was sure they was gone. So I waited ten or fifteen seconds for safety. But that was plenty of time for one more good idea to come into my brain. The idea was this: what if they didn't lock that sliding glass door? If they didn't, a guy could just walk in and do about one minute of detecting pretty easy. I had to get to City Park and all, but if I run a little faster it wouldn't take fifteen minutes to get there anyway. Since they was gone, it wasn't like I was following them or anything, which Officer Mike had advised against. Come to think of it, now that he was retired his advice probably wasn't all that binding any more. And if that sliding glass door was locked, I'd just leave.

It didn't make much sense to crawl down that dangerous downspout with the loose screws when the balcony was such a easy target for jumping. So I jumped down to the balcony and landed pretty light. I listened at the

252

door for a second, just to be extra careful and didn't hear nothing so I pulled at the door. It was locked.

"Dang," I said. Then the light come on inside and I heard voices. There was a thin curtain inside the door so I couldn't see them and they couldn't see me either. For a minute I thought about staying there and listening and if they come out I'd just jump. But if they seen me, they'd know I was on to their new location and they'd move again. I decided I'd just leave.

The ground below had soft dirt, so I climbed up on the railing. What with that dangerous downspout and all jumping was the cautious way to go. Plus I didn't want to be late for the turtle release party. It was only about a story and a half, which I done lots of times.

Two things happened right when I thought that. The first one is I heard them unlocking the glass door. And the other is I seen my Nike bag sitting right there on the balcony. No point in going to a turtle release party without your turtle. But no point in getting shot if you don't have to either.

My training come in as handy as it's ever come in my next three moves. To say it sounds like it took a long time, but to do it took about as long as taking a deep breath. First I jumped back down to the balcony and grabbed the strap of the Nike bag. Second I did a standing jump back up onto the railing. Just when I got there I heard the door slide open behind me. Third, I jumped off the balcony.

While you're in a jump, things go slow in the rest of the world. Since you got nothing else to do until you land you notice them easy. While I was in the air I heard a shout, like a surprised guy would make and then some other shouts. The breeze was cool, like a football season breeze, so I smiled at that.

My landing was OK, but not elegant. I give it about a eight. The Nike bag was heavier than a garbage sack, so it threw me off a little. Plus the dirt was more uneven than it looked. I took off at a pretty good clip. I heard more shouts and then a couple gunshots and seen a spark fly off the sidewalk, so I run even faster.

You can't blame them for shooting at a guy who jumped off their balcony. I'd violated their private property and that pisses people off. So they fired a few warning shots at me to keep me from doing it again. But they couldn't of seen me good enough to make a positive ID, which was lucky.

And I hadn't stole anything, so they couldn't be pissed at that. Plus, since the door was locked, they knew I hadn't even gone in their apartment. You have to figure a balcony ain't as private property as an apartment. I put my-self in their shoes and decided they'd smoke another cigar and have another drink and then they'd forget about it.

CHAPTER TWENTY SEVEN

A turtle release party gets some unexpected guests

I jogged over to City Park. Just to be safe, I stopped a couple times to make sure they wasn't following me. Twice I seen a cool old Cadillac, but no Camaros or Mercedes. Best of all, no guys running after me. I made a note of stuff to bring when I come back later: garbage sacks, and some paper to take notes on, and a wool ski cap in case it got cold. Except for dressing warm I couldn't think of anything else that might come in handy. It was one of my best plans ever.

Even with the incident, I got to the park about 8:57, which ain't technically late. It's a big park, but a road goes through it right by the lake so I jogged down it. With the street lights it was easy to see Holly and Linda and her parents all standing next to a nice new minivan. I got a little nervous about meeting Linda's parents, but then Linda hollered "there he is" and started waving real big. I forgot about being nervous and jogged up to them.

"Hey Mr. Jumper," she said.

"Hey Michelangelo. I didn't recognize you outside the hospital."

"This is my mommy and daddy." She turned to them. "And this is Mr. Jumper."

"At last we meet," her daddy said. "Pleased to meet you. I'm Calvin."

"Howdy," I said, shaking his hand. "Everyone calls me Jumper."

"I'm Jennifer," the mommy said, and I shook her hand too. They were a little older than me and dressed nice but not fancy. Jennifer was a pretty lady, like a older version of Linda. Calvin looked in pretty good shape. He had an expensive haircut so he wasn't a plumber or something like that.

Calvin and Jennifer seemed like they was probably really nice people with clean clothes and good smiles, but I had trouble noticing stuff about them. I ain't sure why, but I tell you what it felt like. It felt like I wanted to be Linda's grown up friend, which I was, but nobody can be as good a grown up friend to a kid as their mom and dad. So when her parents was there, I didn't feel like I was Linda's buddy as much as when they wasn't there. So I might of pretended just a little that they wasn't there.

255

On the other side of the issue, it was easy to remember myself as a kid when I had a mom and dad, and it made me notice that some people still got parents, but I ain't. That didn't cheer me up much either, if I aimed my thinking right at it. So I didn't. It would of been mean to be jealous of Linda just cause she had parents, so I threw that idea out the window. I liked her parents and I was happy she had them, and that's nothing but the truth but it made me sad to pay too much attention to them. So if I forget to tell you anything they done, it ain't because I don't like them. I was probably just looking somewhere else.

"Hi Holly," I said.

"Hi Jumper." She had on jeans and a regular shirt, which made her look different than she did in her uniform, but still nice.

"Is Bartholomew ready?" Linda said and winked at me.

"Lead the way," I said. "Since you got the flashlight."

She reached out and took my hand and led us toward the weedy spot. The rest followed behind us. There was a long stretch of grass and trees before we got to it, so we was like a little parade in the dark following Linda's flashlight. Linda had to walk pretty slow, since she was still weak, and the others kept their distance walking even slower and talking, so we got a little spread out.

"Did you fix your zipper?" she said real quiet.

I felt my jeans, but the zipper was up.

"You got me with that one," I said. Just then I seen some lights moving real slow on the tree branches. It was just car headlights but it looked cool so I turned to see the car. When I did, it turned off its headlights but kept driving closer to the minivan. We was walking across the grass and were about a hundred and thirty feet off the road by then. It didn't seem that ordinary for somebody to turn their lights off while they was still driving, so I kept turning around to watch. When they drove under a street light I seen it was the old Cadillac I'd noticed earlier. It stopped behind the minivan and four guys got out. One was real big and one had a foot in a cast with one of them rubber walker things on the bottom of it.

"We got a problem," I whispered to Linda. I let Holly and her parents catch us. I don't remember ever using my brain as hard as I was doing right then.

"One of you got a cell?" I asked real quiet.

"Sure," Jennifer said. "It's here in my purse."

"Them guys in that Cadillac is bad news," I said. They was out of their car and walking toward us.

"Are we in danger?" Holly asked.

"Well, we ain't yet but in about ten seconds we could be. Are you fast runners?"

"Linda can't run yet. She's still too weak," Holly said.

"I'm calling the police," Calvin said. "I'm not going to be intimidated by a bunch of thugs."

"That's a good idea, sir, long term." I said. "Let's walk while we talk, OK?" We started walking away from the Bones. "If you got a cell phone, you should call the cops. But these guys ain't gonna wait around to get caught, so we need a plan B to stay alive until they get here."

"Stay alive! What are you talking about!"

"It ain't a good time to explain it all right now." I was watching the gang guys moving toward us and I wanted to be polite and all, but Calvin didn't have time to understand the whole situation before we was all getting beat up.

"Look," I said. "You're probably a lot smarter than me, and got more money, and a nice family with a little girl and all, and a car. So in most situations, I'd just say we should do whatever was your idea. But we only got time for one plan right now or we're all in big trouble, and I got one. So how bout we do mine as fast as we can?"

He looked at me real careful, then looked over his shoulder at the gang guys. Then he nodded. "What do we do?"

"OK, it's pretty dark. They can't tell for sure how many of us there is. Linda, you give your daddy your flashlight." She did it and I kept talking real quiet.

"Everybody keep walking pretty ordinary while I tell you the rest of it, but a little fast, like we don't know we're being tailed. Linda, you want a piggy back ride?" I kneeled down and she climbed on without a word. With my backpack on and the Nike bag over one shoulder plus a kid riding piggy back, I had a lot of stuff on me so I probably looked dumb, but it was dark and I had other stuff to think about than how I looked. Linda was about as heavy as a puppy dog on my back, so that didn't slow me down. We started walking again, faster now since we didn't have to be slow for Linda.

257

"They can't see us too good, but they can see the flashlight so they'll follow that," I said. "Calvin, you carry the flashlight so they follow you instead of the women. I'll run ahead and hide Michelangelo so she's safe. Holly, you and Jennifer split off from us gradual, and when the flashlight ain't showing you, change directions and run over to them trees over there. That's to split us up. Calvin, see that big tree straight ahead of us? You lead them right under it. Got it? Keep the flashlight aiming down so they don't see me and Michelangelo. After you get past the tree, just turn off the flashlight and run for it. Jennifer, when you get to them trees call 911."

"What do I say?"

"You tell 'em there's a crime in progress with the Bones."

"The Bones? "

"Gang guys."

"I read about them in the paper!" Jennifer said. "Those guys are killers! What have you gotten us into!"

"Well, we ain't got into anything yet, but if we keep talking instead of thinking and walking we could have some problems," I said. "You ladies start moving away a little." Calvin pointed the flashlight straight down and we all kept walking pretty fast. The Bones was gaining on us.

"What are you going to do?" Calvin said. He didn't sound scared, but he didn't sound happy either. Him and Jennifer was pretty dang upset, as anybody would be and they didn't know if they should take charge, or listen to me, or what.

"After I hide Michelangelo, I'm gonna even up the odds a little till the cops get here. We just need to keep their brains busy so they don't escape. They ain't got that good of brains, so it shouldn't be too hard. Your part is, you lead them under that tree."

"That doesn't sound like much of a plan."

"My plans is pretty much foolproof."

"You can trust Jumper," Holly said. "He's right, this isn't a time for conversation." She already had her cell phone out. "I'm calling 911 while we walk."

"But my daughter..."

"Ain't nobody gonna touch a whisker on her bony little head. You got my word on that one. Hang on, Michelangelo in case it gets bumpy when I go faster. "

258

"What about Bart?" Linda whispered.

"Got him right here." I patted the Nike bag. Then I started running my fastest toward the tree. Linda giggled.

"You're pretty fast for an old guy," she whispered.

"Old guy my foot," I said when we got to the tree. "You get some meat on them skinny bones I'll foot-race you any day of the week."

"You're on," she said. I went to the back of the tree so we was hid. The park people was careful with their trimming, so there wasn't any easy foot holds down low, but the bark was big and it wasn't hard to climb up to the first branches. Linda wasn't that heavy on my back so I took her a little farther up where she'd be hid good. I hooked the Nike bag over a branch.

"OK, now, you ain't afraid of heights are you?"

"Little late to ask that, isn't it? No I ain't afraid of nothing," she whispered back.

"Good. Now you just be real quiet no matter what happens, OK?"

"OK," she whispered.

"No matter what happens. I'll come back for you in a few minutes," I said.

"Promise?"

"Of course I promise, you little knucklehead. Don't let Bart make no getaway."

I climbed down to a big branch that hung out over the side. Calvin was almost to the tree and the Bones was catching up to him.

"Run," I said to him in a loud whisper and he took off and after a little bit he turned off the flashlight. The Bones yelled and started running after him. The big guy was the fastest, but three others wasn't far behind him. The guy in the foot-cast run funny, because of the cast, so he was coming in last. When the first three passed under me I seen they had guns in their hands. I sat on the branch and waited till that last guy was right under me.

"Hey!" I whispered and he stopped. He looked around for who said it, holding his gun out with both hands. The others kept running. Then I jumped. I aimed right behind him. Just as I was landing I put my knee out and caught the middle of his back. He fell forward and landed flat on his face. The gun went flying. He started crawling toward it but his mouth was wide open so I figured he got the wind knocked out of him. I got up fast, threw the gun into the shadows, and duck taped his hands and feet.

259

"You!" he said. Obviously he'd got his wind back so I didn't feel bad about taping his mouth.

I didn't want to leave him under the tree Linda was in, since the others might find him. So I grabbed his feet and drug him over to the weeds we'd been aiming at in the first place to release Bart. It was muddy in there, with about three inches of water on top of the mud, which slowed me down and couldn't of been that pleasant for him either as I drug him into it.

"I'd keep that cast out of the water," I whispered to him. "That cast melts off it's gonna hurt like heck."

You could tell he was cussing at me pretty good, but with the tape on his mouth it didn't have the full effect he was going for. He did bend his knees and raise the cast up. Saying that thing about the cast was a bluff on my part. They mostly make 'em out of waterproof stuff these days, but it give him one more thing to think about. He didn't watch enough TV, that was obvious.

Even taped up, he made a lot of noise with his throat and splashing around in the weeds. I was walking out of the weeds when I seen his buddy sneaking up on us. I had just got out of the mud, but there was still weeds as high as my knee, so I laid down in them to hide. The guy was holding his gun straight in front of him and trying to Indian walk. There was a street light not too far away, so it wasn't all the way dark. He should of been able to see me, but he looked right at the street light. Everybody knows you can't see so good in the dark after you look at a light. That was just a dumb oversight on his part, but it give me a little advantage.

The taped-up guy started to make louder sounds to warn his buddy, but the guy with the gun didn't get it. He lowered his gun and started to run right over to help. When he went past me I got up. He heard me and started to turn around, but I had the element of surprise. He was already running through the weeds toward the lake so I just put my hands on his back and helped him along, only a lot faster than he planned. When the water was about halfway to my knees I give him a strong push and he went flying into the water. He yelled and flailed his arms around, so I knew he never done much jumping. The water ain't that deep so I knew he'd just walk out and help his buddy once he thought about it. But his gun probably got good and wet, if he didn't lose it in the mud, and it would take some time to get his friend untied and get back in the mood for fighting. So I run back up to the grass to look for the rest of them.

Even with park lights, there's lots of shadow places, so I stuck to them. After a while I seen another gang guy hiding behind a tree. He was shadowed himself and looking out on a big open grass area. His gun was aimed out there, waiting for someone to shoot at.

The hidden flaw with his plan was that he couldn't see me behind him. But then, he was young and even I didn't used to think up all the hidden flaws in my plans. I pulled off a piece of duck tape as quiet as I could.

My plan was to sneak up behind him and put tape over his eyes so he couldn't see where to shoot and then grab the gun away. I Indian-walked up behind him.

It was a good plan for a second. I got the tape over his head but not down to his eyes. It stuck on his forehead and he started resisting arrest. But since he resisted so much I had to resist back and his head got knocked hard into the tree. He yelled and grabbed his face. While he was yelling I twisted the gun out of his hand and threw it into the bushes. Then I seen he had a metal thing on his jaw. He must be the one the cowboy hit.

"Sorry, man," I said. "I bet that hurt like heck."

I put my hands on his shoulders and pushed him down to a sitting position. He didn't seem like he wanted to resist any more, so I run tape around the tree and over his elbows a couple times. It seemed mean to tape his mouth shut, with his jaw problems and all. Plus, since his gun was off in the bushes there didn't seem much point. So I didn't. By the time his buddies got out of the water and found him the cops would be there anyway.

So that just left the big guy. He seemed smarter than the others, with his expensive suit and all, and he had a defensive-end kind of body, so he might be a harder problem than the others.

I stayed in the shadows and jogged back to the trees Holly and Jennifer had run to. I heard voices in there. That was a oversight on my part, I thought. I forgot to tell them to be quiet. When I got closer I seen the big guy. He had one arm around Holly's neck and the other hand held a big gun. Calvin and Jennifer was kneeling on the ground in front of him. Holly looked more mad than scared, but I felt a pain in the middle of my chest just from looking at them.

"I tell you we don't know where your money is," Calvin said.

"And I'm telling you for the last time you give it up right now or this stitch gets a bullet in her brain. I ain't fluffing with you any more." He held

261

the gun up to Holly's ear. "And if that don't do it, we'll try stitch number two."

"It's in the minivan," Jennifer said. "The keys are in my purse."

"Yeah, right. I saw that homeless clown walking with you. Maybe I should pop these two and then you and me can go check out that fine ride. Maybe even have a little party."

"He's not homeless," Holly said. "He's an artist."

"Same thing," he said.

"You looking for something?" I yelled. Mercedes swung around so Holly was between us and pointed his gun toward me. Only he couldn't see me because I was in the shadows. And if you remember, it was night time. Sometimes you could see the moon, but mostly there was too many clouds, so between being night and me being in the tree shadows, there wasn't any way he could see me. I could see him a little bit because he wasn't in any tree shadows, but it was too dark to see him good.

"Yeah, I'm looking for something."

"Well, I'm looking for something too. Pepperoni, mushroom, and sun-dried tomatoes."

"I know you," he said, kind of surprised.

"You ain't got the concept of sharing down all that well," I said. He was dragging Holly toward me."

"This is none of your business," he said. "Go listen to your aliens some-where else."

I moved around to where there was more trees.

"They ain't broadcasting but I found some money," I said. "Thought I'd buy me a new pizza with it." OK, so that was a white lie, or maybe even a gray one. I didn't find no money, but it seemed like his lost money was all he wanted to talk about so it seemed like a pretty good ice breaker.

"That money's mine."

"Money you got from selling drugs to kids and minors."

He aimed his gun at my voice and shot the tree I was next to. Shooting at something you can't see is a low percentage deal, so it didn't scare me much. I mean, nobody likes to get shot at, but if someone's gonna shoot at you, this would be a good way to choose. Plus it was dumb. Guns only hold so many bullets so you wasn't thinking clear if you wasted them on

262

low percentage shots. Maybe I had an advantage on this guy on account of being smarter.

"That one's going on your permanent record," I said. "You could put somebody's eye out with that thing." He shot again, but I'd already ducked real low and it wasn't that close. My plan was to get him to shoot until he ran out of bullets, which worked a lot on old westerns, but you couldn't tell how many bullets guns had today. So I was thinking fast on a new plan while I crawled to a different location. The main thing was to keep him busy until the cops showed up.

I bumped into a trash can and he shot at that sound too, but he didn't hit nothing. If I was gonna bluff that I had his money, the plastic sack in the trash can might come in handy, so I pulled it out and moved away again. It was about half full.

"If you had my money you'd be gone," he shouted. It was obvious he was just trying to get me to say something else so he could shoot in the dark at my voice, which worked right into my own plan. I got low behind a tree.

"I got it right here in this trash sack." I shook the sack a little so he could hear it rustling. He didn't say nothing for a minute. After he thought about it, he answered me.

"What do you want?" he yelled. He wasn't all the way sure any more. He'd seen me as a homeless guy and probably had the prejudice they was dumb. It's always to your advantage if the other guy thinks he's smarter than you. We had Presidents who pretend to be dumb just to get votes. People always make a mistake if they think they're smarter than you. Or if they think you're crazy.

"I already said I want a pizza like you swiped. We don't need money on the home planet. A little finders fee might be good though. You know, for the pizza."

"I'm sure we can work something out. Why don't you bring it over here so we can talk?"

"There's too many people. That pizza won't go that far."

"I'll buy two. And one for your spaceship too."

"I'd believe you better if you hadn't of swiped the first one."

He kept moving toward me. Behind him I seen Calvin and Jennifer get off the ground real careful, to make a getaway, but Mercedes heard them and he spun around and shot up in the air.

263

"What I tell you about sitting still?" He yelled at them and they got back down on their hands and knees. They looked pretty scared. He took a step toward them, like he might shoot them just to be mean. He shot that guy in the parking lot pretty easy.

"Hey!" I yelled. "If this is a bad time for you to negotiate on getting your money back I'll just come back some other time."

He spun back around toward me and forgot about them for a minute. But he was still holding Holly tight and every time he turned fast like that, from the sound she made, you could tell it hurt her. I felt a pain in my own stomach just from hearing it. But I had to be a grown up and forget about that and be smart, and pay attention if I was going to do anybody any good. It wasn't the easiest thing for me to do, to keep my whole brain on one subject for a long time, but in this case it seemed pretty important, so I knew I had to do my best work.

"I'd prefer you let the innocent bystanders go. Even if they didn't have no spare change for me when I met them for the first time tonight."

"Blue shirts! They my insurance. You come out or she gets it."

Well, that didn't make no sense to me, even if I was trying to pay attention to the main problems and not get interested in the little ones. I'm a guy who knows something about insurance payments.

"How do you figure that's insurance?" I yelled.

He didn't say nothing for a minute. Then he didn't think up something new to say but just said the same thing.

"I said give me the money or I shoot her."

"That seems like backward insurance to me." I said, as polite as I could.

"Say what?" Now he sounded confused.

"Well, you gotta figure we called the cops already on our cells. Maybe they already got us surrounded, waiting for you to make one false move. Or maybe you still got one minute to make a getaway. So shooting this lady is a crime of murder with witnesses and fingerprints and physical evidence and you ain't thought of a good getaway plan. That's the kind of insurance that insures you go to jail. It might of seemed a good plan when it come to you, but you didn't think of the hidden flaws. Anybody could make that mistake."

"You can't get away from us."

I was moving around. He kept turning to follow my voice.

264

"Us? You mean the Bones?" I said. "The Bones ain't gonna be that useful for a while. They had some more incidents with duck tape." So that was one thing for him to think about.

"You're the fool with the duct tape?"

"Lots of fools got duck tape. I ain't the only one." While he was thinking about that I said, "I wonder if there's a SWAT team guy with your head in his sights right now? I'd be watching for little red laser lights if I was you." Some guys try to keep too much stuff going on in their brain at the same time so they don't do their best thinking on the big one. Mercedes only had one big problem to think about, which was his getaway. Instead, he was thinking about his lost money at the same time, which Holly and me couldn't help him with, and pizza, and spaceships. He should of just walked out of the park before the cops got there and tomorrow remembered where he put his money. The cops was his main puzzle. Instead of solving that, he dumped a whole thousand-piecer out of the box and was trying to solve it all at once.

For me it was different. I was still pissed about the pizza he swiped from me, and pissed he shot that guy in the parking lot, and that he scared Linda. Plus he was scaring her parents and maybe going to hurt them. I didn't know them that good, but I know it's a lousy thing to lose your parents. Linda wasn't going to be losing hers while I was the hall monitor. It just wasn't going to happen. All that stuff hit me wrong but I could have been smart and grown up and pretended it didn't.

But the whole truth is what really pissed me off was seeing him holding Holly and pointing the gun up to her head. When he done that I felt scared for her and nervous and knew I had to keep using my whole brain. But the "nothing but the truth" part is that just seeing his arm around her neck and squeezing her close to him was as bad. My face got hot and my stomach felt like someone hit it and my ears started buzzing. I know she ain't my girlfriend, so it might not make sense. But even if it don't make sense, that part pissed me off more than him shooting at me, and made me want to punch him in the face, even if that was pretty likely to be the last thing I ever done as a live person.

James Bond come up with different solutions to every problem. Sometimes it was scuba diving, sometimes it was a watch that shot out death rays. But he's unusual that way, which is why they made movies of him. Most of us ordinary people find a few tricks we can do and then keep doing them. Ain't nothing wrong with a one trick pony. If he didn't do that trick

265

good he wouldn't be in the circus. But people like to read about different styles of solving problems, so if I was just making this up I'd pretend I shot death rays out of my watch or something. Only that ain't the trick I know. I might be a renaissance guy in lots of ways, with my art process and inventing card games and all, but I know who I am. If it come down to one move and I was in the circus spotlight, I'd want to jump. Unfortunately, I was hiding in the bushes, and he was over there, and so it looked like I was going to have to use some other trick. There was still a pretty good chance I could outwit him.

"The smart thing for you to do," I said, "would be to put down your gun and let me make a citizen arrest on you."

"Yeah, that's gonna happen," he moved toward my voice. He was kind of predictable, walking toward my voice and hoping I'd just stay in one spot and wait for him to get close enough to shoot me. Maybe there was a way I could use that habit of his to outsmart him, but no ideas come into my brain.

"Well, at least I ain't a SWAT guy. I'd let you come peaceful and the judge might take that into account."

"Why don't you just take your finders fee and leave the sack? Ten percent seems fair."

"That's a interesting idea. Let me think on that a minute. How much pizza could I get with ten percent?"

"More than enough to last the rest of your life."

Well, obviously it wouldn't take much pizza to last the rest of my life once he shot me, so I seen through that line. This was like a master chess match, only him and me using words on each other instead of castles and horses. He must of lost more than ten or twenty bucks to be making a big deal on it. But sometimes rich guys make a bigger deal about ten bucks than someone poor as that nun Mother Teresa, who only had one dress. You see that every day. Even if it was only ten bucks, it was worth walking around the park to look for it. I made a note to do that later.

You ain't gonna believe what happened next cause it sounds like it come out of a movie. But sometimes real life is like a movie and you gotta believe it as much. What happened next is that the moon come out from behind a cloud and all of a sudden you could see things a whole lot better. It was a full moon, mostly yellow-white, but with some orange in it, and round like full moons usually is. I was hid behind a bush, so Mercedes couldn't see me even if the sun come out, but now I could see him real good, plus Holly and Linda's parents behind them. All the trees made black shadows, but you could see the grass was green where the moonlight hit it. Which was beautiful and all, but that ain't what made it interesting.

The interesting thing is that the moon showed me one big tree about thirty feet away from me. Before the moon come out it was too dark to see it.

CHAPTER TWENTY EIGHT

The exciting conclusion

I notice trees a lot because of my interest in jumping off them, and some is good trees and others has problems of being lopsided or leaning or have issues with thin branches. I've seen some excellent trees, with fruit, or red leaves, or bird nests in them. But I ain't never seen this good a tree in my life. It had a big round trunk, and then split into five branches about eight feet up, and each one of them branches split into other nice even branches. They was all so neat the whole top part looked like a big green ball. If you was building a Garden of Eden, this was the tree you'd want to keep your best stuff under, like snakes.

Just as soon as I seen it I knew what my new plan was. Since Mercedes kept shooting at my voice and then stepping toward me, maybe I could get him to take a few steps toward that tree by talking to him. Then, when he was under a big branch, I'd jump down on him before he could shoot me. I pictured myself jumping, and seen which branch I'd want to be on, and where I needed to get him to stand. I went over it about three times in my brain and I couldn't see no hidden flaws in the plan. That was a perfect tree for jumping off of. I crawled to my right about twenty feet. Now if he walked toward my voice, he'd be aiming for the spot I wanted him to stand.

"So now that we cleared up how the innocent bystanders ain't good insurance, this seems like a good time to just let them go."

Sure enough, he took a step toward my voice and got a little more under the tree.

"I need to see my money first. What if you're bluffing?"

"I ain't that much of a bluffer."

"I don't know. You seem like a pretty smart guy, maybe you're trying to trick me."

Dang it, I thought. He figured out I'm trying to act dumb.

"Why would I want to trick you? If I ain't got your money why would I come here and let you shoot at me on account of you having innocent by-standers I ain't never seen before? What's in it for me?"

"Maybe you got a message from the home planet."

268

While we talked, he kept walking toward the tree, which I was leading him to with my voice, as I said before. Now he was right under the best jumping branch. Perfect, I thought.

Right then I seen a couple of hidden flaws with my plan. First, I'd have to stop talking so I could run over to the tree, climb it and jump down on him before he moved. But if I stopped talking he'd wonder what I was up to and maybe move. Second, with the moon so bright and him looking in my direction, he'd shoot me when I stood up to run over there. Obviously I was going to have to wait for a cloud to help me with that second issue, but now that I had him under the tree I didn't want him to come to farther. So I had to stop talking some way that wouldn't make him suspicious.

"Uh-oh," I said. "I'm getting a transmission from my space ship. Could you excuse me for a minute?"

"What the..." he said.

He said something to Holly too soft for me to hear and squeezed her a little tighter and she tried to pull away and he laughed. I about stood up and started running straight toward him because maybe then he'd get distracted and she could get away. But even if I wanted to, if I done that I knew he'd just shoot me and probably wouldn't let go of Holly anyway. My face got hot, but I counted to eight to calm down. Some guys count to ten, but that seems like wasting numbers to me. You shouldn't ever get so mad you need to count past eight. But every time I looked at Mercedes holding Holly like that my face got hotter again. I had to count to eight six more times.

Holly looked off to one side and looked startled. Then she turned back, looked right at me and said "Is that one of your friends?" She said it so loud she could have been talking to me.

"Where?" Mercedes said.

"Over there, under that street light."

He looked over there and so did I.

A guy was standing right under the street light. He was wearing a white straw hat and a white shirt, which stood out against the dark shadows, especially with both the streetlight and the moon shining down on him. The guy reminded me of Officer Mike, cause he had a belly, only I ain't never seen Officer Mike in a white hat, so that didn't make sense. Lots of guys got bellies. But then, I had told Officer Mike about the turtle release party so maybe it was him, except I figured he wouldn't come so we didn't wait for him. This guy was too far away to see good, and the straw hat shadowed his face all the way. He had a cane in his hand. What was strange is that he was dancing.

Well, it wasn't "dancing" like a waltz, where there's steps you gotta do in the right order which you about got to be a rocket surgeon to remember. I already told you how I feel about dancing, which is that I ain't good at it, so I don't have to explain that again. This was more unofficial, where some idea for a move comes to you and you just do it, only with a white hat on it looked even cooler. The guy beneath the street light kind of spun around and tipped his hat up with his cane, then acted like he was falling sideways but kept catching himself in a cool way like he planned it all along. He kept coming up with new moves that all looked like accidents until he got his balance again, so it was like he was joking on us, making us think he was falling when he was doing some move he practiced in front of a mirror. He looked like he was having fun. It was never my sport, but I decided maybe some guys like dancing the way I like jumping. If you're not in a waltz class, there ain't no rule book and there ain't any wrong moves except the ones that bust your ankle. Which applies to jumping too. I thought I heard him humming the tune to Wonderful Night for a Moondance, but I ain't sure. Once that idea come into my head I couldn't get it out. Pretty soon I could hear a whole band playing it as loud as an opera star in my head. It was so interesting to watch the guy you didn't have much choice but to watch him, especially with the song in my brain helping out.

Then I realized that Mercedes was staring at the dancer too, like he never seen one before, which meant he wasn't staring at me. This was my chance to run over to that tree. When that guy stopped dancing, or Mercedes got bored, he'd remember me in a New Mexico second. Maybe I already missed my chance by not paying close enough attention to the main problem again.

I stood up as quiet as I could and Indian-walked to the big tree. It was more of an Indian-run as fast as I went, but that ain't a real word. I was careful not to make any sounds. The guy was still dancing when I got to the tree. Standing on the other side of it from where everyone else was, no one could see me. It had the same big bark pattern as that other tree, so I climbed it easy.

I went out on the branch that Mercedes was under. Only while we was distracted by the dancer, he'd moved about ten feet to my right without me noticing, and that voice trick wasn't going to work from up in the tree. Except for that, it had been a foolproof plan.

270

I had brung the trash sack up there with me, which I wouldn't of done if I'd thought about it since it was one more thing to make noise. I just hadn't noticed it, even if it must of made it harder to climb the tree. I wasn't thinking in that direction so it didn't go in my brain. But now it was up there with me and might come in handy. If I threw it down, he'd notice it for sure and maybe I could get him right below me. But it was just one thing, and it would be better if I had something as a spare once I made my first move. Maybe there was a can or something in there I could use.

I started to open the sack, but it made some noise so I stopped. Mercedes heard it, cause he looked around real quick, but he hadn't figured where it was coming from. So getting anything out of the sack wasn't a option. But I could reach back into my backpack with the hand that wasn't holding the sack and so I got out my roll of duck tape real quiet and tossed it in some bushes. It made a good sound on the leaves and he took a few steps toward me. Holly tried to get away but he just pulled her closer.

"I like a girl with some fight in her," he said. "Maybe you can be my new girlfriend." He grabbed her ponytail and twisted her head around and kissed her right on the mouth. She tried to pull back but he was too strong for her. When he was done kissing her he let her pull away a little and then he laughed.

That was the last straw for me. I forgot about being smart. He was still five or six feet to my right, and if I had my feet under me I could of pushed off hard enough to land right on top of his dumb head, but I was sitting on the branch so I could only push off with my hands. I knew I was gonna land right in front of him, but I didn't care. I threw the trash sack behind him pretty hard so it landed before I did and made a big sound. I would of thrown it right at him, but Holly was in front. Then I pushed off as hard as I could and jumped.

As I was falling I seen him twist around real fast and shoot at the sound the trash sack made. Most guys will hear a sound and step away from it, which would of put him right under me. But this guy was more like a bear or a lion who always step toward noises. I should of figured that out from how he reacted to the duck tape and thrown the sack to my advantage. Now, instead of being closer to me, he was seven or eight feet away from me. But that trash sack was one more thing for him to keep in his brain. Then he heard me land, which was another item for his brain and he turned again about as fast as a cat would turn and shot. But he hadn't figured that anybody who jumps won't land standing straight up unless they want to twist their ankle. Like any jumper, I bent my knees when I hit, so I was

271

crouching on the ground and his shot went high. When he focused on me I was already winding up to jump at him. He lowered his gun toward me. But I was the extra item his brain didn't have room for. He accidentally loosened his grip on Holly's neck and she bit his elbow as hard as a dog would and pulled away. He yelled at the pain and she got loose, which distracted him and threw off his aim. Fire shot out the end of the gun, but I didn't care. By then I was already jumping toward him.

I've watched some football, so I know about tackling big guys. You want to hit right at their knees and grab both legs tight, which they call a textbook tackle, so that's what I planned. The jump I did was like a swimmer uses when he starts a race, with my arms in front aimed right at him. I got all my leg muscles into it, and had an excellent push off and I felt like Superman flying for a second. It surprised the heck out of him when he realized what was happening but there wasn't much he could do about it. I caught both his knees while I was still in the air and wrapped around them like a python. His feet come off the ground and he went flying backward with me hanging on like vise grip pliers. He punched my head with his gun as we landed, but his angle wasn't that good and his hand mostly hit me instead of the gun. It probably hurt his hand more than the top of my head, even if I still got a big bump from where part of the gun did hit me. At the time it didn't seem like a big deal.

Most guys would of just lay there after getting tackled like that so I rolled off him. But this guy was tough. Even being foggy headed, he sat up and pulled up his gun to shoot me but I wasn't about to let him, so I jumped back on top of him, grabbed his gun-wrist with one hand and punched him right on the cheek with my other hand. His head jerked sideways. He fell back to the ground and his gun went flying off toward a tree. I figured he was out of the mood for fighting by now for sure, so I got off him again, but I was wrong.

He shook his head like a wet dog does to get the water off him, then started crawling toward the gun.

"I got one more good one for you if you try that," I said. "I ain't hit you my hardest yet, but I'm about in the mood to. So I'd say you ought to just sit there and think about it."

There was a clicking sound behind me and we all froze. Someone just cocked a gun, or took off the safety. I ain't shot a gun before, but I heard their sound in movies lots of times. I turned around slow. Whoever it was stood in the shadow, so you couldn't see them. Dang, I thought. I should of

272

took the Bones' guns when I duck taped them. That was probably gonna be the last hidden flaw I overlooked in this lifetime. The guy in the shadows kind of laughed.

"Steve Atwater would be proud of you, Jumper." It was Officer Mike's voice. I almost couldn't talk, I was so happy it was Officer Mike and not one of the Bones.

"Steve Atwater was about the best tackler the Broncos ever had," I said.

"Until tonight," Officer Mike said. "Sorry I was late for your turtle release party."

"That's OK," I said. "It got crashed and postponed anyway. We'll let you know when we reschedule." Now I sort of started calming down and thinking of things besides guns. I turned around.

"Are you OK?" I asked Holly. She was sitting on the ground rubbing her neck next to Calvin and Jennifer.

"Yeah. Where were you during the playoffs?"

"Where's Linda?" Jennifer said. "I want my daughter."

"She's fine," I said. "She's really brave for a little kid."

"I want her right now!"

"OK," I said.

Officer Mike walked over to Mercedes and picked up his gun. "You know the drill," he said. "Face down, legs spread, hands behind your back."

Mercedes just sat there staring at him and rubbing his jaw, looking at the gun pointed at him. He was still figuring his odds on making a get-away. In his white hat, Officer Mike didn't look much like a cop, so maybe the big gang guy figured he could rush him and get the gun away. Officer Mike took a step or two back as if he was reading the guy's mind. Then he lowered the gun and smiled. "Or, you could make a run for it," he said. "Mr. Atwater, do you think you have one more tackle like that in you tonight?"

"I probably got about eighty-three."

"There you go, big-shot drug dealer from Chicago. Your choice. Hand-cuffs now, or handcuffs after you run eighty-three wind sprints and wind up with your face in the dirt after every one of them. I know what horse I'm putting my money on." He put his gun into a holster inside his shirt and folded his arms across his chest. "And I think your friends the Bones would agree with me."

I couldn't hardly believe Officer Mike was gonna let me do tackling practice on a suspected perpetrator, but I was pretty keyed up and still a little pissed at the guy so I was happy about the idea. I did a couple of stretches to get ready, then a little running in place and made the thumbs up sign to Mercedes to show him I was ready whenever he was.

But Mercedes wasn't in the mood. He looked at me for a minute. Then he shook his head, laid down on his stomach, put his hands behind his back and spread his legs. Officer Mike put one of them plastic handcuffs on him that look like big trash bag ties.

"Do you know who this is?" Officer Mike asked Holly.

"It's the guy in Linda's picture," Holly said. "I recognized him right away."

He turned to me. "And this is the fellow who shot that drug dealer?"

"Yeah, that's him," I said.

About five police cars was pulling up on the road with lights flashing. Cops was getting out and coming toward us.

"I want Linda." Jennifer said. "Where's Linda? Take me to Linda."

"You stay here with Holly," Calvin said. "Me and Jumper will go get her." They both looked white as sheets and shaky.

"You could both come if you want. I bet she's bored by now if she ain't sleeping. But you been through more than she has tonight, and I'm a pretty fast runner," I said. Plus, the cops is gonna want statements. How bout if I meet you back at the minivan? I bet I get her there as fast as you can walk to it."

"They'll want to talk to you, too," Officer Mike said.

"No offense, but cops make me a little nervous," I said. "Except for you, of course. The rest of the Bones is over by the lake. The officers will find them easy. Maybe I could just go down to the station tomorrow and fill out a form..."

Officer Mike didn't answer that, but he turned to Mercedes who was still on the ground.

"Get up," he said. Mercedes got up. Officer Mike made a very elegant gesture that meant, "after you, sir" and they started walking toward the police cars. "The rest are by the lake?"

"Yeah, mostly duck taped."

He nodded and took his prisoner away.

274

CHAPTER TWENTY NINE

The end of the first turtle release party

"Are you in trouble with the law?" Holly asked. Officer Mike was walking up the hill with Mercedes in front of him. Holly brushed little bits of grass out of her hair. "Why don't you want to talk to the police?"

"I'm a little late on some fines."

"They won't care about that."

"Maybe not tonight. But once they think about it they could. Plus, they might think I ain't a reliable witness. Anyway, I got to go get Linda. I'll bring her back up to the minivan."

"What should I tell them?"

"You got to tell them the truth and nothing but the truth. But if you ain't under oath you don't have to say the whole truth, which is my name."

"I'll pay your fines."

"That wouldn't be right, Holly."

"You saved my life."

"They wouldn't of been after you except for your being with me. I was just cleaning up my own mess." The cops was walking toward us. "I gotta go," I said and ran off. In just a minute I got to the correct tree which I had left Linda in. As I walked toward it I couldn't see her, from the darkness and the leaves and all. That was good, because it made it a good hiding place.

"Hey Michelangelo," I yelled when I got near it. "Are you OK?"

"I thought you forgot me," she yelled down from her branch.

"No way," I said. I felt on the bark to find the best climbing spot. "They was pesky but they wasn't that bright."

"Look who's talking," a man's voice said behind me. I turned and seen the guy who went swimming step out from behind the tree. He was all wet and smelled bad and you could see he was still pissed. He had a knife in his hand and he come at me fast swinging it.

See, he was a one trick pony too, and that was his trick, so even if it seems boring to have guys in a book do the same stuff over again, that's just

275

the way it happens most of the time, and you got to keep your integrity about that stuff. You can't just make up that now he had a fire thrower or something just because it would be cool and all. What this guy did was swing his knife at me, like he done pretty much every time we met.

So I ducked, which is what I always done in that situation, even if it's boring. If a guy aims at my head, I grab his wrist or I duck, and this time I ducked. And even if it would be less ordinary to say he whacked me with the knife even though I ducked, I'm a pretty fast ducker and he was pretty sloppy with his knife work, and not that fast a learner. He missed me clean. Maybe you'd like it better if he cut me at least a little to make the story interesting, but in real life you don't ever want to get cut except as a last resort, so I was more pleased than you might be. But that was just his first swing, so now you could wonder if he got me with his next one.

I had ducked with my knees, so now my eyes was about at his belt, and you knew he was going to whack at me again in about a second, only I wouldn't be able to duck since I was already ducked. The tree was behind me so I couldn't go backward. Plus, I was too off balance to tackle him, and I didn't really have time to think up a cool James Bond kind of plan before I fell over. I put all my weight on my left leg, since that's where most of it was already, and the direction I was tilting, and even though I was ducked down and falling, as he started to swing at me again I kicked his knee with my right foot as hard as I could in that position. It wasn't elegant, but I must of got him right on his ACL cause he fell over pretty fast, yelling and holding his knee.

"They're gonna have to put you on injured reserve on the prison team now," I said as I got up. "When you could of just walked away before the cops got here." Then I thought, 'that's what I meant when I said they ain't too bright' but I didn't say it since he'd already had a bad night and there wasn't a point to rubbing his ears in it. I didn't even bother taking his knife away, since it was clear he wasn't going nowhere with it. The cops would be there in a minute.

I climbed up the tree. Linda was sitting right where I left her, and even in the tree shadows she was still about the cutest little girl I ever seen. I noticed how her hair had grown out some more, and it was a little messy. I felt my throat get tight like it does before you cry, which would not have been appropriate so I swallowed a couple of times. I was pretty happy to see she was fine.

276

"Why were those guys after us?" she asked. She sounded like she'd been making a list of questions the whole time she'd been waiting and that was the first one on her list.

"It was mostly me they was after. We had some disagreements about money. I had ten bucks which they thought I should contribute to them and I disagreed. So then they tried to discriminate against me and I had to discriminate back. We just got off on the wrong foot."

"But they tried to kill you."

"Well, they lost some money someplace and for some reason they think I swiped it. That's what happens when you get off on the wrong foot: anything bad happens to you, you think the guy you don't like done it. You seen it in foreign countries all the time. Plus, I seen one of them break a rule and he didn't want to take his consequences. They figured I was a loose end. When people get mad it mostly don't make much sense."

"Is everybody else OK? I heard gunshots. Was that what those sounds were?"

"Yeah, they was gunshots, but they was all wasted ones. I told your mom and dad I'd bring you up to the minivan."

"Cool. Where did you learn to jump out of trees like that?"

"I done it a few times. It wasn't that high."

"Can I do it?"

"Maybe when you ain't so scrawny. But I got a idea. Instead of asking some more questions, you could do a piggyback jump. If you ain't scared."

"Cool!" she said.

She climbed up on my back again and we went to a low branch. "Ready?" I said

"I think so."

"You just hang on real tight and I'll do the hard part."

"OK," she said. Her little arms was about choking my neck, but I held her legs real good too.

And then we jumped.

I ain't never been as careful as I was on that jump. Linda's arms clamped on my neck like a boa contractor snake while we was in the air, but I held my breath so it didn't bother me. She yelled the whole way down like a rodeo cowboy or somebody on a roller coaster. I leaned forward a little to

277

balance her weight when we landed and it was one of my best landings ever. But then it was a short jump so it wasn't a real big deal.

"That's about the coolest thing I ever did," she said, and then she started giggling.

"You're gonna make me start laughing and then I might drop you."

"No you won't," she said. "Let's go find mommy and daddy. And Holly too, of course."

"I said I'd bring you to your minivan. Hang on."

I don't like to show off too much, but my legs felt extra strong. All the excitement had pumped me up and a couple little jumps didn't do much to burn it off. So I run my fastest up to the road. The grass was just the right softness for running, and my hair blew around from the wind we made by running. Linda yelled like I was a bronco, the horse kind, not the football kind. We got to the minivan and Jennifer and Calvin was standing there. They started to run toward us, so I reached up and lifted Linda over my head and handed her to Calvin.

Well, of course they started laughing and crying at the same time and hugging and all that crap you seen in the movies a hundred times so I don't need to tell you all the details.

Then Linda thought of something and she turned to me.

"What about Bart...what about Bartholomew?"

I'd forgot all about him. I had left the guy with the knife and the ACL problem near Bart's tree. The cops would find him pretty soon, so I wasn't crazy about going back over to that particular tree this minute. If they noticed me climbing it to get my Nike bag they'd want to ask me a bunch of questions and make me fill out extra forms. And if I tried to sneak over there, but they seen me anyway, they might think I was one of the Bones and shoot me. They might even think it was suspicious if I said I left my turtle in a Nike bag up in this tree when I jumped out of it. They might have to make up a whole new form for that one.

"You know, I bet old Bartholomew's already gone to sleep for the night," I said. "How about I just go get him without waking him up. Maybe we should have our next turtle release party in the daytime."

"Next Saturday," Holly said, as if she'd been thinking about it the whole time. "Saturday the fourth, right here at noon."

"I'm supposed to work…" Calvin said. Holly looked at him like he was a patient who didn't want to take his medicine, but you knew from her look that he was going to be taking it, and I noticed Jennifer was looking at him the same way. "You know what? Next Saturday will be just fine. They can get along without me for a day. We'll bring a picnic. Jumper, I don't know how we'll ever be able to thank you…"

"Ain't no need to thank me. We was pretty lucky. But what about your job?"

"No job is as important…" he kissed Linda on the forehead. "No job is as important as a turtle, is it honey?"

"Of course not, silly!" she said back at him. She looked pretty happy right then, and so did he.

"We're giving Holly a ride home," Jennifer said. "Why don't we just wait until you get the turtle and give you one too."

"Thanks," I said. "But maybe a different time. I'm in the mood to walk."

"Are you sure?"

"Yeah. This is a pretty good night for walking. See you Saturday," I said, and then I run off toward the tree I just come from.

"Bye Mr. Jumper," Linda yelled. I waved over my head and kept running.

Once I was far enough away so they wouldn't notice, I moved into the shadows and Indian-walked to a spot where I could see the tree in question. Some cops was there helping up the guy whose knee I kicked. It took a guy on each arm to help him walk, since he couldn't put any weight on the leg with the ACL problem. They found the one taped to the tree easy, but I was a little worried about the one in the weeds, with the cast on his foot, since his mouth was taped shut. I had figured his buddy would help him, but he wasn't nowhere to be seen, so maybe he got away. If they got three of them in custody, they might think that was close enough. So I run over there to check.

Sure enough, they'd missed him. He seemed asleep. Now I had the issue of how I was going to lead the cops to find him without filling out a bunch of forms and answering a bunch of questions. If I had to talk to them, I guess I had to talk to them. I couldn't leave a guy duck taped up and lying in the mud with a cast on his foot. That just didn't seem right. So I walked through the mud over to him.

279

"Wake up," I said. "You got some more appointments tonight. Although they ain't gonna be your favorite ones." I pulled the tape off his mouth. He started cussing his loudest, which was about the dumbest thing he could of done from his point of view, but solved my problem for me. I seen police flashlights coming toward us, looking for who shouted. I felt sorry for him, even if he tried to kill me several times. His career choice of being a gang guy hadn't worked out too good for him. Getting your feet busted had to be discouraging. Then, being duck taped and laying in mud with your cast-foot taped to your other one sticking up in the air ain't the glamour side of the gang life, so they probably don't feature it in the recruiting videos. Then yelling so the police could find you easier was a good example of how your instincts wasn't the right ones for the job of being a gang guy.

Them flashlights was getting closer, so I walked over to the shadows behind a bush to watch and make sure they found him OK.

When the cops pulled him to his feet, he yelled at the shadows where I was and said, "He's right fluffing there! That fluffing mo-phone with the foil hat! The plucker who jumps off bridges! He's a crazy duster flock, I tell you! You think I duct taped myself? Arrest him, you smother frocks!"

But the cops just handcuffed him and led him off.

I wasn't in a big hurry to get Bart so I walked over to a park bench and sat down. I watched the cops put each of the Bones into police cars and drive off. They didn't use their sirens or even their flashing lights, so it wasn't glamorous like in the movies. It was more like picking up loiterers, which probably made it even less special for the Bones. If they ever pictured getting caught, I bet they imagined cool music in the background and special effects. This was pretty ordinary, like a day in math class. Now all their days was going to be like that.

Then the park was empty. Them gunshots had scared all the regular family people home a long time ago, and also the homeless people. The cop cars scared away any criminals. That left just me, and I felt pretty good.

It ain't that often you get a whole park to yourself, so I sat on my park bench enjoying it. The stars was extra bright since I wasn't close to any park lights. Some sprinklers come on, making that cool snake-hiss sound they make, and the ones under lights farther away looked like they was shooting diamonds. I could of watched that all night.

I ain't so dumb I'm gonna pretend I'm extra smart. I got mostly C's and C pluses in school, which is a little better than ordinary but not that much. I also got a lot of "if only he'd apply himself's written on report cards.

No, I knew I'd got lucky big time tonight with the Bones. But, like I say, sometimes being smart and being lucky is the same dang thing. I didn't do nothing you wouldn't of done, so you're just as smart as me, and just as lucky too. The main thing about luck is noticing it. Except for jumping, that's about my best thing. I notice when I'm lucky. So maybe I'm a two trick pony after all. Since you read books, you might be a three or four trick pony, unless you use reading books to substitute for one of the more useful tricks. I ain't holding it against you if you done that, I'm just saying you got to count fair.

Sitting there on that park bench in the dark, watching stars that looked like little mirrors reflecting flashlights and sprinklers shooting diamonds I felt lucky about my whole life. I had a new career as an art therapy counselor, which was even more fun than collecting cans and paid a whole lot better. It sounded like maybe Holly wasn't moving to Cleveland, which was better for me no matter what happened with her and Dr. Anderson. The Bones had broke enough laws tonight and got caught in the act that they wasn't going to be a problem again. That freed up a lot of my time right there. Little Linda was getting stronger and seemed like she'd keep being my buddy even if she wasn't in the hospital. And Greg was a pretty interesting friend who cracked me up and drew cool pictures, and was a jumper besides, so there was long term potential there.

Plus we was going to have the turtle release party next Saturday on the fourth, which was a special day every year for me even if nobody else knew it. Holly scheduling it like that was one of them lucky things you got to notice when they happen to you or else you'll think you ain't that lucky. I still missed Mom and Dad, of course, that part don't ever go away. But having interesting friends is kind of like a family too, so even if there was some sad parts inside me, when you looked at all the parts, you had to agree I was about the luckiest guy in the world.

When the sprinklers turned off I climbed the tree to get my Nike bag with Bart in it. It was right where I hung it but, since it was dark in the tree, I put it over my shoulder without opening it to wake Bart and climbed down. Then I walked home noticing how bright the stars was. On an extra lucky night, stars look better even if they're probably just the same as always.

Back at my apartment, when I put the Nike bag on the floor I noticed it was zipped up which surprised me since the zipper had been busted the whole time I owned it.

Then I noticed the bag looked pretty full, which it shouldn't of from only having a turtle in it. Maybe the Bones had found it when I wasn't looking and stuffed newspapers or something in it to bug Bart. So I quick unzipped it.

It was packed full of money, mostly fifties and hundreds, in bundles with rubber bands around each bundle. I dug my hand around in it, but no turtle.

"Sticks!" I said. "I lost him."

At first I thought the Bones had got the last laugh on me, swiping my turtle and hiding their drug money the last place anyone would look for it, which is always the first place you want to hide stuff. They probably thought that was a pretty funny trick.

But when I went over the night in my head to see how they done it, I couldn't remember any time they could of.

Then it hit me like a ton of pumpkin pies: I'd set the Nike bag with Bart down on the roof of the Gentle Arms and maybe I didn't pick him up again when I jumped down to their balcony. The bag I picked up on their balcony must of been theirs and I took it by mistake. No wonder they was pissed.

I zipped up the bag and stuffed it in my freezer for safekeeping. Even if it was late, and I was tired, I jogged back over to the Gentle Arms and climbed the downspout. My bag was there all right, only Bart had made a getaway. I got out my flashlight and it didn't take too long to find him. He didn't seem mad when I picked him up.

"So, you had your own adventure tonight, didn't you?" I said as I put him back in the bag.

Even if I seen how I could jump down from one balcony to the one below it, I didn't want to risk Bart flying out and getting cracked. No way I wanted to explain that one to Michelangelo – she'd go Perry Mason on me in one second. I just carefully climbed the whole three stories down the drain pipe like a regular person and went home.

It took a while to go to sleep, with everything I had to think about. I knew I probably ought to report that I found that drug money but I couldn't see no good reason to hurry on that. Once the cops had all their

282

reports done they'd put out an APB on the money. It didn't make sense to haul it down there before they was ready for it. Better to wait a few days and then have a talk with that new cop and casually work the conversation around to APB's on missing money. If he told me to move along before we got to that part of the conversation, I'd be a responsible citizen and do what he said. Of course, the more times he told me to move along, the longer until that money got turned in, so it was really up to him. And if I had to keep it safe in my freezer, it might be fair for me to take a little bit of interest out of it sometimes, just like banks do.

CHAPTER THIRTY

The second turtle release party

On Saturday, I walked down to the park. In the daylight it looked like a whole different world. Birds was singing and kids was playing. Linda and her parents was already there, spreading a red and white table cloth on a picnic table.

"Hey, Mr. Jumper," Linda said when she seen me and my real Nike bag. She run up to me and give me a big hug.

"Hey, Michelangelo," I said as I peeled her off me. "You're getting about as strong as an octopus."

"I hope you like fried chicken," Jennifer said. She was even prettier in the daytime. Calvin was carrying a cooler of ice and he smiled and nodded his head hello at me.

"It's about my favorite," I said. They had cans of cold pop and potato salad and some ears of corn too. "This looks like Thanksgiving," I said. "And you got enough food to feed an army. Michelangelo must eat like a mule." Of course she rolled her eyes when I said that.

Just then Holly walked up. She was wearing shorts and a white shirt and looked like a actress from the movies.

"Hi, Jumper," she said.

"Yes ma'am," I said back, even if it would have been cooler to say hi back. It caught me off guard seeing her in civilian clothes in the daytime, since I mostly seen her in uniform at night.

"I see you brought Bartholomew," she said.

"We wouldn't let him go till you was here," Linda said.

"Until you were here," Jennifer said.

"Can we let him walk around on the grass before we eat?" Linda asked.

"He's not going to go racing away, is he?" Calvin said.

"No, Daddy, don't be silly! Anyway, Jumper can catch him. He's pretty fast for an old guy. At least as fast as a turtle."

"Hey, I thought I warned you about making cracks about me being an old guy!" I said, and she giggled.

284

"I think we should wait just a little bit," Holly said. She had kind of a mysterious smile, like the one Mona Lisa had that drove everybody crazy from wondering why. Only on Holly it looked good. "There might be a couple more guests."

"Really?" I said.

Holly winked at Linda and Linda winked back at her like they had a secret.

"Maybe," Holly said. "And it looks like they're here." She pointed up to the street where the minivan was parked. An old blue Mustang with a loud muffler come racing down the road about eighty miles an hour. I'd recognize that Mustang anywhere, but it surprised the heck out of me seeing it in the park. It went past the minivan, then slammed on its brakes, squealing and swerving until smoke come from its tires. While it was braking, it spun all the way around exactly right to be aimed back toward the minivan. The engine raced a couple of times standing still, like a tiger growling waiting to jump on a deer. Then it roared, the wheels started spinning and smoking and it about leaped into the air with the front end raised up like it was trying to fly and the back end swerving side to side like a dog trying to break his leash. This time, the driver slammed on the brakes so it spun around and slid sideways and stopped right behind the minivan. Once it was stopped and the smoke settled down, it looked like it had been parallel parked there by a drivers-ed teacher.

"Jim!" I said. I turned to Jennifer and Calvin who was staring at the mustang with their mouths open. "He's about the best driver in the world, and probably the very best one-legged driver, but he don't like to go as slow as most speed limits." I looked at Holly. "How'd you know to invite Jim the thrift store guy?"

"I got my feminine wiles," Holly said. "Plus, we needed someone to drive the rest of the guests."

I looked back up there. Jim was getting out of the driver's side and pulling his crutches out from behind the seat. Then the back door opened and Officer Mike got out. They both had big grins on their faces. Officer Mike dusted off his pants as he went to the trunk and opened it. He reached in and pulled out a wheelchair and unfolded it. Then him and Jim opened the front passenger door and helped the passenger out. It was somebody with casts on both their legs, so it didn't take a Jeopardy winner to figure that one out. I started walking toward them.

"Sunshine? They let you out?"

285

There was something different about Greg and it took me a minute to figure out what it was. It was the grin on his face.

"Not exactly, Dr. Bologna. These two idiots broke me out. Just came in and put me in a wheelchair and rolled me out like they owned the place. No doctors, no forms, no permission. We're all going to jail, that's for sure. Kidnapping, impersonating sane people, you name it. To say nothing of the traffic tickets Hans Solo there should have racked up."

"They got to catch you to ticket you," Jim said. "Luckily, we didn't run into any police. At least none that knew how to drive. My navigator picked a good route."

"Or maybe someone called the police ahead of time and convinced them to look the other way," Greg said, looking at Officer Mike.

"There's a time for rules, and a time to bend the rules," Officer Mike said. He was looking up at the sky and grinning. I never seen so many grins before. "Some people are safe drivers no matter how fast they're going. While others are dangerous before they turn on the car. Plus, there's special circumstances." He looked at me. "How are you doing, young man?"

"I didn't know you guys was that interested in turtles," I said.

"Oh yeah," Office Mike said. "Jim and I try to attend at least one turtle release party a week. They're the big deal these days."

"That's right," Jim said. "Last week we ran into Mick Jagger at one. But he forgot to make a reservation so he couldn't get in."

"That's too bad," I said. "If he'd just asked, maybe Bart and me could of pulled some strings for him. We're pretty high in turtle circles."

Greg was obviously still thinking about his car ride, which I can't blame him for. I been on some rides with Jim myself and it's more like a roller coaster ride than a drive to the mall. "Where did you learn to shift like that?" he asked Jim.

"In a galaxy far away and long ago. It just takes practice. And at least one good leg." Jim pointed at Greg's casts. "And you call me the idiot. Maybe I'll teach you, if you're ever out on bail from that hospital."

"Cool," Greg said, but real quiet so nobody'd think he had went soft. Jim didn't say nothing but he winked at me.

Calvin and Jennifer had been putting paper plates around the picnic table and now they was done.

"So, do I have to eat all this food myself?" Calvin said. Everybody an-

286

swered 'no' at about the same time and started sitting down at the picnic table. It was hard to wheel the wheelchair through the grass, so I picked up one side and Officer Mike picked up the other and we carried Greg to the table. We all sat around the table and piled food pretty high on our plates. Everybody joked with each other like we was old friends even if some people just met each other that day.

I usually do something special every year on the fourth, like maybe I'll have a bottle of beer, or sometimes I'll have breakfast at Denny's or go to a movie in the afternoon. But this was about the best one I had since I was a grown up. I couldn't think of any way for it to get better.

Then Holly got up and said, "I hope you saved some room for dessert."

"Man, you should of warned me about that!" I said. "I must of eaten about three chickens all by myself."

"Good," she said. "Then there'll be more for the rest of us."

She and Jennifer went behind a big tree for a minute and when they come out Holly was carrying a big chocolate cake with a bunch of candles burning on top. She was smiling with her whole face and the little candle fires was reflecting in her eyes so they sparkled. I thought this must be the biggest coincidence in the world that Greg or Linda or somebody had a birthday on the same day as me. Then she set it down on the table right in front of me.

"Get ready to make a wish, Jumper," she said. And then they started singing Happy Birthday, which nobody had ever sung to me since I was a kid. I knew I was supposed to be thinking up a wish, but I was so surprised there wasn't any way a wish was going to come into my brain on time. They was all looking right at me and singing in big opera star voices and I must of looked pretty dumb because a couple of times they almost started laughing. When they sang happy birthday dear Jumper I knew I'd just have to pretend there was something I wanted and blow out the candles. So I did and they clapped their hands.

"How did you know?" I asked Holly.

"You filled out some forms when you volunteered at the hospital," she said. It took me a minute to figure out she was talking about the drug studies.

"You didn't really think we'd come down here for a turtle, did you?" Jim said.

"You mean you guys knew too?"

287

"Of course they knew," answered little Linda. "It wouldn't be much of a surprise party without some of your friends, would it?"

"Thank you," I said. It was all I could think of to say, so I said it again. "Thank you."

"Hey, I just came for the food," Greg said.

"You be careful, buster," I said, "or I'll put you in the trunk of that Mustang while I eat cake."

"Why don't you open your presents," Holly said. "And then we can do the turtle release ceremony, and by then maybe we'll all have room for some cake."

"Man, I don't need no presents after all this."

"It's your birthday," Linda said like I never heard the word before. "Obviously you get presents. Open mine first." She handed me an envelope. "It's from Mommy and Daddy too."

I turned it over in my hand, and smelled it, and then shook it by my ear just to tease her. "Let's see, it don't rattle..."

"Hurry up!" she said, wiggling around on the picnic table bench.

"OK, OK. Didn't you know artists is supposed to be patient?" I opened it up and there was a plastic card inside, like a credit card. It said "Elitch's and had a picture of a roller coaster on it."

"It's a whole year of going to Elitch's for free," Linda said. "And they got me one too, so whenever we want to go we can just walk in without paying any money. Since I know where all the rides are, I can be your guide. Isn't that the coolest thing in the world?"

Elitch's has all kinds of merry go rounds and other rides but it's way too expensive for me, so I ain't been there since I was a kid.

"It's all the way cool," I said. I couldn't even imagine how much a one year pass must cost. "But you shouldn't of..."

"Of course, you can go by yourself if you want," Linda said. "But since we each have a pass it makes a lot more sense for us to go together. Like if we want to talk about art."

"Yeah, I bet art was what you was thinking about when you talked your parents into this idea. I'm gonna hold you to that. Thank you." I give her a hug. "And thank you too," I said to her parents.

288

Jim come over and handed me a present. It was wrapped in the Sunday comics, which was a pretty smart idea. "It's no big deal," he said. "I saw this down at the store and thought you might like it. It's not new or anything. I got a really good deal on it," he said and looked down at the grass. I could tell from the shape it was a book, but I shook it anyway and Linda rolled her eyes.

"Let's see, it ain't a pony," I said and put my hand on my chin like Columbo always done when he was figuring out a mystery. Linda was bouncing her knees up and down real fast like she was a rocket ship about to take off. It's a good idea to always have a kid at a birthday party since they get so excited.

Finally I opened it. Sure enough it was a book. The name of the book was "Dr. Hudson's Secret Journal." I couldn't believe my eyes.

"They made it into a book?" I said.

Jim shrugged. "I guess so."

"Man, thank you. I'll read the whole thing if it takes me two years."

"Here you go, young man." Officer Mike handed me a bigger present that was soft like a pillow wrapped in shiny blue paper. "Happy birthday."

Inside was an official Denver Bronco jersey with the number 27 and the name Atwater. I held it up and tried to say something and I couldn't. When I finally did, it come out a whisper. "It's signed. Is that...?"

"Yeah, signed by Steve Atwater. One of my buddies down at the station knows somebody who works for the Broncos. They heard what you did and made a couple of calls. Atwater was happy they tracked him down. People helping people – we're Americans, that's what we do. He signed it in permanent ink, but you might be careful about washing it anyway."

"This jersey ain't ever getting washed."

"Would somebody pass this down to Dr. Bologna Brain before he starts singing Kumbaya?"

"Sunshine, you didn't have to..."

"I consider it bribing the jailor. Time honored tradition."

"It ain't a bomb is it?"

"Sorry, I didn't have time. Maybe next year."

It was a long skinny box about a foot and a half long and three inches thick wrapped in black paper.

"OK, I can tell you picked out the wrapping paper," I said. "That's a no brainer. But I can't even guess what's inside."

"Face it, Bologna. You can't guess what day of the week it is."

Officer Mike put his hands behind his back and looked up at the sky. "I wonder how long it would take a fellow to crawl back to the hospital?"

"That's OK," I said. "Sunshine and me joke like that all the time. Anyway, I can't stand wondering anymore, so I'm just going to open it." And so I did.

"You got to be kidding!" I said. It was a box with tubes of brand new oil paints and four brushes. I looked over at Greg who was trying to look all bored and James Bond cool. "Sunshine, you got to be kidding!"

"I'm just sick of looking at your dumb pencil drawings," he said. "Oh, and here's a tip: you might try something wild like, I don't know, maybe red for roses. Just to go crazy."

You can't give a teenage guy a hug even if you want to. So I stood up and went over next to him and held out my hand. He wasn't in the mood to shake hands either, but I wasn't going nowhere till he did. "It's this or a hug," I said so only he could hear. So then he shook my hand.

"Thank you Sunshine. I ain't never even thought about drawing something with oil paints. I'm going to give you my very first one."

"That is so not necessary," he said.

"Nope. I insist."

"One more," Holly said. "From me." I went back to my seat and sat down and she handed me a thin present, about a foot square. I figured it was another book from the size, but a tall one without many pages. It was wrapped in paper with big flowers on it and butterflies and it had a white bow.

"You didn't have to get me nothing," I said.

"Nobody has to give anybody anything," she said. "That's why it's fun. Go ahead, open it."

When I seen what it was, my face got hot and I felt that walnut thing in my throat again. It was a wood picture frame with a glass front and behind the glass was a picture. The picture was of me as a little kid standing in front of Mom and Dad. All of us had big smiles on our faces. I'd seen that picture in my brain a lot, but it was never this clear. It was like they was right there.

290

"I ain't seen this picture in years," I said. "Where did you find it?"

"You said your family had a portrait taken down at Broadway Photo. They keep all their negatives, so I had them make a new print."

"That's just...I mean I never thought I'd see them..." My eyes was getting wet and I couldn't think of words.

"Everybody needs to keep their family near them," Holly said softly. "One way or another." Then she turned and started ordering people around like a general, which I was glad of because then I didn't have to talk. "Let's clean up this mess. Linda, would you gather up the plates? Thanks honey. Mike, there's some trash sacks in the minivan." She got Bart out of the Nike bag and handed him to Greg, who obviously didn't want him "You baby-sit the turtle. Try not to teach him any bad words. No, Jumper, you sit still. The guest of honor doesn't have to do any cleaning on his birthday."

"Yes, ma'am," I said. While everybody else buzzed around straightening stuff up, I organized my presents into a neat pile. About every ten seconds I looked at that family picture and seen Mom and Dad smiling at me. And every time, I smiled back at them.

They got the picnic area cleaned up in about two minutes.

"Is anyone ready to reintroduce turtles into City Park?" Holly said.

"I am!" Linda said and raised her hand.

Officer Mike took Bart from Greg and stared into the turtles face. "He looks like a loiterer to me," he said. "He's got that guilty look."

"It's alleged loitering," I said. "I think I seen him look at his watch."

"Well, you're the expert, young man."

Then Calvin took the turtle, even if he looked like a guy who wouldn't like turtles much. He held him up right in front of his face. "You know, Mr. Bartholomew, you were a good friend to my little girl when she needed a friend. I don't care if you are a reptile, that makes you a hero to me. I hope you live a thousand happy years out here." Then he turned to the rest of us. "It seems like Linda, Holly, and Jumper have known Bartholomew the longest. Maybe it would be appropriate if we let them do the honors."

"Yeah," Jim said. "And we'll guard that cake."

"All in favor?" Officer Mike said, and everybody said "aye" at the same time.

291

"Mr. Jumper, you carry him, OK?" Linda said. I took him in one hand and pointed him at the others, like he was a video camera taking a picture of his family.

"Bart, you remember all these nice folks, and if you see them in the park, don't bite them on the ankle or nothing."

"Bart doesn't bite," Linda said. "He's our friend. Let's go." She held out her hands. Holly took one and I took the other with my hand that didn't have the turtle and we walked over to the lake. I handed Bart to Linda and she held him with both hands.

"Will he be OK out here?" she asked. "What if he forgot how to catch his own food?"

"Turtles don't forget stuff like that," I said. "That'd be like you forgetting how to be silly."

"You're the silly one," she said "OK, now Bart, you be a good boy and don't go crossing streets. We'll come back and visit you, OK?" She turned to me and Holly. "We can come back and visit him can't we?"

"Sure, honey," Holly said. "Whenever it's OK with your Mommy and Daddy."

Linda put Bart down in the grass and petted his back for a minute.

"Bye, Bart," she said, and Holly and I said it too.

For a minute Bart sat there getting his bearings. You could tell he liked the way the sun felt on his back. He closed his eyes like he was on a beach. Then he opened them up quick, like he just remembered an appointment for catching grasshoppers, and started walking deeper into the weeds. He wasn't that fast, but he had a real determined walk.

"That's a pretty smart turtle," I said. "I seen him catch a cockroach once by outsmarting him. He's gonna be OK."

"I know," said Linda. She looked pretty sad watching him go. In a minute the weeds was so high you couldn't see him any more. We all watched the spot where he used to be. Then Linda perked up all of a sudden, like little kids do. "I'll race you for the first piece of birthday cake," she said. "Loser is a rotten egg."

"You're on," I said. "Only you're so scrawny I'll give you a head start."

"You count to ten," she said.

292

"Ten seems a little high…" I said, but she was already running back toward the picnic table. Her little legs wasn't that strong yet, so she was slow. Even running half speed counting to ten I could of beat her easy. "One!" I said pretty loud.

"Someday she's gonna be too fast for me," I said to Holly. But winning that race would be cool to her, so I figured I'd let her win. Just this once, even if it was kind of cheating. Bending the rule would be like my own birthday present to myself. "Two!" I yelled.

You ain't gonna believe the next thing that happened. Holly come over so close to me I could smell her perfume, and she grabbed both my ears. That perfume smelled so good I forgot where I was in my counting. Before I knew what she was doing, she pulled my head down toward her face and, for just a second, kissed me right on the mouth.

THE END

293

www.ingramcontent.com/pod-product-compliance
Lightning Source LLC
Chambersburg PA
CBHW061944170626
46813CB00006B/2529